THE KINGDOMS OF CHARTILE
MAGIC

CASSANDRA MORGAN

WHITE WHISKER PUBLICATIONS

MAGIC

First Printing: April 2019
WHITE WHISKER PUBLICATIONS
ISBN: 978-1-7321398-9-3

FOR WAYNE

Because love is the most powerful magic of all.

This book is co-edited by Little Ra, and occasionally the other furry paws of Aila, Aster, Pixie, and Anukis. But mostly Ra and Nuki liked to step on the keyboard.

Thanks, little ones.

WANT TO LEARN MORE ABOUT
THE WORLD OF CHARTILE?

Check out VAULT.AUTHORCASSANDRAMORGAN.COM
and sign up for exclusive **Members Only** access.

GET CHARACTER BACKSTORIES

A DOWNLOADABLE MAP

SPECIAL PREQUEL EPISODES

AND MUCH MORE!

THE REALM OF
THE LOST LEGENDS

Duneland

Outland
Post *

Mt. Kelsii

Cannondole *

The Great River

Elven Palace *

The Belirian Forest

Harpy's Point *

The Neverending Sea

©2018 Jessica Khoury

The Deep of Tomorrow

The Wailing Cliffs

The Tutarian Mountains

The Lesser Tide

The Quiet Green
of Forever

CHARTILE

The circle of life is but boundless,
in time and distance and space,
from the rise and fall of the oceans,
to the moon and sun's endless race.

The Guardian of Light never-ending,
The Bringer of Life upon earth,
The chariot of fire and feather,
The Phoenix, the bird of rebirth.

Across the dome of the heavens it soared,
And ushered in with it the dawn,
With the world out stretched below it,
It hungered to know what it saw.

The forest and woodlands were ravaged,
To ashes and smoldering pyres,
The Phoenix beheld the destruction,
Brought by its life-bringing fires.

It wept for the wilds and woodlands,
Its tears falling light to the earth,
From this the Belirian trees did grow,
And from the flowers the elves given birth.

CHARTILE CREATION MYTH, PART TWO

ONE
LONG LIVE THE QUEEN

IT WAS A COLD DAY along the coast of Harpy's Pointe, but Merrick's blood boiled hot. He watched the waves crash against the jagged black rocks that lined the shore as he stormed through the halls of the castle. The beck-ands leapt out of his way. The guards smiled and acknowledged their young lord, stopping to bow in the proper Elven fashion. Merrick ignored them all. A muscle twitched in his jaw as he clenched a piece of parchment tight in his hand.

A large spray of water erupted off the coastline. A gray whale surfaced, then dove again after the blue mouths that schooled just before a storm. Merrick descended the five stone steps to his father's study. The door banged open, and Savaric, Lord of Harpy's Pointe, looked up from an old tome on his desk. He smiled at his son, which Merrick returned with an icy stare.

"Merrick?" Savaric asked tentatively. He pushed back his chair, but Merrick slammed the parchment on the desk before he could stand.

"She's dead!" Merrick screamed, his voice echoing off the stone walls of the library. Savaric looked from his son to the crumpled paper on his desk. "I just came from town. A missive was received this morning. Queen Piper has been killed in a skirmish against the rebels!"

"Merrick, I—" Savaric began, but Merrick cut him off.

"Princess Taraniz has been dead for fifteen years, Father! Why do you continue to support such nonsense?"

"Because this is no longer about Taraniz's ideals versus the current crown!" Savaric spat. He stood quickly, and Merrick took a step back. "Queen Piper did nothing to hide her magic. She flaunted it, in fact. And the people saw her. They watched their queen using the most outlawed thing in our world, and they saw it as unfair. This is not a battle for the throne. Magic has returned to Chartile, and someone must be a voice of reason among the chaos. We can no longer deny our people what they have been born with."

Merrick crossed his arms, his gray-blue eyes boring into his father's same gray-blue ones.

"Being born with magic does not give someone the right to use it. I was born with the ability to kill. To wrap my hands around a throat and end a life." Merrick reached his hands toward his father as he spoke. "Such an act is still illegal, though my hands would have little difficulty doing so." He lowered his hands and Savaric shook his head.

"It is not so simple, Merrick," he said. "There are people, guards and soldiers, who have the right to kill someone if it means saving a life in defense. Magic can be regulated. It can be used to heal, to save!"

Merrick's face softened slightly, but his voice remained cold. "It's been years, Father. She is not coming back. And legalizing magic cannot save her."

Savaric turned and stared out the window at the water crashing at eye level against the black rocks. "No, but while it failed your mother, it may save others."

Merrick blew out his nose and clenched his fists. He still did not understand how his mother had remained so calm with her husband when he was clearly as stubborn as a manticore.

"The funeral ceremonies are in two weeks. We need to leave immediately," Merrick said.

He took a deep breath, trying to invoke the serenity of his late mother, and the authority of the late queen who had been like his second mother. Now, he had lost them both.

Savaric nodded, though his gaze still drifted across the cold water outside.

Merrick left the library, his footsteps falling softer against the stone floors, and headed to the second floor of the castle. He could smell the evening meal cooking from the kitchens at the end of the hall. The quartermaster's rooms were just outside the kitchens, and it was not uncommon to find Caine snacking within and groping the beck-and girls' bottoms.

Merrick knocked on Caine's door as a shriek drifted from the kitchen. He rolled his eyes and trudged toward the sound. Sure enough, Caine had caught a beck-and girl by her apron strings. She strained against his tug, attempting to scrub clean a stack of potatoes, but the man had his other arm wrapped tightly around her front.

"Master Merrick!" Caine called when he finally noticed Merrick leaning against the doorframe. Caine released the girl and snatched a biscuit from the table.

"Caine, the beck-ands cannot do their job if you're constantly harassing them," Merrick said, his eyebrow raised at the quartermaster.

Caine laughed. "The beck-ands can barely do their jobs as it is. I've known war hounds more intelligent than these Humans. And they like it. Keeps their spirits up, eh?"

"It distracts them—"

"Young Master, a beck-and is just as easily distracted by the rising sun or a flying insect. You put too much faith in our castle rats." Caine patted Merrick's shoulder and headed back toward his quarters, bits of biscuit crumbs hanging in his beard.

"The queen is dead," Merrick said flatly. The hulking man stopped. He turned back to Merrick, his eyes wide and his mouth hanging open. "The funeral ceremonies are in two weeks."

Caine nodded. "Of course." He finished off his biscuit and brushed the crumbs from his beard before hurrying up the hall.

"Can you organize our leave without catching yourself on apron strings?" Merrick called after him.

Caine smirked at Merrick over his shoulder. "Oh, but little master, that is the best part."

Merrick shook his head. He took the narrow, winding staircase to the top floor of the castle. His and his father's quarters were the only rooms here, though Merrick might as well have had the entire floor to himself. His father spent most of his days holed up in his study for the last twelve years. The day-to-day responsibilities of the castle and their little town had fallen mostly to Caine.

Merrick pushed the blond hair from his eyes and began packing the trunk that sat at the end of his bed. This had not been what he expected when he'd visited Harpy's Pointe that morning. A large shipment of clothing from Port Blindmire was scheduled to arrive that day. But the violent storm that had crashed down on their shores earlier in the week must have set them back. There had been no ship, only a carrier bird sent to the old seneschal's home.

Merrick made a point of visiting the place every few days, at least until his father could be bothered to pull himself away from his work and appoint a new seneschal. But Merrick wasn't complaining. His trips to town the last three years were a welcomed break.

He closed the lid on his trunk, then sat on it and hurriedly flipped the latch before the top popped open again. He heaved the chest into the hall and set it outside his door. The beck-ands would be around to load it onto the cart along with his father's possessions soon enough. He unlatched the door between their common rooms and began packing Savaric's traveling trunk as well.

He carefully folded each tunic and hose into the bottom of the trunk like his mother had taught him. Then he placed the separating board over the clothes and wisely packed his father's favorite books, an ink pot and several quills, parchment, and other odds and ends Savaric might need to send messages while away for the next month.

The Elven palace was a good two weeks' ride through the Belirian Forest from Harpy's Pointe. The queen's funeral events would take three days at least, and then it would take two weeks to get back home.

"You will learn to pull your weight, Merrick." He could hear his late mother's voice ringing in his mind. Firm, yet gentle. "It is the way of Harpy's Pointe. It is in your blood. To help and to work and to do."

Merrick could cook and do his own laundry before he had earned his first piece of armor. It was why the other lords and soldiers had taken to calling him "Scullery Boy."

Merrick sat on the edge of his father's four-poster bed and stared out the window at the town below. A ship was still anchored in the port from two days before, and its sails tugged at the ropes that bound it to the main mast. Porters hauled goods from the end of the dock onto the ship where the crewmen loaded the barrels and crates into the hull below. He sighed and leaned his chin on his hand, watching the simplicity of their daily lives.

The door opened, and Merrick spun around. His father stood in the doorway, and both stared at each other in surprise.

"Merrick?" Savaric asked gently.

"I was packing your things." Merrick gestured to the still-open trunk beside him.

Savaric smiled. "Your mother used to do that for me." He placed the large tome he had been reading haphazardly into the trunk and snapped the lid shut. "Come. We have the unfortunate responsibility of announcing the queen's death to our people. And, if I am not mistaken, a seneschal is overdue for our town."

"I could stay, Father. I can take care of things here." Merrick looked expectantly into his father's eyes.

Savaric chuckled and clapped his son on the back. "Nervous to meet your betrothed?"

Merrick sighed. "I've known Ailinn since we were children, Father."

"But you have not met her since the arrangement was made. She has only ever been your friend, not your future wife."

Merrick stared out the window again. The workers on the dock and ship were gone. The shadows that fell over the buildings said it was close to high noon.

"You can't do it all, Merrick," Savaric said. "I'll miss Piper too." He nodded his head toward the door and led Merrick from the room.

TWO
THE WORST DAY EVER

CHARLIE HILL ABSOLUTELY, POSITIVELY, WITHOUT a doubt, hated his life.

There wasn't a single thing he could think of that he liked about it. He stared up at the same ceiling his father had stared at as a child, and in that moment, there wasn't one thing he could think of that he liked about his father, either. His sister was blasting her horrible excuse for music from the bathroom as she showered, and his mother was busy in the kitchen making breakfast. Amanda Hill never made breakfast except for the days they went to visit his father.

Charlie's frown deepened as he thought of the trip he would have to endure later that day. Chelsea was taking her ACTs today and had been permitted to skip her father's visitation this month. No one who listened to that kind of music should be so lucky. An hour-long car ride to the closest veteran's hospital, listening to his mother drone on about being respectful and trying to help his father have a good time, was enough to make Charlie sick.

Then there was the visit itself. He wondered what insane story his father would try to convince him of this time. It had been fun when Charlie was little. His father had quite the imagination. But when Jayson began insisting it was all real, well, it was just too much for anyone to handle.

Charlie rolled over and watched his betta fish, Fred, build a bubble nest in the tank on his dresser. Chelsea finally turned off her music, and he heard her open the bathroom door across the hall.

"Are you up yet?" she called, barging into her brother's room wrapped only in a towel, her hair dripping wet. Charlie gave a yelp and covered his head with his Iron Man sheets.

"Ew! Chelsea! Get out of here!" he cried. "You're not even dressed! *I'm* not even dressed!"

"Oh, please," said Chelsea. She rolled her eyes but still adjusted her towel to ensure it was secure. "I helped change your diapers when you were a baby, for crying out loud. Come on. Get your scrawny butt out of bed. Mom's waiting."

She closed the door in time to miss getting beamed in the head with the pillow Charlie threw at her while still under cover of his sheets.

He sighed and resigned himself to getting up. He pulled a pair of jeans from his dresser and decided on a plaid button-down shirt from his closet. His mother liked it when he dressed nice for his father. Besides, he knew he'd lose the argument of comfort over fashion in the end, anyway. It was easier to do it now, and he could spend more time shoveling food in his face.

He entered the kitchen just as his mother set a plate of bacon and hash browns on the table. Charlie loaded his plate, but Mrs. Hill was still able to squeeze a spatula full of scrambled eggs on, much to her son's displeasure.

"See? That wasn't so hard," said Chelsea from across the table. She was dressed now, sporting a posh little suit jacket and a ghastly pink flower clip in her hair.

"Shut up, Chelsea," Charlie said through a mouthful of eggs. "You don't have to have the last word on everything, you know."

"Well, if you actually stood up to Malcolm Darcy like you do to me, you wouldn't want to stay in bed all day." Chelsea glared at her brother and forced down a kale-and-fruit smoothie.

"Shut up," said Charlie, his tone quieter. He turned away from his sister and shoved an entire piece of bacon into his mouth.

"Malcolm Darcy?" Mrs. Hill asked, her voice feigning a calm tonality. Charlie saw right through it.

"Yeah, the same kid who's picked on Charlie for years." Chelsea rolled her eyes.

"I thought we fixed this," said Mrs. Hill. She plunked herself in the chair beside her son. "Charlie, why didn't you tell me? I'll call the principal again—"

"No! Mom," said Charlie, now sick to his stomach. "It's not a big deal. It's fine. I'm fine."

"You're such a liar!" sneered Chelsea. "Lillie told me your stupid black eye last month was Malcolm pelting you in the face with a dodge ball in your gym class."

"Charles Dimitri!" Mrs. Hill's eyes were nearly popping out of her head, and her bottom lip trembled. "That is not what you told me."

Charlie pushed his plate away, and his fork fell on the floor. He stood from the table so quickly, his chair crashed to the floor behind him.

"Charlie!" his mother cried again.

"Just leave me alone!" Charlie pushed past his sister and ran out the front door. He slammed the door to his mother's SUV closed and ripped off his glasses. He pushed the heels of his hands into his eyes so hard it hurt, but he refused to cry. Crying was weakness, and that was exactly why Malcolm Darcy had tormented him since second grade. That and because he'd believed his father's stupid stories.

There was a knock on the car window. Charlie jumped and turned to see Chelsea standing there. He glared at her, then turned to face the front window, his arms folded across his chest.

Chelsea pushed the button on the fob to start the car and rolled down the window. "I'm sorry," she said, her voice gentle.

"Whatever," Charlie snapped. "I'm the world's punching bag for sadistic fun. You're no better than those jerks at school."

"You're right." Chelsea sighed, and Charlie's head whipped around to look at her. "That wasn't fair. I saw Malcolm make some stupid comment on his social media account today, and I knew it was about you. It made me so mad, and I just—I want you to stand up to him, Charlie. I've tried to do it for you, and I can't anymore."

"No, your stupid college is more important than family."

"Don't say that. You know it's not, Charlie Bear—"

"Don't call me that!" Charlie screamed, and Chelsea took a step back. "No one gets to call me that. Not Dad, not you, not anyone!"

Chelsea stood outside the SUV in silence for several moments until Mrs. Hill stuck her head out the door. "Do one of you have my keys?" she called.

"I've got 'em, Ma!" said Chelsea. She turned back to her brother and held an apple out to him. "Look, I know I pissed you off, and you've got every right to hate me. But I am sorry, okay? And if you ever want to talk about how to stand up to that ass, I'm here to help."

Charlie shot her another glare out of the corner of his eye, snatching the apple from her hand as Mrs. Hill climbed into the vehicle.

"Good luck today, sweetie!" she called through Charlie's still-open window.

"Thanks. Give Daddy a kiss for me, okay?" she replied, handing her mom the car fob. She tousled Charlie's hair before climbing into her red Camaro and driving away.

Mrs. Hill followed Chelsea out of the driveway and through the little housing community to the main road. She pulled her sun visor down as she turned onto the highway, and Charlie saw her angle it to look at him in its tiny mirror.

"Your sister asked me not to say anything—" she began

"Then don't," Charlie snapped. "She's supposed to be the smart one, anyway." He bit into the apple Chelsea had given him and pretended he didn't see his mother wipe away a tear. He finished the apple and pulled a baseball cap from the backseat over his eyes, trying to feign sleep.

The ride to the VA Psychiatric Medical Center of North Central Ohio was too short in Charlie's opinion. He'd only begun to calm down when Mrs. Hill put the SUV in park. He tossed his hat into the backseat again and pulled away from his mother as she attempted to smooth his hair.

"Please don't take your anger out on your father again," she said, her eyes boring their will and desperation into him. "He heard from a friend about a recent archeological dig, and he seems to have taken a regression."

"I know, Mom." Charlie tried to lay his thick, red hair flat, but it was useless. "I heard what Dr. Yi said the last time."

Mrs. Hill nodded and gave a small smile. Charlie ignored her. He exited the car, slamming the door behind him. He walked a single step only to realize he'd caught the edge of his shirt in the door. He freed himself, then hurried to catch up to his mother.

He sat in the waiting area on his tablet for nearly a half hour when Mrs. Hill finally reemerged with her nurse escort.

"Your dad would like to spend some time with just you today, Charlie," she said to him.

Charlie slammed his finger onto the screen of his tablet. His goal had been to clear a line of gems, but he missed and lost the round instead. He threw his head back. He could feel the headache rising in his temples.

"Do I have to?" he whispered so the nurse couldn't hear him. "Please? I don't want to be alone with him."

Mrs. Hill furrowed her brow and turned her back to the nurse. "Charles, he is your father. You have no reason to be afraid of him."

"I'm not *afraid*," Charlie whispered back. "He… He treats me like a little kid all the time."

Mrs. Hill closed her eyes and nodded. "Charlie, you have to understand, your dad came here four years ago. You *are* a little kid to him. Look, the more time you spend with him, the more you can show him what a wonderful young man you've become."

Charlie held his head in his hands as his mother pulled him into a hug. He didn't fight it this time, but he didn't hug her back, either.

"Will you do it for me, then? Please?" she asked, kissing the top of his head. Mrs. Hill was so good at guilt-tripping him. Or Charlie was that much of a pushover—he wasn't sure which.

She let him go, and Charlie handed her his tablet. "Fine," he said.

JAYSON HILL SAT AT A little white table in the hospital's special visitation room. The shelves along the walls were filled with books, pictures of the residents and their families, and an assortment of modern and classic war movies. He picked up another tiny puzzle piece and, scratching his scruffy chin, frowned at the partially completed puzzle before him.

He adjusted the letter from Jack in his pocket. He'd have to decipher the code later. For now, it was all he could do to convince the staff that he was recovering from the traumas of war, and not run from the building because of sheer boredom. But he was the decoy, and he took the job seriously. He thanked God every day that Amanda understood. Charlie, on the other hand…

He heard the door to the room open and watched out of the corner of his eye as the nursing assistant ushered his son in. His shoulders tensed, but he remained fixated on the puzzle.

"Just enter your code to open the door," the assistant said to Charlie. His gentle voice did not match his burly physique, but he was one of Jayson's favorite staff members at the hospital. Jayson heard Charlie walk the length of the room and sit across from him at the table.

"This piece has been bothering me all afternoon," he said quietly.

"Have you tried moving on to something else?" Charlie suggested, picking up a piece in front of him.

The puzzle depicted dazzling sunlight filtering through the canopy of an autumn forest. Charlie placed a piece, then leaned back, crossing his arms in front of him.

Jayson dared a quick glance at him. The boy looked stern, certain his father hadn't even noticed him yet. But Jayson had noticed. He noticed how his son's eyes darted around the room, trying to fixate on something to calm his thoughts. He noticed how he avoided touching his left arm with the same strength he applied to the right. Probably a bruise from that damned bully Amanda told him about. Jayson's mouth went dry. He reached for the glass of water on the shelf beside him as Charlie spoke again.

"Chelsea says hi."

Jayson swallowed the water and smiled. "Thanks, Charlie! I'm so happy for her. I heard she already has some offers from a few colleges."

Charlie glared and looked away before his father could catch his eye. Jayson tried to hold his smile, but his throat was dry again. He wanted to tell him everything. More than just the tales of adventure he had experienced in his youth. He wanted to tell him the truth, the reason he was there. He turned back to the puzzle once more.

"Yeah. It's great," Charlie scoffed. "Real baller or whatever."

Jayson frowned and set down the rogue puzzle piece. "What's wrong, Charlie Bear? Is it that Malcolm boy again? Your mother—"

Charlie's head rolled back in exasperation. "Oh my God! She *told* you?"

"Charlie, it's not your fault," Jayson said gently. He saw a bit too much of himself in his son, and he didn't always like it. "Look, I'm sorry I said anything. Let's talk about something else, okay?"

Charlie sighed and chewed the inside of his cheek. The silence between them was almost palpable. Jayson rose and refilled his cup from the watercooler in the corner. As he sat, Charlie spoke. "I beat his butt at archery in gym class two weeks ago."

Jayson beamed so widely, a dribble of water ran down his chin. "That's my boy!" he cried, giving Charlie a gentle punch on the arm. Charlie tried to suppress a smile. "Taking after your old pops! When I was your age, I single-handedly brought in twelve fugitives with nothing but my bow!" Charlie's face began to fall. "I think it's still in your grandma's garage somewhere. We'll have to get it out sometime. Give it a few rounds. Relive the good times back in Chartile! Once I'm done with my treatment here, you'll see. Your old man'll show you how to do it proper. Not with those newfangled compound bows with sights and their fancy wheelie things."

"That'll never happen if you keep talking like that," Charlie whispered.

Jayson's smile vanished. He cocked his head and furrowed his brow. "What do you mean, Charlie Bear? Don't... don't you want to spend time with me anymore?"

"Of course I do!" Charlie said, letting his crossed arms fall to his sides. "But you've got to stop talking about this Chartile stuff, Dad!"

"But, Charlie. You... You always believed me," said Jayson, his voice weak and strained. "When no one else believed in me, you did. We were a team, you and me."

He had been so sure that Charlie was finally ready. Ready to know that he, Jack and Leo had been working tirelessly for the last twenty-three years to discover the truth about Chartile, Mr. DeHaven's NASA project, and the mysterious Mr. Darrow. He thought Charlie would understand that he was in this hospital as a decoy, and all those years of talking publicly had been to get him in this very facility. But his son's reaction said otherwise.

Charlie shook his head, and Jayson could see his eyes turn glassy with tears.

"Don't you get it? You'll never come out of here until you just let it go! I-I'm sorry I led you on, Dad, but it's not *real*! I know you want it to be, but it's not!

"Yes, it is," said Jayson. He looked at the security camera fixated on their table in the corner as his own eyes filled with tears. "There's so much you don't know. Please don't abandon me."

"It's *you* who abandoned *me*!" Charlie stood up, his hands clenched into fists. "You've ruined my life! Everything that's happened with Malcolm Darcy and everyone else. It's all your fault! You and your stupid delusions! You're my dad! You're supposed to protect me! I'm out there dealing with everything by myself because you're stuck in here! If you would just shut up about it for two minutes, then you could come home! Everything would be normal again. We could be a family again."

Jayson's mouth fell open. He watched his son's face turn bright red, tears streaming down his cheeks. It hadn't been the war that had torn his family apart. It had been Chartile.

When he was young, Charlie hung on every word Jayson ever spoke. He'd been Charlie's hero. Despite Jayson insisting Charlie not tell a soul about Chartile, the secret-keeping abilities of an eight-year-old boy left much to be desired. Rumors spread through the school that Charlie was as crazy as his father.

Charlie had argued every day with anyone who said that Chartile wasn't real. It had even come to blows at times. And Jayson relentlessly defended his son. He'd debated with the teachers, counselors, and principals that taking the side of the nonbelievers was the same as crushing a child's spirit. Every time Jayson was called to the school, he'd made sure to wear his fancy dress uniform and had given the school a piece of his mind. Afterward, he would take Charlie for ice cream and tell him another fascinating story about his short time in Chartile. He'd proudly admit Charlie was his hero too, and their bond grew ever stronger. But after his last tour in Iraq, everything had changed.

Charlie had ceased yelling at his father. He stared down at the man for a moment, his breath coming in short, heavy pants. He wiped his nose on the collar of his shirt and headed for the door.

"Charlie," Jayson called. Charlie stopped but didn't turn around. "I know you don't believe in me anymore, but I'll never stop believing in you."

Charlie entered the code on the keypad. The door slid open, and he stepped into the hall. Before the door had completely closed, he turned to see his father push the entire puzzle to the floor. Jayson grabbed his face in both hands and began to cry.

THREE
MALCOLM DARCY

CHARLIE AND HIS MOTHER DID not speak the entire way back to Swansdale. He refused to even look at her. When she pulled the SUV up to the front doors of the school, he jumped out without so much as a goodbye.

Inside the double doors there were two offices, one to the left and one to the right. Charlie entered the main office to the left and signed his name to the clipboard on the counter.

"Got your note?" the woman behind the desk asked. Charlie nodded and handed her the piece of paper from the VA hospital, explaining his tardiness. She took it, scanned it into her computer, and handed it back.

"Fifth period is almost over," she said, looking at the clock on the wall above Charlie's head. "Why don't you head down to the cafeteria?" Charlie nodded again and left without a word.

It was a stretch to say the stuff the cafeteria served was actually food. But it had one good thing going for it—a smoothie machine. The glorious, fruit-filled sugar boost in the middle of the day was enough to make any teenager excited for a school lunch. Charlie hoisted his backpack onto his shoulder and grabbed one of the plastic cups beside the smoothie machine.

"Chili dog or peanut butter and jelly?" the stout little lunch lady behind the counter asked.

Charlie swallowed his mouthful of smoothie as quickly as he could. "Uh… chili dog, please," he said, his voice taking on a higher pitch than usual. He cleared his throat and turned back to the machine to finish filling his cup.

He could feel the lunch lady's suspicious stare on him as she loaded up his tray. He snapped the lid to his smoothie cup shut and felt a hard shove to his shoulder. He held the cup aloft, regaining his balance. One of his third-period classmates pushed his way to the smoothie machine, a devilish smirk plastered across his face.

"Watch it, fug-face!" the boy said, spittle flying through his braces and his friends laughing more than was necessary.

Charlie ignored them. He accepted his tray from the stern lunch lady, paid for his meal, and shuffled away as quickly as he could. He stayed close to the far wall, avoiding the growing line of high schoolers waiting for their lunches. He plopped himself in the farthest corner of the room, closest to the doors. It was a quick exit if necessary, and the closest seat to the lunch monitor. He sighed and held his head in his hands for just a moment, the relief of quiet solitude spreading over him.

"Yeah, you better be praying, nerd boy!" Charlie's head snapped up, and his eyes met those of Malcolm Darcy. "You owe me more than a dollar after that damn stunt."

Malcolm Darcy stood well over six feet tall, and his coaches claimed he was still growing. He wasn't broad, but he was strong. Charlie knew this from personal experience. His varsity jacket hung off one shoulder, and Charlie noticed a fresh cut on his lip.

Charlie sat straighter. He suppressed the swallow he knew would give away his fear and tried to keep the blood from rushing to his face and ears.

"What are you talking about?" Charlie asked. He watched as Malcolm's friends approached the lunch monitor, Mrs. Baumgarter. They guided her over to the vending machine where another boy pounded the front of the glass. Charlie's hands began to shake. They'd have her distracted long enough for Malcolm to do whatever damage he had in mind.

"I don't think a swirly's going to cut it this time," Malcolm sneered and reached for Charlie's lunch tray.

He slammed the carton of milk onto Charlie's head, then grabbed for the front of his shirt. Charlie pushed his chair away from the table at the last moment, milk coating his glasses, and bolted for the door. Malcolm's long arms stretched across the table, snatching the corner of Charlie's button-down shirt. Charlie tried to twist free, but he was no match against Malcolm's strength. He slammed into the table, sending bits of corn and canned peaches everywhere.

"Let me go!" Charlie's shirt tore as he tried to pull from Malcolm's grasp.

Malcolm readjusted his grip and pulled Charlie across the table toward him. He wrapped his large hand around Charlie's neck and squeezed.

By now, half of the cafeteria was taking notice of the altercation. Some of the students seated by the vending machines stood to block the still-distracted lunch monitor's view. These bi-monthly nerd bashings were some of the only entertainment the small-town school had to offer. Phones were coming out, snapping videos and pictures. Within the hour, there would be a new social media page dedicated just to Charlie's beatings until the school found out and made the students remove it again.

Charlie's arms and hands flailed. Malcolm's grip was becoming tighter and cutting off his air supply.

"Malcolm... I—I can't..."

"What? Can't Breathe?" said Malcolm with a smirk. "Good."

Charlie gasped for air. He dared not try to defend himself, or else he'd be suspended as well. That was the last thing he or his mother needed. But there was something strange about Malcolm. The glint in his eye was no longer one of joy from hurting Charlie. This was true rage and anger. As Malcolm's face turned redder by the moment, Charlie knew things had escalated beyond the bully's usual torture.

The edges of Charlie's vision began to blur.

"Come on, Malcolm. He's had enough," said a girl's voice behind them.

Malcolm ignored her. Charlie watched the boy's face twist with the rage that continued to build within. If Charlie didn't do something soon, he'd pass out, and who knew what Malcolm would do to his unconscious body?

Charlie struggled and flailed like he never had before and felt his hand land on his lunch tray. He grabbed the smoothie cup and poured it on Malcolm's head. The shock of cold loosened Malcolm's grasp just enough. Charlie twisted and grabbed the chili dog on his tray. He slammed it into Malcolm's mouth, and the cafeteria erupted into cries of awe. Some cheered, some booed, and the flashes from the camera phones went wild.

Malcolm staggered back, choking on bits of bun crumbs and canned chili dog sauce. Charlie kicked him in the stomach as hard as he could, and Malcolm fell to the ground amidst the cheers of the growing crowd. His hand caught the edge of the lunch tray, flinging the remainder of the food over Charlie.

Charlie felt the blood pounding in his ears. He stared at Malcolm, his breathing hard and fast for the second time that morning. He felt dazed and wondered whether to run for it or wait for the beating he knew was inevitable once Malcolm returned to his feet.

A shrill whistle echoed off the painted cement walls. Everyone grabbed their ears and parted as Mrs. Baumgarter and the janitor charged their way through to Charlie and Malcolm. Malcolm jumped to his feet and turned to the lunch monitor with a forced expression of fear and concern.

"What's going on here? Malcolm?" Mrs. Baumgarter asked.

"He spilled his lunch tray all over himself, Mrs. Baumgarter. I tried to help him, but he went crazy on me." Several nearby students nodded in agreement, carefully sliding their phones back into their pockets.

Charlie glared. He wanted to scream. He wanted to fight every single person he could lay a punch on. Still, he kept his face void of any emotion, though the anger he'd been feeling all day boiled at the surface. He knew if he let any emotion show, he would cry again, and that would only give his classmates more fuel to add to the fire that seemed to grow every day.

"I think you both need to come with me." The principal, Mr. Umpree, had pushed his way through the crowd behind the janitor who was keeping Charlie and Malcolm apart by placing his broom handle between them. Mr. Umpree surveyed the scene with cool skepticism, though his eyes landed fiercely on Malcolm.

Charlie hopped off the table, and the crowd took a step back. It seemed now that Malcolm had *said* Charlie was crazy, it must be true, and the students feared Charlie would violently lurch at them at any moment. If he weren't on the verge of suspension, Charlie might have made a fake lunge at Malcolm's friends.

He walked past his classmates, and no one dared move closer than five feet, which was fine with him. He followed Mr. Umpree, with Malcolm's football coach, Mr. Echler, close on his heels. Malcolm walked boldly in front of the principal, his head held high. Charlie was certain there was a devious smirk on his face.

They walked into the second office at the front of the building. This one, the guidance office, was run by the secretary, Deb. She was a large woman with an attitude that could rival any rebellious teenager. Few ever saw her softer side, save for Charlie.

Malcolm, Mr. Umpree, and Mr. Echler marched straight into the principal's office and shut the door behind them.

Deb sighed loudly, looking at the closed door and shaking her head. "They're going to be in there a while, what with Mr. Echler along this time." She reached under the desk in front of her. "Here, dear." She handed Charlie a towel and a fresh set of clothes he kept at the school for circumstances such as these.

"Thanks," Charlie mumbled, heading for the staff bathroom behind the desk. As he closed the door behind him, the anger he'd been holding inside seemed to set on him like a weight. He stared at himself in the mirror for a long time before even bothering to clean off his glasses.

He wasn't sure what finally made him snap. It wasn't like him. He wondered if he was going crazy—like his dad. And now he couldn't even talk to his father for another month. Not that Jayson Hill would want to listen to his son right now, anyway. Charlie visibly shuddered at the memory of yelling at his father, his hero.

Charlie shed his shirt and pants and rinsed his hair the best he could in the small sink. He rinsed and wiped his glasses and redressed in the fresh clothes Deb had given him. He stepped out of the staff bathroom, his dirty clothes shoved into a plastic bag he kept with his spare clothes, and the damp towel draped over his arm.

Deb was nowhere to be found. He could still hear voices coming from Mr. Umpree's office, and they didn't sound pleasant. Charlie plunked himself down on one of the plain gray chairs by the windows, waiting for his mother to come. He knew Deb had already called her. He could hear her lecture now. Something about taking his anger with his father out on other people, never disobeying the rules, blah, blah, blah. He sighed and stared out the window, swatting at a fly that buzzed relentlessly around his head.

A white car pulled into the parking lot, its lights blinding Charlie as it whipped in to park. He watched as a tall man stepped out and headed into the school. He walked straight to the guidance office as if he had done it a hundred times before. As he drew closer, Charlie saw the unmistakable resemblance to Malcolm Darcy. He had never met Malcolm's dad before, but this must have been him.

The man pulled open the door, then stopped and stared at Charlie. The door began to close again, hitting the man in the shoulder, but he didn't move. He looked at Charlie with a sad expression. Was it regret? It made the hair on the back of Charlie's neck stand up. Charlie looked away uncomfortably, then glanced at the man again, as he had yet to cease his staring. He looked as though he wanted to say something. The man's jaw twitched, and he opened and closed his mouth a few times.

Finally, Charlie cleared his throat loudly and looked away again.

The man stepped into the office, approaching Mr. Umpree's door. It was then that Charlie noticed the little fly that had been buzzing around his head earlier had somehow stopped—in midair. The man turned the knob and stepped inside the principal's office. Charlie glanced at the clock. It had stopped ticking. The room was becoming very bright, but there were no headlights from cars driving into the parking lot. Charlie could barely make out Deb's desk from across the room in front of him now.

The man opened Mr. Umpree's office door again and stuck his head out. He looked at Charlie, shock spreading across his face as the room filled with more blinding light. Charlie flung his hand up to shield his eyes, and he knew no more.

FOUR
JUST A DREAM

THE FIRST THING CHARLIE NOTICED was the smell. It was the smell of lush, sweet grass, and, of course, his one allergy. He lay there, his eyes still shut, waiting for his body to erupt in a hot, itching rash. But it never came. He dared to open his eyes and found himself in a large clearing in the middle of a dense forest.

The second thing Charlie noticed was that he was stark naked. How he hadn't realized it before, he had no idea. His eyes darted frantically around the clearing. He was alone. Covering himself to the best of his ability, he darted for a mass of bushes straight ahead and found a leaf that was easily the size of a dinner plate. He wiped the dirt off and used it to cover his front.

Panic was beginning to set in. Charlie pictured Malcolm Darcy's sneering face. He wondered if Malcolm and his friends had somehow contrived a way to set him up for a reality TV prank show. He glanced behind him again, searching the canopy above for hidden cameras. He found another dinner-plate-sized leaf on the ground and covered his rear as well. Humiliation was imminent, and exposure was inevitable. Escape was absolutely necessary.

Charlie looked at the trees and bushes around him. Some species looked vaguely familiar, but most everything else was entirely foreign. Not a single maple tree grew anywhere, and Fulton County was notorious for its maple trees.

"Okay, don't panic," Charlie said to himself. He reached up to push his glasses up his nose and realized they weren't there. He was considered legally blind without them, yet his vision was crystal clear.

Charlie glanced around the clearing again, hoping to see his glasses lying somewhere among the fallen leaves. His heart pounded so hard in his chest, he was ready for it to burst out and begin flopping around on the ground in front of him. He closed his eyes, about to begin his breathing exercises, when he felt a warm, humid air flutter across the back of his neck. The little hairs on his neck raised, and he turned around very slowly.

What Charlie saw next was beyond anything he could have expected. He stared into the bright golden eyes of a giant black panther. It grinned back at him, showing a level of intelligence that terrified Charlie even more than being this close to a wild animal.

"If you were to run," the panther whispered to him, "it would be all the more fun for me."

It took only a second for the realization that an animal had just spoken to subside before Charlie bolted back into the clearing. The panther threw back its head and gave a laughing roar before taking off after him.

Charlie was almost to the other side of the clearing when the panther leapt over his head, landing in front of him. The ground shook under its weight, and Charlie stopped dead.

He could see now that this was not a normal panther. Not that talking panthers were normal to Charlie. Jet-black wings, each as large as the boy, quivered at its sides, and more black feathers could be seen hidden among its fur.

This wasn't a prank by Malcolm or his friends. This was a full-blown hallucination. Charlie had finally cracked, just like his dad. Now he understood why Jayson thought his stories about Chartile had been real. The mid-summer breeze across his body was as believable as anything from the real world. And so was the creature smiling before him.

Charlie took a few cautious steps back, looking the panther square in the face. "This is a dream," Charlie said, more to himself than the animal. "You're not real. You can't really hurt me."

The panther laughed again and beat its gigantic wings in the air. "I am as real as

21

any man, tree, or beast, young lad. I only wish I could truly make a meal of you."

"Kashna!" someone called to Charlie's left. Both he and the panther turned to see a boy and girl around Charlie's age staring at the scene in the middle of the clearing.

"Help me!" Charlie called to them and took off running again. This time, however, the panther did not pursue. The strange boy dashed from the brush line and thrust a cape around Charlie's shoulders. Charlie stopped running long enough to see the panther still lying in the clearing where he'd left him, licking its paw and folding its wings nonchalantly.

"It's all right, Ailinn," said the boy over his shoulder. "Common, no doubt, but he's covered now."

"What?" asked Charlie, pulling the cape tighter around him. "I'm not—" He stopped speaking as the girl emerged from behind one of the large trees at the edge of the clearing.

"Oh, please, it's nothing I haven't seen before," she said, her hands on her hips and her brow furrowed. "I helped Mother and the priestesses with the orphans, if you recall."

Charlie felt his face flush. He looked down to make sure the cape was covering all his vital parts.

"Yes, well—" stammered the boy, running his fingers through his thick black hair. "That's different."

The girl rolled her eyes and approached Charlie with a grace and confidence he had never seen before. She glided across the uneven terrain, her head held high and her bright green eyes holding his attention captive. She looked human enough. There weren't any extra appendages – at least none that Charlie could see. But there was definitely something inhuman about her, and it made his heart flutter. She gave a small curtsy, then looked up into Charlie's stunned face.

"I am Princess Ailinn," she said. Charlie stared, his mouth hanging open slightly. She looked back at him with gentle concern. "May I ask your name?"

"Uh—Charlie, Charlie Hill," he replied, finally pulling his eyes away from her. He looked at the boy standing beside her and watched as he raised an eyebrow.

Charlie gulped. He must have been the princess's bodyguard. He was probably trained to know exactly what Charlie was feeling. And thinking. Charlie wasn't sure his face could blush anymore, but he felt heat rise to his cheeks again. He swallowed again and shrank back, hunching to make sure the cape covered everything. It only reached to his knees, which he might have appreciated more in the hot, sticky air at any other time. But right now, Charlie would have given anything for a fully padded snowsuit.

"Can... can you tell me where I am exactly?" he asked, his voice coming out as a high-pitched squeak.

Ailinn tilted her head, scrutinizing him and twirling her curly red hair between her fingers absently. "Charlie Hill?" She began to circle him now, and Charlie hunched even further. "And where are you from, Charlie Hill?"

The older boy rolled his eyes and sighed audibly. "Not this again," he mumbled.

"Hush, Daniel!" Ailinn snapped, then turned her attention back to Charlie.

"Uh... Swansdale? Ohio? Um... The United States of America?" Charlie answered.

Ailinn stopped before him again, grinning. "And is your father Jayson Hill, by chance? The great King Pasalphathe of Chartile, returned as the prophecy foretold? The renegade who single-handedly brought a dozen conspirators back to the castle without so much as a scratch for his troubles? Jayson, the best bowman Chartile has ever seen?"

Charlie shifted uncomfortably. This was most definitely a dream. He'd been thinking about Chartile after visiting his father. That's all this was. It wasn't real. It wasn't. It couldn't be.

"He is nothing more than a crazy fool, Ailinn. Leave him," the boy called Daniel spat at her.

"You remember what Mother taught us. You remember the last part of the prophecy. *And then in kin, come back again.* She warned us something was coming. She knew something was going to happen." Ailinn's attention was fully on Daniel now. Charlie took the opportunity to adjust the cape more tightly around himself.

"Mother was not a good queen," Daniel said gently. "She couldn't handle the stress. She wasn't raised with it."

"Our mother was not crazy. You are only siding with Father to be in his good graces," said Ailinn matter-of-factly.

Charlie seemed nonexistent to them. He took a careful step back, hoping if he walked far enough away from them, he would wake up from whatever this was. Maybe Malcolm Darcy had actually knocked him out, and he was lying across the cafeteria table. Maybe he was still sleeping, and he hadn't even visited his father yet.

Something soft and warm bumped gently against Charlie's back. He jumped, suppressing a squeal as he turned to look over his shoulder. There was the winged panther again. It looked innocently at him with those intelligent, golden eyes and gave a gentle purr.

"I know you sent Kashna to chase him, Daniel. Don't pretend you didn't." Ailinn continued yelling at Daniel.

"He was naked, Ailinn. Completely naked! It was an innocent jest."

"And quite inappropriate for the Prince of the Elves of Chartile."

Daniel glared at Ailinn, his tone turning stern. "You know I haven't held that title for years now, Your Highness. Now, you will accompany me back to the palace, as that seems to be my role lately. Your royal nanny."

Ailinn crossed her arms before her and planted her feet firmly beneath her. "If I must return to the palace, I am taking him back with me."

"He's not a lost little diten mouse—"

"That is final, Lord Nanny." Ailinn turned on her heel, grabbed Charlie by the elbow, and led him off into the darkness of the towering trees. Charlie glanced behind him and saw Daniel shake his head before motioning the panther to follow.

The canopy overhead was so tightly grown together, very little grew at the base of the giant tree trunks. Still, the ground was soft, and several of the trees had merged into one, making their path even more winding than the paths in the woods Charlie was used to exploring back home. Ailinn had let go of him, but he continued to follow her. Despite her obvious frustration with Daniel, he noticed she still moved with the same smooth gait and self-assured air.

"You must excuse my brother's actions," Ailinn said. "Kashna was a peace offering. My father had no interest in him, so Daniel cared for him. Kashna is bonded with Daniel now, and the pair seem to find great joy in terrorizing anyone willing to fall for their tricks."

"Are... Are talking panthers normal here?" Charlie asked. His voice was low and quiet. Ailinn stepped closer to him though it may have only been out of the need to avoid a spiky-looking bush in their path. Charlie knew if he pulled the cape around him any tighter, it might rip.

"I don't know what a panther is," the princess replied. "Kashna is a qarveena, a lost legend."

"Oh," said Charlie.

"But, to answer your question, no," Ailinn continued. "Qarveena have not been seen since the time of the four kings. Savaric will not reveal how or where he found Kashna. It is actually rather worrisome."

Charlie had a thousand questions buried beneath the fog of his mind, but he couldn't focus. His stomach kept doing somersaults every time he looked at Ailinn. His mouth was completely dry, but he thought he would drool at any moment. It was very odd.

"If you're the princess and all," he finally said, his tongue like sandpaper, "why are you out here by yourself? Shouldn't you have an armed guard or something?"

Ailinn heaved a sigh of frustration and thrust her chin in the air. "I was running away. Daniel came after me with Kashna."

"Oh," was all Charlie could think to say at first. "Why would you do that?"

"Because I refuse to be used as a pawn." She stopped and looked at Charlie, her gentle features hardened and stern. "There are things in this world that have changed since your father was here, Charlie Hill. And not for the better. The events your father helped bring about were not the beginning of a time of peace. They were the spark that lit the fires of war."

She held his gaze for several long seconds until he made a swipe at the corner of his mouth to check for any drool. She left him standing alone and stepped out onto a wide dirt path. Charlie looked after her, more confused than ever. He jumped when the qarveena stepped beside him. Daniel sat astride the creature and looked gravely down at Charlie.

"I do not know who you are, stranger, but you would do well not to get involved with anything to do with Princess Ailinn," he said, looking after his sister as she strode up the road alone. "She appears as my father at first, gentle and quiet. But she is as tenacious and dangerous as my mother. Once she gets an idea in her mind, there is no stopping her."

"Then how did you get her to come back with you?" Charlie asked. He tried to adjust the nonexistent glasses on his face. Their disappearance was a stark reminder that he was still dreaming.

"I'm her brother," was all he said, then followed after Ailinn.

Charlie was left alone in the middle of a dark, dense forest with nothing but a medieval cape to cover him. He reached up to pinch his arm, but the cape fell open at the front. He quickly gathered it around himself again before trudging off after Daniel.

The road widened as they went, and the trees thinned. The light that filtered through the thick treetops became slowly brighter. Before he knew it, Charlie stood before a gigantic hedgerow, beyond which rose a towering stone wall. The road ended at a heavy wooden door that measured at least four men wide and three men tall. Charlie saw movement on the wall as soldiers in medieval armor bustled back and forth.

"Raise the gate!" he heard them cry to one another. Chains on either side of the door clanked as the gate was lifted through a slit in the stone wall above.

Ailinn marched through, followed closely by Daniel and Kashna. Charlie hurried after them, and the gate lowered again behind him. They stood in what appeared to be a kind of courtyard. A group of soldiers in the same medieval armor parted before the pair of royals, bowing as they did so. Ailinn opened her mouth to speak to one of the men when a voice echoed off the cobblestone surrounding them.

"By the Gods, Ailinn!" The soldiers bowed even lower and Daniel followed suit. Even Kashna lay flat on his stomach as a blond-haired man in sweeping, embroidered robes approached. Behind him, several older men in various embroidered tunics and heavy jewelry hurried into the courtyard.

Ailinn did not bow. She thrust her chin out as she had before and squared her shoulders back.

"Father," she said, the cold in her voice icy enough to chill the summer air. Charlie ducked behind the soldiers, who still bowed to the man. If this was Ailinn's father, he must be the king. Charlie had no intention, whether real or in a dream, to appear naked before the King of the Elves of Chartile.

The king grabbed Ailinn's shoulders and shook her. The princess did not flinch. "You. You and your damned, bullheaded—" He stopped abruptly, releasing Ailinn from his grasp. He took several deep breaths and continued. "You will not do this to me, Ailinn. I will not stand for it."

"Nor will I," Ailinn countered. "I am not a trinket to be given away at will. I am not your pawn, Father." Her green eyes flashed with cold, hard anger.

"I am the King of the Elves of Chartile, and you will bow before me as any other man. You may be Princess, but you are still my daughter. Your fate rests with me until the day you wear your mother's crown." He leaned closer to Ailinn, ice-blue eyes meeting green. "I will discuss this with you further in private. Take her to the tower," he called to the guards.

"No, wait!" Daniel cried, rushing ahead of the armored men to his sister's side. Kashna followed, giving the smallest growl at the soldiers approaching from the rear.

Ailinn glanced sidelong at her brother, now clearly quite afraid.

"Let me take care of her, Father," said Daniel. "I will make her listen."

Ailinn glared at Daniel, fidgeting nervously and rubbing her wrists.

"Out of the question," the king countered. "You disobeyed my orders as well. You are no better than she!"

"But she'll listen to me, Father! Please." Daniel grabbed his sister's hand, but Ailinn immediately pulled free.

From out of absolutely nowhere, Charlie sneezed violently. He covered his face with the cloak and tried to bow lower. The king and the noblemen behind him looked stunned to see the strange boy covered in naught but a cloak and crouching behind the guards.

"Who are you?" one of the elaborately dressed men asked. Charlie looked up at the faces surrounding him, all staring with intense curiosity.

"I—I—" he stammered, slowly creeping out from behind the guards to stand beside Daniel. He gave Kashna as wide of a berth as possible. "I'm Charlie, sir."

At this point, he had no idea what to do. He knelt on the stone ground on both knees, the edges of the cloak now completely covering him. He felt his body go numb as the blood rushed to his face. Oh, what he wouldn't do to not be naked at that very moment. Forget not fitting in at school—this was just ridiculous. Charlie was completely convinced at this point. This was unquestionably, without a doubt, the worst dream ever. Clothes, any clothes, especially clothes to help him fit in for a change, would have been fantastic at that moment.

"It is as Mother predicted," said Ailinn. "Nobles of the Conclave, I bring you Charlie of the Hill, son of Jayson. It is as the prophecy foretold."

"Quiet, Ailinn." Daniel grabbed his sister's arm again and hissed in her ear.

"Leave me, Daniel," she said, pushing him away. "*And then in kin, come back again.* Mother said it was not as we first thought. Jayson, Jack, and Leo will not be returning to us as those born of Chartile. The prophecy has brought us Jayson of the Hill's son. She was right. We cannot ignore this!"

There was a long pause of silence, broken only by the uncomfortable shuffling of the soldiers' boots and the swish of the noblemen's capes and tunics.

Eventually, the king spoke. "Take the princess to the tower. And please escort Daniel to his chambers."

Ailinn and Daniel did not argue this time. The change in their father's tone must have meant something only they knew. Ailinn turned to look at Charlie one last time as she was ushered away, a grin spreading across her face. Charlie wasn't sure why. All he knew was his neck and wrists were suddenly very itchy.

"What of this one, Majesty?" one of the soldiers asked the king.

Charlie rose and nearly fell over. The cloak slipped from his shoulders, and he made a mad grab for it. But the tunic that had not been there a moment before pulled at his underarms. The cloak fell at his feet, and Charlie looked up at the king and noblemen with as much awe as they stared back with.

Charlie was now garbed in a blue-and-white tunic. Sparkling, golden thread ran through the entire garment, and the cuffs around his collar and wrists were a delicate lace. The hose on his legs shimmered in the dim light as if made of pure gold.

The king stepped forward, presenting a hand in greeting. Charlie took it and offered a small shake. The king smiled at him and gave the smallest of bows.

"Well, Charlie of the Hill, welcome to Chartile."

FIVE
DREAMS AND ACTUALITY

OF ALL THE OUTRAGEOUS THINGS his brain could have thought up for him to wear, this get-up was the worst. Charlie scratched at the lacy collar as he followed a group of guards through the Elven palace.

In that moment, as he knelt before the king, his mind could focus on nothing else except his immediate need for clothes. Anything would have been satisfactory, but of course, the lingering fear of being different made itself known. Charlie had pushed it away. Of course, he wanted to fit in. He'd always wanted to fit in. And somehow, his mind contrived a way for him to be both clothed and normal. Not that lacy cuffs were normal for Charlie. But apparently, they were in Chartile.

It was all too much. He was going completely crazy. *As crazy as Dad*, Charlie thought to himself. He regretted yelling at him now more than ever. It made perfect sense how Jayson could have believed his hallucinations were real. Charlie's footfalls echoed through the gold hallway the guards led him down. The glint and reflection off the brightly polished marble tile appeared real enough as well. Even the smell of BO and armor funk from the guards beside him was plenty realistic.

They turned down another corridor, this one lined with towering tree trunks carved into elegant pillars and inlaid with gold. It was exactly as his father had described it. Even the golden tiles on the floor, worn in some areas and polished bright in others, were just as Jayson had said.

The guards who escorted Charlie stared sidelong at him as they walked. When Charlie looked at them, they turned away quickly, only to look back at him again moments later. Charlie tried to ignore them. He remained silent, pressing his tongue to the roof of his mouth. Sometimes, in his dreams, he knew he shouldn't say or do something, but his dream-self did it anyway. He was determined to keep quiet no matter what his dream-self wanted to do.

The guards stopped before a carved wooden door built through the tree trunks that supported the stone walls. A guard pulled the door open and held it for Charlie, bowing as he did so.

"Your quarters, Lord of the Hill," he said. Charlie stood frozen, looking at the four guards who towered on either side of him. He had, unfortunately, inherited his father's height, or rather, the lack thereof. It seemed his dream was going for full-out authenticity, which only heightened his sense of awareness.

"We will stand watch here, Master Charlie," another guard said, giving Charlie a small smile and nod. "You are safe now." Charlie peeked into the room, then stepped carefully through. He jumped when the door closed behind him, and a chill ran down his spine as he heard the clink of armor from the guards outside his door.

"So weird," Charlie whispered to himself, turning to survey his quarters. He'd never stayed anywhere with quarters before. It looked like just a room to Charlie, though, an admittedly fancy one.

The four-poster bed was as intricately carved as the pillars in the hall, and its canopy held a few of the dinner-plate-sized leaves caught on top. The single window overlooking a garden and courtyard a few feet below was built into a stone wall between the towering tree trunks. The trees were tall and thick, their boughs laced together to create the ceiling.

Charlie stepped to the window and the sweet scent of flowers met him instantly. The drop down into the courtyard was almost four feet. He didn't remember going uphill, but clearly, he had. Or had he? Dreams were weird like that.

Charlie pulled himself away from the window, scratching at the lace around his neck and wrists again. He spied a wardrobe carved to match the four-poster, and inside hung an assortment of tunics, plain shirts, vests, and hosiery. While better than what he currently wore, Charlie had hoped to find a pair of jeans and sneakers. He sighed and closed the wardrobe door. This dream had been anything but convenient so far. He shouldn't have expected it to start being so now.

A carved vanity sat to the left of the wardrobe, and a bowl of fruit and a plate of crackers and cheese had been laid out on top. Charlie's eyes widened at the sight of the food. He made a grab for the crackers and stuffed at least three in his mouth at once. He hadn't realized how hungry he was. His confusion and fear must have kept his hunger pains at bay, but the sight of the food had brought them ravenously back. He wondered if his dream-stomach would recognize food and end its growling and rumbling.

Charlie polished off the crackers and moved on to some sort of apple-pear thing. He wasn't sure what it was, but he didn't care. He took a bite, and juice dribbled down his chin. He was halfway through the fruit when it dawned on him: What if it was poisoned? He threw the fruit back into the bowl and wiped his hands and chin on his tunic. Stupid dream-self. But if he was dreaming, did being poisoned even matter?

Charlie walked back to the four-poster bed and hopped onto the mattress. It wasn't very firm, and it smelled funny. He fumbled with the tiny buttons on the front of his tunic and peeled it off his sweaty torso. Why couldn't his dream have air conditioning?

After stripping off the rest of his clothes and searching the wardrobe to no avail for anything resembling boxers or briefs, Charlie gave up and sprawled on the bed. Hallucinating was exhausting. He hoped that as soon as he woke up, he'd find himself in his bed back home, or maybe even sleeping in the high school office.

For a moment, an image of Princess Ailinn flashed into his mind. He felt angry and scared. Then the feelings faded into something different. The more he thought about her, the more his stomach wanted to do flip-flops.

"I really am going crazy," he whispered to himself. Charlie bunched up the smelly pillows underneath him, closed his eyes, and drifted into sleep.

THERE WAS SHUFFLING TO CHARLIE'S right. Still paralyzed by sleep, he could only listen. He heard the creak of a door hinge, then more shuffling. It sounded like his grandmother when she walked down the hall in her little house slippers. A loud clank like silverware on a platter made Charlie jump. He bolted upright, his eyes wide. He screamed when he saw the tiny figure of a man cleaning up the uneaten food still spread across the vanity. The little man jumped as well and dropped the platter of food. Crumbs, crackers, and bits of the clay plate went flying everywhere. Charlie pulled the blankets up over his naked body.

"What the hell, man. Just… What the—?"

The little man was so old, Charlie half-expected the breeze through the window to blow him over. His brown eyes were slightly clouded, and what little hair was left was a tuft of white cotton at the base of his head. His skin was the color and texture of tanned leather, and he walked with a small hunch, always looking at the floor.

"Forgive me, Master Charlie. I did not intend to frighten you," he said, his voice a raspy squeak.

"I'm still here," Charlie murmured. He took several deep breaths, but his heart still raced. "How am I still here?"

The tiny man bent to retrieve the pieces of shattered pottery at the foot of the four-poster. Charlie heard his bones crack loudly and the man's labored breathing as he reached under the bed. When he emerged again, with many grunts and groans, his arms were full of crackers and broken plate. He nodded to Charlie but did not meet his gaze. He turned to retrieve the fruit bowl and Charlie saw a thin line of blood running down the man's arm. A jagged piece of pottery poked deeply into the thin and withered flesh, though the man did not seem to notice.

"You're bleeding," said Charlie.

The man looked at his arm. He adjusted the broken shards of plate, but the blood still dripped. He emptied the contents of his arms into the fruit bowl and headed for a little door Charlie hadn't noticed across the room.

"Wait!" Charlie called to him. He wrapped the tunic still lying on the floor around his middle and hurried to the wardrobe. Sifting through the strange clothing, he grabbed what looked like very long arm or leg coverings. He had no idea what they were, but they were made of some kind of linen or cotton, and he knew this would be absorbent. Charlie wasn't squeamish about blood, and his father had taught him a thing or two about first aid from his days in the war.

Jayson had fulfilled his dream of flying, but not as a fighter pilot. He was a skilled field medic and had flown the emergency medical helicopters into the war zones to rescue his fallen soldiers. He'd taught his son basic first aid before he'd been ten years old.

Charlie hurried across the room, reaching out for the little man. The man recoiled, taking a tentative step back.

Charlie stopped. "I know how to wrap your arm for the bleeding. My dad showed me." He kept his voice calm like his father had taught him, even though he felt his knees and hands begin to shake. He had convinced himself that when he awoke, he'd be back in Swansdale. The fact that he remained in Chartile made his head spin. He still had no idea whether any of it was real, but he wasn't about to let someone bleed all over, dream-blood or not.

The man stared at the floor, watching as the blood dripped off his elbow and landed on the wood below. His eyes darted back and forth, and he blinked rapidly. Eventually, he set his armload of broken plate back on the vanity and turned to Charlie, though he still refused to meet the boy's gaze.

Charlie approached him slowly and reached for his arm. He felt the little man jump and stiffen at his touch, but he didn't pull away.

"What's your name?" Charlie asked as he wiped away the blood to look at the wound.

The old man hesitated. He swallowed hard and replied, "Phillippe, Master Charlie. I am your assigned beck-and."

He reminded Charlie of his Aunt Jessica's puppy. She'd rescued him from a home where he'd been beaten and abused. But there were no outward signs of abuse on Phillippe. No bruises or cuts. At least not that Charlie could see beneath his plain white tunic and the layers of dirt and grime.

Charlie tied the ends of the wrapping and leaned back. Phillippe stared at his arm, wrapped and bound under Charlie's skillful hand. He looked at the boy for the first time, then quickly away again, but not before Charlie noticed the tears that had formed against his cloudy brown eyes.

"What's wrong?" Charlie asked. "Did I do something wrong?" He tried to reach for Phillippe's arm again, worried that he had perhaps wrapped things too tightly. But the beck-and let his arm fall to his side, ignoring Charlie's gesture.

Charlie watched as he scuttled to the wardrobe and began rummaging through the clothes inside. He pulled out a pair of the skinny-looking pants, a tunic, and an assortment of other clothes and laid them on the bed with delicate, bony fingers.

"I have not the words to express my gratitude, Master Charlie. The generosity of your house precedes you, though I did not believe it."

Charlie furrowed his brow. "What do you mean?"

Phillippe hesitated. He scratched at his wrapped arm and stared at his feet as he shuffled back and forth. "Humans are not granted the same respect as the greater races, Master Charlie. It is our punishment."

Charlie bit his lip and tightened the tunic he had wrapped around himself. There were certain cultural differences in Chartile that had made Jayson uncomfortable, and he had spoken very little about beck-ands. What he had told Charlie, the boy pushed from his mind when his father was sent to the psychiatric center. It was only now as Charlie watched the little man across the room, did he realize why Phillippe would not look at him and it seemed difficult for him to speak.

"Well, I'm not from Chartile. I'm not an elf or dwarf or whatever, so you don't have to act like that around me," he said.

Phillippe's gaze shifted to Charlie once more, and this time, he didn't look away.

Charlie walked to the bed and looked at the clothes the man had laid out for him. "You're not my slave, okay? But I could use some help figuring out how to put this stuff on." He lifted what looked like a wad of white cotton and shrugged at Phillippe.

After much fuss and embarrassment, the beck-and helped Charlie dress in the strange clothes common to the elves of Chartile. Charlie hated to admit it, but the undergarments were more comfortable than the boxers he had wished for earlier.

Charlie sat on the edge of the bed again, fidgeting with the hem of his tunic. He watched the little man continue to clean up the shards of broken plate that had managed to make their way to all four corners of the room. Phillippe declined Charlie's offer of help, and the boy decided not to push. His mother used to tease her husband about needing a beck-and or two, but Jayson never much appreciated the joke.

There had been a brief period when the sunlight filtered through the open window. The dense construction of the trees that made up the palace made it almost impossible for sunlight to get through except for when it shone at just the right angle. And now that the sun was setting, even the slight ambiance of light had all but faded.

"What were you saying about beck-ands before?" Charlie asked Phillippe as he stood with a last fragment of pottery in hand. He dropped the shard in the fruit bowl with the rest and began lighting several lamps placed around the room. When Phillippe did not answer, Charlie continued, "You said it was your punishment."

Phillippe lit the last lamp and extinguished the lighting taper in his hand. The light from the lamps scattered the shadows in the room, but not before bouncing off the golden cuffs adorned with black gems that the beck-and wore tight against his wrists.

"How much do you wish to know, Master Charlie?"

Charlie sighed. "Everything."

THE ORENITE CUFFS WERE ITCHY and too tight. They needed sent to one of the Dwarvik smiths for readjusting, but King Valin would not allow it. It was one of the few things he had some semblance of control over within his kingdom, though his daughter was slowly slipping through that grasp since his wife's death.

Ailinn sat in her favorite chair, scratching at the cuffs on her wrists and reading from several books and journals her mother had left her. She pulled the table closer to her and opened three books at once, spreading them out before her.

She heard talking outside her door and scrambled to gather the journals and books. She lifted the seat on a second chair and opened a hidden compartment. With a swift and practiced routine, she dumped the books in and situated the cushion back into place as the lock on her door clicked. She spun around, knocking a lamp on the table to the floor and plunging the room into semi-darkness.

"Ailinn! Are you all right?" asked Daniel's voice from the door. The three men who had stood guard outside her door rushed in, hands on their hilts.

"I'm fine," she said. "I'm sorry. You startled me is all."

Daniel nodded to the guards behind him, and they exited the room once more. Ailinn sighed and sat in her chair as Daniel retrieved a lamp from the mantel.

"Researching again?" Daniel asked. He lifted the cushion of the chair and pulled out a few stray scrolls before setting the new lamp on the table between them.

"Father will destroy this kingdom if I don't do something," Ailinn said, snatching one of the scrolls from her brother as he sat.

"You *can* do something," he prompted.

Ailinn glared. "I will not marry Merrick."

"You were betrothed to him once, Ailinn. He's our friend—"

Ailinn snapped her fingers, cutting Daniel off. "He is not our friend! His father supplied the rebels who killed our mother! I refuse to marry a traitor."

Daniel rolled his eyes. "You're thinking about this all wrong." For all her disdain towards him, Ailinn was an over thinker, exactly like her father. And though Daniel had never met his half-human, half-dwarvik father, Dimitri, he seemed to be the only level-headed one in the family. He assumed the trait was from him. He ran his fingers through his black hair and leaned forward. "Savaric has agreed to discontinue his support of the rebels if you marry Merrick."

"He claims such, but I don't believe it."

Daniel nodded. "Which is why your marriage to Merrick is even more important. A spider in a glass cage is not nearly as dangerous as a spider left to his own devices. Savaric will spend much of his time at the palace attempting to gain a place among the Conclave of Nobles. This will make monitoring his movements much easier than having him skulk about up in Harpy's Pointe."

"And Merrick?" Ailinn crossed her arms and raised an eyebrow. "You mean to tell me that Savaric's own son will not keep his father informed? Savaric will continue to be a step ahead of us no matter what we do."

"Then you haven't heard the rumors."

"Oh, I have." Ailinn stood from her chair and paced before the fireplace, scratching at the orenite cuffs again. "You honestly believe Merrick left his comfy little castle and has been masquerading as a commoner in his own town for the last two years? I'm sorry, Daniel. I know you think me crazy to believe some of the things I do, but that—"

"He was like a second son to Mother," Daniel retorted. He sighed and stood, pulling a small key from his pocket. "Here," he said, reaching out a hand to her. "I nicked it from one of your guards."

Ailinn smirked as her brother unlocked the cuffs. "I thought you said you were ashamed of your father. A common thief, I believe you called him?" She let out an audible sigh as she pulled her hands free of the cuffs. Daniel set them on the mantel beside her.

"Now that I have renounced my claim to the throne, there's no point in denying who I am. I have no need to sweeten the king toward me."

"You still try." Ailinn laughed. "Don't deny it, Daniel."

"You think it's easy staying so close to you when I have no real purpose here? With Mother gone, who's left to protect you?"

Ailinn sat on the arm of the chair beside Daniel and took his hand in hers.

"Who's left to protect *you*?"

Daniel laughed. "I can take care of myself just fine, little princess. You're the one with the wild ideas and rampant magic."

Ailinn raised an eyebrow. "Hmph," she said and stood from the chair arm. "Well, my wild ideas might just save me from this idiotic marriage." She lifted the scroll she had snatched from Daniel and held it out to him.

"It's the prophecy," he said, not bothering to read it.

Ailinn smirked again. "Exactly. Read the last stanza for me."

Daniel rolled his eyes but obliged his sister. "*And then in kin, come back again, joining two worlds as one.*" There was but a moment's pause before he groaned. "Oh, Ailinn, no—"

"Yes," she said, sticking her chin out again. "I will marry Charlie of the Hill."

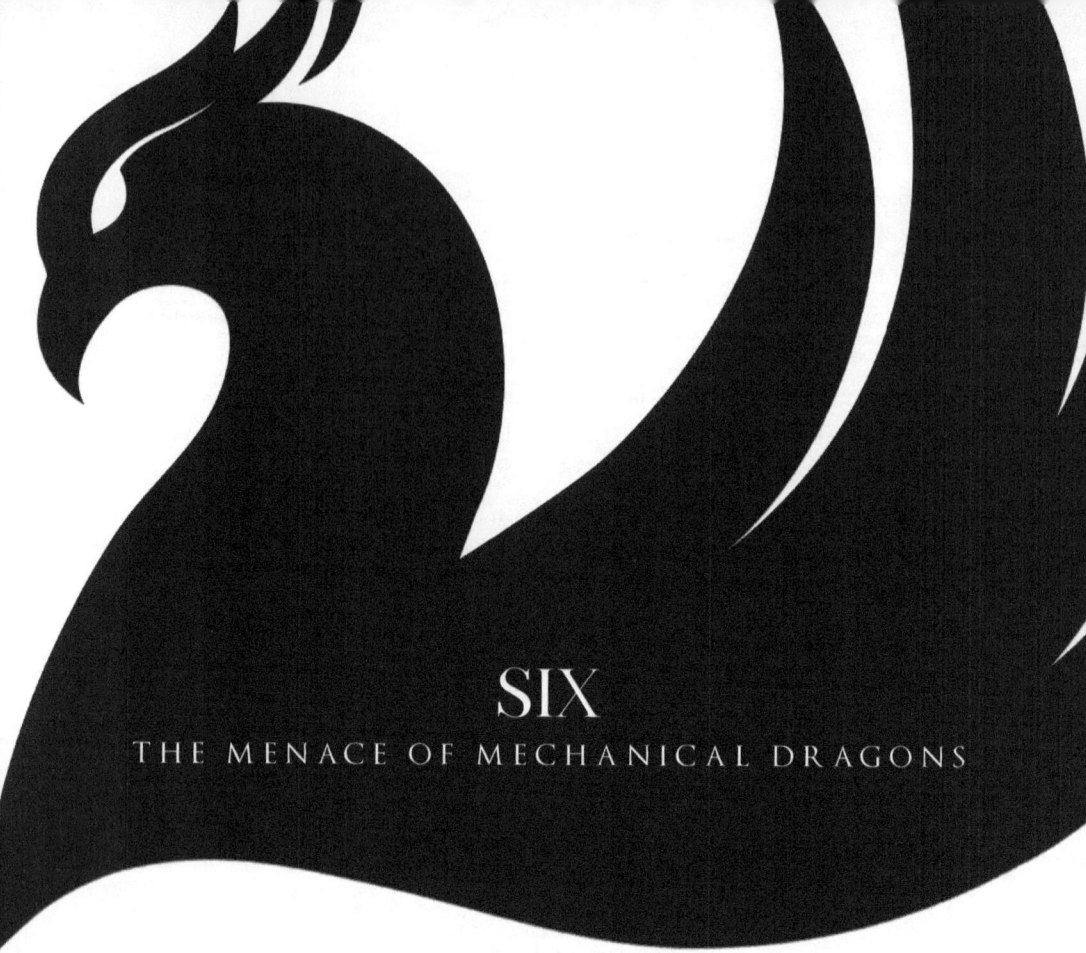

SIX

THE MENACE OF MECHANICAL DRAGONS

THERE WAS A SHARP KNOCK on the door, causing both Charlie and Phillippe to jump. The old man scurried to his feet so quickly, he winced at the pain in his joints. He stood beside the door, his head down. Charlie just stared, unsure what to do. Phillippe cleared his throat and glanced again at the door.

"Uh, who is it?" Charlie called.

There was an uncomfortable silence that followed, then a man's voice replied. "King Valin wishes to invite Lord Charlie of the Hill to dine with him and the Conclave tonight." Even through the wood, the voice sounded confused as to why he was addressing the front side of the door and not the tenant within.

Charlie looked at Phillippe, his eyes pleading for guidance. The little man looked at his master for only a moment, then nodded and opened the door.

"Master Charlie will attend King Valin this evening. Will he send an escort, or shall one be requested from the captain?" Phillippe replied.

"A full escort will be provided," the guard said, looking past the little beck-and to the boy inside. He bowed to Charlie, then headed back up the corridor.

Phillippe closed the door and shuffled back to Charlie, whose face had gone completely pale.

"Dinner with the king?" Charlie said.

"It is a great honor, Master Charlie," Phillippe said as he resumed his seat on the floor.

Charlie stood and began pacing fervently. He felt his heart begin to beat faster and his hands shook. "I don't know anything about being around royalty. Who do I bow to or where do I sit? What am I even supposed to say? This isn't a dream. It's the longest nightmare ever."

"King Valin and the Conclave want to know *you*, my lord. They are well-versed in their own customs."

"But what if I accidentally offend someone's honor or something? I could be beheaded or thrown in the dungeon!" Charlie flopped across the bed and buried his head beneath the strange-smelling pillow. He'd already tried pinching himself a hundred times. Every time Phillippe had told him something outrageous, like how his childhood hero, Queen Piper, had been killed. Or how Princess Ailinn was betrothed to some guy whose name reminded Charlie of a Christmas shop. Each time he pinched a different part of his body, but to no avail. He knew the truth, but he wasn't ready to accept it yet.

He sat up and saw Phillippe perched at the end of the bed.

"What about Princess Ailinn?" he asked the little man.

"What of her?"

Charlie blushed and felt his stomach give a jolt. "Wh-What if I embarrass myself in front of her?"

In the flickering light of the candles and lamps scattered about the room, Charlie could still see the smirk on Phillippe's face. He looked away and smashed the pillow over his head again.

"If it is the Elven etiquettes that you are so concerned with, Master Charlie, I am more than happy to instruct you," Phillippe said gently.

Charlie pulled the pillow off his head again. "Really?"

This time, Phillippe did not try to hide his smile, though he still would not look Charlie in the eye. "Of course, young master. I have lived in the palace most of my life. I may not be Elven, but I know the customs and etiquettes. Even the courtships."

"Well, I—I'm not worried about that, but... can you just teach me at least the bowing stuff?"

Phillippe spent the next hour teaching Charlie what he called "the basics," though Charlie found it all far from basic. The different bows were the most confusing. He repeated them over and over in front of his beck-and while the little man chased him around the room, attempting to redress him in his golden tunic and hose.

Even still, he always got something wrong, like whether the palm was turned down or upright, or if the hand was draped across the front or the back. There were even different heights to the bowing. One bowed lowest to the king, and only slightly bent for the lords who were not part of the Conclave. Conclave members, regardless of any other title, were given the same level bow as a prince or princess, but the hand placement was different.

"This is crazy. I'll never—"

There was the same sharp knock at the door again, and Charlie nearly fell over from his bowing stance when he heard it.

"You will do fine, Master Charlie," Phillippe whispered as he shuffled to the door. "Remember, it's you they want."

Outside, two guards waited, both much younger than the other guards Charlie had thus far encountered. They smiled at first, then seemed to remember their manners and training. One nudged the other, and they bowed in unison.

"Your escort, Master Charlie," the first one said.

Charlie swallowed hard, squared his shoulders, and joined them in the golden hall. It wasn't until he heard the door close behind him and knew Phillippe was no longer with him that his heart began to beat wildly again. He tried to distract himself, both from his anxious thoughts and the guards' body odor by running through the different bows in his mind as they walked.

After several twists and turns down winding halls and crooked corridors, they approached two ornately carved wooden doors. Flanking them were two statues, one of a man on the right and of a woman on the left. Charlie supposed they were food gods or something like that. He didn't study them too close since the statues were naked. He didn't want his escort to think he was some kind of pervert. That sort of news wouldn't exactly be received well. The guards pulled the doors wide, revealing a room already full of onlookers.

Silence fell across the room. Many of the nobles from the courtyard earlier that day were seated there, as were the king and Daniel. Charlie stood as straight as he could and walked forward. He could hear his heart pounding in his ears, and his legs felt like lead weights as he approached the table. The nobles at the two tables flanking the head table stared wide-eyed as he walked past them.

Charlie stopped at what he thought was the right distance from the king. The spot on the floor was slightly worn, so he hoped it was right. King Valin eyed him with a flat, impassive expression. Charlie tucked his left hand, palm up, around his back to rest nearly on his right hip. He bent his knees, his left almost touching the floor as his right hand crossed his chest to rest on his heart. He felt more like a pretzel than ever with the room watching him.

"King Valin," he said, and his voice cracked, "I am Charles Hill, son of Jayson Hill. It is with great honor and—um…" The shift of a skirt to his right caught Charlie's attention. The words Phillippe had taught him would no longer come. Princess Ailinn sat at the very end of one of the side tables. She looked back at him, her face set and stern, though her eyes were red and glassy, as though she had been recently crying. She glanced at her father, and Charlie blinked at her.

"It is with great honor and delight that we have *you* to join us, Charlie Hill," the king replied.

Charlie snapped back to attention. He hadn't realized how much he had turned to look at Ailinn. His hands had fallen out of their appropriate positions, and his knee was completely touching the floor now. He staggered to his feet. If he offended the King of the Elves, hiding these strange feelings he felt around Princess Ailinn would be the least of his concerns. He dared a glance at the head table and saw King Valin smiling beneath his beard, his blue eyes twinkling in the candle light.

"Please, come join me." King Valin motioned to the seat between himself and Daniel. Charlie nodded, rose from his bow, and hurried around the table opposite from Ailinn. Every pair of eyes in the room continued to follow him. Some smiled, others remained skeptical.

Charlie sat in the chair the king had indicated. He tried to scoot closer to the table, but the cobblestone floor made it difficult. He lifted the chair, moving it closer to the table with a loud scraping sound across the stone. The hall was silent, save for the clatter of Charlie's chair until he smacked his knees on the underside of the table and made Daniel's chalice wobble precariously.

"Sorry," he whispered to no one in particular, quickly removing his elbows from the table.

When Charlie settled, King Valin clapped his hands, and a door across the room swung open. A parade of beck-ands emerged bearing trays of various foods around to the tables. They offered their fare first to King Valin, Charlie, and

Daniel, then to the nobles seated around them. Charlie knew they were beck-ands, not only by their warm, tan skin and tattered clothes but by the assortment of black and gold cuffs they wore.

"Thank—uh, that's enough," he murmured, stopping himself from thanking the beck-and who placed a hunk of bread on his plate.

Charlie sighed and turned his attention to the crowd before him, which thankfully had picked up its chatter once more. His eyes drifted to Princess Ailinn as she accepted a cluster of berries from a tray. Though the forest-castle was balmy and stifling, she wore a long-sleeved and heavy-looking dress. The other nobles seemed dressed more appropriately in shorter sleeves and lighter, airy fabrics. She dabbed at a bead of sweat rolling down her temple with a handkerchief and pulled out a fan made from some sort of woven tree leaves. Charlie thought he caught the faintest glint of gold under the sleeve, but her arm moved so quickly in an effort to cool herself, he wasn't sure. He tore his eyes from her and focused on the food before him.

There was more food than he had ever seen. A full medieval feast. The beck-ands moved back and forth behind the long tables, heads down and trays held high. Every time the nobles snapped and barked at the beck-ands, Charlie saw them jump. It made him uncomfortable, and that was a feat, considering he had to cross his legs every time he caught Princess Ailinn's eye.

He had just bitten into a piece of cooked pork when one of the nobles called to him above the din of conversation. "What happened to your father after he returned to your world, Master Charlie?" he asked.

Silence fell again. Even the clinking of the cutlery diminished.

Charlie swallowed hard and took a gulp from the goblet before him. The bitter taste of wine, not water as he had expected, saturated his tongue. He coughed and set the goblet down.

"Well," he said, his voice still strained, "he started to do better in school." He cleared his throat, ignoring the eyes that stared intently back at him, and continued. "He joined the Air Force when he graduated. We had a war too. He was a medic, and he flew planes and helicopters to rescue the injured soldiers from the war zones."

A hum started around the tables as small conversations broke out. Charlie sat, waiting for the interrogation to continue.

"Your father can fly?" another noble asked in sheer amazement. "How is this possible?"

Charlie blinked. These people had no idea what an airplane was. His brain couldn't possibly have come up with that sort of twist on its own. Or perhaps his condition was worse than he feared. He swallowed the bite of bread in his mouth, trying to think of how to describe a helicopter. "It's a machine. He flies a machine that he sits inside. I don't know how it works. It's complicated with instruments and compasses to help him navigate."

"Can others fly these machines in your world?" the first noble asked.

"Oh, yeah," said Charlie, nodding his head. "And not just for the Air Force and stuff, either. We have all kinds of planes and helicopters. Some rich people have their own, private planes and pilots. Er—those are what the people who fly the planes are called. Pilots."

The nobles murmured among themselves. Charlie sat in silence, picking at the mounds of food on his plate. Had he said something wrong? Those who had once appeared uncertain that Charlie was truly the son of Jayson Hill now looked somewhere between excited and frightened. The murmurs and stares continued. Charlie needed another drink, but the wine was terrible. Instead, he picked up his knife and began sawing into a roll he had grabbed from a passing beck-and. He hoped the conversation would continue without him, but it did not. He looked up, searching the table for butter, and noticed every noble had their eyes on him again. Even Princess Ailinn was looking at him, her green eyes narrowed and a smile pulling at her lips.

"Mechanical dragons," she said at last, breaking the silence. "Your world is full of its own wondrous magic, isn't it, Charlie?"

Charlie shrugged. "I guess so. It's different." He eyed the goblet of wine again, his mouth growing more like sandpaper by the moment.

"Wondrous indeed," said King Valin, patting Charlie on the back and passing him another goblet, this one filled with water.

"What do you plan to do during your stay here?" asked another of the nobles. He was much younger than most present, but his hair was already beginning to gray.

Charlie shrugged. "I don't know. I didn't exactly plan to come here like on a vacation or anything."

"You must come shooting with me!" the noble said. "Surely, your father taught you his skills with a bow."

"A little," Charlie said, his face turning bright red. He attempted to hide it in the goblet the king had given him. "I didn't really want to learn it, though, so I'm not very good."

"It is no trouble at all, Master Charlie. There have been countless men who denied the teachings of their fathers, only to learn it was in their blood all along. My name is Torvald. I would be honored to attend you at the range."

"Now, don't be trying to keep him to yourself, Torv," said the noble beside the younger man, slapping him on the back. "You must have joined your father on a hunt at one time, surely. Riding across the countryside with nothing but your men and your horse." He looked at the treetop ceiling, lost in nostalgia before turning his expectant face back to the boy.

Charlie shook his head. He dared a glance at Ailinn. Her smirking face had fallen into sadness again. She fidgeted with the cuffs of her dress, scratching at the golden bands beneath the fabric. He tore his eyes from her and replied to the noble. "My family doesn't go hunting. My dad says guns only belong in war. And my sister was a vegetarian for a while, so…" Charlie trailed off, picking at his food again.

"M'boy, the greatest horse master of Sutton Low will teach you to ride. Fear not."

Before the meal had finished, Charlie's schedule was filled with archery lessons, horseback riding, sword fighting, even dancing lessons. He felt dizzy, unsure what to say or do. He didn't want to offend anyone, but neither the king nor Daniel seated beside him offered any sort of help. Perhaps this was how things were done in Chartile, and how guests of honor were treated. Or maybe, if he slipped off his horse or fell while dancing, he'd hit his head hard enough he'd wake back up in his own world. He could only hope.

The beck-ands were taking away the remnants of a minty lemon dessert when Ailinn finally spoke above the chatter of excited nobles. "And what of your magic, Master Charlie? Have you given thought to refining those skills while you're here?"

The room fell silent once more, save for the clash of a piece of cutlery as it hit the floor. Most of the nobles looked at the princess with sheer terror, and Charlie worried they would behead her, or something equally terrible. But soon, they turned their gazes to Charlie again as Ailinn had not taken her piercing green eyes off him.

Charlie scratched at the lace around his collar. He knew magic was outlawed from his conversations with Phillippe and what his father had taught him growing up. What he couldn't understand was why Ailinn had fought so hard to prove who he was, now only to appear determined to have him thrown in the dungeons.

"I—I don't have any magic," he replied flatly. The tension in the room lessened, but only for a moment. For the first time since he had met her, Ailinn flashed a wide, toothy smile at him, clearly holding back laughter.

"Yes, you do," she said, her voice much calmer than her face portrayed. "You see, my mother made that cloak you wore earlier today. She spun it with magic. Only those who have the gift of magic could draw on the magical reserve in those fibers and bend it to their will. Tell them how we found him, Daniel. Tell them why he wore Mother's cloak."

Clearly unprepared, Daniel spluttered as he took a drink. He wiped his mouth on his sleeve and replied, "I do not know what you mean, dear sister. Charlie was not injured in any way. He was quite... whole... in fact. Very much... intact." Daniel cleared his throat and nodded at his sister. He lowered his head and stared her down. Charlie recognized the secret language of a brother and sister almost immediately, but that was the least of his concerns at the moment. If the entire Conclave of Nobles and the king learned that Princess Ailinn had seen him naked, his fate could be worse than if they learned he possibly had magic.

"Don't mock me, Daniel. You know perfectly well what I meant. The clothes Charlie wore when he fell in the courtyard were not there when we found him, were they Daniel?" Ailinn pushed her chair back, ready to stand.

Daniel shook his head at her, but Ailinn stormed to her feet, ignoring him. Before she could speak, King Valin stood.

"Guards, escort the princess back to her tower immediately," he said. His booming voice, exactly as Charlie had heard in the courtyard, brought any side conversations to an abrupt halt. "I will not have my guest harassed in such a manner."

From behind the tree pillars along the outer wall, several guards converged on Ailinn.

"Tell them, Charlie!" she screamed as the guards yanked her away from the table. "You were brought here for a reason! You can't deny the gifts you have been given. Let me go! Charlie, please!"

Charlie stood. His heart was racing, and any form of reason all but left his brain when Ailinn began to cry.

"Wait!" he said, though the room was already silent. The only sound was Ailinn struggling against the guards, and Charlie's racing heartbeat pounding in his ears.

Daniel grabbed Charlie's arm so hard, he knew it would leave a bruise.

"Don't do this," he hissed in Charlie's ear.

"I have to," Charlie whispered back.

Daniel tightened his grip, but Charlie turned back to the crowd.

"Ailinn's right. I wasn't wearing those clothes when I got here. But if the cloak was magic like Ailinn says, then maybe it works different on people from my world."

He breathed a small sigh of relief. He hadn't admitted he had magic, but at least the whole room didn't know Ailinn had seen him butt-naked, either.

Daniel released Charlie's arm, and Charlie looked at the king who still stood beside him. King Valin nodded at the guards, and they pulled Ailinn from the room. As the sounds of her protests faded into the distance, each of the nobles stood. They walked before the king, bowed, and left hurriedly. Soon, Daniel, King Valin, and Charlie were the only ones to remain.

"I take my leave, Father," said Daniel, and Valin narrowed his eyes at him.

"You will leave her, Daniel," he said warningly. "She is dangerous, and you will not continue to protect her."

Daniel only bowed to the king, then turned quickly toward the double doors. As his footfalls echoed away, Charlie became uncomfortably aware that he was now alone with a very angry king. He wiped his mouth on his napkin and stood.

"I'm just gonna go back to my room now," he said, jabbing his thumb over his shoulder at the door. He turned on his heel and walked as quickly as he could toward the double doors without running.

He realized halfway across the room that he had not bowed nor addressed the king as Phillippe had taught him. But King Valin seemed to take no notice of Charlie. He took a long drink from his chalice and rubbed his temples. Nevertheless, Charlie gave a sort of bow that wasn't really like anything the beck-and had shown him, then fled the hall. He breathed a heavy sigh of relief when the large double doors closed behind him.

SEVEN
PRIDE AND PEDESTALS

CHARLIE RACED ALONG THE GOLDEN corridors of the Elven palace, passing carved pillar after carved pillar. It was completely dark now, and the only light in the halls came from the lanterns or torches that burned every so often along the way. It wasn't until his Elven shoes made him slip and stumble that Charlie realized he had absolutely no idea where he was going.

Every hall looked the same, and this one was no exception. He passed dozens of doors, most carved through the trunks of the enormous Belirian trees like his own, with the occasional one set in the stone that ran between the trees.

He rounded yet another identical corner and stopped short. On the wall before him, flanked by two brightly burning and ornately etched lanterns, was a painting of three teenaged boys, the silhouettes of kings standing behind them. One was a little pudgy with glasses. The other was very tall and thin with flowing locks of brown hair. And one was short and freckled with messy red hair. Charlie knew who they were even before reading the engraved plaque on the frame: *The Returned Kings*.

His stomach lurched, and every hair on his neck stood on end. Even though the portrait carried little resemblance to his father, there was no denying who he and the other two were in the painting. His hands and arms felt numb as he realized the pedestal the people of Chartile had put Jayson on. The one he was expected to rise to.

Charlie rounded on his heel, his ears turning redder by the minute. He stormed along the corridors again, this time not caring that he was lost. He had no idea how long he had been walking when he found his way to a metal gate fitted between two trees. He pushed on the gate without thinking and passed into the garden beyond.

He walked along the stone path, guided only by the dim moonlight and occasional hanging lantern. He looked past the strange plants and flowers, not really seeing them at all. The trees above him appeared to have been trimmed away so sunlight could filter through to the plants below, but he paid little mind to it. He passed a fountain with little silver fish darting toward the surface to catch the water bugs resting on top. He sat on the fountain's edge and looked up at the dark sky above him.

He felt more conflicted than ever. It was easy to believe you were something you were not when everyone around you believed in you. But the fact of the matter was, Charlie was not his father, and he had no intention of ever becoming like his father—the man who had abandoned his family. Every person he met here placed their expectations of an upgraded Jayson of the Hill onto Charlie's sixteen-year-old shoulders. He didn't want that responsibility, but he doubted anyone would listen.

There were quiet footsteps on the other side of the fountain. Charlie reached to his hip, expecting some kind of dagger to be there, then smacked his forehead for the sheer ridiculousness of the instinct. He peered around the tall stone structure and saw Ailinn. She had changed into a simple gown, her hair piled on top of her head, and a bag in one hand. She sat on the edge of the fountain, sprinkling breadcrumbs into the water. The silver fish darted and splashed in their haste to devour the bread, and a smile pulled at the princess's lips as she watched them.

Charlie watched her. He couldn't move or speak. She was the prettiest girl he had ever seen, and the mere sight of her completely paralyzed him. He had absolutely no experience with girls. Not that he had ever felt any inclination to. Not in that way. Charlie wasn't exactly dating material in Swansdale. As she watched the silver fish, Charlie caught the truth in her smile. He recognized it well. Sadness. Loneliness. He wanted to put his arm around her and let her cry on his shoulder. Though he was sure Princess Ailinn was not a crier. He didn't know her story, but she must have been very brave to stand up to everyone the way she did. Two times, in fact, in the short while Charlie had been in Chartile. He wondered how long it had been since a tear slipped down her ivory cheek.

She sprinkled another handful of breadcrumbs into the water and smiled again.

"I know you're hungry," she whispered to the fish. "I'll take care of you. Don't worry."

She bit her lip, and Charlie suddenly wanted to kiss her. He had never kissed a girl before and wondered what it was like, what it tasted like.

"Probably strawberries," he whispered.

Ailinn stood up so fast, she dropped the bag of breadcrumbs into the water. The tiny fish frenzied with excitement and splashed her dress as they ate.

"I'm sorry!" said Charlie, coming from behind the fountain, his hands raised in surrender. "I didn't mean to startle you." He hoped that was the only thing he'd said out loud.

Ailinn placed a hand over her heart and chuckled. "Charlie, you gave me a fright."

"I'm sorry. I didn't mean—"

"No, it's all right." She smiled and sat on the edge of the fountain. She fished out the little bag, wrung it out, and laid it beside her to dry. "I'm glad it's you," she said, ignoring the flush rising in his face.

"Oh?" said Charlie. He still felt paralyzed as her piercing green eyes studied him.

She chuckled again. "Yes. We haven't been able to talk since this morning."

"Oh," Charlie said again. He realized how stupid he must have sounded. He tried to flatten his hair and think of something cool to say, but his brain wasn't working.

"Come sit." Ailinn patted the ledge beside her. She had to stop herself from laughing when she saw the panic on Charlie's face. His awkwardness was adorable and a refreshing change from the usual pompous and overconfident sons of the nobles she typically encountered. He wore on his sleeve the way she felt but could never show.

"Okay," Charlie said. His body felt like jelly as he found his way around the fountain beside her. He had to hurry or else his legs might seize up like cement. He hoped he didn't appear too eager. He sat beside her, then leapt back up again, pulling the wet breadcrumb bag from his rear. Ailinn attempted to stifle a laugh and snorted instead. She clasped her hands to her face, her eyes wide. They stared at each other for a moment, then laughed again.

"I thought your dad sent you back to the tower," Charlie said after the giggles had died down. He was trying not to look too closely at her. He didn't want her thinking he was a creep or something.

Ailinn smirked and raised an eyebrow. "I have my ways of sneaking in and out of this place."

They sat in silence for several long minutes. Ailinn stared at the sky and the trees beyond. Charlie's stomach did flip-flops against the meal he had just eaten.

"My mother often talked about running away from here when I was little," Ailinn finally said, still staring at the sky. "I didn't understand why she wanted to leave until after she died." She turned to Charlie, and her laughing green eyes were hard once more. "There are things in this world that are not what my father and the Conclave believe—or want you to think."

"Like what?" Charlie asked. Phillippe had already told him more than he could possibly imagine to be true.

Ailinn sighed and fidgeted with the gold band beneath her dress sleeve. "Like the drought this last spring. I don't believe for a moment it was because our High Priest did not perform his due diligence to Einsentar. Or that the disappearances across the kingdom are coincidental. Mostly, I do not believe Lord Savaric has the proper intentions with the treaty he's proposed."

"A treaty?"

Ailinn nodded. "Lord Savaric has been supplying the rebels with food and medicine, and we suspect weapons as well. He's a supporter of birth parity."

"Birth pear-what now?" Charlie asked.

"Birth parity. When the four kings, Jenemar, Pasalphathe, Florine, and Kasmalin, finally defeated Duke Noraedin, it was agreed that magic would be eradicated from the world. All but Kasmalin agreed. They made very specific marriage arrangements among the nobles so their children would not be born with magic. Except there was a problem they did not expect."

"They had magic anyway, didn't they? That's what happened to Piper."

"In a manner of speaking. It was the commoners they did not factor in. Arranged marriages are common among the nobles, but not the simple folk. However, as magic had been outlawed, the commoners were forced to hide their magic. Some resorted to killing their own children."

"Holy-what?" Charlie cried, then clapped a hand to his mouth as his voice echoed off the surrounding stone.

They waited until the sound died away and they were sure no one had heard.

"It is terrible. But when they saw my mother using her magic against Taraniz's supporters, it was like they had permission to come out of the shadows once more. Birth parity is what Savaric refers to when he speaks of no longer punishing people for the way they were born," said Ailinn more quietly.

"That makes sense," Charlie whispered back.

"Except Savaric's surrender was too sudden and too convenient. He agreed to stop supplying the rebels and to give his full support to the crown once more *if* I would marry his son, Merrick."

"Why don't you, I don't know, just arrest the guy? I mean, Valin's the king, right?"

Ailinn shook her head. "If it were only so simple. The last thing we want is for Savaric to become a martyr. If he is arrested, there's no telling what his supporters would do. During the time of the four kings, well… many lives were lost for the sake of who was right and who was righter."

Charlie scratched his nose, suddenly wishing he had paid more attention to Mr. Carroll during social studies and world history.

"Besides," Ailinn continued, adjusting her skirts. "who's to say he or his rebels wouldn't just help him escape using magic?"

"I guess that makes sense," said Charlie. "But what about Merrick? Maybe he isn't bad like Savaric. Maybe he really can help. And Savaric's gonna be watched closely because Merrick will be, like, important and stuff. So, if he tries any funny business, you'll know, right?" Charlie snapped his mouth shut as Ailinn squinted at him. What he had said probably made as much sense as putting a piece of bologna in a CD player and expecting that song from the grocery store to start playing. He didn't understand why he could talk to any girl at school without issue—if any girl actually wanted to talk to him—but Ailinn turned his brain to mush.

She blinked at him. "How do you know such things?" she asked, breathless.

Charlie shrugged. He didn't want to tell on Phillippe, especially if he wasn't supposed to have told Charlie all the politics of Chartile. "I don't know. *Is* Merrick a nice guy?"

Ailinn shook her head. "Merrick, my brother, and I were playmates when we were younger. My mother wanted to spend as much time in Harpy's Pointe as she could. She wanted to learn about where she came from. About my grandmother and great grandparents."

"So, you're friends with Merrick then." The disappointment in Charlie's voice was unmistakable.

Ailinn sighed and fidgeted with her golden cuffs. "It's complicated. When Merrick discovered his father was supporting the rebellion, he left Harpy's Pointe. He does not support his father and has written to me and Daniel several times assuring his loyalty to the Elven crown. Or so he claims anyway." Ailinn looked at Charlie, her eyes dazzling with admiration. "But how could you have known this?" she asked him.

Charlie's eyes widened. Clearly, Ailinn mistook his lucky guesses and conversations with Phillippe for some kind of prophetic ability or something. The last thing he needed was for her to start telling everyone he was the next Nostradamus. He simply shrugged at her and shook his head.

Ailinn smirked, making Charlie's already weak knees tremble more. "The wonderment of you never ceases to amaze, Charlie of the Hill."

"Me? No, I—I'm not my father, I—"

"Don't judge yourself against the grandeur of diamonds, Charlie. You are destined for greatness." She rose and for a moment, felt herself reach for Charlie. She stopped as her hands began to tremble and Charlie's eyes stared up at her, wide and afraid. She pulled back and picked up the breadcrumb bag instead. She was royalty after all. Not a commoner as her mother had been raised. Her mere presence was meant to strike fealty and fear into the hearts of those who looked upon her. She was foolish to think anyone could have feelings for her, let alone someone like Charlie Hill. Besides, her feelings couldn't be real. The prophecy said she was meant to marry him. It never said anything about love.

"You will save us. I know it," she said, and she headed up the path, disappearing behind a flowering hedgerow.

Charlie exhaled loudly. He hadn't realized he had been holding his breath when she'd reached for him. He stood and paced around the fountain. The little fish followed him in circles, hoping for another feast of breadcrumbs. He lifted a hand to remove his glasses, then remembered they were still not there. He stopped and looked at the castle of towering trees and stone behind him.

Even in Chartile everyone expected him to be something he wasn't. Charlie wasn't a fighter, or archer, or horseback rider. He wasn't a miracle sent from the Heavens or some reincarnated king. He wasn't his father, and he definitely wasn't the next Romeo. He had no idea who he was, and that thought alone rather terrified him. Maybe Chelsea had been right about finding some direction in his life, some sense of purpose. Then at least he wouldn't be a total loser.

"Oh! Master Charlie, sir," said a winded voice behind him. Charlie spun around and saw Phillippe bent double, clutching a stitch in his side. "I am so relieved I found you, sir. When you did not return from the banquet, I—"

"Were you trying to find me?" Charlie asked, astonished.

"Of course," said the little man, now standing as erect as he could. He still would not meet Charlie's gaze, but at least he was looking at the boy's feet instead of his own now. "I could not raise an alarm for your disappearance without first confirming. All the beck-ands are looking for you, sir. I asked for their help. It was one of the princess's ladies' beck-ands who informed me you were here with her, Master."

"I'm sorry," said Charlie, hanging his head.

Phillippe squinted at him, not bothering to look away this time. "Sorry, sir?" he asked in a pitifully raspy voice.

"I'm sorry I worried you. I didn't mean to. I just needed to get away, to think."

Phillippe looked at Charlie, though this time, it was Charlie who would not return the beck-and's gaze. Phillippe shuffled forward and raised his hand to Charlie's shoulder.

"Come," said Phillippe. "I will take you back to your quarters."

EIGHT
FEAR AND FAMILY

CHARLIE WOKE THE NEXT MORNING with a horrible stomachache. He couldn't remember his dad ever talking about getting ill from the food in Chartile, save for the time he'd gotten drunk on Dwarvik pearl wine. But the Elven food was richer and heavier than the simple meats and vegetables Jayson, Jack, and Leo had eaten during their first weeks in Chartile.

Phillippe was a lifesaver. The beck-and had teas, crackers, and soups, all hot and ready before Charlie even requested them. He would disappear through his little door for a half hour at a time, only to return with a steaming bowl of soup and news that Charlie's lessons with the nobles had been rescheduled to next week.

Despite being in a strange world, a strange room, and a strange bed with smells and sounds as unfamiliar to him as being dropped in the middle of Ethiopia, Charlie was able to rest well thanks to his new friend.

Ailinn came to visit Charlie on the third night, accompanied by several guards. She'd returned to wearing a thick, heavy dress, and she looked more uncomfortable than ever. Two of her guards stood sentry at the door, speaking to

Charlie's guards who remained stationed outside his room at all times. The other two followed close behind her, and Charlie wasn't sure if her discomfort was due to the dress or the overbearing presence of her escort.

Phillippe produced a chair for Ailinn, and she sat delicately, arranging her skirts around her just so. She was on edge, her carefree ways from the night before seeming buried inside again.

Charlie tried sitting up to greet her, but he felt his stomach start to heave and thought better of it. Instead, he lay in bed, his hands folded across his belly, looking pitiful and nothing like the savior Ailinn believed him to be.

"I heard you were not well," she said softly. "I would have liked to make you some of Gran's ginger cakes, but..." She trailed off, glancing at the guards over her shoulder.

"It's okay. I'm sure I'll be fine tomorrow," said Charlie more weakly than he had intended.

There was an awkward silence between them as the guards shuffled back and forth behind the princess's chair. Ailinn scratched at her wrists, and Charlie tried to fluff his pillows. Seeing her made his stomach jump and twist, which was not a good feeling when he had purged his gut only an hour before.

"Everyone was quite disappointed you needed to cancel your lessons," Ailinn continued. Even her tone had changed. It was quieter, more proper. "Many of them wanted to visit you today, but I would not allow it."

"Thanks," Charlie mustered.

Ailinn smiled like he was some kind of injured animal. "It would not do to have our Charlie of the Hill seen at anything but his best."

Charlie inwardly scoffed. He would rather make a fool of himself in front of every noble than have Ailinn sitting in front of him right now, especially while he was still trying to keep down his soup.

"Yeah, probably not good," he said. Not that anything about his current situation was good.

Ailinn tried to smile again. A thousand thoughts ran through her mind. She had not yet told her father her intentions to marry Charlie, though she was more concerned about whether Charlie would accept the news or not. Prophecies were a tricky thing. Her father clearly did not believe in them, and it was hard to tell what Charlie believed at all.

"Your Highness," one of the guards called from the doorway. "Your lessons, my lady."

"Rest well, Charlie," Ailinn said.

"You too—uh, be well." Charlie could have smacked himself in the face, but at least he managed a genuine smile from Ailinn. She curtsied and left with her escort trailing close behind. Charlie watched her until the door had closed behind the last guard. Even then, he still held the image of her in his mind for several long moments before curling back under the blankets and drifting off into a peaceful sleep.

Soft footsteps approached from across the room. Charlie almost ignored them until he heard the distinct difference between Phillippe's shuffling steps and the hard step of a boot heel. He reeled over, throwing the thin linen sheet off, and immediately regretted it. He barely made it to the chamber pot in time, though thankfully, nothing came up. Someone handed him a cool towel, and Charlie buried his face in it. He sat back in bed with a muffled "thanks" through the towel.

"You are quite welcome," a familiar voice replied.

Charlie ripped the towel from his face. He watched as Daniel lifted the chamber pot without hesitation, left the room, and returned moments later with a fresh one.

"Thank you," said Charlie, quite shocked.

"I often heard how my father cared for Jayson and his friends when they were here. It seemed rather fortuitous I should do the same for you." Daniel jumped onto the bed, and Charlie grabbed his stomach, wincing.

"Yeah, I suppose so." Charlie studied Daniel. He looked nothing like Valin or Ailinn.

Daniel seemed to notice Charlie's gaze. He smirked, and at least that was familiar to Charlie. "Go on, ask me," he said.

Charlie swallowed and sat up slowly. "Is Dimitri your dad?"

"Well, that's the most polite way anyone has ever asked me about my family," Daniel chuckled.

"I'm named after him," Charlie replied, and Daniel raised an interested eyebrow. "Charles Dimitri Hill."

"How fortuitous indeed." Daniel leaned against one of the four-posters at the foot of the bed, his feet stretched out, and his shirt half-unbuttoned. Charlie wondered if he was trying to appear sloppy, but all it did was intimidate him.

"You aren't like everyone else around here," said Charlie when the bed stopped bouncing. "You aren't all fancy and proper and all that."

"But I'm not like everyone else, am I? Dwarvik, Elven, *and* Human. It's why

Ailinn is first in line for the throne, not I."

"But Piper was your mother. Doesn't that still make you royal-ish?"

"No," Daniel said flatly, his tone turning more serious now. "Everyone knows who I am, but we all pretend it isn't true. I am the son of my mother's first and true love, the half-dwarf, half-human, Dimitri, who was the nephew of the late Dwarvik Empress Nefiri. But that doesn't make me Dwarvik royalty either. Mother married Valin shortly after your father left Chartile in order to conceal my illegitimacy. But it was rather obvious." Daniel gestured down his body, indicating the dark complexion that was anything but Elven.

"When I was thirteen, I denounced my claim to the throne, portraying my wishes to become my sister's personal bodyguard. This was all Father's, Valin's, doing. Had I refused to renounce my claim, I would have been cast out and brought shame to my mother's name. Valin did raise me as his own, even if it was begrudgingly. I have no more ill-will toward Valin than what is normal for any son. Now, Ailinn, on the other hand. She and Valin have practically hated each other since birth."

Charlie heard Phillippe's beck-and door creak open. He shuffled to the bed and set a serving tray on Charlie's side table. Charlie grabbed a piece of spiced bread and chewed absentmindedly. He barely noticed the little man start to clean the room even though he had done so earlier that morning. Daniel watched Phillippe for a moment, then turned his attention back to Charlie.

"Well, you can't really blame her, though," Charlie replied, his mouth full. "I mean, she's being married off to someone she doesn't love, and her dad won't let her do magic, even though he let her mom do it."

"Yes and no," said Daniel, snatching a piece of bread from the tray as well. "I understand my father's reasons for attempting to control her magic. It was not right for my mother to use hers, at least in public. But since we are now fighting both the rebels and the Court of the Rogue who want to use magic with no restraint or consequence, to allow his daughter to do so would be hypocrisy. That is not a good thing if you are king. And Merrick is a good friend. Ailinn is simply being stubborn."

"The Court of the Rogue?" Charlie asked as a piece of bread dangled from the corner of his mouth.

Daniel nodded. "An organized group of thieves that have risen to power among the commoners. They are at the heart of this rebellion."

"Oh." Charlie tried to catch the piece of bread with his tongue, but only managed to knock it out of his mouth and into the sheets. He took another bite, hoping Daniel had missed what had just transpired. "I still don't get how Merrick and Savaric aren't working together. Isn't it a bit coincidental that Merrick doesn't agree with his dad and just happened to go off to live in another town? But he's okay with Savaric's idea to marry Ailinn. I don't know. It seems a little funny if you ask me." Charlie reached for his chalice of water. It was empty. He tried to sit up and winced. He wiped at the sweat beaded across his forehead.

"Here," said Daniel, swinging his legs over the bed. "Let me." He poured the cool water from the pitcher Phillippe had brought and handed the chalice to Charlie before resuming his seat against the four-poster once more.

"Thanks," said Charlie, but there was something about Daniel's demeanor the boy couldn't place. Perhaps it was because he was still on the verge of puking, but something about Daniel had him on edge.

"Before Savaric turned rogue, Merrick was one of our dearest friends. He is the future Lord of Harpy's Pointe, where my grandmother was born. We spent many summers playing in these hallways together. I would be happy to call him my brother. He only agreed to marry Ailinn to end the fighting."

Charlie shrugged, too weak to put up more of an argument or to think of a good one in the first place. Daniel tossed the last bit of his bread in the air and caught it in his mouth. He turned to Charlie, his face cold and serious, which also looked exactly like Ailinn's. This time, Charlie saw they had the same cheekbones and eye shape.

"That is why I'm here, Charles Dimitri Hill," he said. "I saw you in the garden last night with my sister."

Charlie gulped down his last bit of bread and froze. That was why Daniel was acting so strange.

"I can't have you distracting her. We need this treaty, and Ailinn has some crazy idea that she is supposed to marry you."

This time, Charlie's stomach lurched so hard, he nearly vomited on Daniel. He reached for the clean chamber pot and held his head over it for a moment. Finally, he looked back to the young man sitting on the bed across from him, eyebrows raised, but his face still stern.

"I'm only sixteen!" Charlie protested. "I can't get married!"

"I'm glad you think so, but Ailinn can be very persuasive, and I have seen the way you look at her."

Charlie's eyes widened again, and his face flushed at Daniel's words.

"The prophecy says *and then in kin come back again, joining two worlds as one.* Before our mother died, she had a vision. A vision she claims of your world. She said the prophecy was not what we once believed it to be. And it is true. You have returned, but not as the soul of one of our ancient kings in a new body. My sister has taken this a step further."

Daniel rose from the bed, towering over Charlie. "If you do anything to lead her on, to make her believe you two could be wed, you will find your time in Chartile coming to a swift end." Daniel bowed to Charlie, then turned and headed back into the corridor beyond the tree-trunk door.

Charlie stared at the closed door again, but this time, it was not fanciful images of a lovely princess in his mind. His brain was filled with visions of death. He jumped, smacking himself in the chin with the chamber pot when Phillippe laid a gentle hand on his knee.

"I'm doomed, Phillippe," he said.

"*Doomed* is a rather strong word," Phillippe reassured him.

"You heard Prince—er, Daniel. Whatever he is, you heard him! He could pulverize me into dust if I so much as look at Ailinn."

"Daniel is a rather intimidating individual, but I think dust may be an over-exaggeration." Phillippe gently took the chamber pot from Charlie and set it back on the floor. "Is it your wish to marry Princess Ailinn?"

Charlie reeled back. "What? God, no!"

"Then what do you have to fear?"

Charlie held his face in his hands. "It's more complicated than that, Phil. I—I'm only sixteen. I've never even kissed a girl before. I don't want to marry her, but I can't help some things. When I'm around her, my brain just stops working. I like her, Phil. I can't help that."

Phillippe nodded and turned his attention to lighting the lanterns as darkness filled the room. "Princess Ailinn needs more people in her life who love her," he said. "There are many kinds of love, Master Charlie. Whether you are here to fulfill a prophecy or simply devour my bread, it could be that love will save us in the end."

Charlie barely slept. Every little sound woke him from his poor excuse for sleep. His stomachache had subsided, but the dread that had replaced it was almost worse. He took no visitors the next day and felt rather disappointed in himself when he told Phillippe to send Ailinn away. He was still too much of a coward to face her. He sulked beneath the covers, trying to find a comfortable position and fight his curiosity to explore the palace.

"Master Charlie, you cannot lie in bed all day," said Phillippe, pulling back the curtains to let the sunlight in. The beck-ands had their timing down perfectly for each room when the sunlight would enter. Their schedule was impressively precise.

Charlie shielded his eyes from the bright rays. "What else am I supposed to do while I'm here?" he protested. "I've got all these… lessons… with these nobles, and I know nothing about any of it."

"But this is why they're offering to teach you, Master Charlie," said Phillippe, tying back the drapes. The beck-and still would not meet Charlie's eye regularly.

"But, Phil, they *expect* me to be good at this stuff. My dad had this knack for things. When he was here, he could just do it. I can't! I don't know how to ride, I don't know how to dance. But everyone expects me to."

Despite the much-needed sunshine, Charlie flopped back onto the bed and covered his head with his pillow. He felt Phillippe sit beside him and begin to peel the pillow back.

"If anyone expects anything from you, then it is their own failing to get to know the true Charlie, whom I find to be far more interesting than any Elven noble I have ever met. And I have worked at the palace a very long time."

"But I can't exactly be myself. I might offend someone." Charlie moaned.

He sat up beside Phillippe and hugged the pillow to his chest. They sat quietly for several moments, and Charlie realized how much he was whining. Phillippe was so patient, and Charlie was acting like an absolute brat.

"I'm sorry I'm such a loser. I don't know why everything scares me so much."

"I think, Master Charlie, that it is time you learned some balance. Involve yourself with the nobles and the Elven people. Show an interest in our ways. But do so in your own Charlie-way." Phillippe smiled, his eyes almost meeting the boy's. Charlie couldn't help but smile back.

"Well, can you at least show me some stuff, so I don't look like a total idiot next week?"

NINE
NOBLE GESTURES

THE BECK-ANDS HAD ALREADY LIT the lanterns in Daniel's room before he returned. He shielded his eyes and extinguished most of them. Kashna watched him from his place before the cold hearth, his tail twitching anxiously.

"It happened again, didn't it?" Kashna asked.

Daniel flopped into a chair close by, still holding his head. Kashna barely saw him nod in acknowledgment.

"Can… Can you tell me if I at least talked to him? I don't remember if I made it there or not. It—it's all black. If Ailinn is determined to fight Savaric, Charlie needs all the information he can get," Daniel said, his voice barely a whisper.

Kashna rose and padded softly across the room toward Daniel. He leaned his forehead against Daniel's temple, and his mind went quiet. Then the memories came. He sat on Charlie's bed, facing the boy. What Ailinn saw in him, he had no idea. He was weak and frail of both body and spirit. The words were muffled. He couldn't make out anything, but so far, it all seemed familiar.

The edges of his vision grew darker, and the images were warped. He saw himself standing over Charlie, still speaking to him. It was brief, but perhaps there was more that Kashna could see that he couldn't. He left Charlie's room and tore through the golden halls of the palace.

Kashna pulled away, and the whir of a thousand thoughts and voices slowly filled Daniel's mind again.

"I cannot say for certain," Kashna said quietly. He knew the pain Daniel felt. It was more than a headache, and he had felt it when he connected with him. "You did speak of Savaric, Ailinn, and the treaty."

Daniel sighed and looked into the qarveena's golden eyes. "I'll have to trust I did what I intended to do."

Kashna nodded and laid on the floor beside him, his head resting on Daniel's feet. Daniel wished Kashna could take his pain away, but even Kashna's magic was not enough.

There was a soft knock on the wall behind a tapestry. Kashna rose with a slight growl though Daniel did not move. The qarveena flicked his head, and the tapestry moved aside, revealing a small door. He flicked his head again, and the little door opened. Ailinn stood on the other side. She looked into the room beyond Kashna and her face fell.

"Again?" she asked, stepping through the door. Kashna turned, allowing the tapestry to fall over the princess. She took a moment to free herself but shrugged off her annoyance with the creature. "Should I fetch a beck-and for some tea?"

Daniel stirred at the sound of her voice. Ailinn rushed to her brother, missing the qarveena's tail as he conveniently flicked it in front of her. "Ailinn?"

"Shh, I'm here," she whispered, and she held her brother's face in her hands. "What can I do?"

Daniel sat up and shook his head. "It's so loud today. More thoughts and voices than ever. So much screaming." He pulled away from Ailinn, holding his head again and gripping tightly at his hair.

Ailinn watched him for several minutes until beads of sweat formed on his temples. She patted them away, and Daniel sat up.

"It's quieting now," he said, smiling weakly at her. "I visited Charlie this evening." He tried changing the subject. The tension in his sister's face was almost as awful as he felt.

"So did I," she replied. Somehow this did not surprise Daniel. "I'm worried about him."

Daniel raised an eyebrow at his sister. That *did* surprise him.

"Oh?" he asked, hoping his voice didn't sound too eager.

Ailinn nodded. "He's so unsure of himself. Mother said Jayson did not believe the truth either when he first came to Chartile."

"And the returned kings lived with her for weeks before they were called to Mount Kelsii, let alone left to confront Aunt Ani."

"True," said Ailinn. She carefully stepped over Kashna, who resumed his post at Daniel's feet, and sat in the chair beside him. "I haven't told him yet. About the prophecy and marrying him. I'm afraid it might frighten him away."

Daniel paused and shifted uncomfortably in his chair. "Several of our visiting and resident nobles have agreed to train him. Let him prove himself to himself, and to you. If he's unfit to be a leader, no matter what the prophecy says, Ailinn, you deserve someone levelheaded and confident."

Ailinn rolled her eyes. "Like every other damned lord's son in this place?"

"No, I said confident, not insecurity disguised as arrogance. There's a difference and you know it."

"And I know exactly who you speak of as well, Daniel." Ailinn had dropped her sweet, whispered tone. Clearly, her brother was feeling better.

"Do you even have feelings for him?"

Ailinn stood, absently twirling her hair as she paced. "I think that's the scariest part. I think I do, Daniel. Or else I have myself so delusioned I've forced myself to believe it. But there's something there, something different." She caught sight of herself in a mirror that hung on the wall. Her green eyes stared back at her, a doe-eyed expression she had never seen before reflected in them. She huffed, returning to the chair beside Daniel and refusing to look at him until she composed herself again. "Besides," she continued, "it's too dangerous to marry Merrick."

"I wouldn't count Merrick out yet. I've got... a feeling. I don't know for sure, but it wouldn't surprise me if we saw Merrick sooner rather than later. Then we can decide for ourselves whose side he's on."

The tip of Kashna's tail twitched and his golden eyes stared at the wall before him as he listened to Daniel and Ailinn. He too had a feeling, but he couldn't put his flight feathers on it. Something was brewing, and someone was coming.

WHEN CHARLIE'S FIRST LESSON WITH Lord Torvald came to pass, it was as though the lessons Phillippe had taught him over the last week had never occurred. Shooting a handmade recurve was very different from the ones they used in gym class. It took over two dozen tries before Charlie managed to hit the target, and that was after the beck-ands had moved the target closer—twice.

The day after found Charlie in a grand ballroom with enough candles to give the illusion that there was actually sun. At least he managed to remember some of his lessons with Phillippe even if they were steps from three different dances. He heard a chuckle at one point and saw Princess Ailinn peeking through the doors to watch him as he twirled rather ungracefully. He felt his ankle begin to roll as he stopped spinning to look at her. He caught himself but still managed to fall to the floor. Ailinn covered her mouth, her eyes wide, and disappeared behind the door again.

He continued to stare at the door, beet red and his heart pounding. He felt a hand on his shoulder and heard the soft voice of Lord Tristian. "The art of dance is not for everyone, Master Charlie." He helped Charlie to his feet and straightened his tunic. "As well as the art of love."

Charlie's eyes widened, and his embarrassment flushed all the way to his ears this time. Lord Tristian smiled and patted his shoulder. "Best steer clear of that one, lad. She's more than anyone can handle right now." He turned to the musicians seated in the corner and dismissed them with a nod. "You did well! Practice your pivas and posture. Until next time." He bowed, and his embroidered dress cloak billowed behind him as he exited the room after the musicians.

"Thank you!" Charlie called, but he had already vanished. Charlie sighed and wondered if he should put out all the candles before leaving. After several moments, he left and hoped he didn't just cause the entire Elven palace to burn down.

His two guards waited patiently for him in the hall. Charlie had gotten to know Jock and Drustad rather well over the last several days as they'd escorted him to his various lessons throughout the palace grounds.

"I'd like to have lunch in my room today," he said to them. Jock nodded and walked off toward the kitchens. Drustad, a stout man with flowing blond hair and a bright smile, fell in behind Charlie as he headed back to his room. The boy knew the way by heart now, and his feet carried him to his door before he even knew he had traveled the distance. Drustad held the door for Charlie and bowed as he entered.

The room was quiet. Phillippe was nowhere to be found. Charlie crossed the room and flung open the drapes, which should have already been pulled back.

The fresh air, humid as it was in the heat of the Chartilian summer, was just what he needed to clear his mind.

If Lord Tristian knew Charlie had feelings for Ailinn, he wondered how many others knew. Not that he entirely understood those feelings himself, but there was definitely something there.

In the distance, Charlie could hear children belonging to the resident nobles splashing at the fish in the fountain just beyond his sight. He still didn't know if Ailinn had true feelings for him, or if she was only being nice to him in order to fulfill the prophecy she so desperately believed. No one else seemed to believe her interpretation, as far as Charlie knew. Could the Conclave have sent Daniel to threaten him?

The children's voices faded away, and Charlie heard the familiar creak of the little beck-and door. But it was not Phillippe's familiar shuffling that Charlie heard next. A young girl, huffing and puffing with a heavy tray, pushed her way through the door. He rushed to assist her, and the girl stopped with a tiny squeak of fear. The tray began to tremble even more, and she clamped her eyes shut.

Charlie stopped before he reached her. "Here, let me help you with that," he said gently. The girl, no more than ten, opened one eye as Charlie held out his hands for the tray. When she did not move, Charlie carefully took the tray from her and set it on the vanity.

"For-Forgive my weakness, Master Charlie," the girl whispered.

"It's all right. Here, you want one?" He held out a small fruit tart to the girl. A wave of excitement, confusion, then fear, spread across her face, and she took a step back. "It's not poisoned," Charlie said. "Well, at least I hope it's not. That'd be really bad for me right now."

Charlie saw the tiniest smile tug briefly at the girl's lips. Tentatively, her entire body shaking, the girl took the tart from Charlie and ate it in three bites. Charlie picked up the rest of the tray and moved it to the tiny table and chair beside the window. He tore into the meat pie as the little girl continued to watch him.

"Where's Phil?" Charlie asked her through a mouthful of steamed carrots.

She was so quiet, Charlie barely heard her reply. "He's fallen ill, Master."

Charlie looked up, his brow furrowed, and the girl took another step back. "Ill? Is he going to be okay? Is he at the doctor or something?"

The girl began to tremble again, and Charlie saw her eyes dart for the little beck-and door. He sighed and took a swig of water to wash down the mouthful of rather bland carrots.

"Okay, what did Phillippe tell you about me? Anything?" he asked.

The girl just shook her head.

Charlie sighed again. "What's your name?"

The girl hesitated, her eyes still darting toward the beck-and door. "Saajee'a," she whispered.

"Saajee'a, I'm not sure how much you know about me, but I'm not from around here."

Saajee'a nodded, her eyes now dancing across the floor in front of her.

"Where I come from, we don't have beck-ands, so I'm not gonna hurt you or dismiss you or whatever, okay? You're here to do your job, and I appreciate that. And believe me, so does my stomach right now." Charlie took another bite of meat pie.

Something about Chartile had certainly changed him. It had barely been two weeks, but Charlie was sure something had happened. For as long as he could remember, he had shut off his ability to care for anyone outside of his father. The harassment he suffered at school had hardened him, and the love he felt toward his father had begun to fade as well in the last few years. But the feeling of being truly and utterly alone when Charlie first came to Chartile seemed to open his heart again.

Phillippe was the first person in a very long time whom Charlie could say he truthfully cared for, and not out of family obligation. That had been like a chain reaction. He might have looked past other kids being bullied at his school before. He had his own issues to concern himself with, and he'd tried to avoid swirlys at all cost. The part of him his father had tried to foster for years was blossoming under the Belirian trees these days.

He turned back to the serving tray and picked up another small fruit tart. After his recent bout of illness, Phillippe had made sure that Charlie's foods were well-monitored. They were often plain and simple. The fruit tarts were one of the few indulgences his stomach would allow him to have.

"You can sit down if you want," Charlie said. "I know Phil doesn't like sitting in the chairs, but he usually sits on the rug."

Saajee'a took the invitation immediately. When she settled, Charlie tossed her the last fruit tart, and he heard her giggle.

"What's wrong with Phillippe?" he coaxed again.

Saajee'a swallowed her mouthful of tart, and replied, "We don't know. Lots of the beck-ands are sick."

"But there's a doctor, right? I mean, they're getting medicine, right? They'll be okay?"

Saajee'a shrugged. "Well, my momma and some of the other beck-ands are trying to take care of them, but…" She trailed off, biting her lip, the look of fear returning to her face.

"You can tell me, Saajee'a. I won't tell anyone."

"Momma thinks it might be magic, but she can't make it better because of the magic stoppers."

"Magic stoppers?" Charlie asked.

Saajee'a clinked her orenite cuffs together, and Charlie's face fell.

There was a sharp knock on the door, and Charlie recognized it as Drustad. The young guard found it amusing to use his sword hilt to knock on doors, knowing it made the inhabitants startle. Being on the other side of the door with him *was* amusing, but Charlie still jumped a mile every time Drustad did it to him.

Saajee'a leapt to her feet and bounded across the room for the door. She squeaked again when she realized Charlie was right behind her. He nodded reassuringly to her and opened the door.

"Lord Kharas is waiting for you in the stables, Master Charlie," said Drustad.

Charlie's shoulders slumped. "Already?" he muttered. His horseback riding lesson was the one thing he had dreaded out of all the nobles' polite offerings to teach him. He wasn't afraid of animals, but horses were huge and powerful. And now that he suspected Ailinn spent most of her time spying on his lessons, he had no intention of breaking his neck in front of her.

"Aye, sir," said Jock, and he tugged at his big, red beard. "Lord Kharas is the finest horse master across all the Elven territories. Sutton Low is on the outskirts of the Belirian Forest, close to the deserts. They say the land is filled with thousands of horses running wild and free, and only the best horse masters can catch and tame them."

"I am not a horse master," Charlie grumbled. He glanced at Saajee'a behind him. "Meet me back here later, okay?" he said.

Saajee'a nodded and hurried off through the beck-and door as Charlie begrudgingly followed Jock and Drustad to the stables.

VALIN DRAINED THE REMAINDER OF his goblet of wine and promptly refilled it. He set the half-empty decanter beside the already empty one. His advisor had been sent a missive that morning, which had forced The Conclave to hold an emergency meeting. Now the king hoped more wine would help him think of a clear answer. He had even sent a carrier bird to his father in Cannondole, but he knew he wouldn't hear back for at least a day—if at all. Valar had removed himself from any more dealings with politics, save matters to do with his hometown.

Unfortunately, the wine wasn't working, and Valin had exhausted his supply of brandy last week when Charlie of the Hill had shown up in Chartile. The child was a menace. He was nothing like Jayson, but almost worse so. Jayson had had ambition and drive. Charlie was a mindless keradoe being pulled along with no sense of right or wrong, safety or danger. He was more trouble than he was worth, but possibly his last hope.

Valin walked to the main door to his quarters, his movements straight and poised. He wrenched open the door.

"Bring me Ailinn and Daniel!" he growled to his guards before slamming the door again. He couldn't wait for the next shipment of brandy.

THE TRIP TO THE STABLES was far longer than Charlie remembered when they'd passed it on their way to the archery range before. He wasn't sure if his guards were stalling for time for him or intentionally trying to get his nerves up, but it left plenty of time for Charlie to think.

Just before they reached the large wooden doors that led to the stable area, Charlie stopped.

"I need you guys to do something for me," he whispered, pulling them into a small alcove.

Jock and Drustad exchanged serious looks, then turned their full attention to Charlie.

"Anything, little brother," Jock whispered.

Charlie swallowed hard, hesitating. "I… I need a favor. How do you know if a girl likes you?"

Jock did a better job of hiding his smirk than Drustad. Both men shifted to block Charlie from the view of any passersby.

"If you are referring to the princess—" Jock began.

"I never said…" Charlie stopped speaking as soon as he saw the looks on Jock's and Drustad's faces. "I know she wants to marry me because of the prophecy, but, like, what does she *think* about me? Does she just want to marry me because of the prophecy, or does she, you know, have feelings? Not that I want to get married. I still don't want to get married."

"Why don't you ask her?" Drustad asked.

"You can't just ask a girl if she likes you! I'd look like an idiot!"

"Then how are you to know?" Jock asked.

"Can you ask around to some of the beck-ands and guards? Ask them if they've heard Ailinn talking about me? But she can't know I'm asking! You have to keep it secret from her."

Jock and Drustad grinned. "As you wish, Master Charlie," said Jock. They bowed and headed back up the hall, leaving Charlie alone before the doors to the stable.

It took several minutes for Charlie to get his heart to stop pounding. He'd heard that animals could sense fear, and he didn't want his horse getting the wrong impression.

He stepped through the doors and onto a dirt aisle, lined with stalls on the far side. The smell was just as bad as Charlie remembered from when he had visited the county fair. The stamping of hooves to his right made him turn.

An older gentleman held the reins of a graying black mare who pawed at the packed dirt floor. Behind him, his beck-and held a towering chestnut stallion who shook like a dog in anticipation of the ride. But what terrified Charlie the most was the rider of the white mare standing behind the black horse: Princess Ailinn. She smiled at him as she adjusted her seat in the saddle.

"I hope you do not mind the princess joining us, Master Charlie," said Lord Kharas.

"It's been too long since I've gone for a ride," Ailinn said. Her horse snorted as if in agreement. She patted its neck and leaned forward to scratch between the mare's eyes.

"You mean, I'm not going to a pasture or an arena or something? Shouldn't you just make me, like, walk in a circle on the end of a rope first? Like the ponies at the fair?" Charlie asked, completely unable to hide his nerves. Between the princess, three huge animals that could trample him at any moment, and Lord Kharas, who was taller than any of the nobles he had yet met, Charlie was no match to keep his feelings in check.

Lord Kharas laughed. "We'll tie you on if we must. I promise we'll go slowly, and you will be right beside me." He nodded to his beck-and, who handed the reins off to his master and set a wooden block beside the horse.

There was much fussing over how to get on the horse the right way, how to hold the reins, and keeping his heels pointed down. Charlie's horse, Cinders, took a step forward. The boy flattened himself onto the horse's neck, hoping to hang on for dear life, but then quite nearly fell off.

"She won't harm you," said Ailinn. She'd walked her horse beside Cinders and grabbed the reins so Charlie could sit back up.

"Not on purpose anyway," Charlie grumbled.

"You're too tense. You must relax. Animals can sense our emotions. They can feel what we feel and will reflect it back. The last thing Cinders would ever want is to hurt you." She handed the reins back to Charlie with a sympathetic look. Charlie's hands shook when her fingers brushed across his knuckles, and Cinders snorted under him, making Charlie jump.

Lord Kharas walked beside Charlie and led him out onto the main road away from the palace. It would have been a rather enjoyable day. The wind had picked up, taking the humidity out of the air. It had been hanging around for several days, creating a constant and uncomfortable sticky feeling. The sunlight filtering through the dense canopy overhead was warm, and the songs of the birds were comforting, if different from the usual array of robins and blue jays back home. After a few instructions on proper posture, Lord Kharas instructed Charlie to walk several paces with his horse, then turn her around and come back.

Charlie felt like such an idiot, trying to squeeze his legs to make the horse walk. When the mare finally did, he lurched and tried not to drop the reins. When he had reached the small clearing Lord Kharas indicated, he was able to get Cinders to turn around at least part way before she completely stopped. He squeezed his legs as hard as he could, but she would not budge. She lowered her head to nibble a flower and nearly pulled Charlie over her head in the process.

"She's testing you, Charlie," Ailinn called to him. "Pull her head up and give her a nudge with your heels."

Charlie did as Ailinn instructed, though it must have felt like more than a nudge to Cinders. The horse bolted, and Charlie found himself flat on his back, staring up at the treetops above him. A guard retrieved his horse, and another helped him to his feet, brushing earth and leaves from his clothes.

"You're still too tense," said Ailinn. She had dismounted and retrieved Cinders from the guard, leading her back to Charlie. Begrudgingly, Charlie accepted the help from the various guards to re-ascend his steed. Then, much to his shock, Ailinn pulled herself up behind him in a single, fluid motion. His heart raced as he felt her pressed against his back. She reached under his arms and put her hands over his.

"Relax your grip," she whispered in his ear. He had to stop himself from tightening his hands as her breath tickled his ear. "She can feel the energy and vibrations through your hands." Ailinn clucked her tongue and nudged Cinders forward.

They walked back to Lord Kharas and the guards without incident, save for the damage Charlie wondered was happening to his heart as it ravaged the inside of his chest. Ailinn dismounted and Charlie breathed a sigh of relief.

"Try it again," she said to him with a curt nod. Lord Kharas opened his mouth to protest, but Ailinn shot him a look. "He can do it," she said, her voice flat.

Lord Kharas looked at Charlie and nodded. Charlie sighed, still flush and his heart still pounding from moments before. He squeezed his legs, and Cinders walked forward. Ailinn was following close behind on foot. He went to turn the horse, and she stopped again.

"She's not a ship. Pull your wrist and elbow toward your navel." Charlie did as the princess instructed, and Cinders began to turn. "Wonderful! Now nudge her forward."

Charlie barely touched the horse's sides. Cinders turned her head to look at him, then lowered her head to eat the grass again.

"Come on!" Charlie cried, yanking on the reins to pull the horse's head up. Cinders snorted angrily and shook her head. Charlie kicked her sides again, and Cinders took off toward the group ahead once more.

Again, Charlie found himself staring up at the trees, his rear and shoulder protesting in pain. Ailinn hurried to him. "Are you all right? Charlie, you cannot get angry at her. You're making her nervous!"

"*You're* making *me* nervous!" Charlie screamed at her as he tried to sit up.

Suddenly, his face was on fire. Ailinn had smacked him hard across the cheek and was now walking back to the group. She swung up onto her horse, nodded to her guards, and cantered back to the palace. Charlie stared after her, not sure whether to grab his sore face or aching butt. Lord Kharas approached Charlie and knelt down to him. Cinders was being held by one of Kharas's men, calm as could be.

"I think you've had enough lessons for today," Kharas said to Charlie quietly. He reached out a hand to him, and Charlie accepted it. What little pride he might have had left had been smashed into the dirt by his rear and left in broken shambles.

He rode in the saddle in front of Lord Kharas on the way back to the palace. He was sure he had broken his butt bone and was dreading thinking of having to ask Saajee'a for some kind of ice pack to sit on. Before they rounded the last corner, Kharas called for a halt.

"Everyone, dismount," he said, and the guards did so, rather confused. The man handed Charlie Cinder's reins again. "We'll walk the rest of the way. It will not do for everyone to see you riding with me when you left on your own. I do believe your ego is hurt quite enough for today."

Charlie blushed and looked at the ground. "Thank you, my lord," he mumbled.

Kharas patted his shoulder. "You aren't your father, but I find it foolish for anyone to expect you to be. You'll find your own way here, just as he did, and probably just as hard as he did as well."

Charlie huffed. "My dad had it easy. He could do everything without even thinking. He had the reincarnated soul of a king to guide him. I've got nothing."

"You've got yourself—and your friends," Kharas said. "Your father may have found the use of his bow easy, but he still had many lessons in magic from my understanding. And he caused plenty of mayhem on his own while he was here as well."

Charlie squinted at Lord Kharas. "Did you know him?"

Kharas smiled and shook his head. "I'm a lover of history and a good tale. There have been plenty of accounts written about your father and his friends. Queen Gemari of Mount Kelsi and our own Queen Piper among them."

Charlie was silent for several moments. He could hear the guards growing restless behind them, and the horse's tack clanked and squeaked.

"I'm sure I have something with me if you'd like to read it."

"Sure," Charlie replied quietly.

Lord Kharas called the team forward, and they headed back to the stables.

TEN
THE KING'S TASK

AILINN GALLOPED THROUGH THE FRONT gates of the palace, headed straight to the stables. She pulled her mare to a halt, her guards bringing up the rear and dismounting behind her. She swung from her saddle, tossing the horse's reins at the stable beck-ands, and stormed through the doors to the castle.

"Ailinn!" someone called to her from a side corridor. She ignored them though her guards stopped long enough to allow the speaker to pass. "Ailinn, I've been looking everywhere for you." Daniel ran to her, but Ailinn held up a hand to silence him before he could speak again.

"Don't! Daniel—just—no," she said.

"Ailinn, it's Father. He needs to speak with us."

Ailinn took a deep breath and stopped. News traveled through the Elven palace faster than the wind through the Belirian trees. She'd stepped out of bounds. She had pushed Charlie too hard, too fast. She had struck him out of pure frustration. She knew there would be consequences.

She turned to her brother, not daring to meet his gaze. Daniel turned to his

73

sister's guards. They handed him the key to Ailinn's orenite cuffs, and Daniel dismissed them.

"Sometimes I wonder why I even bother trying," Ailinn mumbled. Daniel tucked the key in the pouch on his belt. He pulled Ailinn into a hug and squeezed her tightly. "Because you're just like Mother."

Ailinn shook her head and pulled away. "I wish I was."

"You want to tell me about it?"

"Oh, I'm sure Father will tell us all about what I've done wrong this time, and how I've brought shame to our family once again."

Daniel took Ailinn's hand and led the way toward the throne room. "I know you think you are, but you're not alone, Ailinn."

ONE OF LORD KHARAS'S GUARDS escorted a very disgruntled Charlie through the castle and back to his rooms. Neither said a word, which wasn't unusual for Charlie, but there was a tension in the air that was as palpable as the lump rising on Charlie's backside. He didn't wait for the guard to open the door for him. He wrenched the door open, unprepared for its surprising weight. He fumbled getting through, then swiftly locked it behind him.

Saajee'a was still there, scrubbing the floors on her hands and knees. She looked up, her large brown eyes filled with surprise and a touch of the same fear Charlie recognized from when he'd first met Phillippe. She rose, wiping her hands on her dingy tunic, but Charlie looked straight through her. He ran to his bed and tossed himself across the mattress, landing face-down on his smelly pillow. He heard Saajee'a return to her scrubbing, and he quickly sat up to draw the curtains of the four-poster around him. He didn't want Saajee'a to look at him. He struggled with the ties, his vision blurred through salty tears. His nose was filling up and he could hardly breathe.

The rap of Drustad's hilt against the door made Saajee'a squeak. She rose again and hurried to open the heavy door. Charlie pulled his other pillow over his head, blocking out whatever conversation the two might have had.

It was at least ten minutes before Charlie's sobs had subsided into hiccups. He sat up and noticed someone had set a handkerchief on the edge of the bed.

Charlie blew his nose loudly. He sat staring at the burgundy curtain before him for several long moments until he dared a peek into the room beyond.

Saajee'a was tying back the window curtain for the midday sun, but she wasn't alone. Jock and Drustad stood patiently by the door. They stopped their whispering when they caught sight of Charlie peering through a gap in the bed curtain. Jock hurried forward, a chalice of cold water in his hand. Drustad followed close behind with the silver pitcher he'd picked up from the dresser on his way.

Jock handed the chalice to Charlie, and the boy took a long drink. His guards exchanged worried glances but did not speak. Charlie set the empty chalice on his nightstand and stared at the floor.

It was pretty clear now how Princess Ailinn felt about him. And, if she ever had any feelings for Charlie, they were as long gone as his pride. He would have to remember to write Lord Kharas a thank-you letter or something. Maybe send him a basket of fruit or cookies. Charlie wasn't sure what the appropriate gesture would be, but the man had saved him from even more humiliation when they'd reentered the palace grounds.

Charlie heard Phillippe's little door open and close again. His shoulders fell as he watched Saajee'a, not Phil, struggle with a heavy tray of food. They all watched as she set it on the dresser and disappeared through the door again. Phillippe was somewhere in the palace, sick and probably dying, and Charlie was feeling miserable about a sore bum.

"Jock? Drustad?" Charlie heard the words leave his lips before he could stop himself. "Can I talk to you?"

Drustad sat on the end of the bed, and Jock pulled up the chair, straddling its back and fighting against the sword at his side.

"What's on your mind, little brother?" Jock asked.

Charlie took a deep breath. He scratched the bridge of his nose, a habit he had developed since he no longer wore glasses.

"I messed up major today. Like, big time major," he began. His guards remained quiet as he continued. "I yelled at Ailinn and she... she hit me for it." The memory seemed to sting more than his cheek or tailbone. "Guess I know how she feels now."

"I wouldn't be so sure of that," Jock said gently.

Charlie scoffed. "Yeah, right. Any chance I might have had is long gone now. She thinks I'm someone special. Everyone thinks I'm someone special, but I'm not. I'm not! I can't do this anymore. I can't do it here or at home. I don't want to keep being something I'm not." Charlie took a deep breath, willing himself not to start crying again.

"And what gives you any indication that anyone believes you're more than who you are?" Drustad pressed.

Charlie paused and shrugged. "I mean, all these lords are trying to teach me how to do stuff, but I can't do it."

"I believe *teach* is the important word here," said Jock.

Charlie finally looked up and met the man's blue-eyed gaze.

Jock stood swiftly from the chair. He unsheathed his sword, and Charlie leaned back into the bed. But the young guard didn't advance on him. Instead, he removed his glove and carefully balanced the sword on the back of his hand. Charlie watched in awe as he stepped back into the center of the room. He stepped backwards and forwards in a kind of dance, the sword barely swaying as he moved.

"My uncle is the Baron of Icefjord. We don't see many palace guards or soldiers so far East. When the war began, the usual palace guards were called into battle, leaving the palace scrambling for guards. I never anticipated I'd be anything more than a fisherman with a knack for counting coffers. But the recruiters came, and I was chosen. I was not the best. In fact, my lack of any formal training in fighting held me back for quite some time. But I practiced. I trained. I *tried*."

Jock tossed his sword into the air and caught the hilt in a single movement, sheathing it just as quickly. He sat in the chair again and leaned towards Charlie.

"Charlie, you have never pretended to be anything other than who you are, and that is what Princess Ailinn admires most about you."

"You never give up, despite how many times you miscount your dance steps or miss the archery targets," said Drustad. "A leader is not someone who does everything on his own. He inspires those around him and knows when to ask for help from those greater than himself."

"Well, considering I'm not really great at anything, I guess I have that going for me."

Drustad clapped Charlie on his shoulder, and Charlie stifled a wince. Apparently, he had landed on his shoulder too when he'd fallen.

"You're great at being you, and that's refreshing for the princess," said Drustad.

"And a small disagreement is nothing a meaningful apology can't fix." Jock leaned close to Charlie and lowered his voice in a mock whisper. "I hear moonflowers and salted chocolates are her favorite."

When Charlie didn't respond, Jock and Drustad both rose. They each placed a hand under Charlie's arms and pulled him to his feet.

"Whoa! Hey—"

"Moping around and hiding in your quarters isn't going to solve anything," Drustad said more sternly this time.

Jock snapped his fingers loudly and called toward the little door, "Oy! Beck-and!"

"Her name's Saajee'a," Charlie snapped.

Jock smirked. "I'm sorry?"

"Her name's Saajee'a," Charlie repeated, quieter this time.

"Say it like you meant it the first time," Drustad said. "No one else would have dared correct someone over a beck-and, but you do. It's what makes you different. Be different like you mean it."

Saajee'a appeared in the doorway. "Master Charlie?"

"We need ice and bruise balm," Jock said to her.

Saajee'a nodded at the floor. "Master Charlie, it's Phillippe."

Charlie's head shot up. He looked wide-eyed at the girl and felt the blood leave his face. "What's wrong?"

Saajee'a wouldn't look at him. He saw her swallow and bite her lower lip. "H-he's getting worse. So are some of the others. Can... Can you help them? The nobles, they say Jayson of the Hill is a healer."

There was a knock on the door, and Charlie darted across the room before Saajee'a could answer it. He wrenched it open, prepared this time for the heavy weight. One of the king's personal guards stood outside. Charlie saw Jock and Drustad straighten out of the corner of his eye. The king's guard scanned the room, his eyes finally landing on Charlie.

"King Valin wishes to speak with you immediately, Master Charlie," said the guard, his tone gruff.

Charlie looked from Saajee'a and back to the king's guard several times. Phil needed him, but Charlie was no doctor. The king's guard stared down at him. Finally, Charlie turned back to Saajee'a, who continued to stare solemnly at the floor.

"I'll talk to the king," he said to her. Saajee'a nodded and disappeared through the little door. "Lead the way," Charlie said to the king's guard. The stern man raised an eyebrow at the boy, then swiftly turned on his heel. Charlie hurried after him and heard Jock and Drustad follow close behind.

THE THRONE ROOM OF THE Elven palace was less intimidating to Ailinn than it was to most of the Conclave. The princess had spent countless hours sitting beside her mother, listening to the formalities of court and politics, and learning the laws of her people. She squeezed Daniel's hand, released it, and pushed the doors wide.

Much like the great hall, the boughs of the trees scattered throughout the room had been woven together to create the domed ceiling. Only this room was much taller. The first Belirian tree from which the elves had been born sat at its center, and King Valin slouched in the throne that had been carved from it.

"Phoenix Harbor agrees to pay fourteen hundred gold per year for three years to the Birchwood Barony for their clay mines," said one of the noblemen who stood at the base of the dais.

"Only three years?" said another noble. "My king, Lilliana is my second daughter. She and the heirs she may produce are second in line to the barony, as her elder sister and her husband have yet to produce any heirs in the last three years. Surely, she is worth more than that. Ten years at least."

"Five years, and not a month more," declared the first noble obstinately.

Valin took a long drink from the chalice beside him and promptly refilled it from the wine decanter. "Is five years reasonable to you, Ronan?" he asked. There was a long pause, and Ronan nodded. "Do you wish to hold the wedding while you are here in residence for the summer?" Valin continued.

"If Lord Ronan would permit a delay, the wedding could be held in accordance with an annual sailing event in Phoenix Harbor. It is said to bring good luck to a marriage. No dowries need be transferred until that time. The Winds of Fortune cast off is held at the end of the month, and travel from here to Phoenix Harbor would take only two weeks. If Your Majesty would allow it, I can send a carrier bird ahead to begin the preparations."

King Valin nodded and took yet another drink from his chalice.

"Agreed," the noble from Birchwood Barony said loudly.

The king staggered to his feet, carefully treading the steps of the dais. He approached a young couple who had been standing to the side for the duration of the negotiations.

"Then I wish Gullhad and Lilliana the greatest happiness and prosperity in their future life together. May you be blessed in all that you do," Valin said slowly.

The group gave a formal bow to their king and turned to leave. They bowed to Ailinn as they passed, and Ailinn noticed the glares at Daniel as they departed.

"You wished to see us, Father," Daniel said after the doors had closed behind them.

Valin staggered back up the steps to the throne. He half fell into the chair and immediately reached for his chalice.

"Have you been drinking?" Ailinn asked.

"Not just drinking. You're drunk," Daniel stated flatly.

"This is a damn thankless job. It helps me cope," Valin snapped.

"Perhaps if you spent more time with a clear mind, your job would be less daunting," Ailinn said as she approached the dais.

"I am more clear-minded now than I have ever been." Valin waved the chalice before him, mocking his two children.

Ailinn opened her mouth to speak, but Daniel laid a hand on her shoulder.

"What can we do for you, Father?" he asked.

Valin's face fell. He swirled the wine in his cup and set it down again. He pushed himself to a standing position though he still leaned against the arm of the throne.

"Savaric is on his way," he whispered, and Daniel and Ailinn exchanged worried glances. "He will arrive in ten days' time."

"No," Ailinn breathed. "I thought they weren't coming for another month. Savaric was supposed to finish his rounds at the tournaments before coming."

"A messenger was sent ahead. He bore the crest of Harpy's Pointe on his person. He is coming, Ailinn, and I cannot stop it."

"Please reconsider this, Father! You and Mother promised me—"

"Things have changed since you were a little girl, Ailinn," Daniel said. His hand flew to his forehead, and he doubled over in pain.

Ailinn reached for him though Valin took no notice. He refilled his chalice again and steadied himself against the throne.

"I'm all right," Daniel whispered sternly. He stood straight again and nodded reassuringly.

"Father, you married Mother for the betterment of our kingdom. You must agree that neither of you were ever fond of each other. I cannot accept this for myself. I want to love my husband, not live in contempt of him."

"Ailinn, Daniel is correct," said Valin, his speech continuing to slur. "Times have changed since that promise to you, and it is a promise I never should have made. I did grow to love your mother in time. And you will love Merrick too. You were friends once. And Merrick does not hold the same beliefs as his father. He is a good man."

"But I don't love him." Ailinn could no longer look at her father. Her hand found its way to Daniel's, her voice failing to hide the defeat she knew was coming.

"We cannot change who we are born to be any more than we can change the rising and setting of the sun," Valin replied. He swayed down the steps of the dais and set a hand on Ailinn's shoulder. "You were born to be the future ruler of the Elves of Chartile, Ailinn. I am sorry that does not suit your spirit at this moment, but even your mother learned to put her own interests aside for the greater good of her people. You will too, in time."

The doors to the throne room opened behind them and one of the king's guards stood framed at their center.

"Charlie of the Hill, Your Majesty," he said. The group of guards who surrounded Charlie stepped to either side of the double doors, leaving Charlie feeling quite exposed. He glanced sideways and saw Kashna standing patiently in the hall, his golden eyes glinting with mischief.

Charlie hurried into the throne room, not daring to take his eyes off the creature until he was safely through the doors. They shut behind him with a resonating boom. It was then his eyes took in the size and wonderment of the room. He almost didn't notice the three people staring back at him. When his eyes fell on Ailinn, his cheek started throbbing again. He swallowed hard and walked toward the dais, stopping at what he hoped was the appropriate distance from King Valin. The floor appeared slightly more worn in that particular spot, and he hoped it was from people stopping on this spot often. Though for a brief moment, he wondered if it was where the king beheaded criminals, and if the floor was worn from cleaning and scrubbing up blood. He shuddered before rising from his awkward bow.

"Thank you for meeting with me, Charlie," said Valin. "I trust your stay in the palace has thus far been enjoyable?"

"Yes, sir... er, Your Majesty." Charlie quickly corrected himself and bowed again in apology.

"I hear your ride with Lord Kharas and my daughter was rather eventful."

Charlie didn't dare raise his hand to his cheek, but his backside gave a sudden throb, and he could feel his face growing flush. He heard Ailinn shift uncomfortably next to him.

"I'm not very good at riding, Your Majesty," he replied.

Valin nodded. "We all have our strengths and our weaknesses. And one of Ailinn's weaknesses is trying to help people. A trait she must have inherited from her grandmother."

This time, Charlie did glance at Ailinn. She stared at the floor and fidgeted with the cuffs on her wrists. Charlie stayed quiet. He wasn't sure whether he was still at risk for punishment or even death. He dared not risk saying more than necessary. Years of being bullied had taught him to remain silent, even when his mind was screaming to be heard.

King Valin took a step toward Charlie, and the boy stiffened. "Fear not, young Charlie. Ailinn's behavior was out of line, and I do apologize for her indiscretions and temper."

"Father, I—" Ailinn began. Valin held up a hand.

"I have not asked you here to reprimand you. I have a task for you."

"For me?" Charlie asked, all manner of formality gone in an instant.

"Him?" Daniel asked with disdain.

"But I can't do anything. I can't even dance," Charlie said.

Valin laughed loudly and stumbled where he stood. He threw out a hand, leaning against Charlie. The boy could smell wine on Valin's breath. Charlie looked at Daniel and Ailinn. They looked as embarrassed as he felt.

Valin finally straightened himself and continued. "There are few who can keep up with the likes of Lord Tristian. Do not vex yourself. No, Charlie, the task I have for you has weighed on my mind for some time now. Since the day you arrived in fact."

"You want me to marry Ailinn, don't you?" The words tumbled out of Charlie's mouth before he could stop himself. One thing Chartile had *not* been good for was keeping his emotions in check.

"Of course not!" Valin's brow furrowed hard, and Charlie could see where Ailinn got her stern looks. "Who has suggested—?"

Valin turned slowly toward his daughter, and Ailinn took a step back.

"It's the prophecy, isn't it?" Charlie said quickly, and Valin returned his drunken gaze back to him. "My-My dad told it to me. When I got here, I-I just thought…"

"This prophecy will be the death of me," Valin whispered, holding his head in his hands and walking back to his throne. He stepped up the dais and plopped into the throne. "My dear boy, I am terribly sorry. It is no wonder you have been so worried these last several days. You truly need have no fears while you are here. Come here." He motioned to a small chair beside the great throne. It was likely meant for Daniel or Ailinn, as it was intricately carved with a blue velvet cushion. Charlie hesitated. He felt as nervous as the time he'd had to give a speech for his sixth-grade graduation, and that hadn't ended well. He pushed his jitters and nausea away and ascended the dais to sit beside the king.

"Charlie, I do not wish to set on you the same pressures that were placed on your father and his friends. Jayson did many great and wonderful things, but he was only a child. He was younger even than you. It was not fair to ask so much of him. However, if the blood of Jayson Hill runs in your veins, then I have little doubt that you do carry the... *gift*... of magic." The word *gift* seemed to cause a rather nasty taste in Valin's mouth. He swallowed and continued. "I have received word that Lord Savaric and his son, Merrick, are ten days' ride from the palace. They are coming as my guests to negotiate the treaty and marriage arrangements between Merrick and Ailinn. But it would do well to show Savaric that I and my home are not so unprotected as he believes. Will you train with Ailinn? Will you allow her to teach you how to wield your magic and prepare a show of force when Savaric arrives?"

Charlie blinked at the king sitting before him, absolutely and utterly confused beyond belief.

"Father, you're mad!" Ailinn cried. "By the Phoenix, you're playing right into Savaric's hands!"

"Ailinn's right, Father," said Daniel, still massaging his temples on occasion. "By allowing even the son of Jayson Hill to use magic, you are condoning its very use."

"And, isn't magic illegal? I thought you had forbidden Ailinn to use it," said Charlie.

Valin closed his eyes, and the shadows that fell across his face made him appear older and worn. "We are in desperate times. If anyone would be given the right to wield such power, it would be the son of our returned king. It would be the one who has come to fulfill the prophecy, the one who can bring to right the wrongs. You are not Chartilian. You are neither Elven, Dwarvik, or Human. We cannot hold you to our same laws."

"Father—"

Valin stood from the throne, cutting off Daniel and towering over him. "The chosen one came to *me!*" he shouted. "Not Savaric. Not the Court of the Rogue, and not the cursed rebels who break criminals from our jails and usurp every seneschal from Hollycrest to Sutton Low! I have the right to use him—"

Valin paused. His hand twitched toward the chalice wine. Charlie saw Ailinn's lip trembling in fear, and Daniel stepped closer to her.

The king sighed, finally giving in. He threw back a mouthful of wine, his features returning to calm once more. "I am not asking you to use your magic to fight as your father was forced to against Princess Taraniz. I am only asking for a show of force. Make a spectacle of it. Show Savaric that the son of Jayson Hill came to us, not him. I know Ailinn has learned many tricks from her mother that will yield themselves well to such an endeavor. But she cannot be the one to do it. I have my suspicions that Savaric has other reasons for wanting his son to marry my daughter."

"And what makes you believe that I would agree to this in the first place?" said Ailinn. She crossed her arms before her and raised a sinister eyebrow.

"I need time," Valin snapped. "Time to figure out Savaric's plans. If he can be distracted by Charlie's ability to use magic, he may not press for your wedding as quickly, which gives me the time I need to investigate his motives while he is here. Your own blasted stubbornness may, in fact, work to my advantage, little girl."

"What kind of plans? Will Ailinn still have to marry Merrick anyway?" Charlie asked.

Valin smiled at him. "Never mind yourself with such things. These are the burdens of a king. And I have others looking into the matter. Adults." He nodded and laid a hand on Charlie's shoulder, though the gesture did not comfort him. "No one must know. Savaric will get quite the awakening when he sets foot in my castle."

"The returned kings had weeks to train. I trained with Mother for years. I can't possibly teach Charlie in ten days," Ailinn argued.

"The time frame is rather improbable, Father," Daniel agreed.

"Charlie is the son of the returned king of Chartile!" Valin shouted, rising from his throne and making them all jump. "And he came to *us*, not Savaric. It is proof that only the worthy may wield such treachery."

"Mother would—"

"Your mother left me to rule a kingdom I never wanted!" Valin interrupted Ailinn. His eyes bulged from their sockets, and the top of his head was bright red where the hair had begun to recede. "I told her I would not stand in her way of what she wanted to do as queen. I never wanted this. Not becoming the Lord of Cannondole and certainly not the King of the Elves. I am doing what I think is best for us all and I'll be damned if I'm going to let three small children tell me otherwise."

Ailinn took a step forward. The fire and determination in her eyes had returned.

"I'll do it," Charlie said, standing swiftly and stepping between Valin and Ailinn. The room fell silent once more, and Charlie cleared his throat. "I'll do it, but... but on one condition."

Valin raised an eyebrow. "A condition?

Charlie swallowed. "Y-Yes. Your Majesty. Phil, my frien—my beck-and. He's sick. Most of the beck-ands are sick."

"It's the Desert Death," said Daniel. "It affects only the Humans. One of them must have come in ill with the new lot."

"We'll get more," said Ailinn gently. "I'm sorry about your beck-and, Charlie."

Charlie felt his mouth fall open. He stared at Valin, Ailinn, and Daniel, waiting for one of them to crack a smile and tell him it was all a joke. But it never came. "Are you serious right now? These people are dying!"

"They're just beck-ands, Charlie," said Daniel.

Charlie shook his head. "No. No, I don't think you believe that for one minute! My dad told me that your grandma was Human. You're telling me you're totally okay with letting these people die? Well, I'm not. No magic until these people get some help." Charlie crossed his arms in front of him. His hands shook, but he pushed his fear of being thrown into the dungeons aside.

Finally, Ailinn spoke. "Perhaps I can take a look at them. It... could be good training."

Valin nodded. "Daniel, you will be their guard and their cover. No one must know. You are all dismissed."

Ailinn and Daniel bowed to Valin and headed for the doors. Charlie hurried after them, then remembered to turn and bow as well. King Valin had already turned to his chalice again and took no notice. When Charlie reached the hall, he found Daniel leaning against a carved pillar.

"What's wrong?" Charlie asked. "Should I get the guards or—"

Daniel stood straight, rubbing his temples, and breathed an audible sigh.

"Are you all right?" Ailinn asked.

"Yes, but I—"

"Later. Are you well enough to walk?"

"Lean on me, Daniel," said Kashna, stepping from the shadows.

"I'm fine. I swear it."

"You're definitely not fine. Is it that Desert Death thing? Because you're part Human?"

Daniel glared at Charlie. "Of course not. I have very little Human blood in me. I simply need rest."

"Of course," said Ailinn. "Kashna, please, take him."

The creature nodded and leaned against Daniel as they headed up the golden hall.

"What is—"

"Thank you, Charlie," Ailinn interrupted. "Thank you for not telling my father about... about our marriage being my idea."

Charlie watched as Ailinn's face contorted itself into a blank stare. At least, it would have appeared free of emotion to anyone else. Charlie recognized it immediately. She was hurt so deeply, there were no emotions that could possibly express her anguish. And she was also thinking. By now she must have had at least three plans on how to escape from her impending marriage to Merrick. That look was dangerous.

"Oh, uh... you're welcome, I guess." He still couldn't bring himself to look her in the eye, but her mere presence was making him incredibly uncomfortable again. Girls were so very complicated. "Listen, Phil and the others, they're really sick. We have to help them now."

Ailinn shook her head. "I will send my physician to look at them and administer medicine. There are things we can do to slow the disease. We must train you first."

"But—"

Ailinn held up her hand. "When Daniel has recovered, I will send him to fetch you. Until then, remain in your quarters. We have much work to do."

Charlie thought he saw the faintest smile as she turned to leave. Her guards joined her from where they had waited across the corridor and blocked her from his view. It was a good thing, too, as Charlie realized he was staring far too intently at her backside. He heard footsteps approach and turned to see Jock join him.

"Drustad's shift ended when you reached the throne room," he said. "How did it go?"

ELEVEN
THE MANY MOODS OF MAGIC

THE AFTERNOON SUN PASSED OVER the royal wing of the Elven palace, and the beck-ands hurried about their daily task of lighting the lanterns as the shadows stretched through the halls. Though they kept their heads down and attentions toward their lantern-lighting, it was difficult not to notice the late queen's son as he staggered through the hall, held upright by the massive qarveena.

They reached the door to Daniel's quarters. Kashna had only to flick his head, and it opened with a creak. Daniel leaned against the doorjamb, then stumbled through. Kashna nodded toward the door again, and it closed behind them. With practiced control, the beck-ands kept the tug at the corners of their mouth at bay. Instead, they moved further down the corridor, lighting the torches and lanterns as they went.

Daniel collapsed into the first chair he came to and held his head in his hands. The torrent of voices in his mind whispered over each other, creating indiscernible nonsense. The last thing he remembered was standing before the king with Ailinn. Somewhere along the way, Charlie and Kashna had arrived, but it seemed the conversation had ended by the time he came to again. Kashna pushed his forehead to Daniel's. Within moments, the whispers subsided, and Daniel found himself thinking of a small stream not far from the palace. He could even hear the water falling over the large rock and the echo inside the cavern.

Kashna pulled away and settled at Daniel's feet.

"Thank you, Kashna," Daniel whispered. "Did you hear what happened?"

Kashna shifted his wings and crossed his paws before him. "As always." He paused, licking at the pads of his feet. "King Valin wishes Ailinn to instruct Charlie of the Hill in the ways of magic."

"What?" The only thing keeping Daniel from leaping to his feet was the qarveena that conveniently lay across his boots. "That's absurd!"

"Among other creative adjectives," Kashna said, still licking his paw.

"How can he possibly believe condoning the use of magic in front of Savaric will help our cause? If the rebels get more of a foothold, we'll be having the beck-ands revolting soon."

"Charlie is neither Elven, Human, or Dwarvik. He is not Chartilian and has pledged no allegiance to Valin or Savaric. He is as neutral a pawn as we could hope for."

"A neutral pawn is more dangerous than one who has sworn allegiance. There is nothing stopping him from being corrupted by Savaric or even Merrick when they arrive." Daniel's feet were beginning to fall asleep. He wiggled uncomfortably, but Kashna didn't budge.

"You are forgetting who Charlie secretly wishes to pledge his allegiance to."

Daniel's brown eyes met Kashna's golden ones, and he watched the creature smirk as he began to purr.

"My sister is more unpredictable than Charlie. He can be controlled more easily, but Ailinn? She fears nothing." Daniel finally pulled himself free from Kashna's bulk and walked to the empty hearth, leaning against the mantel. "Though I fear I am becoming more unpredictable by the day. Kashna, these… voices, the lost time and memories. I cannot protect Ailinn if I am not in control of myself."

"Your mother said for the two of you to take care of each other. You do not have to weather this alone," said Kashna.

Daniel nodded. "I know. Which is why I have you. Promise me that if whatever is plaguing me grows worse, you will come with me. We'll look for your family. Ailinn may be young, but she can take care of herself. This palace would welcome having one less bastard walking its halls."

"I THINK HE'S GONE A bit crazy, to be honest," said Charlie. He sat on his bed, rubbing his feet. He still wasn't used to some of the Elven clothes, and his boots had yet to fully break in. Though King Valin had instructed them not to reveal their plan to a single soul, Charlie knew he could trust Jock. The guard listened intently as Charlie spoke not only of the king's plan but also his outburst and anger toward the late queen for leaving him alone to rule.

"I mean, his eyes were totally bugging out of his head. And I don't think a normal person would tell his kids that he doesn't want to be the king. That's like the president saying he never really wanted to be president. It just doesn't work that way, man."

"I don't know this president, but I believe I understand you," said Jock, shifting around his sword as he sat in the chair. "It's no secret that King Valin wanted nothing more than to hang on the arm of the queen. Responsibility never suited him, though he has tried to pretend otherwise."

"That sucks," Charlie muttered. "Ailinn's supposed to be queen. Her mom dies, so she can't teach her, and her dad doesn't really want the job, so he can't teach her."

"If her marriage to Lord Merrick is successful, I believe his experiences will help fill in the gaps of her education."

"*If* she marries him. I don't know if she still wants to try to marry me." Charlie gulped and shook his head. "Why are girls so confusing?" He leaned back into the pillows and stared at the canopy above him. Someone, probably Saajee'a, had cleared out the leaves from his overhead canopy, but a new one had already taken their place.

The pair sat in silence for several minutes. The sun was nearly set, and he could hear the chorus of strange frogs chirping in the woven branches that made up his ceiling. The temperature had dropped rather significantly throughout the day, and Charlie could have fallen asleep right there if a sharp knock on his door hadn't brought him to again.

Jock leapt to his feet and hurried to the door. Daniel towered in the doorway. He looked at Jock, surprised to find Charlie's guard inside rather than guarding the door.

"It's okay. Let him in," said Charlie. Jock stepped aside and bowed as Daniel stepped through, ducking slightly to keep from hitting his head on the door.

"Where's Kashna?" Charlie glanced tentatively into the hall beyond.

"With Ailinn," Daniel replied flatly. He looked from Charlie to Jock and back again.

"It's all right. He's with us," said Charlie.

Daniel sighed and ran his fingers through his hair. "You were told to remain silent on the matter. How many more have you told? You may compromise our entire operation. We don't know if Savaric has spies within the palace."

"I can assure you, my lord," said Jock, "that your secret is safely guarded. It is my duty, after all, to guard Master Charlie."

Daniel glared but bit his tongue on the matter. Instead, he snapped at Charlie. "Come. We must hurry before anyone sees."

"Wait. What about Phil?" Charlie asked.

Daniel blinked at him. "What about him?"

Charlie furrowed his brow. "What about him? I told the king I'm not learning any magic until Phil gets help."

Daniel cleared his throat. What else had transpired during their conversation with Valin that he did not know? "You can discuss the matter further with Ailinn."

Charlie huffed but turned to the chair Jock had previously occupied to put his boots back on.

"If it would please Master Charlie," Saajee'a said as she peeked out from the beck-and door and tried to bow, "you may take the beck-and passages."

"Good idea!" said Charlie. He beamed at Saajee'a, who bit her lip to hide her smile. "Then no one will see us."

"Except for the beck-ands, who talk nearly as much as the nobles." Daniel stared down at the young girl in disgust.

Saajee'a hung her head and took a step back into the shadows. "Forgive us, Lord Daniel," she murmured.

"No," said Charlie to Daniel. "You don't need to be sorry, Saajee'a. It's a good idea, and I say we do it. You might learn more if you actually listened to your beck-ands, Daniel." Charlie stood from the chair. He glanced at Jock, who winked at him.

"I will cover for you," he said.

"Thanks, Jock. Come on, Saajee'a. You lead the way."

Saajee'a hesitated for a moment, caught between the appalled look on Daniel's face and Charlie's words of encouragement.

Charlie did not wait for an answer from either of them. He walked to the little door and bent down. He couldn't see two inches in front of his face. It looked like nothing more than a black void and smelled like musty earth. A light appeared, and Charlie looked over his shoulder to find Saajee'a handing him one of the oil lamps from his vanity.

"Where are you heading, Master Charlie?" she asked.

"Princess Ailinn's quarters," said Daniel from behind them. Charlie looked up and saw him carrying a lamp as well. His frustration seemed to have softened.

Saajee'a nodded and headed into the blackness of the beck-and passage.

Four large steps led down to a packed dirt tunnel that was barely tall enough for Daniel to walk through, and a small mattress sat in a shallow alcove at their base. Charlie winced as he walked past this, now realizing this was where Phillippe, now Saajee'a, slept. At every crossway, were four stones, one large and one small smooth stone, and one large and one small rough stone. Saajee'a explained it was how the beck-ands knew which direction to turn in the dark. Due to the lack of ventilation in the passages, mounting permanent lanterns or torches was dangerous. And carrying one wouldn't allow the beck-ands to take as much back and forth in one trip. One learned the passages by feel alone.

They approached a set of steps larger than most of the others, and Saajee'a stopped.

"Would you prefer to enter from the hallway or directly into her room, Master Charlie?" she whispered.

"The hallway. Definitely the hallway," Charlie replied. Saajee'a nodded and ascended the steps.

Daniel grabbed Charlie's arm. "If we go into the hallway now, what will have been the point of enduring this filthy trek? It is fortunate that we haven't encountered anyone. It should remain so. And if these passages mirror the halls above, which I am sure they do, we are very close to her rooms."

Charlie pulled his arm from Daniel's grip. "Dude, I ain't risking... ya know... She could be changing or something."

Daniel raised an eyebrow at him and shrugged. "Turnabout's fair play. She's seen *you* naked."

Charlie was glad for the darkness. He could feel his face blushing hard at the mention of his first encounter with Ailinn.

Daniel didn't wait for a reply. He hurried forward and caught Saajee'a by the hem of her tunic. She squeaked and nearly fell down the stairs.

"Hey!" Charlie shouted, hurrying forward to catch Saajee'a before she fell.

"You will take us to the princess's quarters directly," Daniel spat. He let go of Saajee'a so violently, she fell back into Charlie's arms.

"Not cool, man," Charlie said glaring at Daniel as he descended the steps back into the passage.

"Eat dragon dung," Daniel sneered, continuing along the passage.

"You okay?" Charlie asked, straightening the girl's dingy tunic. Saajee'a stared at the ground but nodded. Charlie patted her back and followed Daniel.

Daniel had been right that Princess Ailinn's quarters were close. They ascended another stair but did not see any mattresses like the one for Phil.

"Where are her beck-ands?" Charlie whispered in Saajee'a's ear. He didn't want to walk in on any of them undressing, either.

"The princess is attended by her ladies-in-waiting, Master Charlie. They each have a beck-and that may be called upon to assist them or the princess."

"Oh," said Charlie sheepishly.

Daniel waited at the top of the stairs. He knocked quietly. Three knocks, two knocks, then three again. It was only a few seconds, and Ailinn opened the door.

"I did not expect you to come this way," she whispered, standing aside for them to enter. Daniel ducked through the small door, and Charlie followed.

What little nerve Charlie had gained since his meeting with the king was waning quickly. Ailinn was dressed in a plain white shirt with fitted slacks. They weren't like the hose Charlie and Daniel wore, but they still showed off her figure.

He hardly noticed how spacious the room was in comparison to his own. He followed along behind the pair, the look of a lost little puppy in his eyes. He continued to stand long after Ailinn and Daniel had taken seats around a small table set with clear chalices of water. He must have looked like an idiot, but he could feel the muscles in his legs slowly freezing him in place to the floor.

"Charlie," said Ailinn, "you may sit."

Charlie jumped at the sound of his name. Her voice gave him the power to move, and he quickly sat in the chair closest to Daniel.

"Is Kashna outside then?" Ailinn asked Daniel.

"Naturally," Daniel said. He twirled the glass in his hand and lounged in his chair as though he were the king himself. "I can't have the two of you running off now. Especially you." He indicated his sister, who glared at him fiercely. It was amazing how quickly her green eyes could go from warm to cold.

"Well, where to begin?" Ailinn said, turning to Charlie. He gulped his water, which dribbled down his face and tunic. He wiped his chin and sat as straight as he could, hoping Ailinn hadn't seen. "I have ten days to teach you how to use magic, and in what forms we are going to use it when Merrick and Savaric arrive."

"Forms?" Charlie asked. "Like weather magic versus moving stuff around? Those were the things my dad mostly talked about."

"On a basic level, yes," said Ailinn. She stood and began pacing the room, her arms crossed before her, and her little pinkie hanging on the corner of her mouth. "But there are many moods to magic. I could create a thunderstorm to appear overhead in a matter of moments. With this, I can instill a sense of wonder or a sense of fear in those watching it."

"So it's like mind control then," said Charlie. He thought he was beginning to understand.

"Not exactly," said Ailinn. Charlie's face fell. Perhaps not then. Ailinn continued. "It's deeper than that. I'm not forcing anyone to feel anything. They can sense it on their own, and their bodies are interpreting it. Daniel, would you, please?"

She held out her arms to her brother. A pair of golden cuffs with a rainbow of gems were clamped tightly around her wrists. The largest stones were pure black, exactly like the ones Phillippe, Saajee'a, and the other beck-ands wore.

"On the first day, Ailinn? Is that really necessary?" Daniel asked her.

Ailinn's shoulders dropped, and she rolled her eyes. "Ten days, Daniel! Or would you like to explain to Father why I was unable to teach Charlie how to use his magic?"

"You swear you aren't going to run." Daniel glared just as fiercely back at his sister, brown eyes meeting green as he rose from his chair.

"And where would I go that you couldn't find me?" she whispered.

Daniel patted Ailinn's cheek with a debonair sort of grin. "Nowhere," he whispered back, and he walked through a door into an adjoining room. They heard another door open and shut farther away, and another set of feet joining Daniel as he hurried back.

Kashna was steps behind him as he reentered the room. The qarveena smiled and shook his great wings. Charlie froze.

"So, the little king is learning magic," Kashna sneered. Charlie's heart began to beat wildly. "Frightened, are you, little king?" Daniel sat on his chair again, but Kashna continued to pace the room. "Give me five minutes with him again in one of the training pastures and I'll get the magic out of him." He walked straight up to Charlie, his golden eyes the exact height to meet the boy's.

Charlie sat motionless in his chair. He felt the hot breath of the animal on his face. He tried to force himself not to swallow, but a hard lump formed in his throat.

"That won't be necessary, Kashna," said Ailinn. "Father has asked me to train him."

"Has he, now?" Kashna turned, and Charlie let out the breath he had been holding. Kashna sat beside Daniel and licked at his paw. "Then we best not defy the great King of the Elves." It was more sarcastic than sincere.

Ailinn rolled her eyes. "I suppose asking you to wait outside and guard the door is out of the question."

"I'm not taking the chance you won't try to run," Daniel said.

"Oh, yes, because I couldn't have done so all the other times you removed them. You're being dramatic, and you want Kashna to torture and scare Charlie."

"Perhaps it is a lesson in control," Kashna said, grinning at Charlie.

"Well, you aren't helping." Ailinn held out her wrists again, and Daniel produced the key from his pocket, finally removing her cuffs.

The skin beneath was just as red and raw as Phillippe's had been. Ailinn sighed aloud in relief, closing her eyes and rubbing her wrists for several moments. She walked to a carved desk in the corner and pulled a jar from one of the drawers. Charlie could smell something like eucalyptus or peppermint as Ailinn slathered a cream onto her wrists.

"Now who's being melodramatic?" Daniel called to her. "You had them off last night."

"Yes, but they need taken to Tutaria for adjusting," she snapped back. "In case you haven't noticed, they have become a bit tight."

"Then perhaps the princess should not eat so many sweets," Daniel chided back.

Ailinn flicked a small cube of ice at him that she had somehow made appear from nowhere. Daniel picked up the cube from his lap, plunked it in his glass, and toasted his sister.

"You are hopeless," she said to him.

Charlie barely remembered much of his first magic lesson with Ailinn. He spent most of the time holding her hands, praying that she didn't notice them trembling.

She began first by transferring a warm, tingling energy into Charlie's hands and instructing him to tell her the emotion of the energy. It was extremely difficult at first. Charlie was pulling guesses out of thin air. But when he locked eyes with her and concentrated, he knew exactly what emotion she was sending him. It took all his effort not to smile a big, stupid grin.

Then, Ailinn announced it was Charlie's turn to send an emotion back to her. This too took quite a bit of practice, as he had to learn how to focus the energy down his arms and through his hands.

According to Kashna, a diten mouse could tell what emotion he was sending as it radiated out of every pore in his body.

By the time their lesson had ended, Charlie was physically exhausted, but his mind buzzed.

Daniel left Ailinn's quarters for his own with Kashna in tow, leaving Charlie to return through the pitch blackness of the beck-and passages on his own. To his relief, Saajee'a had waited in the darkness for Charlie to return. He didn't dare say anything. Not until they returned to his room, and the little door to the passage closed behind them both. He flopped on the bed, hugging his pillow with a grin a mile wide.

"She likes me, Saajee'a," he said. "I know it."

THE NEXT WEEK WENT BY much faster than Charlie would have liked. He spent his days training with the lords and nobles. By the end of seven days, he could successfully parry with a small, thin sword that looked much like a fencing rapier. His training master called it a *firon tutor*, an ancient word that meant "Little Spine."

Charlie was also becoming more comfortable on Cinders. Lord Kharas seemed to have learned his lesson during their first excursion. They practiced in a clearing a half mile from the palace. Kharas would attach a long rope to Cinders' halter and lunge her while Charlie practiced his balance.

But it was his evening lessons Charlie looked forward to the most. Under Daniel's and Kashna's watchful eyes, Ailinn pushed Charlie as hard as she could. He left each lesson exhausted and exhilarated. He would fall instantly into sweet, blissful dreams before Phillippe could secure the door to the beck-and passages behind him. As she had promised, Ailinn sent the palace physician to treat the beck-and. He was still considerably weak, and Saajee'a stayed on per Charlie's request to assist him, but Charlie was thrilled to have him back.

With only three days left to prepare before Savaric's arrival, Ailinn felt her confidence waning as Charlie's grew.

"We need to practice in the throne room," Ailinn said. She watched Charlie extinguish and ignite a single candle on the table over and over again.

"The throne room is guarded at all times, Ailinn. Unless you can convince Father to call off the guard for a night, it's not possible without revealing ourselves," said Daniel as he nonchalantly stroked Kashna's ears. The big cat purred loudly and flicked the end of his tail in contentment.

"There's always the banquet hall," said Charlie, lighting the candle once more and turning to face the three. "The beck-ands have access to it via the kitchens, and I'm sure there are passages that lead to the kitchens from here. I've seen beck-ands go in and out of there as a shortcut when I've had my lessons with Lord Tristian." Charlie cleared his throat. He hadn't told Daniel or Ailinn he'd decided to continue his dancing lessons and was slightly embarrassed at the admission.

"And who will take us through the passages? Your little beck-and, whom I am sure has told half the other beck-ands what we're up to by now?"

"Phillippe wouldn't do that, and neither would Saajee'a. He's my friend. And yes, he could show us the way."

Daniel laughed loudly, and Kashna joined in, the subtle reverb of a purr in each guffaw.

"You hold too much faith in that old man. He's a slave, nothing more, nothing less. He has no education, no training of any sort. Explain to me, little king, how someone like that could ever keep a secret?" Daniel ran his fingers through his thick black hair and eyed Charlie with an all-knowing look to rival Ailinn's.

"Because he has no reason to betray me. If you treated me the way you treat your beck-ands, I wouldn't wanna help you, either." Charlie stood, even as Kashna tilted his head and grinned up at him. "If Ailinn says we need a bigger place to practice, and we need to do it in secret, then I think Phil will know where we can do that. Even if it's not the banquet hall."

There was silence for a long stretch, the only sound being Kashna's continued gentle purr. Eventually, both Daniel and Charlie turned to Ailinn. She chewed her nails, staring at the floor.

"All right," she finally said. "We'll ask Charlie's beck-and for assistance. I have faith in the prophecy, and therefore I have faith in Charlie."

Daniel shook his head and rolled his eyes. "So be it."

Charlie led Phillippe into Ailinn's quarters, with Saajee'a trailing close behind. He told the little man about needing a larger practice space, but Phillippe immediately dismissed the banquet hall. More stone had been used to build it than other places in the palace, which meant it echoed more than other rooms. Instead, he recommended an old meeting room close to the library.

"It was part of the original palace built centuries ago," he told them. And there was no stone to be found anywhere in the room.

He led Charlie, Ailinn, Daniel, and Kashna through the passages and up a steep slope. Cobwebs hung in thick sheets, and the latch to the door stuck. Daniel eventually pried it open, sweat beading along his forehead. The door creaked loudly as it swung inward, and the group stayed in the shadows of the passageway, listening intently for any sound that might signal a guard to investigate the strange noise. But no one came.

They stepped cautiously into the room. It was minimally decorated, with only a dusty wooden table, several chairs, and a large chandelier made of antlers with dozens of candles wedged securely onto the points. The trees in the room were so old, they had grown into and through each other, making it difficult to know where one tree stopped and another began. The branches overhead held no leaves, leading one to believe the trees might have died, or at least that those branches no longer gained enough sunlight to produce leaves. But the twigs and branches were so intertwined, the leaves weren't necessary.

Ailinn and Daniel looked at the room in wonder.

"How did I not know about this place?" Daniel asked. "I know every inch of the palace."

"Where is this?" Ailinn asked, turning to Phillippe, who was creeping back into the shadows of the passage.

Phillippe dared a glance at Charlie, who couldn't stop smiling. He shuffled forward across the mossy floor and pushed on one of the gigantic tree trunks. It gave way to a large room, filled with towering shelves that went on much farther than could be seen, and it smelled faintly of must and parchment.

"The library," Ailinn whispered. "This is off one of the antechambers. I remember finding Mama here looking for anything to do with the prophecy."

"I wonder if she knew about this place," Daniel said, poking his head through to the room beyond, then quickly pulling the door closed. The seam of the door was entirely invisible against the cracked bark of the Belirian tree.

"This is fantastic, Phillippe. Thank you," said Charlie, smiling at the beck-and. Phillippe smiled back, gave his master a small bow and returned to the passageway with Saajee'a.

They wiped the dust and cobwebs from the table and chairs and sat. Ailinn stared at the chandelier above her and raised her hands. A swift wind filled the room and shook the dirt and cobwebs from the candles. One candle fell with a loud thud, nearly hitting Daniel on the head.

"Watch it!"

Ailinn ignored him. "Charlie, would you mind putting this back?" she asked, handing the candle to him.

Charlie looked at her, confused for a moment. He took and candle and began to climb onto the table.

"Not that way," she said to him. Charlie sat back in his chair, squinting at Ailinn and furrowing his brow. "Like this." She held out her hands, and Charlie felt the candle twitch in his grasp. It lifted into the air, higher and higher until it was level with one of the empty prongs of the chandelier. She lowered the candle back to the table where it hovered in front of Charlie. "Now, you try."

Charlie took a deep breath and reached out to sense the energies that were the candle and Ailinn. He could feel the playfulness in the mood she had set with her energy. She was flirting with him in a way that Daniel couldn't sense.

The candle almost fell, but Charlie recovered enough to keep it afloat. It rose into the air, perhaps not as quickly as Ailinn had made it, or as stable, but Charlie eventually had it secured in place again.

"Wonderful," said Ailinn. She flashed her toothy smile at him for the first time since Charlie's first night at the banquet. "Now light them. Light them all. At once."

Charlie looked at the chandelier which had at least thirty or more candles. "I can't concentrate on all the wicks at the same time," he said, utterly bewildered at her request.

"Of course you can," she said. "They are all made of the same material. You simply need to identify the energy combination of the elements that create the wick, then broaden your senses to encompass them all instead of staying focused on just one."

It took some time. A long time, if Charlie were being honest. He felt like he'd been sitting there for hours. He had to close his eyes and block out everything else in the room. He could hear the steady breathing of Daniel, Ailinn, and even Kashna, who stood guard at the secret panel into the library. But he couldn't think of that. He couldn't feel that. Ailinn's energy whirled with hope and encouragement. Daniel's was flat and tired. He blocked it all. There was nothing in the room except him and the chandelier. Nothing but him and the candles. The candlewicks that were growing warmer. He could feel their energy moving faster and faster, creating a friction in themselves. He thought he smelled smoke, but he couldn't think about that, either. The wicks were growing hotter, vibrating faster and faster.

Ailinn let out a cry that broke Charlie's concentration. She gasped and leapt from her chair, cheering and clapping. Charlie looked at the chandelier above him. All but eight candles were burning.

Daniel looked at Charlie in open-mouth amazement. He licked his lips, closed his eyes, and leaned back in his chair. "Hmm," was his reply. "Took you long enough."

"Hush, Daniel," said Ailinn, but she continued to smile. "Charlie, if you can light all the chandeliers in the throne room at once, that will surely gain Savaric's attention."

"You'll have to do more than light and extinguish candles to make him fear you," chided Daniel. "That's what Father wants. You've spent seven days teaching him how to work with fire and move small objects. A Human child who has not yet gained their orenite cuffs can do that." He stood and leaned across the table. The light from the chandelier threw shadows across his face that made him seem even more mysterious. "You need to master the art of illusion if you want to get through to Savaric."

"Daniel, there's no time for that. It took the returned kings weeks to learn basic control of the elements. What Charlie has accomplished in a week is amazing. We must continue to hone these skills and use this to our advantage."

"No," said Charlie, "I think Daniel's right. These tricks wouldn't scare a fly. I'll cancel all my other lessons over the next three days. We're going to work all day, every day until Savaric gets here. It's our best shot of teaching this guy who's boss."

"No time like the present to begin," Daniel replied, smiling at Charlie and plopping back into his chair.

"Daniel, it's late. Charlie must be exhausted after lighting the candles. We need to—"

"Someone's coming," Kashna growled.

Panic spread between them.

"Your damned beck-and did this," Daniel sneered.

"No, he wouldn't!" cried Charlie.

"Into the passage," said Ailinn. She reached out her hands, and a gust of wind whirled around the room. Dead leaves that had fallen on the floor slapped Daniel and Charlie in the face. The wind extinguished the candles, but the chandelier began to rock. It fell, crashing into the table, and sending Daniel and Charlie tripping backward into Kashna.

The two tumbled out into the library antechamber, knocking several books and scrolls from the shelves as they did so. They could hear the clanking of armor as guards rushed toward the sound.

"I'll distract them. You get Ailinn out of here," said Daniel. He pushed Charlie back through the panel and Kashna leapt through to join his master.

"You there!" Daniel cried. "A beck-and must have removed their cuffs. This way!"

Footsteps pounded away from the panel. Charlie was frozen. He felt someone grab his wrist. He twisted, pulling the person into him as his sword master had taught him.

It was Ailinn. Both caught their breath, staring up into each other's eyes.

"Let's go," she whispered, fleeing into the dark passageway.

The lantern they had left with Phillippe was burning dimly. The old man couldn't run as swiftly as Ailinn and Charlie, but he led the way through the dark passages. The princess's quarters seemed farther away than they had remembered.

As they reached the steps to Ailinn's quarters, Ailinn pushed on the door and fell into the room, Charlie narrowly avoiding tripping over her. They closed the door behind them and lay on the floor, completely out of breath.

The stitch in Charlie's side was just beginning to subside when he heard Ailinn giggle. It was quiet at first, then it grew louder and louder. Her laughter was contagious, and Charlie soon found himself chuckling along. They lay on the floor, laughing long and hard until their sides ached again.

"You should have seen the look on your face when you fell!" said Ailinn, breathless, and she guffawed so hard, her next sentence was incomprehensible.

"You could have blown the whole castle down with that wind!" said Charlie, wiping a tear from his eye as he laughed. "What were you thinking about, a damn hurricane?"

Ailinn went quiet. She took several deep breaths and turned to look at Charlie lying beside her. "You," she replied, flashing her toothy smile at him again. She sat up and pulled Charlie into a sitting position. "I imagined standing there in the throne room, with Savaric walking down the aisle toward me and Father. I thought of you standing at the base of the dais, fulfilling the prophecy."

Charlie's face fell. He pulled his hand from Ailinn's.

"Is that all I am to you?" he asked angrily.

Ailinn leaned back, her brow furrowed in confusion. "What do you mean?" she asked, still breathless from laughing so hard.

"This returned king? The one who's going to fulfill the prophecy your mother was obsessed with? That's all you care about, isn't it?"

"No, I—Charlie, it's not like that at all! I—"

"You don't care about me or anyone except you and your mom and that damn prophecy." Charlie stood, his face turning red. He wasn't sure whether the tears stinging his eyes were from their previous laughter or from the anger that was rising inside him. "I know exactly what this is. You'll lead me on, make me believe I'm something special. Then, as soon as you're done with me, you're going to leave me! You're going to abandon me like my dad and everyone else! Well, I'm not going to let that happen here. I'm going to make my own destiny, and I don't need you to do it!"

Charlie wretched open the beck-and door, hitting Ailinn's feet as he did so. He raced down the steps and turned the corner back up the passageway, Phillippe bobbing far behind him, and attempting to catch up with the diminishing light of the lantern.

Charlie pushed the door to his room open and nearly slammed the door in Phillippe's face before he remembered the little man. He caught the door, looking down at the beck-and who stared up at him with shock and confusion. It was too much. Charlie burst into tears. He ran to his bed and buried his head in his pillow.

Phillippe poured him a cup of water and set it on the nightstand before drawing the curtains around the four-poster and extinguishing the tiny lantern light.

TWELVE
KASHNA

BATHROOMS ARE A GREAT PLACE to think. And a bathroom in the Elven palace was no exception. The one Charlie used was shared among several of the nobles and visitors in that part of the castle. It had to be reserved when used for bathing, as beck-ands needed to be scheduled to attend the fires that heated the water.

Somehow, Phillippe had managed to find an available time that day. By the time the sun came up, the gigantic fires were rolling and the pots of water steaming. Much to Charlie's disapproval, Phillippe pulled his master out of bed and pushed him down the hall toward the bathroom. A tub of hot, steaming water sat in the middle of the room, surrounded by dense, fluffy moss and smooth stepping stones. A door opened to the left, and another beck-and carrying a large pot of steaming water entered the room. He did not look at Charlie, but he dumped the water into the tub, nodded to Phillippe, and closed the door behind him.

"You dragged me out of bed for a bath?" said Charlie sleepily. The heat and humidity were like a sauna and did little to help Charlie feel more awake.

"Yes," was Phillippe's short response. Charlie looked at him, surprised at the little man's bold response. He was so surprised, in fact, that he did not argue but simply walked to the other side of the tub, hung his clothes on the bar on the wall, and entered the bathtub.

Once he had settled, Phillippe dropped a small ball of salt and herbs into the water.

"What's that?" Charlie asked, lifting himself half out of the water in disgust.

"It is to help you relax, Master Charlie," Phillippe said with a smile. Charlie watched it sink to the bottom, then saw the herbs rise back to the surface as the salt dissolved, giving off a floral and earthy scent. It *was* rather relaxing.

Charlie watched as Phillippe shuffled out of the room and stared at the back of the closed door. It wasn't the custom in Chartile for nobles to bathe alone, and Phillippe had helped him with his last few baths. Mostly scrubbing his back and handing him his towel and clothes when he finished. Not that Charlie needed the help, but he didn't want to offend anyone by refusing their customs. He had already caused enough stir among the nobles and beck-ands when he'd insisted Phillippe be treated for the Desert Death.

Charlie shrugged and reached for the bar of soap and a long scrub brush. Without Phillippe hanging around, it was easier for Charlie's mind to wander. Immediately, it fixated on the incident that had occurred the night before.

Ailinn had been playing him all along. He was sure of it now. She wanted to make him into the vision of the returned king she had in her mind. She didn't really like him. Not that Charlie blamed her. He was weak and worthless. He still wasn't holding his sword properly during lessons. His pivas during his dance lessons looked more like leg spasms, and he was still terrified Cinders was going to take off on him again. Ailinn deserved someone who was stronger and more confident, someone who could live up to his father's reputation. And that wasn't Charlie.

Charlie scrubbed his body until every last inch of skin was pink and raw. He washed his hair and dunked his head beneath the water, then scrubbed again to make sure all the soap was out.

When he lifted his head from the water again, Charlie screamed. It was sort of a scream, anyway. It sounded more like the squeal of a half-drowned pig. He wiped the water from his face and sunk down into the tub until only his head was sticking out.

Kashna stood there, looking down at him with that far-too-intelligent grin. His golden eyes sparkled with a sort of hunger, and Charlie now wished Phillippe had stayed. He really didn't want to be eaten while sitting completely vulnerable in a bathtub. Not that he wanted to be eaten at all, but the thought of the nobles coming to stare at the crime scene, which included his naked body flopped over the side of the tub, sent a chill down his spine. It was a recurring theme he didn't wish to repeat.

"What are you doing here?" Charlie finally asked as it seemed Kashna was not about to speak first.

"Your beck-and asked me here last night. Resourceful little man. He's quite fond of you. I can't say I've seen many beck-ands as loyal to their masters as Phillippe and Saajee'a are to you," Kashna replied. His voice was surprisingly gentle, and not mocking at all.

"Phil?" Charlie asked, more to himself than Kashna. "But why?"

The qarveena settled himself on the mossy ground. He did not flap his wings or snap his teeth. He looked at Charlie, his golden eyes full of sincerity. Charlie wasn't sure if this disturbed him more or less.

"According to your beck-and, and various other accounts, both you and Princess Ailinn spent hours crying in your chambers last night, thus leading both of you to the conclusion that neither of you wants anything to do with the other any longer. However, with Lord Savaric's impending arrival, we cannot waste any time in your training over trivial adolescent tendencies toward some form of romance. I have been told that love is a learning process in your kind."

Charlie's stomach felt queasy. Ailinn had been crying? Perhaps he had gotten her all wrong. But it didn't matter anymore. She wanted nothing to do with him now. The best that Charlie could hope for was to learn his magic as quickly as possible and... and then what? Charlie blinked at Kashna as his mind raced. He had never been particularly good at thinking long-term. Mostly he focused on making it through his days without being tripped or shoved into a locker. Once he learned his magic, once Savaric was... defeated? Then what?

"So," Charlie began, trying to keep his voice from cracking, "Who's going to teach me then?"

"I am," Kashna replied. He stood and took several steps closer, golden eyes level with Charlie's blue.

"You?" Charlie asked. Several snappy comebacks came to his mind, but he swallowed them.

Kashna crossed the room toward the bar where Charlie's clothes and drying towel hung. "What you must understand, little king, is that though I know little of where I came from, I am still what the people of Chartile call a Lost Legend." He grabbed the towel in his teeth and handed it to Charlie. "I have the same ability to wield magic as any Human or Elf who has been given the gift. At one time in the history of this world, it was not a gift, but something as common as learning to walk or fly. It was passed down from parent to offspring. We all had our unique talents, even amongst races and species."

Charlie stepped from the tub. He dried himself thoroughly and followed the stepping stones to his clothes hanging on the bar.

"So, you're going to teach me then," was all he could muster. His mind was whirring with too many conflicting thoughts. He was lucky his sentence had been coherent at all.

"Yes," Kashna said in a near whisper. "I will meet you in your chambers in one hour." He turned to leave, the tip of his tail twitching in some sort of aggravation.

"Wait," Charlie called to him. The creature's wings drooped as he turned back to Charlie. "What about Daniel?" He stared hard at Kashna, trying to convey more than what his words alone meant.

"Ailinn has told Daniel nothing of your confrontation. He believes this is all Ailinn's doing. Which, as far as she is concerned, it is. She knows nothing of your feelings from last night, or your decision to refuse to continue training with her. It was, in part, Daniel's idea to have me train you. Though I admit, your beck-and and I discussed the topic at length before my master rose from slumber. One hour, little king."

Kashna flicked his head at the door, and Charlie heard the latch click. Slowly, the door swung open, and Kashna sauntered from the room. Charlie watched as the door closed seemingly of its own accord behind the creature. He stared at the back of the closed door before quickly dressing and hurrying back up the corridor to his room.

Saajee'a was laying out a small tray with an assortment of Charlie's favorite breakfast foods and his favorite honey and herb drink when he burst into the room. She did not startle as she would have a week ago. She finished pouring the drink into a chalice, then turned to face him.

"Where's Phil?" Charlie asked.

Saajee'a clasped her hands behind her back and looked toward the little beck-and door. "He... he is not well, Master Charlie," she whispered. "He returned from your bath and—and fell, sir."

"Where is he?" Charlie's heart raced. Not again. He didn't care about his lessons with Kashna. The qarveena, or whatever he was called, could wait. Phil could not.

"Resting, Master." Saajee'a looked toward the little door.

Charlie grabbed the chalice and a tart from the vanity and rushed to the beck-and door. He opened it slowly, trying to keep it from creaking as much as possible. Phillippe lay on the dingy mattress, his face tense even as he slept. Charlie knelt beside him and laid a hand on his shoulder.

Phillippe jumped, then relaxed as his cloudy eyes found Charlie. The boy lifted the chalice to Phillippe's lips and helped him drink. He wiped the dribble from the man's chin with his sleeve and set the tart in his weathered hand.

"Are you angry with me, Master Charlie?" he asked weakly.

Charlie shook his head. "Of course not, Phil."

Phillippe smiled weakly. "I wished only to do what I thought was best for the kingdom. Your training is important, and I—I know what love feels like. I know what a mess it can make the world." He shifted and gasped in pain.

Charlie set a comforting hand on his shoulder. He would send Saajee'a for Ailinn's physician again.

"I've seen the way you two look at each other," Phillippe continued before Charlie could rise. "I know that look myself."

Charlie never thought to ask Phillippe about his family before. "Do you have a family, Phil? Should I go get them?"

Phillippe pulled a thin blanket around himself, and his brow slowly relaxed, if only a little. "Beck-ands are not permitted relationships. Marriages may be approved by a beck-and's master. Most birth arrangements are decided upon by the Chamberlain and their council."

Charlie swallowed. It sounded worse than an arranged marriage. "Oh," he said. "But you… you were in love once?"

Phillippe closed his eyes, and the faintest smile pulled at his lips. "I fell in love with the most remarkable young woman. Najilah. She would have been a wonderful mother."

"Would have?"

Phillippe was silent for so long, Charlie thought he had fallen asleep. He stood quietly and turned back toward his quarters, but Phillippe finally answered. "When they discovered Najilah was pregnant, she was put to death. She had broken the laws of her station, as had I. For two days they tortured her, trying to discover who the father was. She never once revealed my name."

Charlie wasn't sure if it was time or practice that steadied Phillippe's voice. Still, his words hung cold in the darkness between them. He stared down at the little man, trying to imagine what he might have looked like decades ago. He saw a man, young and in love, and it made his stomach sink more.

"If I had ever had a son, I would pray to the Gods he would be like you, Charlie." Phillippe touched the golden orenite cuffs on his wrists with trembling hands. This time, his voice cracked, and tears escaped his cloudy eyes. "I wish I could have helped you, Master Charlie. I wish I could have been the one to teach you, but I can't. I can't." He made to turn away from Charlie, but the boy was faster. Charlie grabbed the man's hands and squeezed them tightly.

"You *have* taught me things, Phillippe. One thing Ailinn told me is there are different kinds of magic, and I think that people caring for each other is one of them. Since I came here, you've always been there for me. I need that more right now than learning how to levitate a candle."

The door creaked beside them, and Saajee'a peeked carefully around the corner.

"I'm sorry to disturb you, Master Charlie," she whispered. "Shall I return your breakfast to the kitchens? Mother can make you something else."

"No, it's fine. Thank you, Saajee'a. I'll be out in a moment. Can you bring me one of the pillows from my bed?"

Saajee'a nodded and hurried to fetch the pillow. She handed it to Charlie, who helped arrange it behind Phillippe's head.

"How's that?" he asked.

Phillippe smiled. "More comfortable. Thank you," he squeaked.

Charlie squeezed Phillippe's hand one more time, then left him to rest. He closed the beck-and-door as quietly as he could and turned back to Saajee'a. She stood beside the vanity, her hands clasped behind her back again.

"Phil needs to see Ailinn's physician again. Can you deliver the message to whoever is in charge of that, Saajee'a?" he asked.

Saajee'a's face grew serious. She nodded and half-ran across the room and out the beck-and door.

Charlie sighed as he watched her go. He took the tray of breakfast to his bed and stuffed an entire fruit tart into his mouth. He leaned back, staring up at the canopy above him. The leaves had shifted slightly, like a breeze had caught them just right. Outside, he could hear the familiar splashing of the water fountain and wondered if Ailinn was still feeding the little fish. He reached nonchalantly toward the chalice sitting on the bedside table and jumped. He bolted upright, turning to see what his hand had brushed. It was Kashna, sitting beside his bed grinning, the tip of his tail twitching.

"How did you get in here?" Charlie asked.

"I can walk unseen and unknown if I so desire," Kashna purred.

"Well—I... Don't do that! You can't go around sneaking up on people like that!" Charlie cried. He sat straighter, attempting to regain some measure of composure.

"And why not?" Kashna asked, tilting his head innocently. "The reactions are so entertaining."

Charlie glared at the creature who chuckled back.

"So, no one knows you're in here? Won't Daniel suspect you're up to something with you being gone?" Charlie asked, swinging his legs over the side of the bed and trying to relax.

"I do not accompany my master in his daily duties about the palace. For my part, I am believed to sleep soundly in his quarters when in fact I roam the castle and its grounds, unseen by those who are already riveted by their own workings."

Charlie thought he understood. He had to listen closely to Kashna to understand him. His words were muddled with growls and purrs. Even when he was able to make out the words, Kashna never seemed to give a straight answer.

"So, it's like, because people don't want to see you, they can't see you. And since they don't even know you're there in the first place, then how could they know they want to see you at all? They're busy thinking about other things."

Kashna smiled wide, his sharp, pointed teeth glinting in the lantern light of the room. "Now you are beginning to understand the finer points of magic, little king." He stood and began pacing the room. His tail trailed behind him, just above the floor, and his wings tucked courteously beside him so as not to knock anything over.

"Magic is more than feeling for the individual energies that make up something or someone. It's more than understanding the emotions that are contained within the person at that moment. Magic is also about choice.

"You can choose not to act. You can choose to act in a way that, if a person wishes the same outcome that you put into motion, only then will it occur. And it is about the choice to force your will upon someone. The ancient laws of magic say the latter is forbidden, but as most have forgotten those old ways, except those of us with memories not our own, there are no rules anymore. I have been shaped into someone who decides my own rules, and I obey my master when I choose and when I must. Who do *you* wish to become, Charlie Hill?"

Charlie sat in silence for several long minutes. Kashna had ceased his pacing and now stood looking at the boy, patiently waiting.

Finally, Charlie spoke. "I don't know," he said flatly. "I haven't been shaped by magic. Not yet anyway. I grew up without it, so I can't decide what kind of person I'll be with it. I gotta learn more about… about—I don't know. I don't know who I am or anything about my own magic yet."

"The two are one, Charlie," said Kashna. His voice remained gentle, which was even more unnerving to Charlie. "You cannot wait to learn who you are until you've discovered your magic. Your magic is part of who you are. And who you are may define which magic path to take."

"Then I guess I'll just have to wait and see."

Kashna smiled and nodded approvingly. He flexed his wings and began pacing again. "When you begin to understand that you can change a person's will, their desires, it opens a door to new thought that you may also change an object's will. Now, how is this possible? An inanimate object has no conscious, no soul. It cannot breathe or move or think. It is not alive. But by some will or another, the individual forms of energy that make up that object allowed themselves to be arranged in such a way that it would become a chalice, a rug, a door. And they choose to remain that way unless acted upon by outside forces that change their will. Water may turn steel to rust. The wind may loosen the seeds of the Belirian flowers and carry them to new lands."

Charlie perched on the edge of his bed. He leaned toward Kashna, hanging on each purred word the qarveena spoke.

"Therefore," Kashna continued, "by enacting my will, my desires, upon an object, I can force it into something new. Within reason, mind you. Without adding or removing more particles of energy, I could not will your chalice into a curtain. A chalice is made of metal and gems. Your curtain is made of fabric. However, I *can* will it to reshape itself."

Kashna stopped pacing. He turned and stared intently at the chalice on Charlie's nightstand. The air around the chalice moved and warped, like heat rising from a hot surface. Charlie watched as the chalice began to melt, but not in any way he had ever seen before. Globs were dripping and morphing, rising and falling, until they formed themselves into a metal bowl. The air calmed, and Charlie looked from Kashna to the bowl and back again.

"How do I know you aren't trying to force your will on me and make me *think* it's just a bowl?" he asked.

Kashna threw his head back and laughed. "You are an astute learner, little king. What you speak of is called by some an illusion. An illusion can only be perceived by sight. If someone were to touch an object that was not truly as it was, they could feel the difference, and thus know that something was wrong."

Kashna blinked at Charlie and nodded toward the bowl. "Please, touch it," he said.

Hesitantly, Charlie reached for the bowl. It was warm but remained intact at his touch. He poured some of his honey and herb drink into the vessel and held it up to look through the bottom. Carefully, he lifted the bowl to his lips and drank.

He set the bowl back on the side table and looked at Kashna.

"How am I supposed to learn this in three days? And what am I going to do with it?" Charlie's voice had turned from awe to frustration. It had taken him a week just to learn how to lift a stupid candle. This was more than even his dad had learned how to do.

"Do you understand the theory of what I have told you, little king?" Kashna walked to him, slow and steady, his golden eyes piercing through Charlie's blue ones. Charlie nodded. "Then you have little need to worry about learning it. Doing it is going to be your challenge, and your task."

"But that's what I mean," Charlie mumbled to himself. Kashna stood inches from him now. He growled and bared his teeth for the first time.

"Then say what you mean, little king. Words are yet another form of magic that this world has yet to understand. Words have many meanings and many forms. Say what you mean and mean what you say."

Charlie gulped and nodded as Kashna turned from him, walking back to the center of the room.

"Kashna?" Charlie asked timidly. "Where did you learn all of this stuff?"

The creature sighed and looked out Charlie's window to the courtyard beyond. He stood there, seemingly lost in deep thought. Charlie wondered if he was trying to will the stone into something new, but eventually, he spoke.

"I have few memories of my time before coming here. I remember a place barren and cold. It was winter. Someone found me. There are fleeting and unfocused memories of suckling milk from a towel dipped into a bowl and being given scraps of meat. I remember the ride in the carriage to the palace. I was placed in a dark chest. I was frightened. I could not see. I could not breathe. Then a voice spoke in my mind. It said to me: *Remember, little one. Remember your past and be my will.*

"When the chest was opened, King Valin dropped it. I attempted to fly, but I was too young. I fell and slid across the floor. Daniel came to me. I looked into his face and I knew that he felt the same as I. Unloved, unwanted, not belonging. Neither of us fit into this world, and we needed each other. Since then, I have had flashes of what I assume are memories of a life long since passed. A great qarveena, larger even than I am now, wielding magic. I know his thoughts, and I can sense what he feels. I once knew these things long ago, and I can know them again."

He turned just as the sun was beginning to pass across the window. He lifted his head, reveling in the sun's warm rays. Charlie stared at him, and for the first time, felt sympathy for Kashna. He remained silent as the qarveena warmed himself in the momentary sunny spotlight. As the sun began to shift and shadows fell across his face once more, Kashna turned to Charlie again, his eyes more sad than ever.

"Your first lesson is to will your chalice back to its original form." Kashna turned and headed to the door. He opened it with a gesture of his massive head as he had with the bathroom door. Jock and Drustad stood outside. They did not seem to notice the door opening behind them. They did not notice the great winged creature passing between them. They continued their conversation about the princess's ladies, and which was eligible for marriage. They did not notice the door latch behind Kashna, and again, Charlie was left staring at the back of a closed door.

THIRTEEN
TO KNOW, TO WILL, TO DO

IT TOOK HOURS BEFORE CHARLIE was able to turn the bowl back into a half-deformed version of the original chalice. By then, Saajee'a had crept back through the beck-and door carrying a bag of freshly laundered clothes. She hung them in the wardrobe as Charlie sat staring at his creation. When he finished reforming the metal vessel, he collapsed onto his bed, a small smile pulling at the corners of his mouth. He was already asleep by the time Saajee'a tiptoed around the bed and pulled the covers over him.

Charlie felt as though he had barely shut his eyes when something pulled him from his sleep. He hadn't heard a sound but somehow found himself drifting out of a pleasant dream that had involved him shooting fireballs out of his hands at a group of orcs. He opened his eyes, and this time stifled his scream. Kashna was staring at him, his teeth bared in an unnatural smile.

"Stop doing that!" Charlie cried. He sat up and rubbed his forehead. His head was pounding from a headache he had not noticed before. It was completely black outside the small window, though he knew that didn't mean much when you lived in the middle of a giant clump of massive trees. Thankfully, Saajee'a had left a single lantern burning across the room on the vanity.

"Perhaps one day, but not today," Kashna said. He leaned forward and touched Charlie with his nose. A cool sensation brushed across his skin. He felt his headache subsiding, then it was gone.

Kashna sat back and eyed Charlie. "Better?" he asked.

Charlie nodded but continued to rub his head until the cool sensation had gone as well.

Kashna turned to the chalice on Charlie's bedside table. It was less like a chalice than Charlie remembered before falling asleep. Far from it, in fact. It resembled some form of modern art, and Charlie was completely embarrassed.

"Well done," Kashna said softly.

Charlie raised his eyebrows at the qarveena, shocked. "Well done?"

Kashna turned to Charlie and nodded. "Yes. You have done well applying the concepts of your first lesson. Expecting perfection when attempting any task for the first time is unreasonable. You have done well." He looked at the deformed mass again, and within moments, had reshaped it into its original chalice form. "Now it is time to work with other mediums. Shall we begin?"

"What time is it?" Charlie asked, looking out the pitch-black window. He knew the garden was out there, but he couldn't see a single flower.

"Late, but not yet tomorrow. Then again, it is always today. Do you have any particular feelings about this rug?"

Charlie peered through the darkness. Kashna sat on the rug in the middle of the room. It was a simple woven rug, nothing spectacular, he supposed. But at least Kashna had had the decency to ask, which Charlie found rather odd.

"Uh… n-no. Not really," he answered.

"Good." Kashna nodded and stepped off the rug. He turned to face it, and Charlie watched as it unraveled before his eyes. The pieces of yarn or fabric, or whatever was holding it all together, rose and fell from the air like little helicopter seeds. Soon, there was a small mound of what used to be a rug in the middle of the floor.

Kashna walked toward Charlie's vanity and gulped down a small meat pie that still sat on the tray from earlier.

"Now, restore the rug. This time, I will remain here," he said, helping himself to another pie.

Watching Kashna eat made Charlie's stomach grumble. He poured himself another glass of the honey drink into the newly restored chalice and sat on the floor before the mess of string and fabric.

He reached out with his mind, sensing every little piece and every little fiber of what used to be his rug. He began searching for pieces that had similar energy patterns, knowing they must have fit close together at one time. He was beginning to divide the pieces into large and small when Kashna's smooth voice broke his concentration.

"Charlie, you are simply using your ability to levitate. You must will this rug back into existence," he said.

Kashna joined Charlie. He fluffed out his wings and shook from his head to his tail. He settled next to the boy, his golden eyes piercing through the darkness and glowing ominously.

"Place your hand on my back."

Timidly, Charlie reached his hand toward Kashna. Immediately, thoughts and feelings that were not his own raced into his mind. It was a blur, and Charlie gasped in terror. He tried to pull his hand away, but he seemed to have lost control over his body. A gentle voice rose above the noise of the memories. *It will pass. Relax your mind.* It was Kashna. Charlie took several deep breaths, and the memories began to slow.

A single image swam into focus, and Charlie realized he was staring at himself from Kashna's eyes. But he was no longer afraid. There was a feeling of concern and an attempt to remain calm. When Charlie's brow finally unfurrowed, Kashna turned his attention to the pile of material in front of him.

An image of what the rug had looked like before formed in his mind's eye, and the Kashna-Charlie hybrid willed the remnants of the rug to form themselves whole again. It was strange to Charlie. Rather than being remade by an outside force creating it anew, the pieces seemed to want to become a rug again, binding to their previous neighbors with ease.

Kashna stood and broke the connection with Charlie. The boy's mind reeled as it attempted to reorient itself into being just Charlie once more. Eventually, the room stopped spinning. He opened his eyes to see Kashna sitting on the newly reconstructed rug, smiling smugly.

"I get it now. I totally understand!" Charlie said, his face bright with excitement. "And it's not even that hard. Like, you just *do* it! Oh, man. This is so cool!" He tried to stand, but his head started spinning again. He sat down quickly, though his smile never faded.

Kashna bowed his head. "Well done, Master Charlie. I do believe our continued lessons are no longer necessary."

"Wait," said Charlie, his head still spinning. "That's it?"

Kashna blinked. "Nothing is ever complete if that is what you are asking. I take my leave of you, though I would encourage you to use your newfound skills whilst practicing your other lessons. I believe you have a riding lesson in the morning. Good night."

The qarveena left the room as he had before, completely unbeknownst to Drustad standing outside the door.

Charlie leapt from the floor as soon as the door had latched behind Kashna's trailing tail. He fist-pumped the air and jumped up and down in excitement.

For the next two hours, Charlie practiced reforming various objects around his room. Certain things took more concentration, especially if they were constructed of more than one type of material. He was even able to reconstruct some of his clothes into something that more closely resembled what he would have worn at home. Still no jeans or tennis shoes, but he was glad to not have to wear the hose anymore.

It was only when the singing frogs outside had ceased their chirping that Charlie finally fell into bed for a few short hours of rest.

THE BIRDS WERE SINGING MADLY outside when Charlie woke. He stretched and yawned, staring out the window with a smile on his face.

The clothes he had reformed were laid out on the end of his bed, but neither Phillippe nor Saajee'a were anywhere in sight. He pulled on a pair of light blue trousers that had once been a linen shirt. The trim that had run along the sleeves, collar, and bottom hem had been redone as stripes down the outer sides. He rummaged through the clothes to find a tunic that had once been two separate shirts. Now, the once-plain white shirt sported shorter sleeves, a slimmer fit, and a collar covered in material taken from a pair of blue hose.

He pulled on his riding boots and cinched his belt over his shirt. Even if it wasn't the fashions of Chartile, or even the Middle Ages on Earth, Charlie felt more like the hero he was striving to be.

He heard the beck-and door open, and the clanking of a tray as Saajee'a's hands shook under its weight. Charlie spun around and dashed toward the little girl. He caught the tray just before Saajee'a dropped it and set it on the vanity beside him.

"Good morning, Saajee'a," Charlie said brightly, popping a fruit tart in his mouth. "Did your mother make breakfast again?"

Saajee'a blinked at Charlie. "Y-Yes, Master Charlie," she stammered out.

"Tell her I said thanks." Charlie polished off the eggs and wrapped a pastry in a cloth, stuffing it in his pocket.

"Did the physicians come to look at Phillippe yet?" Charlie asked. He inched toward the beck-and door, not wanting to wake Phillippe.

"Yes, Master Charlie," Saajee'a said. "They-They gave him a medicine to help him sleep. They said there isn't much more they can do, sir."

Charlie stopped just outside the beck-and door. He peeked carefully through and saw Phillippe lying on his dingy mattress. The only signs of life were his slow breathing. Charlie closed the door quietly. He found himself staring at his hands, the same hands he had used to levitate candles and shoot fireballs in his dreams. Illness had to be caused by something, and something had energy. Energy that could be willed into something else.

Drustad's sharp hilt-knock startled Charlie from his thoughts. Saajee'a hurried to the door and opened it.

"Lord Kharas wishes to inquire whether you have canceled your lesson with him for today, or only your lesson yesterday," said Drustad.

"Oh, man. I totally forgot!" Charlie smacked his forehead and hurried to gather an apple from the food tray. "No, I wanna do it. It's not too late, is it?"

"Not at all," Jock replied from behind Drustad. "Your lessons do not start for another hour. I'll send word myself." He winked at Charlie before heading out, and Drustad closed the door behind him.

Charlie breathed a sigh of relief. He still had time. He wolfed down another tart and a handful of sausages, then heard Saajee'a clear her throat.

"The throne room is currently unoccupied, Master Charlie," she said. Charlie blinked at her, but Saajee'a bustled to the vanity, lifted the remnants of Charlie's breakfast, and left.

It was several moments before Saajee'a's words struck like lightning in Charlie's mind. He bolted for the main door and wrenched it open. Drustad turned to look at him, confusion spreading across his face. His hand went to his sword hilt, and he looked over Charlie's shoulder into the room.

"You wanna go for a walk?" Charlie asked him.

It took very little bribery in the way of some of Saajee'a's mother's pastries for Charlie to convince Drustad to escort him to the throne room to prepare for Savaric's arrival in two days. He puffed his chest out and smiled at every passerby. It was hard to tell whether they were more surprised at his new demeanor or the fanciful clothes he wore. Either way, Charlie felt exhilarated.

Drustad stepped inside the throne room to ensure it was unoccupied, then he shut the doors tightly behind Charlie, and the boy was thrown into pitch blackness. Charlie stood still, waiting for the echo of the doors to dissipate. He took several deep breaths and closed his eyes.

First, he practiced lighting and extinguishing the candles on the great chandeliers until he could snuff them out without hesitation. Then came the wind. He loved the dramatics of wind in all the movies he had ever watched that helped make the entrances of his favorite characters more epic.

He was still working out how to make the wind stop more suddenly when the throne room doors opened. Lord Kharas stood framed in the doorway. The wind billowed out his robes and tossed his long beard to the side as it slowly died. The man looked around the room, listening to the whistle of the wind subside. He turned to Charlie and smiled.

"Lord Savaric will have quite the show when he arrives," he said. He walked toward Charlie, who stood frozen halfway up the aisle and laid a hand on his shoulder. "King Valin has asked me to be his advisor after Princess Ailinn's marriage to Merrick is complete. I know what the king has instructed of you. Your secret is safe with me, Charlie."

Charlie breathed out a sigh. Then he remembered he was now supposed to be a powerful wizard or king or something like that. He squared his shoulders and looked up at Lord Kharas sternly.

"I'm ready for my lesson, my lord," he said. Lord Kharas chuckled, his eyes twinkling with admiration.

"Then come along. Cinders is waiting for you."

Drustad fell in behind the pair as they trudged toward the stables. Charlie felt his hands begin to shake despite trying to act the part of a returned magical king. He had come a long way since his first disastrous ride with Cinders, but the fear of being trampled to death or bucked off and breaking his neck still loomed inside him.

The big black mare was saddled and ready to go when they entered the stables. The sight of her made Charlie suddenly weak in the knees. Any courage he had gained the last few days was gone in an instant. He paused at the entrance to the stable and gulped. Cinders caught sight of him. She snorted and shook her head.

Charlie approached her cautiously and reached a hand out to stroke her nose. He pulled a piece of citrus fruit from the pouch on his belt and held it out to her. Cinders sniffed the air in front of her as Charlie came closer. She lipped at the fruit and gently took it from his hand, biting into it and sending a spray of juice across his boots. Charlie raised a trembling hand to her neck and stroked her softly as she chewed.

"Good girl, Cinders," he said. It was then that he noticed the rope Lord Kharas used during their lessons was not tied to his saddle.

Kharas noticed Charlie's gaze and smiled. "I think you're ready to try your hand at a free ride," he said.

Charlie took a deep breath and turned back to the mare, who had moved on to nibbling his belt pouch for more treats.

"Okay, girl, I know we got off on the wrong foot... er, hoof," he whispered. "But we gotta figure out how to work together now, okay? You and me. We're gonna do this. We have to do this."

Charlie closed his eyes. He formed an image in his mind. He and Cinders riding through the Belirian forest. They were in sync, riding with perfect form. He held the thought in his mind until the detail was as if he was looking through his eyes. Cinders tossed her head as he willed her to see what he saw and feel what he felt. She shivered under her saddle but soon settled.

Charlie opened his eyes and patted her neck again. The horse nudged him with her nose and lowered her head to meet his eye. Charlie knew she had understood, and he nodded to her.

"Shall we begin, Master Charlie?" Kharas asked, swinging himself into the saddle of his own chestnut stallion. Charlie had no idea how long he stood there with Cinders. Time seemed to move more quickly when he worked with magic. He blushed and nodded. He turned to the saddle and swung himself up with little effort. He suppressed a smile as he fitted his feet into the stirrups. It was the first time he had not needed the mounting block the beck-and had brought. Cinders tossed her head and nickered.

Kharas nudged his horse forward toward the large training paddock just outside the stables. Charlie followed, trying to calm his still-shaking hands. Though somehow, the ride seemed smoother. He looked up, and for the first time, he noticed the surrounding landscape. Hardly anyone was about, and those that were, were all busy at their own tasks. It wasn't the parade of eyes he had imagined it would be. He straightened in his saddle, and Cinders lowered her head and sighed.

Kharas halted at the gate to the paddock, and Charlie pulled Cinders to a stop beside him. "You two seem to have finally come to an understanding," he said, patting Cinder's neck.

"I think so," said Charlie.

"Let's find out, shall we? Follow me." Kharas nodded at the stable hand to open the gate. The man obliged, but not before Lord Kharas called over his shoulder at Charlie. "A race to the clearing then?"

He trotted through the first gate, then the second on the far side of the paddock, disappearing around a turn in the path through the trees ahead.

"Let's go, girl," Charlie whispered to Cinders. He nudged her gently, and Cinders took off into a canter.

Charlie started. He fell forward and grabbed Cinders' neck. The horse stopped, and Charlie sat up. He took a deep breath and nudged her again. Cinders began with a walk this time. Charlie clicked his tongue, and she increased to a trot. They rounded the first bend and caught sight of Lord Kharas not far ahead. Charlie nudged Cinders one last time, and she launched into a canter. Charlie felt the rise and fall of her gait beneath him. They flew past Kharas and on toward the clearing. Lord Kharas whooped behind him and matched Charlie's pace.

Charlie felt himself smile. The pounding of Cinders' hooves beat in time with his heart as the two raced through the forest. The trees were a blur as they ran past. Carefully, Charlie reached out with his mind. He could sense the excitement in Cinders, the thrill of finally becoming one with her rider. It was hard for her to contain her joy, he noted. Her muscles twitched. She wanted to fly faster and farther, but she seemed to be holding back for the sake of Charlie. She was happy simply making him happy.

The break in the trees ahead was the only clue to the clearing ahead. Charlie guided Cinders through the opening and turned her sharply to head back up the trail again. But it was too much. Cinders dug into the ground and leaned hard, trying to keep her balance. Charlie wasn't ready. He felt Cinders dip and went flying from the saddle again. He slammed hard into the earth and rolled to a stop at the base of a Belirian tree. The sound of hooves signaled the approach of Lord Kharas, who pulled his mount to a stop as Cinders sauntered over and lipped at Charlie's hair.

Kharas laughed a hearty belly laugh as Charlie pushed himself to his hands and knees. "Getting a little carried away, are we?" he asked. Charlie smiled back at him and pushed Cinders off his hair. "Are you well, Master Charlie?" Kharas asked with slight concern.

Charlie nodded. "Yes, I'm fine." He stretched his neck and shoulders and brushed the dirt from his knees. Pulling himself into the saddle was a bit more difficult now that his rear and shoulders were screaming in pain, but at least he managed to swing his leg over on the first try. He patted Cinders' neck and urged her into a walk.

He joined Kharas at the opening to the path, and the man brushed earth and weeds from Charlie's shirt.

"How well can your magic remove grass stains?" he asked, chuckling.

The sound of more hooves approaching down the path stifled their laughter. Drustad pulled an unsaddled horse to a stop before them. Both horse and rider were breathless.

"My lords, forgive me," Drustad began and coughed. Kharas unhooked a tiny waterskin from his belt and handed it to the young man, who drank and continued. "You must return immediately. King Valin's orders. Lord Savaric and his son have just arrived."

FOURTEEN
LORD SAVARIC

IT WAS TOO SOON. IT may have only been by a few days, but Ailinn wasn't ready. Her ladies' beck-ands had informed them that Lord Savaric and his son had arrived at the palace gates seemingly out of nowhere. Her father had stalled for time, as Charlie wasn't even in the castle. The Lord of Harpy's Pointe and his son were escorted to their old quarters and instructed to wait to be received by the king and the Conclave.

Ailinn paced before the tapestry that led to her brother's quarters. She heard the soft knock signaling his presence, and she hurried to pull back the heavy drapery.

"Is it him? Is it really him?" she asked before Daniel could close the secret door.

He straightened and brushed dust from his black hair. "Yes, it's him."

Ailinn cursed under her breath and began pacing again. "He wasn't supposed to be here yet. Charlie's not ready. I know he's not. And it doesn't matter anyway. We have no plan. There's no way to get out of this!"

Daniel grabbed Ailinn by her shoulders, holding her steady. "He hasn't even signed the official order to cease his support of the rebels. We have time."

He stared hard into Ailinn's eyes until she sighed and nodded.

"Do you think he will?" she asked. "Sign the order? Do you think he'll actually do it?"

Daniel released his sister. He ran his fingers through his hair and sat in one of the chairs close by. "I don't know. Part of me believes he will, but whether he will follow through is another matter entirely. I need to talk to Merrick."

Ailinn's face turned cold. "Merrick's as much of a traitor as his father," she snapped.

"I don't think so," said Daniel.

"I know you don't, but people change, Daniel. Much can happen in a few years' time."

"He's our only chance at gathering any information."

Ailinn bit her lip, halting the retort that almost dared to escape. She watched as Daniel straightened the quilt across the back of the chair. He was calm, and much more collected than he had been the last several weeks.

"How are you feeling?" she asked, sitting in a chair across from him.

Daniel smiled. "Better, actually."

"Did Kashna help you?"

Daniel shook his head. "No, the pain subsided on its own."

"And... no more periods of missing time?" Ailinn fidgeted with her orenite cuffs as she spoke. Daniel's temper had been rather close to the surface of late, and now was not the time to anger him. She needed him on her side. But she also needed to know she could count on him.

Daniel continued to smile. "No, I haven't had an episode in at least two days." When Ailinn didn't respond, Daniel tugged at a strand of her hair. "Here now, you have enough to think about besides me. I'm fine. Promise."

Ailinn finally flashed her own smile, but it vanished as quickly as it had come. She certainly did have more than enough to worry about. She had planned to speak with Charlie that afternoon, but that was no longer an option. Her guards would be around any moment to escort her to the throne room, and she still had no idea what to do if they forced her to agree to a marriage with Merrick on the spot.

She regularly devised three different strategies for her endeavors, and not having even one was torture. She rubbed again at the orenite cuffs on her wrists. Her father would never permit her to arrive with them removed. Savaric knew her and her mother since she was a child. He knew she possessed magic. She would have to change to cover them.

"My guards will be here soon," she said. "I need to fetch my ladies to prepare me."

Daniel rose and nodded. "I'll come 'round and wait outside." He kissed Ailinn's forehead and patted her shoulder. "You are the heir to the Elven throne, Princess Ailinn. Muster your courage and wit. There will be plenty of time for stubbornness later." He tugged a strand of her hair once more and disappeared behind the tapestry.

CHARLIE'S HEART POUNDED AS HE raced through the corridors with Drustad in tow. He wasn't ready for Savaric yet, at least not in his heart. His skills in magic had definitely grown since his training with Kashna, but the thought of confronting the man who had caused so much fear and strife in the Elven territories of Chartile was enough to make him want to crawl under a rock again.

Jock was waiting for them outside the door to Charlie's quarters. He held the door for the boy who rushed through and began stripping off his dirty clothes, leaving a trail behind him as he ran toward the wardrobe.

Phillippe peeked through the little beck-and door and quietly shuffled inside. "Master?" he asked hesitantly.

Charlie spun around, his head and one arm through a clean linen shirt.

"Phil!" he cried and ran to the little man. "You're up! How are you—I mean, are you okay? What happened?"

Phillippe held Charlie's shirt so he could push his other arm through and slowly staggered toward the wardrobe. "Saajee'a brought the princess's physicians again. And her mother."

"Her mother?" Charlie asked.

Phillippe nodded. "She was able to instruct the physicians in more specific care for Humans. They increased my medicines."

Charlie beamed. "That's great! Are... are you better now?"

The little man handed Charlie a pair of shoes like the ones the nobles wore. They looked sort of like the short boots he saw some the girls in his class wear.

"I am not cured, if that is your question, Master Charlie. But I am well enough to return to my duties."

"I'm really glad, Phil, because I've got a major problem."

Phillippe handed Charlie a pair of hose that had not been altered. Charlie took them begrudgingly and removed the comfortable pants he had made.

"Is it the princess?" Phillippe asked.

Charlie shook his head. "Savaric's here. He wasn't supposed to be here for another day or two. Now everyone's freaking out. There was gonna be a big welcoming thing in the throne room, and now it's just crazy!"

Phillippe looked from Charlie to the little door and back again. "They will need my help in the kitchens, Master—"

Charlie cut him off. "No, Phil. You're just now feeling better. I want you to stay here."

Phillippe smiled and for the first time, Charlie noticed he was missing several teeth. "Do not believe for a moment that Saajee'a and her mother will not be watching me like birds of prey. And it may give me an opportunity to speak with Lord Savaric's beck-ands as well."

Charlie furrowed his brow and thought for several moments. "All right. But if you start to feel bad, you come back and lie down for a bit. You can even use my bed. I don't mind."

"Will you be all right?" Phillippe asked, his tone more friend than servant.

Charlie sighed. "I mean, I'm as good as I'm gonna be." His hands had started shaking again, and he fumbled with his belt. He had somehow managed to twist it and had to start again.

Phillippe reached out a hand and undid the knot Charlie was making again. He pulled tight, tighter than Charlie had expected. Then he looked up, his clouded eyes meeting Charlie's with stern confidence

"Show him courage the likes of which he has never seen," the old man whispered, then shuffled across the room as quickly as his old bones would allow toward the beck-and passages.

Charlie watched him go until the little door creaked closed behind him. He shoved on his boots in a mad flurry and bolted back toward the door and his guards still waiting outside.

The halls were full of nobles, their families and even a few beck-ands, all processing to the throne room in an unorganized bout of chaos. This was the first time Ailinn and Merrick would be officially presented to each other as betrothed. It was customary for such meetings regarding royalty to be done publicly. And though the atmosphere buzzed with excitement, Charlie could sense fear in many whom he passed on his way. His new abilities seemed to have made him more aware of the emotions of those around him.

He entered the throne room through the great double doors, squished between Jock and Drustad. Charlie saw Daniel and Kashna, who stood at the base of the dais. They each caught his eye. Kashna nodded and winked at him. Daniel glared and clenched his jaw.

Charlie spied Lord Kharas amongst the throng. He stood at the front of the crowd close to the dais, and Charlie hurried for him. If Lord Kharas already knew of Charlie's training in magic, he would not suspect anything of his deep concentration during Savaric's entrance. He could trust the man and knew he was safe there.

"On your guard, little king," Kharas whispered to Charlie. His usual cheerful demeanor was sharp and on edge. Charlie nodded and squeezed in beside him, half-hidden behind Jock so as not to stand out too pretentiously.

The double doors closed behind a pair of ladies-in-waiting, their skirts flying as they hurried into the throng of onlookers. A hush fell over the crowd, and Charlie's fingers tingled.

The doors opened again as King Valin and Princess Ailinn walked in, accompanied by more armed guards than Charlie had seen in one place since his first day arriving at the palace. Their feet marched in perfect sync, and the sound echoed throughout the room with a terrifying authority.

Valin held his head high and acknowledged a few of the nobles who bowed as he passed. Ailinn, however, took little notice of anyone or anything. She was ghostly white, as though she might be sick at any moment. But her eyes, which stared transfixed to the stone floor beneath her, were like daggers.

Daniel and Kashna bowed to Valin as they approached. They whispered quietly, and the king smiled, nodding at something that was said.

King and Princess ascended the dais to their thrones and turned to face the crowd of eager faces staring up at them. Valin gestured to the guards still stationed at the double doors. They stood aside, and a herald called loudly, cutting the thick air with his voice.

"Lord Savaric of Harpy's Pointe and his son, Merrick of Harpy's Pointe!"

The man who sauntered in was not what Charlie had expected. He was clean shaven with thick black hair cut short. His clothes were not as extravagant as Charlie had anticipated, either. Rather, he wore simple blue trousers fitted in the Dwarvik fashion, and a plain white shirt with a modest gold and blue embroidery around the collar and cuffs. He was flanked only by two young men, neither of whom carried any sort of weapons or armor,

His demeanor, however, was exactly as Charlie had predicted. Cool and charismatic. He flashed a broad smile at the crowd who clapped softly as he entered. Savaric dramatically swept out his arm before him as he gave a full bow to King Valin. When he rose, he continued to smile wide, his gray-blue eyes surveying the room as he did so.

A young man dressed as casually as Savaric, stood close by, and Charlie assumed this must be Merrick. He bowed to King Valin as well and gave a gentle nod toward Ailinn. Ailinn ignored him. She stared transfixed at the double doors at the back of the room, clenching and unclenching her jaw.

"Valin!" Savaric cried, and his voice drowned out the dying applause of the crowd. "So high and mighty you've become. Won't even embrace me like the old friends we are. Come now. Come greet me as you once did. Enough with the formalities." He held his arms wide, but Valin did not move.

Merrick stepped forward and attempted to push his father's arm down. "Don't do this," he whispered to Savaric sharply.

"I wish only to be embraced as a member of this family," said Savaric, not only to his son but to the entire room. "For am I not the future father-in-law of the future Queen of Chartile?"

"You are as yet considered a brigand for your actions and associations, Savaric," Valin said curtly. "It has not escaped my notice that your entourage carry no weapons. At least, none that would be permitted."

Savaric's eyes widened, and he clutched at his heart. Behind him, Merrick turned away, holding his head in his hand.

"Valin! You crush me! Truly, I am hurt, old friend. For how is it that you may call *me* an outlaw when you have been training your own little king in the ways of magic?" Lord Savaric pointed straight at Charlie.

Charlie felt his face begin to flush. He tried looking down the row of embroidered tunics, as though searching for the culprit, but the crowd parted slightly. All eyes were transfixed on him.

Lord Kharas set his hand on Charlie's shoulder and eased him forward. The crowd began to murmur and whisper as he stepped from the throng before Savaric. The man smiled coyly at him and urged him forward. Charlie dared a glance back to Kashna and Daniel. The creature grinned encouragingly at him.

"Charles Dimitri Hill," Savaric breathed. "It is good to finally meet you."

Charlie remained silent. He knew this tactic well and refused to give in to Savaric's taunts, though it was odd that the man knew his full name. Savaric swept his cloak behind him, bending into a deep, dramatic bow. When Charlie did not respond, he stood straight again.

"Come, little king," he pressed. "Show us your might."

Charlie squared his shoulders and narrowed his eyes. Savaric's belittling was worse than King Valin's. "I am Charles Hill, son of the great Jayson Hill, returned soul of King Pasalphathe. You will mock me no more."

The lights in the chandeliers extinguished at once, and the room was thrown into darkness save for a single candle burning directly above where Charlie stood. Charlie raised his hands, and the double doors flew open. A gust of wind blew through the hall. Several ladies screamed, and everyone ducked for cover.

Before Charlie could will the soldiers standing at the door to advance on Savaric, the man laughed. He threw his head back and clapped his hands together. The wind began to die as Charlie's concentration broke. The boy waved his hand, relighting the chandeliers, and everyone saw Savaric wipe a tear from his eye.

"Marvelous, little king," he said and turned again to Valin. "He is a darling, Valin. But you have yourself a bit of a quandary."

Charlie was shocked, and it appeared so was Valin. The king's worried eyes darted around the room to the various members of the Conclave, and even to Daniel.

"You see, Your Majesty, it is not right and just that you would allow someone to train in the ways of magic when you have worked so hard to deny that right to so many of your own people."

"Magic was outlawed for a reason, Savaric," Valin chided. "There are no laws that can govern against an unseen force. A force that can so easily corrupt a greedy heart and become uncontrollable."

"Oh, yes," said Savaric, his eyes widening in mock understanding. "For you did work so hard to control your own queen, did you not? Of course not. You used her to fight fire with fire and then sent her to her death."

Savaric turned to address the entire room now. His voiced carried across the curved boughs of the treetops so not a single person could mistake his words.

"You follow a king that turns the law to suit his personal gains and twists it when it threatens his high and mighty status."

"Charlie is the son of our returned kings," Valin argued, but even his booming voice could not match the charm or authority of Savaric. "He has returned to us, here at the palace, to fulfill the prophecy. Not to you, Savaric, who try so desperately to attain that which will never be yours."

"You and your princess proclaim this little boy to be the son of Jayson Hill." Savaric stepped toward the crowd and pointed to a member of the Conclave. "Lord Raphael, how is your daughter?"

A murmur spread through the crowd.

The man named Raphael glanced toward the double doors before squaring his shoulders at Savaric. "She is well, Lord Savaric. Studying her letters in our quarters at this moment."

Savaric chuckled. "I am glad to hear it, but I was not referring to Adelaide. Raph, how is Justine?"

Raphael's face grew pale. He swallowed hard and cleared his throat. "She-she is no longer with us. She returned to the Phoenix several years ago."

Several nobles nodded in agreement, one patting Raphael on the shoulder.

"I find that incredibly fascinating, my lord. You see, I have reason to believe that Justine is safe and well serving as a basket weaver's daughter in Hollycrest. She is quite nimble with the reeds. So much so, the weaver's business is, in fact, booming. It's almost unnatural how quickly she can create those baskets. But perhaps my information is false. Ah, Lady Beatrix. Your son, Arian. He is well?"

A woman across the aisle from Charlie flushed a brilliant red and wrung her hands. "Arian? I—I'm afraid I don't—"

Savaric held up a hand to silence her. "It has been many years. I understand you may not remember him." He gestured toward one of the young men who had accompanied him into the throne room. "Arian was so frightened when you sent him away, Lady Beatrix. But he has found a new family now. Someone who appreciates his gifts and talents."

Savaric's arm encircled the young man, who appeared dazed. Charlie would have pegged him for a druggie if he were back on Earth. His eyes were glazed, and his skin was pale with a yellow tint.

Lady Beatrix clapped her hands over her mouth. Her eyes filled with tears, and she nearly fainted on her feet. Her neighbors caught her as she began to fall, helping her to sit on the cold tile floor where she fanned herself feverishly. Savaric ignored her. He hugged Arian, then dismissed him.

"The royal family would have you believe that magic no longer exists in the Elven lines. They have every one of you afraid of the consequences and sending your children to live in hiding, pawning them off as the commoner's problem. Or worse, smothering them in their sleep. Your own late queen is proof that magic runs within our Elven blood stronger than ever. It is no more a curse than our abilities to walk and speak."

"Lord Savaric," Daniel said, interrupting. "With all due respect, I was born with hands that can grasp and squeeze. It doesn't mean it is good and well for me to wrap my hands around the throats of every person who would do me wrong and send them to the Creator. Even if we were to acknowledge the existence of magic within our race, it doesn't mean we can allow it to thrive."

Savaric's hands flourished before him and he gave a small bow to Daniel. "'Tis a shame they forced you to relinquish your claim to the throne, young man. But you are no more Elven than the creature that stands beside you. Such a shame." Savaric turned his back to the dais and addressed the crowd again.

"Lords and ladies, Nobles of the Conclave. You have been deceived in your own right. While your king allows this so-called Charlie of the Hill, his own wife, even his own daughter, to perform magic, you must hide away your children in fear. I urge you to see that King Valin is unfit to rule."

Merrick, who had remained silent and mortified behind his father, suddenly moved forward. He stepped before Savaric, blocking his father's view from the king. Merrick's eyes narrowed as he reached for Savaric's shoulders.

"Stop this, Father!" he seethed, but his voice was drowned out by Valin's own. "Enough! Guards!"

Savaric pushed past his son as the king's guards advanced down the center aisle.

"I make a motion that Princess Ailinn and Merrick should be wed immediately," he said, his voice never wavering. "See how he stands for what is right and just." Savaric swung his arm around Merrick's shoulders and held him in place. "He stands against his own father for what he believes is right and true. My son is the class of king Chartile needs at this very moment. And whether he will uphold the cause that I have worked so hard to achieve or no, I will surrender to his verdict."

One of the guards grabbed Savaric's arm, but Valin held up his hand.

"You surrender to your son, but will you still surrender to the king?" Valin asked coldly. The room grew quiet. "Will you sign the order to cease your treacherous support of this rebel cause?"

Savaric turned a stern eye back to Valin and slowly pointed a single finger at the king. "I will never bow to the man who sits upon that throne now. Release him from his service, good nobles, and help us move toward a future that no longer punishes us for the actions of our ancestors."

Charlie finally saw what it must have looked like to want to be invisible.

Merrick continued in a vain attempt to push his father off him. If it weren't for the single voice that rose above the deafening silence of the room, Charlie was sure Merrick would have discovered a way to melt into the floor if he could have.

"No," came Ailinn's voice. It was the first time she had spoken, and her voice cut through the silence like a knife. "I refuse to follow in the footsteps of my mother. I will not marry for what some believe to be the good of the kingdom. I will not allow my heart to fall victim to one I do not choose, and I will not let someone as deranged as this man, who has carried on without a soul to stop him, get one step closer to power."

Valin smacked Ailinn across her cheek so hard, it brought immediate tears to her eyes. "Take her to the tower," he whispered to the guards. This time, Ailinn did not fight them. She looked at her father with absolute and utter betrayal.

Savaric laughed again. He released Merrick and pushed him away so violently, he fell to the floor before Charlie. The boy pulled Merrick to his feet, and the two stood together, watching Ailinn leave, both helpless to do anything.

"I see your method for regaining control." Savaric smirked at Valin. "You simply remove those who would defy you." He threw his arms wide and gave a mock bow again. "How simple-minded of you."

Charlie's feet carried him several paces before he realized what he was doing. His fists were clenched, and his face was red. He stopped before Savaric so tense and angry that even though he wanted to knock the man square in the nose, his arms felt like lead.

"No one bullies the king or Princess Ailinn," he said. "You think you're so great coming in here and-and... *mocking* everyone. Well, we won't stand for it!"

Savaric smiled at Charlie, a small and understanding smile that made Charlie's skin crawl.

"But you see, little king, everyone here knows that if they attempt to stand against me, I can reveal which of their families hold the baneful curse of magic. And your king cannot offer them clemency without showing those who have not yet turned from him that what I speak is the truth." Savaric grabbed Charlie's chin and his smile widened. "I'm sorry to disappoint you, little king, but I am that great."

Charlie pulled his face from Savaric's grasp and darted from the room as the man's hearty laugh echoed off the trees and followed him into the hall.

FIFTEEN
TOWERS AND TRAITORS

CHARLIE KNEW THE CORE OF the palace by heart. He'd spent enough time following Jock and Drustad to and from his lessons with the nobles. The areas dedicated to lesser nobility and the tradesmen who lived on the premises in service to the crown weren't as clear to him, but he knew the way to Princess Ailinn's tower, and that was exactly where he was going.

The castle was eerily quiet as he ran through the halls. Most of the nobles were in attendance in the throne room, but even the beck-ands seemed to be strangely absent.

Charlie halted before a plain wooden door. He reached for the handle just as he heard another door close at the top of the winding stair beyond. He heard the boots of the guards descending toward him and leapt back in time for the wooden door to swing open.

The guards startled when they saw him. Their eyes darted across Charlie's face with a fearful anticipation. Charlie could feel his jaw clenching. What was wrong with them? They stood frozen on the steps, their hands twitching to stay off their sword hilts. It wasn't until Charlie remembered he had just demonstrated his magical abilities only minutes ago that he reigned in his anger.

He bowed politely to them. "I need to speak with the princess, please," he said.

The guards exchanged worried glances. There were no words spoken amongst them. They nodded to each other, then stepped off the stair, clearing the path for Charlie. Charlie gave a small bow in appreciation and bolted up the stairs.

As he reached the top, he found himself staring at another worn, wooden door. This time, it was his own thoughts keeping his hand poised before him. He had no idea what he was going to say to Ailinn. For all he knew she was still angry with him. Finally, he knocked.

There was no answer.

"Ailinn?" Charlie called through the door. "It's Charlie. Um… can I come in?"

There was a long pause. Charlie wondered if Ailinn was asleep. He realized it was more likely she was ignoring him. She was definitely still mad. He sighed and turned to leave.

"Yes," said Ailinn's faint voice.

Very slowly, Charlie opened the door, his heart hammering in his chest. His eyes widened, and he rushed to the bed where Ailinn sat.

Manacles attached to the wall bound Ailinn to the bed. A vanity and a bookshelf sat across from the bed, but she would have been unable to use them in her current state.

"What the—hold on," said Charlie. He reached for the chains bound to the wall and stupidly tried to pry the metal apart with his bare hands.

"Leave them, Charlie," said Ailinn. She turned away from him and looked out the tiny window at the treetops outside. Charlie's fingernail bent, and he shook his hand violently, trying to keep from shouting. He watched Ailinn, but she did not move. The hair rose on the back of his neck as he sucked his sore finger. This wasn't like her.

She must have felt his eyes boring into her. She turned her head slightly, replying over her shoulder, "They are made from orenite. It is the same material as my other cuffs. The magic may rebound on me if you tamper with them."

"Ailinn, this-this isn't cool," Charlie said. "This isn't right. Let me help you."

Ailinn stifled a laugh and turned to face him again. "You wish to help me? Only days ago you adamantly believed I didn't care for you. Something about abandoning you as others have? Now you come rushing to my aid, like a hero saving the lost damsel in the children's tales of old. Has your newfound magic made you so bold?

Should I believe my father that eventually magic corrupts all hearts?"

Charlie sat down on the edge of the bed. He crossed his arms in front of him and chewed on his lip. Maybe his magic *was* going to his head. Even so, chaining someone to the wall? The orenite cuffs and the slavery of the Humans made him uncomfortable, but he hadn't wanted to interfere. His father would have told him it was disrespectful to think all cultures should dress and act the same as him. But this was a step too far.

"I'm sorry," he said. He looked up into Ailinn's weary face and saw her eyes were red from crying. "I—I *was* abandoned. At least I thought I was. I know my dad didn't do it on purpose, but… it hurt. And I didn't want to get hurt again."

"Sometimes anger makes me feel stronger," said Ailinn. She turned herself to sit next to him, her legs hanging off the edge of the bed and arms pulled across her chest by the shackles. "I used to think I could protect myself with it. I hated everyone. Even my mother after some time. I was so angry when she died. I blamed her for leaving me and Daniel, for using her magic and teaching me magic. I know it's not true now, but it took a long time for that hurt to… well, it hasn't gone away if I'm honest. It's just a little more dull. Being angry didn't make me feel any better. It just—"

"Pushes people away," Charlie finished.

She looked at him, her eyes still bloodshot, and nodded.

They sat in silence for several minutes, feet shuffling back and forth on the floor or chewing at their nails.

"So, what are we going to do about your upcoming marriage?" Charlie asked.

Ailinn's head snapped around, glaring at Charlie until she saw the grin that curled at the corners of his lips.

She grinned back, but her smile quickly fell away. "I want to trust Merrick, but I haven't seen him in so long, I can't tell where his loyalties lie," she said, fidgeting with her hair.

"Trust me, if anyone knows embarrassment, it's me, and that guy was full-out embarrassed hardcore," Charlie said.

"Yes, almost too much so," Ailinn said quietly. "It seems almost too perfect, Merrick's situation, doesn't it? He can so easily leave Harpy's Pointe, and Savaric simply lets him go? He hates his father for all he has done, and yet he agreed to our marriage. All communication has been between my father and Savaric. We only have Savaric's word on where Merrick stands. I don't know what to believe." Ailinn sighed. She flung herself back on the bed and covered her face with her hands as best she could.

Charlie chewed at his nails, watching Ailinn stare at the ceiling above them. Finally, he said, "Then it sounds like he's our guy to talk to."

IT WAS PHILIPPE'S RECOMMENDATION THAT Charlie lay low for a few days. The palace was buzzing with a frantic sort of energy that had everyone on edge. King Valin had ordered Savaric and his two young companions to be guarded at all times. Even Merrick was under strict observations, though he rarely left his room within his father's quarters.

Charlie's lessons were also canceled for the time being, which left Jock and Drustad plenty of time to reprimand their young charge.

"You should have told us about your magic lessons," said Drustad in a hushed whisper.

"We could have helped you," said Jock.

Charlie raised an eyebrow at his guard.

"Well, not with the magic part or anything like that." Jock immediately turned red.

"You're going to need some more allies with Merrick and Savaric here now," Drustad said. "You might as well start with us."

"And those two beck-ands of yours." Jock gestured at Saajee'a and Phillippe as they carefully crept through the tiny door carrying trays loaded down with food. Jock and Charlie immediately relieved the two of their burdens as Drustad offered them pillows to sit on. Phillippe still refused to sit equal to Charlie, but due to his illness, he eventually gave in to accepting one of Charlie's pillows. Saajee'a followed suit after her old mentor and charge.

The five ate their meal in between the candid conversation about Savaric and Merrick.

As it was, Savaric seemed to conveniently pop up wherever Charlie went. In the corridors, the library, even the stables. Phillippe had arranged several meetings between Charlie and a few trusted beck-ands. But there Savaric was each time, bright-eyed and boisterous. He was never without his two companions, who remained glassy-eyed and dazed.

"Ah, little king!" said Savaric. Both Charlie and the guard Drustad had arranged a meeting with jumped. "Such a pleasure, these coincidental meetings. Care for a ride with me? I am certain you are better company than all the palace guards forced to follow my every move night and day." Savaric gestured toward Cinders, who pawed the ground in her stall.

Charlie and the guard exchanged courteous bows before parting ways. The boy turned to Savaric, his shoulders squared. "Maybe if you weren't trying to break the law, you wouldn't have to be followed around all the time."

Savaric placed a hand over his heart and pouted sardonically. "Aw, Charlie. From one lawbreaker to another, I am hurt. Surely, you of all people here in Chartile understand the plight of inheriting a gift you did not ask for. I have heard of your struggles in living up to the great status of your father."

Charlie rolled his eyes and bit his tongue. It was like this every time with Savaric, and Charlie had learned not to antagonize him. Instead, he gave a small bow and turned on his heel.

"Until next time, little king!" Savaric called after him. Charlie suppressed the urge to shoot an obscene gesture at the man over his shoulder, but he knew Savaric wouldn't understand it anyway.

He trudged back to his room, Jock and Drustad close behind. Several of the nobles jumped when they saw him and hurried out of the way. Others took the time to bow or curtsey or even greet him as he passed.

In the last few days, it had become rather obvious who likely had magic hidden in their family lines. And either there were more non-magic nobles in favor of allowing the use of magic back into the realm, or the number of nobles with magic within their families was greater than anyone could have imagined.

Ailinn suggested it was probably somewhere in the middle. Since her outburst in the throne room, King Valin had ordered her to remain in the tower without visitation. Even Daniel and Kashna were not permitted to see her. Fortunately for Charlie, Jock, Drustad, and a handful of beck-ands were able to distract Ailinn's guards so Charlie could sneak up to her. Unfortunately, there wasn't much to discuss.

As usual, Phillippe had not been idle in Charlie's absence. Several letters sat on the bedside table beside a platter of spiced meat, cheese, and bite-sized vegetable tarts. Charlie jumped onto his bed and grabbed a tart and an envelope as Phillippe finished sweeping his little pile of dirt down the steps into the beck-and passage.

Under Saajee'a's mother's guidance, the physicians healed most of the beck-ands back to health. The Desert Death had taken its toll on Phillippe, though, and Saajee'a nagged after him constantly to be cautious and rest often. At this moment, however, Saajee'a was off helping her mother in the kitchens, and Phillippe seemed to have been more productive in her absence.

Charlie took a bite that was a bit too big and tore open the first envelope. It was from one of the palace tailors requesting an audience with him. He wished to discuss the clothes Charlie had made, as several of the noble children were requesting them. He set the paper aside for Phillippe to arrange the meeting. He seemed to know more about Charlie's schedule than he did these days.

The second was from Lord Kharas. He had questioned one of Savaric's companions during a ride and learned the boy was either deaf and mute or transfixed in a state of perpetual captivation. Kharas was sure the boys were being bewitched in some way, but, as several guards and beck-ands had already reported, it did not appear as though Savaric himself had any magical abilities. Charlie was glad he had entrusted Lord Kharas as one of his allies. He understood why Valin had asked him to be the king's advisor. He read the letter three times to memorize it, then set it aside to burn.

Charlie reached for a chunk of cheese and the last letter on the table. He opened it and a smile spread across his face. It was from Ailinn. Phillippe had been able to work with a beck-and who served one of Ailinn's ladies-in-waiting. The two now secretly traded letters every day in addition to their almost daily meetings.

Charlie,

Today the ruStling of the leaves outside my window is more crisP, more lIke rain on glass. Autumn is nipping at the hEels of Summer, and I am witness to its reminder, As I can see the first of the BeLirian Leaves turnIng orAnge in the far distaNce. Father has traded my Chains for my rEgular cuFfs, thOugh I begged him to have them sent to the DwaRves in Mount KelSii or TutAria for adjusting. He says this will take seVeral weeks, and that I cannot be bound to the wall of my chaMbers for so long. ThOugh I agRee, if he only knEw the Chains Are bUt a physical represeTation of my daIly prisOn.

The strawberries and cream were a lovely treat. Thank you for having them seNt to me. I have sent a Letter to DaniEl, asking him to talk to Father on my behalf. I miSs my time in the gardenS with my little fish.

*Please **T**ake care of them fo**R** me? They need to eat more before the cold begins to set in. They do not eat as m**U**ch when the weather turn**S**, and they need to fa**T**ten up to survive winter.*

All my love,
Ailinn

Carefully, Charlie studied her note. Ailinn's unique style of handwriting lent itself well to cryptic messages. A sort of half-print, half-calligraphy that anyone who knew her writing would think nothing of. They discussed sending such messages, as Ailinn learned information from her ladies-in-waiting. This message read: *Spies alliance for Sav. More caution. Less trust.*

It was with a heavy heart that Charlie got up and burned Ailinn's and Kharas's notes in the lamp sitting on the vanity. There hadn't been an opportunity to see her today, and his chest ached when he was apart from her.

Phillippe shuffled back from the passageway and reached for the note from the tailor. Charlie watched the beck-and's age-worn hand tremble as his fingers closed around the parchment. For an instant, he wondered if he could trust Phillippe. The little man was one of the oldest beck-ands he had seen in the castle. Surely, he knew things. Secrets and rumors. Things that could be used against the crown, against Ailinn and Daniel.

Charlie shook his head. If there was one person in all Chartile that Charlie could trust, it was Phillippe.

"Phil," he called to the little man. "I need your help with something again, and I need you to be the one to do it."

Phillippe's eyes twinkled, and this time he did not hide away his smile.

It took two days for Charlie's message to get delivered to Merrick.

First, Phillippe needed to learn his routine, which was easy enough in the end. Merrick hardly ever left his room. Next was coordinating a false trail for Savaric to follow. His incessant stalking of Charlie hadn't ceased in the slightest. Somehow, he always knew when Charlie was meeting with someone, which gave the boy a sickening feeling that one of his allies was a traitor after all.

Only Charlie and Phillippe knew about the meeting with Merrick, and only they knew the secondary trail they left was false. Jock and Drustad helped to plant the information for the false trail which forced Savaric far away from his quarters and away from his son.

Phillippe conveniently came across the young beck-and girl taking Merrick his afternoon meal. He graciously offered to assist her and slipped a piece of paper under the platter of cooked vegetables.

When Charlie returned from his false meeting with one of the stable hands, Phillippe turned from his work of hanging fresh laundry in the wardrobe and gave Charlie a thumbs-up, beaming as he did so. Charlie had taught him the gesture to use as their secret signal, and Phillippe seemed empowered by it.

Jock entered on Charlie's heels. He closed the door behind Drustad and latched it. As it turned out, the two were more than brawn with shiny swords. They were extremely observant. They could read body language and speech nuances better than anyone Charlie knew. He was glad he had accepted their offer for help.

"He got it then?" Charlie asked, sitting on the edge of his bed as Jock and Drustad drew up chairs.

Phillippe poured everyone a chalice of water, then carefully lowered himself onto the pillow at Charlie's feet.

"He did, Master Charlie," Phillippe squeaked with delight.

Jock and Drustad looked at each other, then back at Charlie.

"Did who get what?" Drustad asked.

Charlie hesitated, but he needed his guard's help.

"Merrick. I'm sorry I didn't tell you guys before. It's... it's Savaric. He always seems to be one step ahead of us. I—I had to keep this one on the down low, if you get me."

By the looks on Jock and Drustad's faces, they did not.

"You don't trust us?" Jock asked. His lips barely moved as he spoke.

"No! I mean, yes, I do. I mean... I do trust you. I want to trust you. I don't know how Savaric is learning about my meetings, but he is. I had a fake meeting today so Savaric would follow me and leave Merrick alone so Phillippe could pass him a note. I'm sorry I didn't tell you before. But I'm telling you now, right? And... I need your help for the next step."

Charlie couldn't bring himself to look Jock and Drustad in the face. They looked heartbroken. "Are you mad at me?" he asked.

"Of course not!" Drustad's booming voice caught Charlie off-guard. He looked up and saw the two guards smiling.

"It was a brilliant idea. Very clever of you," said Jock.

"Oh, thank goodness," Charlie mumbled to himself.

"But if you ever find out someone was ratting on you, Charlie, you leave them to us," Drustad whispered sternly.

Charlie forced a laugh as Jock and Drustad looked at him, their faces set and serious. "Right, sure. Um, just one more thing." The two guards leaned closer to him. "You can't tell Daniel. Or Kashna."

"Do you suspect them as the traitors?" Jock asked.

"No, I—I don't think so. It's just, Daniel hates Merrick. At least I think he does. If he found out I was trying to talk to him, he'd probably tell Kashna to rip me to pieces or something!"

"The smaller our circle, the fewer mistakes may be made," Phillippe said.

"What do you need from us?" Drustad asked.

Charlie rose from his chair and carried a small stack of books back to his guard.

"If Merrick accepts my offer to talk, he'll be in the palace library at noon wearing a red tunic," said Charlie. "I will be at the archery range, and hopefully, so will Savaric. I need one of you to return these books and see if Merrick is there."

Drustad took the books from Charlie and nodded.

"How will we know if he's playing us?" Jock asked. The tension in the room grew thick. "He could play along, pretending he's on our side, and still relay everything to his father."

No one dared look at each other or speak for several long moments. A gust of wind blew the curtain wildly, and the boughs overhead creaked.

"Lord Savaric knows half of our moves before we even make them," said Phillippe calmly. "If Merrick goes to him, he will have learned nothing more except that you wish to speak with him to learn his true feelings and intentions in his own words. Savaric cannot fault anyone for wanting to know that. Your conversation with him will reveal nothing on our part."

"And if he is on our side, we have gained another ally," said Drustad.

Charlie nodded and studied the dust pattern on his riding boots. He sighed and took another drink. The books he borrowed from the library recounted the history of the returned kings. Most were rather inflammatory, even compared to his father's own accounts. But Jayson, Jack, and Leo had spent most of their time in the Dwarvik mountain of Mount Kelsi. The elves didn't even know they existed until they had killed Princess Taraniz. However, among the books had been a retelling of events from an interview done with Queen Piper herself. This seemed to be the truest account and lined up the most with the stories Charlie heard as a child.

The Chartile of Charlie's bedtime stories were of a world full helpful mentors and an obvious evil that had to be destroyed. The more he thought about Savaric's words in the throne room, the more his stomach churned. Savaric was right in one regard: people shouldn't be punished for how they were born. At least, that was what Charlie believed. His father and his friends had come to Chartile trying to change the world for the better, but perhaps they had only made it more complicated. Queen Piper had not lived happily ever after, and neither had Jayson. Stories didn't end when the book closed. People went on living, making mistakes and saying stupid things. He only hoped he didn't say something stupid when he talked to Merrick.

DANIEL'S EYES SHOT OPEN. THE light that filtered through the trees was growing dimmer. He sat up and reached a hand toward his belt. He had no sword. The hairs on the back of his neck stood on end. The leaves in the trees above him shifted in the wind, and something large landed on the path up ahead.

"Rest easy," said a calming voice in his mind.

Daniel breathed a sigh. "Kashna," he said as the qarveena's glowing eyes emerged toward him out of the darkness.

"I would have found you sooner, but I was tailing Savaric as you instructed. Are you all right?" Kashna asked.

Daniel leaned against a tree and closed his eyes. His headaches had not gone as he had said to his sister. They had become stronger, and the blackouts were more frequent. But he couldn't worry Ailinn about such things. Not with Savaric and Merrick loose in the castle.

"Where am I?" Daniel asked.

Kashna cast a casual glance at their surroundings and sniffed the air. "The Rill of Kelf," he said.

"The Rill of Kelf? That's... that's at least a day from the palace. How long have I been gone?"

Kashna swept his tail behind him and looked at the boughs of the trees above. "It is difficult to say. I have been busy. But it cannot be more than a few hours."

Daniel held his head in his hands. At least the darkness was keeping the pounding in his head at bay

"A few hours. How is that possible?"

"I think such matters would be more easily thought through in the comfort of one's own bed."

"No. No, I don't think I can go back. Kashna, this is dangerous. What if I hurt someone? What if I… what if I kill Ailinn or my father? No, I have to work this out."

"You will only cause more chaos by not returning. The last thing Ailinn or Valin need is to worry where you might be."

Daniel sighed. He knew Kashna was right, knew his sister was safer if he remained at the palace. But something had to be done. He had to figure out what was causing this… whatever this was. He ran his fingers through his tangled hair, knocking loose the dirt and silt that had dried in it.

"When did this start? It had to be… how old was I? At least ten. Over ten years. But it's gotten worse. Three? Four years, now? What's happened since then? Mother's death. No, the headaches were there before. Ailinn's betrothal? Perhaps?"

Kashna stood and walked toward Daniel. He set a heavy paw on the young man's knee. "Our connection does not allow me to will you onto my back, but you realize there are other, more painful ways for me to force you home."

Daniel looked into Kashna's golden eyes, his own beginning to brim with tears. "I need help, Kashna. I need help before something happens."

Kashna bowed his head and pressed his forehead to Daniel's. The pain subsided. Daniel's vision became clearer. He wrapped his arms around the creature's neck and buried his face in the thick, black fur.

"You are always safe with me."

SIXTEEN
MAKING PLANS

CHARLIE BARELY SLEPT THAT NIGHT. The smell of the feathers from his mattress and pillows seemed more overwhelming than usual. He tossed and turned until he had twisted himself up in the covers and became hot and sticky. He threw the blanket off, only to have to pull them over himself again minutes later. His mind raced with a thousand thoughts, and he wondered what Merrick's decision would be. He lay staring at the canopy overhead until Phillippe and Saajee'a came to light the morning lamps.

Charlie sat up in bed and heard the loud *thwack* of Drustad's hilt against the door. He nodded to Phillippe, who shuffled to the door and knocked back three times—their secret code for *yes, but stand by*.

Charlie quickly dressed in the clothes Phillippe tossed to him and attempted to lay his hair flat again. He needed a haircut before coming to Chartile, and it was now becoming desperate. He buttoned his shirt and nodded again to the beck-and.

No sooner had Phillippe opened the door a crack, than he was nearly knocked to the ground. Daniel pushed the door open with such force, it left Phillippe leaning against the wall for support. Saajee'a shrank into the shadows, inching around the edge of the room toward Phillippe. Jock and Drustad stood in the doorway, torn between wanting to help Charlie and Phillippe and reprimanding their lord.

Kashna followed close behind. His wings drooped and trailed on the floor behind him. His shoulders hunched, and his golden eyes had lost their luster. He appeared exhausted and lacked the intention or energy to keep Daniel from pouncing upon Charlie.

"What do you think you're playing at?" Daniel snapped, pointing a finger at Charlie.

"What are you talking about—" Daniel grabbed Charlie by the collar of his shirt and lifted him a few inches off the floor. Jock and Drustad's eyes flicked from Charlie to each other, and then to Kashna.

"I thought my instruction to stay away from Ailinn was clear, but apparently not. You must be as daft as you are useless." Daniel turned and slammed Charlie against one of the four posters of his bed. Charlie's face met the hard wood, and he felt as though his eye would explode out of its socket.

"We need this alliance, little king," Daniel continued, holding Charlie firmly against the hard wood of the bed frame. "And now I discover you're not only undermining everything we've worked to achieve these last several months with your plotting and scheming, but you're filling my little sister's head with ideas!"

Daniel pulled Charlie's head back away from the four-poster and slammed his face into the wood again. This time, Charlie's eyes swam with stars. The edges of his vision turned black, but he forced himself to stay conscious.

"Daniel, I—" Charlie tried to speak. Daniel lifted Charlie's head away from the wood again, but Kashna spoke first.

"My lord, how will our king know what he has done wrong if he is unconscious and unable to hear it?"

Daniel paused with Charlie's head pulled back and ready to strike again against the wood. Charlie released his breath in a spluttering cough. Daniel glared, seeming to catch his breath as well. He flung Charlie onto the bed and punched him in the stomach. Charlie twisted himself into a ball, grabbing his middle to protect himself.

"You don't understand." He coughed. Daniel rounded on him and lifted Charlie's head up by his hair.

"What don't I understand? That you're doing everything in your power to keep this marriage from happening? Ailinn is not a normal person. She is a princess, and therefore an asset, a tool in negotiation." Daniel threw Charlie's head forward, and the boy felt his neck crack. "She belongs to the Crown and the Conclave. It is for them to decide what happens to her."

"I'm just trying to protect her," said Charlie, barely audible now. He wasn't sure which part of him hurt worse at the moment.

"How could you possibly protect her any more than our palace guards? Do you really believe you are better suited to protect her than me? You still cannot hold your sword properly. Your archery targets are set to half the distance as our newest recruited archers. Though I hear your pivas have improved. Tell me, how does learning The Maiden's dance help to save my sister?"

"If you would allow my master to speak, he would tell you." Everyone turned to see Phillippe peeking from behind Drustad. His was the last voice Charlie had expected to hear. Phillippe was turning bright red, inching farther behind the guard as everyone stared.

"I see you've taught your pet a few tricks," Daniel spat.

"I haven't done anything except be nice to him, which is the same thing I'm trying to do for Ailinn," said Charlie, sitting up and still clutching his stomach.

Daniel tore his eyes from the shriveling beck-and, but Charlie held up his hand.

"Hang on," he said. "Just let me finish before you go beating me again. Anyway, I can take more than you think."

The beck-and door creaked, and Saajee'a crept quietly around the crowd in the room. She poured cool water from a pitcher she carried onto a cloth, and more into one of the many chalices on Charlie's bedside table. She handed the cup to Charlie and began dabbing at a cut on his cheekbone. Charlie graciously took a drink, then laid a hand on Saajee'a's arm.

"I'm fine, Saajee'a. Thank you," he whispered. She bowed to him and joined Phillippe behind the massive form of Drustad.

"Savaric's up to something," said Charlie before Daniel could speak. "I've been trying to get information from people to learn what it might be. I'm not trying to stop Ailinn's marriage because I lov—because of anything to do with me. I just want to make sure she's going to be safe. Plus, Merrick marrying Ailinn puts Savaric closer to King Valin and the Conclave. I'm trying to protect everyone."

Daniel was silent. He looked down at Charlie, who was carefully flexing his neck and shoulders. He turned to Kashna, and the two stared at one another for quite some time.

Finally, as Charlie was assessing whether one of his front teeth was loose, Daniel spoke. "Why didn't you come to me, then? I'm her brother. You think I don't care about her?"

Charlie glared up at Daniel. He took a deep breath and shifted his position on the bed. "Frankly, no, I don't. Honestly, I'd be pretty mad if the guy who was supposed to be taking care of me turned his back on me. Valin doesn't have a drop of royal blood in his body. He's king by marriage. You at least have royal blood. Elven and Dwarvik, if I remember what my dad told me about Nefiri's brother. You should never have been denied the crown. It wasn't right. And it's really hard to tell whether you care about Ailinn as a person, or if you only care about her because she's an asset." Charlie spoke these last words with as much contempt as he could muster in his condition. "Dude, no one would blame you if you wanted to turn your back on your family based on how you've been treated. It doesn't make sense that you'd want to protect the Crown, but not Ailinn. So, I'm sorry if I doubted you and all, but you're a really confusing person. I couldn't take a chance that you were actually working with Savaric."

A bell tolled the noon hour. Charlie looked at Drustad, who nodded and left the room.

"What's going on?" Daniel asked, looking after the guard. "Kashna, follow him."

The qarveena bowed his head, then padded after the guard.

"You can beat me more if you want, but I can't tell you. Not yet." This time, Charlie did stand, his arm still cradling his stomach. "You take care of Ailinn your way, and I'll take care of her mine, okay? Besides, it's probably better that we have two separate plans going on. This way, it's harder for Savaric to learn everything. He's got spies everywhere, Daniel. So be careful."

Daniel's nostrils flared. His hands clenched into white-knuckled fists. Charlie stood a little straighter, waiting for the beating to resume. But it never came. Daniel stomped out of the room, slamming the door shut behind him so violently, it shook some of the boughs in the ceiling overhead. Charlie breathed a sigh of relief and collapsed onto the bed.

Saajee'a rushed forward again with the cloth and pressed it onto Charlie's eye, which was beginning to swell.

"I'll fetch the palace physicians," said Phillippe.

"No, it's okay," Charlie said, his voice a whisper as he gave into the pain.

"My mother then," said Saajee'a. "Let me at least get my mother to look at you."

"I'll be all right, guys," said Charlie. "I've had worse." He winced and clenched his jaw as he removed his tunic to see what visible damage had been done. Faint bruises rose around his side, but it seemed his face had taken the brunt of the damage.

"I can teach you to block attacks, sir," said Jock. Charlie's eyes opened wide, or as wide as they could under the circumstances. He held up a hand and cried, "No! No more lessons." His stomach hurt, and he returned his hand to its resting place, applying pressure to his abdomen. "That's the last thing I need."

Saajee'a whispered to Phillippe, then took off down the passages, mumbling something about ointment for Charlie's eye and cheek. Jock gave one last look at Charlie before heading back to his post in the corridor. He opened the door and nearly collided with Drustad.

Drustad peeked his head through the doorway and gave Charlie a thumbs-up, an enthusiastic smile plastered across his face. Merrick had worn his red tunic in the library. He was on their side. Or at least Charlie hoped. Charlie returned the gesture, then collapsed onto the bed.

PHILLIPPE ONCE AGAIN HELPED DELIVER messages to the nobles who were still continuing their instruction with Charlie. He canceled all of Charlie's lessons for the day and bade him to rest. The ointment and tea Saajee'a's mother had brought tasted and smelled awful, but it seemed effective. Most of his pain had subsided by evening, and the swelling around his eye had diminished to an array of purples and reds.

Phillippe also helped deliver another message to Merrick through his network of trusted beck-ands. Merrick was to meet Charlie in the gardens by the fountain after nightfall. Charlie didn't know what he'd do without the little man. He promised himself that as soon as the situation with Savaric was done and figured out, he would work on finding Phillippe a family who would treat him well and possibly let him retire. His father had only been in Chartile a few months. Charlie couldn't guarantee he'd be around long enough to take care of Phillippe himself.

As the lamps across the palace were extinguished for the evening, Charlie dressed to meet Merrick. He left his altered clothes in the wardrobe and opted for a more traditional Elven look in the hopes it would offer some show of respect to Merrick.

"I shall keep a candle lit in the window," said Philippe, straightening Charlie's tunic, "in case you need to find your way back through the gardens, rather than through the palace."

"I wish you would let one of us accompany you," said Drustad, and Jock nodded behind him.

"No," said Charlie, shaking his head. "You've already stayed here too long. You need to get some rest. Besides, it might draw too much attention."

This didn't seem to satisfy the guards. Jock raised his eyebrows at Charlie, and Drustad crossed his arms, planting his feet firmly beneath him.

"I'll be fine!" said Charlie, forcing a smile that hurt his tender eye. "You said I need to trust him. It doesn't look very trusting if I show up with Human Shield and Super Muscle in tow." The joke was lost to Jock and Drustad, but they nodded their heads and yielded.

Carefully, Charlie climbed on the windowsill and stared at the four-foot drop below. It didn't look far, but his body still ached from his encounter with Daniel. He had decided sneaking into the gardens through his window would draw less attention than walking through the palace at such a late hour.

Phillippe handed Charlie a small bag which he tucked into his belt. He jumped and landed on his feet, feeling the impact rise through his bones before fading away. He turned back and waved to the three heads peering out at him, then took off into the darkness.

Guided by little more than a sliver of moonlight through the boughs of the trees and the occasional lantern that hung on hooks along the path, Charlie eventually found his way to the fountain where he was to meet Merrick. He walked around the fountain twice, his quiet footfalls muffled further by the sound of the falling water. Merrick hadn't come yet.

His hands trembled as he undid the knot of the little pouch and tossed a handful of breadcrumbs into the water. Ailinn's silver fish darted to the surface, gulping food and air in their haste for a meal. It was a good cover in case he was discovered, and Ailinn had genuinely asked him to help care for her little fish. He missed his betta fish, Fred, and hoped his mom or sister would remember to feed him.

He tossed another handful of breadcrumbs into the water, just as the sound of approaching steps caught his attention.

"Charlie?" a voice whispered from the shadows.

SEVENTEEN
MERRICK

CHARLIE PEERED AROUND THE FOUNTAIN. A tall, blond-haired young man stepped out of the darkness. Charlie's hand flew to his hip, where his sword hung, and he began to draw it from its sheath.

"I am unarmed," came Merrick's smooth voice, as he held up his hands.

Charlie relaxed, but his fingers twitched, wanting to feel the comfort of the Dwarvik steel. He dumped the rest of the breadcrumbs into the fountain and joined Merrick on the other side.

"Thanks for coming," Charlie whispered, holding his hand out to Merrick. Merrick looked at it, then slowly offered up his own. Charlie reached for his hand and gripped it hard with a single shake. "It's a greeting where I come from," he said. "Sort of like a bow, but you don't have to worry about getting it wrong."

Merrick squeezed Charlie's hand with a smile and gave a single shake back. "Thank you," he said.

"No problem," said Charlie, his voice cracking. He cleared his throat and released his grip before Merrick could feel his hands begin to shake.

Merrick was as tall as Daniel, maybe even taller. He had Savaric's blue-gray eyes, but they were much kinder against his sandy-blond hair. He was built, too. His shoulders were broad, and his hands looked calloused and weathered. He oozed nobility from every pore. It took little effort for Charlie to imagine him as the next King of the Elves of Chartile, and his confidence began to waver.

Merrick cleared his throat as well and sat on the edge of the fountain. "You wished to speak with me?"

"Yeah," said Charlie. He swung his arms at his side until he realized it probably didn't look very noble or proper. He thrust his thumbs into his belt as he had seen Kharas do.

"I hear you're gathering information about my father," said Merrick. "How can I be of assistance?"

Charlie blinked. Merrick was certainly straight to the point. Charlie paced a few steps, then replied, "Well, with you, I guess."

Merrick sat straighter. He turned himself square with Charlie, his hands folded in his lap.

"I want to know your side of the story in all this," said Charlie. "I like Ailinn, and I want to make sure she's gonna be okay." He was ready for Merrick to snap back with a quick-witted remark like his father, ready for the taunting, or even a hearty guffaw. But it never came.

Merrick nodded at Charlie, his face set and stoic.

"That is fair," he said, nodding. "And I must admit, I'm impressed. Ailinn has lost much favor within her family and the Conclave since her mother's death. I have heard of few who would stand up for her as boldly as you have."

Charlie blushed, thankful for the darkness that surrounded them.

"My father was not always this way. Not until Queen Piper ascended the throne," Merrick began.

"When we learned she was the reincarnated soul of one of the ancient kings and could wield the magic of old, several townsfolk in our Harpy's Pointe joined with a secret faction that was still in favor of Taraniz's idea to join all the kingdoms of Chartile under one rule." Merrick shifted uncomfortably on the edge of the fountain. He sighed and continued.

"You mean the Court of the Rogue?"

Charlie half expected Merrick to turn and look at him like he had six heads. Everyone always seemed surprised when he knew things. But Merrick did not flinch. He shook his head and replied, "no, the Court of the Rogue has many agendas. Some of them at times contradictory. But you are correct that they are involved. They were some of the first supporters of this secret faction."

"Do you think your dad's part of the Court of the Rogue or that secret faction? Is that why he changed?"

"I cannot say why my father changed, only that he did. His love of antiquity became an obsession. He poured over books, manuscripts, and even artifacts that he had acquired over the years. When he began taking food from Harpy's Pointe and sending it to the rebellion, I could not stand idly by. I confronted him, but he would not see reason."

"What was he looking for in those books?" Charlie asked, feeling more and more like an investigative detective by the minute.

"I don't know," said Merrick, shaking his head. "He babbled about the opportunities that magic could open for all the races, including medicine and warfare. He wanted to study it, but my father has never been a scholar, even if he was curious. So I left. I found board at the inn in Harpy's Pointe and began looking for odd jobs in a few of the surrounding towns."

"And no one knew who you were?"

"Of course they did," said Merrick, waving a dismissive hand. "But I never flaunted it. What my father does not know, or perhaps he did and he simply does not care, is Harpy's Pointe was ready to overthrow him and name me lord. I did not want this. I feel I am still too young even to be a prince, and certainly not Lord of Harpy's Pointe. I found an ally in the town's regent, and we worked together to maintain the peace in Harpy's Pointe. We gathered as much information as we could about my father's movements and actions, but there was little to track. He has kept everything very quiet."

"So why did you agree to go along with his plan, then? If you hate him so much?" asked Charlie. A strange pang of guilt stung his stomach as he thought of his own father.

"Please understand, I do not hate my father," said Merrick, sitting straighter again, his eyes more vibrant in the low lantern light. "I hate the things he has done. There is a difference. When he came to me and told me I could end all this by marrying Ailinn, I agreed. Queen Runa was born in Harpy's Pointe, and Queen Piper spent much time there in her early days on the throne learning of her heritage. Daniel, Ailinn, and I became friends. For me, the decision to stop the war was an easy one, and it also meant I could marry someone dear to me. That is rarely a luxury among nobility. I have not seen Ailinn for some time now, but I have cared for her as my sister, and I will continue to care for her and do what I can to heal this kingdom."

Charlie sat in silence for several long moments. He chewed his nails and listened to the splashing of the fountain behind him. Merrick sat quietly beside him, still and patient.

Finally, Charlie spoke. "You realize your story is all pretty convenient. I mean, talk about being the golden boy. People are already talking. They say you and your dad are in this together to gain control of the kingdom."

Merrick gave a single laugh and shook his head. "Yes, I've thought much of this myself. When my father first sought me out with his proposal, I rejected the offer. I refused to be a pawn in his games. I did not want to be seen as being in league with him, especially as I cannot agree with what he has done. It was Seamus Vidal, the Regent of Rams Isle, who convinced me to do so. I have many allies who are willing to vouch for me that I am not working for my father but working toward ending this war."

"And *how* are you going to end the war?" Charlie asked. "Whether people like it or not, magic's back. And it sounds like it's been back for a while. Piper had magic. Ailinn has magic. You can't just pretend it doesn't exist." Charlie crossed his arms and raised an eyebrow at Merrick.

Merrick nodded again, his expression apathetic. "I've thought about this as well. My father claims he will stop supplying the rebels, but that does not mean he won't work politically to help them. Magic is a very dangerous thing and is the cause of why Chartile is in the mess it is right now. You're right that we cannot continue the way we have been. Ignorance is not the answer. But I am not convinced that full acceptance is the answer, either. How do you rule over something intangible? Magic is not a thing that can be taxed or regulated like livestock or tavern income, any more than hatred or love. It would make sense to slowly reintroduce it into our society through educational institutions, but how can one know who to trust? King Pasalphathe trusted his brother. He was blood and look where that trust in magic has led us. This is not a decision I feel I can make entirely on my own or even after a single meeting with the Conclave. It is a decision that does need to be made, it needs to move forward, but not too quickly."

Charlie's head was beginning to pound, whether by straining to see Merrick in the dim light of the garden lamps or by trying to keep up with the young man's train of thought. But there was also something that gurgled in the pit of Charlie's stomach. It made his hands tremble and his jaw clench. Merrick would definitely be able to take care of Ailinn and Chartile better than Charlie ever could. Even though he had learned to wield his magic rather quickly, he was losing faith that he was the one sent to fulfill the prophecy after all.

He swallowed hard against the lump in his throat and forced a smile. "I believe you. And I believe you'll be good for Ailinn. And Chartile. Are you willing to help me figure out what Savaric is up to then?"

"Of course," said Merrick. "What would you have me do?"

"I don't know yet," said Charlie. "Right now, we're just trying to collect as much information as we can about Savaric. He's got to have some kind of plan. Why else would he suddenly change his tune? You marrying Ailinn has to be a piece to something, or he never would have suggested it to King Valin."

"You're right," said Merrick, resting his elbow on his knee and scratching at the blond stubble on his chin. "But my father confides in no one. My grandfather, I have heard was… less than affectionate with his children. I'm sure it didn't help that my father's arranged marriage was so my grandfather could gain more lands. As I said, most marriages among nobles are for political gain. He loved her, though. He loved her more than anything. After she died, he trusted no one." Merrick paused, and his eyes seemed to stare through Charlie as he puzzled over a distant memory.

"I'm sorry," said Charlie meekly.

Merrick shook his head. "I was very young when she left us. It was my father and me for a very long time. Queen Piper was like a second mother to me. Though now that I think on it, it was after my mother's death that my father began to learn more about the magic of old."

A shudder ran through Charlie. "You don't think he's trying to bring her back to life, do you?" Zombies were only something in TV shows and movies back on Earth, but so was magic.

"No," said Merrick, shaking his head. He looked at Charlie, a skeptical gleam in his eye. "That's not possible, is it?"

Charlie shrugged. "I don't know. I've heard about doctors doing, like, finger transplants in my world, but as far as I know, zombies aren't real."

Merrick blinked at Charlie, and the boy realized he likely had not understood a word he had said.

"I'll look into this more and report back to you if I learn anything." Merrick stood and held out his hand to Charlie. Charlie rose stiffly and took Merrick's outstretched hand with a smile. "If you remain in Chartile for longer than your father, Charlie of the Hill, I would welcome your counsel any day."

EIGHTEEN
THE PRINCESS AND THE PROPOSAL

"YOU DID WHAT?" AILINN STOOD from her bed, her fists clenched, and her green eyes looked ready to pop out of her head.

Charlie held his hands up. "Just hear me out, okay?" he said. Ailinn huffed, her lips pierced tightly together, but she remained silent. "I talked to as many people as I could. Every beck-and Phillippe trusts, every guard Jock and Drustad trust. I've talked to Lord Kharas and a lot of other nobles he recommended. No one can find any dirt on Savaric. Besides, I told you I was going to talk to him."

"Yes, but I didn't think it would end with you believing I should go through with this!" Ailinn cried. She heaved a sigh and sat back on the bed. "Agreeing to marry Merrick after I have fought so hard to retain my independence would do nothing but show my people that I hold no power. Once my father renounces his claim in favor of myself and Merrick, I will be seen as nothing more than a pretty pawn upon a pretty chair."

Ailinn had been permitted to return to her usual quarters. This made meeting with her much easier since Charlie took the beck-and passages to avoid her guards.

Her living quarters where she would receive guests were spacious and echoed. They had opted to talk in her bedchamber, which was rather small compared to the rest of her quarters.

"I don't think that's going to happen," said Charlie. He leaned forward in his chair. He wanted to reach for her hands, but they were still clenched in her lap. "*You* are the one with magic, not Merrick, and your people want guidance and leadership when it comes to that. You're the best person to do that."

"The preparations for the wedding are already underway, regardless. Announcements have been sent out. In six weeks' time, I will be married whether I wish it or not. It feels wrong to just give in." Her voice was barely a whisper now. She stared down at her white-knuckled hands and breathed deeply, her eyes blinking back the tears.

"Ailinn, we need this wedding to move forward so we can try to figure out what Savaric is up to. We've hit a dead end. If it's a marriage he wants in order to enact his plans, then that's what we have to give him."

"And hope we're still two steps ahead," she added coldly.

A knot formed in Charlie's throat. A realization had hit him shortly after his meeting with Merrick. If Ailinn was going to marry Merrick, regardless of Savaric's plan, Charlie had to start distancing himself from her. Merrick was good and loyal and just. He was calm and brave and handsome. He was strong, both physically and mentally. He was absolutely everything Charlie was not, and he was everything Chartile needed. He was what Ailinn needed, too. He was older and smarter, and he was probably the one who would fulfill the prophecy, not Charlie. He was almost sure of that now.

There was a knock on the little door to the passages. Charlie's and Ailinn's heads snapped around as Phillippe opened the door and peeked around the corner.

"Master Charlie, you must return to your quarters immediately. Allies have come to seek an audience with you."

"Who?" Charlie asked. He had not scheduled any meetings that afternoon except the one with Ailinn.

Phillippe stared hard at Charlie, then dared a glance at Ailinn. Charlie's eyes widened, and he stood quickly. He took a step, ready to bolt for the passageway door, but turned instead as Ailinn stared up at him. Her eyes were bloodshot from holding back her tears. He wanted to reach out to her, to kiss her. He wanted to be the one to not just tell her it would be all right, but to prove it to her.

"We'll be three steps ahead of him before he realizes it." Charlie smiled and darted toward the passage.

The passageways were dark as usual, though Charlie had learned how to navigate them as well as the beck-ands. He turned blindly to his left, and his shoulder barely nudged the corner of the stone and earthen wall. Phillippe's shuffling steps ahead of him made it easier to follow.

"What does Daniel want?" Charlie asked, trying to keep his voice low in the echoing passage.

"I cannot tell you, sir," Phillippe squeaked.

Charlie stopped for a heartbeat, taken aback before continuing on. "Why?" he asked.

"That cursed Kashna said he would eat me, Master Charlie." Phillippe's words were more anger than fear, and Charlie felt himself smirk at his increasing confidence. "And lord Daniel said you would not come if he told you. Jock has accompanied them in your room. Drustad continues to wait at his usual post."

They rounded another corner, and this time Charlie smacked his shoulder square into the side of the wall. He stumbled, rubbing the spot where his shoulder had connected with the stone. He took a deep breath. He needed to focus. He could not let fear get the upper hand when dealing with Daniel.

Phillippe held the door open at the top of a small incline, and the light that poured in was nearly blinding. The beck-and must have moved the curtain for the day's sun before coming to fetch his master. Charlie staggered into the room still holding his sore shoulder and squinting through the sunlight.

He stopped in the doorway and stared at the sight that awaited him.

Jock stood sentry at the door, his arms behind his back, and a blank expression on his face. Kashna lay on the rug in front of Charlie's bed licking his paw. Daniel rose from one of the chairs, his brown eyes narrowed in frustration.

"I thought your beck-and may have gotten lost." He sneered and crossed his arms before him.

Merrick rose from the other chair beside Daniel and gave a small bow of welcome to Charlie.

Charlie's eyes darted from one corner of the room to the other. The hair on the back of his neck stood out. He fought the urge to cast out his magic and levitate his sword to him.

"What's going on?" Charlie asked.

"We have a plan," said Merrick. "Will you join us?" He indicated the chair he had sat in before. Charlie took a few steps forward, and Phillippe shuffled past him to pour chalices of water for everyone. Kashna rose from his place on the floor to stand beside Daniel.

"A plan for what?" Charlie asked as he drew closer. He was watching all three of his visitors very carefully.

"A plan to save Ailinn *and* find out what Savaric is up to," said Daniel. He sat back in his chair and began stroking Kashna gently between his ears.

Charlie nodded to Jock, and the guard joined Drustad in the hall once more, his eyes lingering across Charlie's face with a grave look of suspicion. Charlie sat in the chair across from Merrick and Daniel. He accepted the chalice of water Phillippe handed him, waiting for Daniel to continue.

"Ailinn has protested from the beginning that she does not wish to marry unless it is for love," said Merrick, also accepting a chalice from Phillippe. "I truly do not wish to force her into something she does not want. It will only make things worse in the end. I believe that a relationship between us could work in time, but not if she has any animosity."

"But this is exactly what Savaric wants," said Daniel. "Whether or not she wants to, when Ailinn marries Merrick, this will be playing right into the hands of whatever he has planned. We need to disrupt his plan, and Ailinn's refusal to marry Merrick is not good enough."

"So, what are you thinking?" Charlie asked. He was still on edge, looking from Daniel to Merrick and back again. Neither seemed to give any indication they were being dishonest, at least as far as he could tell.

Daniel glanced at Merrick and took a long drink from his chalice. "We need you to convince Ailinn to change her mind about marrying Merrick," he said.

Charlie sat a little straighter.

"But it's only for appearances' sake," said Merrick, holding up his hand in defense. "We need Ailinn to appear as though she has given in and resigned herself to the marriage. Then we will enact the second part of our plan."

"Second part?" Charlie asked, raising an eyebrow.

Daniel nodded. "If Savaric thinks everything is going according to his plan, he will not expect a kidnapping."

Charlie leapt to his feet, nearly upturning the chalice that had sat on the floor beside his chair. "Kidnapping?" he cried. "Whoa—hold on—just... push the back button and freeze!"

"Ailinn will be in no danger, Charlie," said Merrick reassuringly. He stood to meet Charlie's worried gaze. "Lord Valar of Cannondole, Valin's father and

Ailinn grandfather, has agreed to house Ailinn for a short time."

"By staging a kidnapping, Savaric will no longer believe he is in control of the situation," said Daniel. "He will panic. He'll get slack and careless. His next actions and discussions will bring us closer to discovering his plans."

Kashna's rumbling purr ceased. He blinked and looked at Charlie with his bright, golden eyes. "He will never suspect such a thing," he said, rising from the floor and shaking like a dog caught in a rainstorm. He paced, clearly bothered by the conversation, and lay back down on the rug, licking his paw again.

"Who is going to do the kidnapping?" Charlie asked.

"A few trusted guards—"

"No," Charlie said, cutting Daniel off. "We don't know where Savaric has his spies placed." He looked at his door, then back to the young men before him. "Jock and Drustad will do it."

"They will suspect your involvement," said Merrick. "They will accuse you of attempting treason against the crown and undermining the marriage."

"Everyone knows about your feelings for my sister," Daniel breathed quietly.

"Not if I ask for replacement guards," said Charlie, though a knot formed in his throat as he spoke the words. "I think it's time I had a talk with King Valin, anyway. I can arrange a meeting to ask for new guards. Especially if I say that I suspect Jock and Drustad have been slacking off." Charlie finally sat back in his chair. He looked at Phillippe. "We have a system of communication. I don't need them with me to be able to send them messages."

"You will do this then?" Merrick asked. "You will convince Ailinn?"

Charlie bit his lip, then nodded reluctantly. He'd already started doing it, anyway. Now, there was no turning back.

"We must tread slowly and cautiously," Daniel added. "If too many of these events happen too close together—Ailinn's change of heart, Charlie's change of guard, the kidnapping—it will look suspicious."

"The wedding is only a few weeks away, though," said Charlie. "The guests will start to come in the next week or so. It's going to be harder to work around more people."

"I can arrange your meeting with King Valin before tomorrow night, Master Charlie," Phillippe said. "And, if I might be so bold…" Charlie nearly laughed as Phillippe looked to him for permission to continue. The gesture was only for the formality of their guests. Charlie nodded, and Phillippe cleared his throat. "If they see the princess speaking with her future husband, her change of heart might be more easily believed."

Merrick and Daniel turned back to Charlie as he fidgeted with the chalice in his hand. His mouth had turned dry as everyone in the room stared at him. It was one thing for him to believe that Ailinn should marry Merrick. It was another thing entirely that others were trying to execute that very plan. Any hope that Ailinn could still be his girlfriend was slowly fading, like the sunlight across the floor. It was yet another cruel reminder of how different Chartile was from his own world and how much he longed for home.

Finally, Charlie nodded his agreement.

"There's something else," Merrick said, breaking the awkward tension that surrounded the room. "I may have found something. I'm not sure."

Charlie leaned forward in his chair, and Daniel set his chalice on the floor beside him. Even Kashna lifted his head, ears pricked forward.

"When our families, mine and Ailinn's, when they agreed on our marriage, I learned to speak, read, and write in several of the old languages. Of course, any noble can read the Dwarvik runes and the old Elven script, but my father insisted I learn ancient Draconian and Merspeech as well. He said there was much to learn from our history that could help advance our future."

Merrick stood and began pacing, twirling the chalice in his hand until he nearly dumped the water and finally thought to set it down.

"I acquired a few tricks during my time working in Harpy's Pointe. I worked at the local inn, and we occasionally had reason to suspect some of our guests of theft. I learned to pick locks well. While my father was away from our quarters yesterday, I picked the lock on his traveling chest. Inside was the large tome I have seen him reading since I was a child. I've never looked at it until that moment. The entire book is written in Merspeech, and it references very ancient magic. One page in particular seemed more read than the others. A recipe for a sort of elixir or potion of sorts."

"A potion?" Daniel asked.

"What does it do?" asked Charlie.

Merrick continued his pacing. "It's strange. It speaks of biped physiology, and the effects of certain compounds on the mind. It is a very odd sort of magic, but this elixir puts the drinker in a state of… unnatural bliss. They perceive no danger and are therefore immune to such habits as lying and can be easily persuaded."

"Why would someone use such a thing?" asked Daniel. His brow had furrowed more deeply, and his lip curled in disgust.

"In times of old," Kashna said, still sprawled on the floor between them, "magic was used in combination with herb-lore and medicine. A concoction of this type would likely be used to subdue patients for healing treatment."

"Wait," said Charlie. The room shifted out of focus as he thought. Daniel, Kashna, and Merrick turned to look at him, but his mind was focused on an image from a particular moment.

When Savaric first arrived in Chartile, he entered the throne room with two young men in tow behind him. At first, Charlie had thought they were his beck-ands, but their skin and hair were too pale to be Human. Charlie brushed them off as Savaric's personal servants and had given up on any sort of lead after Kharas reported the two seemed to be deaf and mute or... "In some sort of state."

"What?" Daniel snapped.

Charlie lifted his head and finally noticed the three sets of eyes staring at him.

"Okay, maybe I'm being weird or whatever, but do you think Savaric is using that potion on his two servants? Maybe to keep them from revealing anything?"

Daniel and Merrick exchanged glances and shrugged.

"But if they are loyal to him, why would they have any desire to reveal anything?" Daniel asked.

"Are they loyal?" asked Charlie, looking at Merrick.

Merrick thought for a moment. "I suppose I never questioned it, but it's entirely possible they aren't. I don't know."

"And you said it would keep someone from lying?" Charlie continued, his tone rising with excitement now.

"What if the reason he is always a step ahead of us is because he's poisoning everyone around him and then interrogating them?"

Merrick scratched at his stubble, and Daniel ran his fingers through his hair.

"Wouldn't we have noticed others within the palace in this... state you speak of?" Kashna asked. "Surely he couldn't have enough elixir to interrogate and keep quiet the entire Elven palace."

Charlie slumped back in his chair. He was so sure he had figured it all out. He was sure Savaric intended to use the potion on Ailinn and Merrick once they ascended the throne so he could rule through them. But Kashna was right. If Ailinn and Merrick suddenly started acting like zombies, it'd be too obvious.

"I still believe you're on the correct path, Merrick," said Daniel. Charlie looked at him, surprised, but he noticed the words seemed to surprise Daniel as well. "Can you look at this book again? Perhaps there are other potions or uses of magic that may help us understand his intentions."

Merrick nodded. He had finally resumed sitting again. "I can try."

"Good," said Charlie. "So, that's it then? That's kind of our plan?" Something felt wrong to him, but he wasn't sure why. All the pieces of their plan were moving forward without issue, but maybe that was it. It was all too easy.

"I'll arrange your meeting with the king at once, Master Charlie," Phillippe squeaked behind them.

"I cannot guarantee I'll have another chance to look at the book," said Merrick.

"Perhaps I can help with that," Daniel said. "If I ask for a meeting with Savaric, perhaps I can convince him I'm in favor of Ailinn's marriage to you. That should draw him away long enough."

This time, it was Kashna who shook his head. "I believe it is too risky," he said. "It may draw too much suspicion with everything else moving."

"I have to agree with Kashna," said Charlie reluctantly. "I'll try to get my guards changed, and then I still have to talk to Ailinn and convince her. We should lie low for a few days. Like, not get together and limit our notes and stuff."

"Agreed," said Merrick.

The tension in the room rose again. Merrick drained the water from his chalice and stood.

"Would your beck-and escort me back to my quarters through the passages?" he asked.

Phillippe bowed to Merrick and held the little door open for him. When they had disappeared into the darkness, Daniel stood as well.

"This isn't a game, little king," he whispered, towering over Charlie. "One wrong step and we may never be able to recover."

Kashna rose from the floor. He shook his head and paced in a circle before joining Daniel at the door. He seemed agitated, like a fly relentlessly buzzed around his head. Charlie wondered if qarveenas could get headaches.

Charlie crossed the room and pulled the door open. He was much shorter than Daniel but did his best to meet the lord's gaze.

"You worry about you. I can handle myself."

Daniel smirked, shook his head, and left Charlie alone with his thoughts and that awful feeling in the pit of his stomach.

NINETEEN
OVERTURE

TRUE TO HIS WORD, PHILLIPPE arranged a meeting between Charlie and King Valin the very next day. Charlie had no idea how the beck-and was able to pull off such tasks. Beck-ands were servants and not permitted certain jobs within the palace. Charlie suspected Phillippe's age had gained him so many connections through the years. Still, the knowledge that Charlie was safe under the extended, watchful eye of his beck-and and Phillippe's many friends was of little comfort as he marched toward the massive throne room. Jock and Drustad were at his sides, their footsteps echoing in the empty room as they headed toward the small annex off the main room.

When Charlie first spoke to them, they'd been far from pleased at the thought of being replaced to say the least. They argued for Charlie's safety. They argued that it would be more difficult for them to collaborate together. Mostly, they argued they would miss Charlie, as they had taken him on as a sort of adoptive little brother. It was Phillippe who convinced them it was the only way to ensure Ailinn's absolute safety, and to make sure Charlie would be clear of any accusations.

There were already two guards waiting outside the annex door. Charlie nodded to Drustad and Jock. They looked back at him with the saddest expressions Charlie had ever seen. He thought it might even rival the pitiful stares of his grandmother's Jack Russell Terrier when she begged for food scraps. Charlie turned away from them and walked through the door to the small room beyond.

King Valin rose from one of the chairs that lined the outer wall as Charlie entered. The boy took a few steps forward and made to bow to the king.

"There's no need for such formalities here, Charlie," said Valin as he gestured toward a chair beside his own. Charlie stopped mid-bow. He couldn't move for a full five seconds. Already things were not going the way he had rehearsed them. He took the seat Valin had indicated and tried not to fidget. He didn't want the king to see he was nervous.

"I'm glad you asked to speak with me," Valin continued, also taking his seat. He was dressed less formally than the other times Charlie had seen him. He wore hose and a tunic like Charlie's. He smiled at the boy, but it only made Charlie more uncomfortable. "I hear you have been asking questions about Savaric."

"Your Majesty—" Charlie began, but Valin raised a hand to silence him.

"There is no need for apology, Charlie," he said, waving his hand between them. "If I were to promote any investigation, it could jeopardize the marriage arrangement, and thus my chances of ending this war. Have you found anything?"

Charlie was stunned. This was definitely *not* the way he had rehearsed things. He was now rather grateful for the times he had unexpectedly run into Savaric. It had forced him to think on his feet. Not that it was difficult. Staying one step ahead of Malcolm Darcy had been good practice.

"Not much, your Majesty," Charlie said. "But I know Merrick's on our side. He doesn't like what Savaric is doing, and..." Charlie swallowed hard, suppressing a sigh. "I think he'll be really good for the kingdom and Ailinn."

Valin laid his hand on Charlie's shoulder. It was more comforting than he had expected. Charlie looked up into the man's icy-blue eyes. They were not dilated or bloodshot, and Charlie realized there wasn't a cup of wine or brandy in sight.

"It is a relief to hear you say such," Valin said. "I was wrong to doubt you. How true it is that age is no more than the cycles of the sun. When I was your age, my mother was running Cannondole, and I was taking all the credit. My father was playing advisor to the king, and I was playing little Lord of the City."

Valin laughed, and Charlie watched a memory pass through the king's mind as he did so. It was all Charlie could do to smile back, if uncomfortably.

"Savaric did not shirk his duties as the future Lord of Harpy's Pointe growing up. He learned the ways of politics and negotiations whilst I was sneaking into the local tavern to gamble the town's money. You can't imagine how dangerous this makes him to me now. I am glad to know I have you on my side."

"Why did you become king then?" The question fell from Charlie's mouth before he could stop it. He turned away and pressed his knuckles to his lips.

Valin sighed. He rose from his chair and sauntered across the room. He stopped before one of the tapestries that hung along the walls of the room. "It was my father's recommendation. Most of the Conclave had been corrupted by Taraniz's, or rather Noraedin's, manipulation. There were few people left who had the ability to stand as the royal advisor. It was a way for my father to help Piper rebuild Chartile, and I wasn't going to say no to such a just and worthy cause. Once again, I could sit back and reap the rewards of others. I would be seen as the king who helped resurrect Chartile, and I needn't do more than attend meetings and look the part. I was rather content to let my wife make the tough decisions. After all, she was born royalty. When she died, I was lost in more ways than anyone knows."

The silence that followed was a mix of emotions for Charlie, and he assumed for Valin as well. The tension was thick, and the room stuffy. He wasn't sure whether he felt sorry for Valin or appalled, but it was probably both.

Valin turned back to Charlie, the joy and laughter now gone. Charlie stood as he approached and looked up into the king's ice-blue eyes again. They had changed in just the space of a few moments leaving Charlie to wonder which emotion lingered within them. Fear, doubt, regret, or something else.

Charlie swallowed again and licked his lips. "I'll do whatever I can to help."

Valin nodded and smiled weakly. He sighed again, appearing to release the last of the emotion held within him. He seemed relieved to once more place responsibility into someone else's hands.

"What did you wish to speak with me about?" he asked, taking his seat again.

Charlie had nearly forgotten his whole reason for coming to see Valin. He straightened a bit, finally ready to deliver the lines he had rehearsed with Phillippe.

"It's my guards, your Majesty. I—I came to ask for replacements."

Valin sat straighter as well, his brow furrowed in concern. "What happened? Are they working for Savaric? I knew he had spies within the palace, but I never would have suspected Jock and Drust—"

"No, it's nothing like that!" Charlie cried. "I just—I don't think they're taking things very seriously. Or maybe the hours are too much for them." His breath caught in his throat, and he struggled to recover his practiced speech. "I caught them sleeping the other night. I don't want them to get in trouble or anything. I'm sure everyone's on edge. Maybe they just need a vacation for a little while."

Valin's jaw tightened, and he breathed through his nose. Finally, he spoke. "Of course, Charlie. I cannot apologize enough for their actions. I will have them questioned by our captain and replaced immediately."

Charlie nodded and forced a smile. "Thank you, your Majesty."

He stood to bow to Valin but found the king's arm extended toward him instead.

"Your father taught me your custom long ago," said Valin with a smile. "Remember?"

Charlie took the man's hand and squeezed it as his father would have. He released his grip and had to steady his walk, so as not to full-out run for the door.

Outside, Drustad and Jock stood waiting for him. Neither gave any indication they knew the contents of the conversation that had transpired. They stepped in line behind Charlie as they walked up the main aisle of the throne room and out into the palace once more.

Charlie wanted to tell them everything that had happened, but they had all agreed it would be best if it appeared as though Charlie were distancing himself from them. As he stopped outside his bedroom door, waiting for one of the guards to open it for him, he fought the urge to turn and hug them.

Drustad reached for the handle and pulled the door open. Charlie dared a glance up at them. They smiled back reassuringly, and his heart still sank.

THE CHANGE OF GUARD OCCURRED more quickly than Charlie had imagined. By the time he awoke the next morning, two brawny and broad-shouldered guards stood sentry outside his door. Their faces were less kind and more rigid than Jock's and Drustad's, and they addressed him as only "my lord" before and after each encounter. It was with both relief and unease that Charlie sat on his window ledge before dusk, ready to meet Princess Ailinn. If it wasn't for Phillippe's reassurance that his former guards were fine, he might have copped out.

"We must proceed with the plan, Master Charlie," said Phillippe, lighting the candle he would place on the ledge after the boy left.

"I know," Charlie whined. "I just feel really bad is all." He readjusted his tunic, then shrugged.

"They understand, and they agreed to the plan," Phillippe continued to console him. "Do not let their actions be in vain."

Charlie nodded and leapt from the windowsill. He landed on his feet, a painful tingle running up his legs again. He turned and looked up at his beck-and, smiling and giving him a thumbs-up. Phillippe returned the gesture and placed the candle on the ledge.

There was still a bit of sun shining through the trees. The boughs above the garden areas were trimmed back as sparsely as possible to allow light through for the plants. Still, the lamps had already been lit, casting strange double shadows in the light of the fading sun.

Charlie traversed the gardens more easily this time. His hand remained at the ready on the hilt of the blade that hung at his waist.

He rounded the corner and stopped. Someone was singing. He peeked around a phoenix feather bush and saw Ailinn sitting on the edge of the fountain, her fingers trailing in the water as the little fish darted back and forth beneath the ripples.

"In the spring of ancient wood,
Beneath the willow down,
Your voice it whispers like the flame,
Adorned in royal crown.

Upon the wings of phoenix breath,
Arise above the ashes left,
And with her love Anatha bless,
Into Creator's arms to rest.

Farewell, my darling flame,
Farewell, we merry met,
Farewell until we cross anew,
Into the blazing sun to set."

Ailinn's voice seemed to trail off, and a stifled sob broke the eerie stillness that had followed her song.

"I miss you, Mama," Ailinn whispered.

Charlie felt sick, and he clutched a hand to his chest. Thoughts of his own parents flashed before his mind's eye. Would he ever get home to them, or would their last memory of him be of a little boy with a hot temper?

Carefully, he stepped from the shadows. Ailinn held her face in her hands and rocked back and forth on the edge of the fountain. Charlie reached out and placed a hand on her shoulder.

She jumped to her feet, quickly wiping the tears from her cheeks.

"How long have you been there?" she demanded, her voice tight.

"Just a minute," said Charlie, taking a step back.

Ailinn took a deep breath and wiped away another stray tear. She swallowed several times, her eyes darting back and forth.

"I was charged with giving the overture for my mother's funeral," Ailinn finally said. She looked at Charlie with her usual fiery stare. "It is considered a great honor among the elves to deliver the overture before the funeral pyre is lit."

She turned away from Charlie, and he saw her pull a handkerchief from her sleeve and wipe her nose. He wanted to comfort her, but his feet wouldn't move.

"My mother hated fire," Ailinn continued, speaking to the darkness that closed in around them. "I know it's tradition. We return by fire and earth as the first of our kind were created. But it still seemed wrong. I've witnessed many nobles' funerals, but it was different with my mother. I—I don't know how, but I suddenly realized why she married my father. I hated her for so long for it. Her actions condemned me to the same fate. I forgave her today, and she is not even here for me to tell her."

Another sharp intake of breath escaped Ailinn, and she wiped her cheek again.

"I want to tell her so many things, and I can't." She turned to Charlie, her face streaked with tears she didn't bother to wipe away this time. "Everyone seemed to forget her so quickly. It's only been two years. She made me strong, and I feel so powerless without her. I feel trapped and angry and worthless, and no matter how hard I try, I see her in my dreams every night. I want to let her go, but I can't. I can't."

Hot tears stung Charlie's own eyes. If he were home, he would have forced them away. He would have buried his emotions and said something cruel or nothing at all. His parents weren't dead, but he felt the same longing as Ailinn to want them in his life again. He was a different person now, but it didn't change his feelings of wanting to see them again.

"I miss my family too," he whispered.

He had but a second's warning before Ailinn rushed at him and buried her face in his neck. She wrapped her arms around him and squeezed him tightly. Charlie hugged her back, smelling the sweetness of her hair as it fell across his face. She trembled against him, her tears hot and soaking through his tunic.

They stayed wrapped in each other's comfort until the sun had completely set, leaving them in a half-darkness as the lantern light glowed around them. Ailinn's shudders had subsided along with her tears, but her grip on Charlie remained solid. When she pulled away, even the warm summer air felt cold.

Ailinn wiped her face again. It was red and splotchy, but Charlie still couldn't take his eyes off her.

"I know what I have to do," she said, her voice barely audible above the splash of the fountain beside them. "I know I have to marry Merrick. It's the right thing to do."

"That's what I came to talk to you about," said Charlie. Their hands had somehow found each other. He rubbed his thumb over the back of her hand. He smiled and guided Ailinn off the stone path toward the tree line.

"If this is about us—" Ailinn said before they had left the light of the lanterns.

Charlie interrupted her. "Not here."

They stopped beneath a pink willow, letting its leaves cover and conceal them. Shrouded in darkness, Ailinn turned to Charlie, the furrow between her eyes barely visible.

"What is it?" she asked.

"Daniel, Merrick, and I have a plan."

Ailinn opened her mouth to argue, but Charlie pressed a finger to her lips, stunning her into silence. "We're going to get you out of here, but you need to pretend you're going to marry Merrick."

"Charlie, I am not pretending." Ailinn's tone had turned defensive. "I understand what I must do."

"That's what I'm saying. You don't have to anymore," replied Charlie. "We're going to take you to your grandfather just before the wedding. But we need Savaric to think you're going through with the wedding. You and Merrick need to be seen together. Once Savaric sees things are working out for him, we're hoping his complacency will reveal the next part of his plan. By then, you'll be hiding in Cannondole, and we'll be one step closer to getting rid of this guy."

It was hard to see Ailinn's face in the darkness beneath the tree. Charlie caught the smallest glint in her eye. It could have been from her tears, but it reminded him of the gleam of excitement he saw in her, especially when she tried to hide a smile.

"Then… I don't have to marry Merrick," she said, the realization in her voice was almost palpable.

"I guess not," Charlie said with a shrug.

Ailinn's free hand found its way to Charlie's shoulder. She stood close to him, so close he could feel her breath against his face. She shook again and looked into Charlie's eyes. Charlie lifted his hand to her face, his fingers brushing against her ear.

"Your ears aren't pointed," he said as his heart pounded faster.

Ailinn giggled. "An ancient superstition," she whispered.

Charlie leaned toward her, his lips brushing against hers. He hesitated, his hands shaking and his legs feeling as though they would give way under him at any moment.

Ailinn pressed her lips to his, and he wrapped his arms around her again. She did taste like strawberries. He wondered if her heart was beating as wildly as his, if the only thing holding her up was being pressed to him, like he was to her.

Charlie felt a tug and nearly fell forward. He bent a knee and caught himself from falling spread-eagle on the ground.

"Char—" he heard Ailinn scream before something stifled her cry.

"Ailinn!" Charlie called after her. The mess of nerves filling him kept him frozen in place. He heard shuffling through the trees ahead of him, and someone cried out in pain.

"Charlie!" Ailinn called again.

It was the push he needed. Charlie bolted from the ground, fumbling with the sword in his hand. He could barely see and nearly ran into a branch or tree more than once. The shuffling was getting farther away. He felt something slam against his body. He stumbled and fell to the ground, his sword flying out of his hand.

"You bloody coward! You let them get away!" a voice screamed somewhere above him. "Ailinn! Ailinn!" It called in the dark.

Charlie struggled to his feet, holding his ribs. He headed in the direction he heard his sword clang against a tree but was stopped mid-stride. The frantic stranger grabbed Charlie's shoulder, pushing him to the ground.

"I knew you were in league with them!"

"Daniel?"

TWENTY
INTO THE NIGHT

DANIEL WAS RUNNING SO CLOSE behind Charlie, one false step and they'd both come crashing down. They tore through the gardens back to Charlie's bedroom window. The candle fell to the floor and slid half the length of the room as Charlie and Daniel tumbled through the open window.

Phillippe emerged from the passage holding a small knife in a surprisingly steady hand.

"You've armed your beck-and now?" Daniel stared wide-eyed at Phillippe as he pushed himself up from the floor.

Charlie ignored him. "Phil, they've taken Ailinn!"

"The princess is gone?" Saajee'a peered through the beck-and door, her eyes as wide as Daniel's.

"Saajee'a! What are you doing here?" Phillippe demanded, setting his knife on the vanity.

"Looking after you, of course," she said. "Do you really think Mother would let you do everything you've been doing without someone reporting back to her?"

"We don't have time for this," said Daniel. He headed toward the beck-and door, and Saajee'a shrank into the darkness as he approached.

"Wait," Phillippe called.

Daniel stopped, from what appeared to be more shock than following the beck-and's orders. Phillippe hurried toward Charlie's wardrobe and pulled a large, heavy bag from its depths.

"I've... had this... ready," he huffed and tried to pull the bag onto his shoulder. "For... Cannondole."

Charlie hurried to his side and struggled to lift the bag himself. "What did you pack in here, Phil?"

"We have no time for this," snapped Daniel again. "The trail is getting cold. We need to alert my father of this, not sneak around like rogues and criminals!"

"If we alert everyone, Savaric will have an easier chance of getting away in the chaos," said Charlie. "We need to be quiet and discreet. Send some extra guards to his rooms or something."

"I will handle things my way, little king," said Daniel, his eyes narrowed, and his jaw clenched. "I'm going after her, with you or without you. I'm getting Kashna and leaving."

He pushed past Saajee'a and disappeared into the darkness.

"We have to warn the king. We have to find Savaric before he runs off." Charlie hoisted the bag onto his bed. His eyes searched Phillippe's, waiting for someone else to tell him what to do. He stood frozen in place, his lips still tingling from his kiss with Ailinn only minutes ago.

"Master Charlie," said Phillippe gently, "it's time for you to do what you came here to do."

"But Savaric—" Charlie argued.

Phillippe held a hand up to silence him, and Charlie blinked in disbelief.

"I will send word to Jock and Drustad immediately. They have friends who are always watching Savaric . Let us do our part in this, Charlie. You must do yours."

Charlie felt tears sting his eyes again. He blinked them away and swallowed hard.

"I'm scared," he whispered. He sank to his knees and wrapped his arms around himself.

Phillippe knelt before him, his knees creaking as he forced himself to the floor. He laid a weathered hand on the boy's shoulder. Charlie looked up, staring at the worn eyes shrouded in lines and wrinkles.

"We all are," Phillippe whispered.

WITH PHILLIPPE'S MYSTERIOUS PACK HOISTED onto his back, Charlie tore after Saajee'a through the beck-and passages as quickly as the darkness would allow him. Phillippe had taken a separate path several turns back, hurrying to find Drustad and Jock. Saajee'a had promised to get Charlie safely and secretly to the stables.

His heart raced from more than just the exertion of running with the heavy bag. Daniel had been right. The trail to Ailinn's kidnappers was getting cold. And even if he found it, he had no idea what he would do to save her. Charlie's skills with a blade left much to be desired.

They headed up a gentle slope, and Saajee'a pushed open the double doors before him. They were in the kitchens, and the smell of cooking meat greeted him as they hurried past the large prep table. Several beck-ands tended the fires, turning the giant spits of fowl carcasses. They stopped after Charlie had only taken a few paces into the room.

"Master Charlie?" A young boy stood almost hidden behind the scrubbed wooden prep table. Charlie recognized him as one of the regular beck-ands to the stable hands. More beck-ands were emerging from the shadows, their eager faces refusing to look at his.

"Saajee'a!" A plump woman bustled out of the pantry, slamming the door behind her. "What is the meaning of this?"

"Mama, I—"

"Master Charlie, please forgive us."

"No, Mama, listen," said Saajee'a defiantly.

Her mother glared at her, a look that could have rivaled Princess Ailinn's. She reached a hand toward her daughter, but Saajee'a pulled away.

"Listen!" said the young girl. "Princess Ailinn has been kidnapped."

The silence that had fallen when Charlie first entered was quickly replaced with whispers and mumblings.

"The princess?"

Saajee'a nodded and finally looked back at Charlie.

"I'm going after her," he said, and the whispers grew more frantic.

"It was Lord Savaric, Mama," Saajee'a continued.

"That is a severe accusation—"

Charlie quickly defended her. "It's true."

The whispers stopped. Charlie glanced around the room. He recognized several faces as beck-ands Phillippe had spoken to and helped him deliver messages. These people had been his silent army, a network of secret spies. If Phillippe and Saajee'a trusted them, then so did he.

"I know it was him," continued Charlie. "Or at least someone who works for him. Savaric wouldn't do the dirty work himself."

"He's probably asleep in his chambers, sir," said a middle-aged beck-and whose hair had gone white long before its time.

Saajee'a's mother rounded on him and smacked the back of his head. Beck-ands were not permitted to speak to anyone besides other beck-ands unless first prompted. He rubbed the spot she had struck, but another beck-and spoke.

"He would need to appear innocent, so no one could link the kidnapping back to him," he said.

Charlie saw Saajee'a's mother's grasp on the beck-ands quickly slipping. Her nostrils flared, and her shoulders tensed.

"He can't escape," said Charlie before the woman exploded with anger. "He can't leave the palace."

The reaction from the beck-ands was almost instant. They bustled back and forth through the kitchen, Saajee'a's mother barking orders at them. They gathered trays, food, cups, and pitchers. Several beck-ands darted past Charlie and into the passages beyond.

"You leave him and his party to us, Master Charlie." Saajee'a's mother hurried back into the pantry and emerged with a small bottle of herbs.

"The stables are just past the servants' area. Through those doors there," said Saajee'a beside him.

Charlie knelt down, the weight of the pack making his knees crack as loud as Phillippe's. "Stay out of the way, Saajee'a. Savaric knows you and Phillippe have both been my beck-ands. I don't want you to get hurt."

"I'll be all right, Master Charlie," she said, flashing a bright smile against her terracotta skin. Charlie reached for her, and she did not back away. He pulled her into a hug, and he felt her wrap her arms around his neck and squeeze. She released him quickly, red rising in her cheeks, and hurried off around a corner.

The young boy who had first spoken wove his way through the mass of frenzied beck-ands and grabbed Charlie's sleeve.

"You'll be needing Cinders saddled, yes, Master Charlie?" he asked.

Charlie looked down at him. He saw a smile spread across the boy's face, and his eyes flicked up to meet Charlie's for just an instant. Charlie smiled back, though he was still sick to his stomach with nerves. The boy led Charlie through the throng of workers and into the servants' area of the palace.

There was little light, save for a few large candles here and there. Several Belirian trees had been hollowed out, and Charlie saw they were just large enough for a small mattress to fit. A few beck-ands pulled the doors to their tree beds closed as he and the stable boy passed by. He wondered how they stayed warm in the winter and shuddered at the thought.

They rounded a corner, the little boy still pulling Charlie by the cuff of his tunic. The stables were completely dark. There were no lanterns or candles anywhere, but Charlie did not need light to know where Cinders' stall was. He set the heavy pack on the ground and approached the horse. She whinnied loudly, and the other horses answered her, pawing at the ground in their stalls.

Charlie stroked her velvet nose, and she blew hot air into his hand.

"Easy, girl. It's just me," Charlie whispered. Cinders lipped at his palm, and he rubbed her nose again.

A loud crash down the stable aisle made Charlie and several of the horses jump. He could barely make out the silhouette of the stable boy through the cracks in the building where the light of the lanterns outside shown in. The beck-and boy was on the ground beneath a heap of saddle that was as big as he was.

Charlie rushed to him and pulled the saddle off.

"I can do it, Master Charlie," he said, reaching for the saddle now in Charlie's arms. When Charlie handed him only half the weight, the boy stumbled again.

"Why don't you get Cinders?" Charlie said as politely as he could. The hairs on the back of his neck were still on end. The trail was getting colder by the minute, and Daniel still had not arrived. Charlie wondered for a moment if Daniel had intentionally left him behind.

The stable boy hung his head and hurried to grab a lead rope from the tack room.

"Turn around slowly," said a cold voice. Charlie felt the tip of a blade in the middle of his back.

Charlie turned as instructed, cursing that his arms were trapped beneath the saddle and unable to get to his sword. The silhouette was tall and broad, and completely shrouded in darkness. The horses had gone eerily quiet. They weren't even pawing at the ground anymore.

"What do you mean by sneaking off in the middle of the night?" the voice demanded. "Hoping to deliver a message from Lord Savaric, are you? Perhaps running off to meet some of those rebels for a midnight attack on the palace? State your business here with my horses, and I may let you live to see another sunrise."

Charlie knew that voice, or at least he hoped he did. He squinted in the dark, trying to catch the familiar glint in the man's eye.

"Lord Kharas?" he finally asked.

The man lowered his weapon and took a step back.

"Charlie?" he asked. "What are you doing?"

Charlie set the saddle on the ground. "Ailinn's been kidnapped. The beck-ands are trying to keep Savaric from running away."

"Have you confirmed he is still in his quarters?" Kharas asked. Charlie heard him sheath his sword and watched his silhouette adjust his stance.

Charlie closed his eyes and rubbed his forehead. "No," he said, "I didn't think of that. But I have to go after Ailinn. They're getting away. It's probably been, like, twenty minutes!"

Lord Kharas sighed. "Wait here." He turned and headed through a door that led to the main entrance from the stable to the palace.

The stable boy emerged from the shadows again and bustled past Charlie to take Cinders from her stall. He barely came to the top of the horse's front leg, but she remained calm and gentle.

Charlie heard a sound like a wooden chest opening from beyond the door Lord Kharas had disappeared through. He ignored it and instead approached Cinders to place the saddle on her.

"She's my favorite horse, Master Charlie. I'm so glad you're riding her," the beck-and boy said as Charlie tightened the girth on the saddle. "And you're my favorite lord, Master Charlie, so I like that you two are friends."

Lord Kharas appeared out of the shadows once more, carrying something large over his shoulder. He tossed a coin to the stable boy who gasped as he scrambled in the dirt for it.

"Run along to your father, boy. Tell no one what has happened here, or I'll have you strung up by your ears, you hear?" Kharas's voice was kinder than his words implied.

"Yes, Lord Kharas!" the boy said. "And you're my favorite lord too!"

Charlie stifled a laugh as he took off back towards the servants' area. His joy was short-lived as Lord Kharas put a hand on his shoulder.

"If Savaric is behind this kidnapping, he is cunning enough to know to stay behind, at least for a little while. You were wise to have him watched, but he will suspect as much. The entire palace needs to be put on alert. Every noble and beck-and accounted for and in their chambers. But you, Charlie. You must find the men who did this. It may be our last hope in discovering Savaric's plans."

"Find Jock and Drustad. My old guards. They can help you. And Phillippe, too. He's my beck-and. You can trust them," said Charlie. He pulled the bridle from a hook beside Cinders' stall and slipped it over her head.

"I am afraid you will be the first person Savaric will accuse of this treachery. Your guards can hold their own, but your beck-and may be in danger."

Charlie's eyes widened. He made to run back to the palace, but Kharas's firm hand steadied him.

"Princess Ailinn is more important than your beck-and, I'm afraid. The fate of this war lies with her."

Footsteps pounded on the ground behind the pair. Daniel's silhouette stood out against the lantern light filtering through the cracks in the stall behind him.

"I can't find Kashna anywhere!" he cried, joining Charlie and Kharas. "I think Savaric may have taken him too, but I can't imagine why."

"Kashna is a rare creature indeed. Perhaps he means to use him as part of his negotiations. It's difficult to say what goes on in Savaric's mind."

Daniel stopped when he heard Lord Kharas's voice. Charlie watched his outline look between the pair.

"It's okay," said Charlie. "He's with us."

"How many people do you have involved in this?" Daniel spat, hurrying to gather tack for his own horse. "No wonder Savaric knows everything that's going on. Everyone else seems to."

Charlie opened his mouth to speak, but Kharas squeezed his arm and gave a single shake of his head. Charlie understood. Arguing with Daniel wasn't worth it.

Kharas slung the burden he carried over Cinders' back.

"My gift to you, little king," he said, buckling a pair of saddlebags to the horse's saddle. "Though I intended on giving it to you when I left for Sutton Low."

Charlie suddenly remembered the pack Phillippe had given him. He hoisted it onto his shoulders once more before shuffling back to Cinders and Kharas. The man barely stifled his laugh.

"Compliments of your faithful beck-and?" he asked.

"How'd you guess?" Charlie huffed against the weight of the bag. His saddle weighed less.

"For one, this is a servant's pack, and I know you would have never thought to bring that many items with you." He pulled the pack from Charlie and began moving things from the pack to the saddlebags.

Daniel had finished tacking his horse in record time. He led the horse from its stall and pulled himself into the saddle with ease.

"Let's go!"

Kharas finished filling the saddlebags and returned to Charlie a much lighter pack. Charlie slung this over his shoulder and attempted to find a mounting block in the darkness. He felt Kharas pull him back, and he could barely see the man hold his clasped hands out. With Kharas's help, Charlie mounted Cinders, who nickered quietly and bobbed her head.

"Bring her back, Charlie," Kharas whispered. He nodded to Daniel, though Charlie barely saw it in the darkness himself. Without a word, he headed back towards the main entrance into the palace, and Charlie heard him lock the door.

Cinders bobbed her head again and stomped the ground. Charlie patted her neck and turned her towards Daniel.

"Where are we going?" Charlie asked as they raced out of the stables. He was still bouncing far more than he would have liked in the saddle, but at least he wasn't falling off. "These lanterns won't last forever. How are we going to see in the dark?"

"I know where to go," Daniel called over his shoulder.

"How?" Charlie asked, rather unnerved.

"I had a vision."

Charlie watched Daniel duck beneath a branch and narrowly missed thwacking his own nose. "A vision?"

"I can't explain it," Daniel called back. "I didn't know what it meant at the time. Now I do. We need to get to the Rill of Kelf."

"The what?" Charlie yelled over the pounding of the horse's hooves. The Rill of Kelf sounded like something out of a movie. "What's a rill? What's a kelf?"

"It's a small stream where my sister and I once played. A short way past it is the tributary that meets with the Great River."

Charlie hesitated. "How do you know that's where they'll be?"

"Because I saw us fighting," Daniel said.

The lanterns finally ended after a mile, and Charlie and Daniel were forced to dismount. They led their horses along the dark path as quickly as they could. Charlie created a small fireball in his hand, which shed at least a few feet of light in front of them.

If it weren't for the fear of tripping over a loose rock or a rogue tree root, Charlie might have let his thoughts wander more. It seemed awfully convenient that Daniel just happened to be in the gardens when Ailinn had been kidnapped. Tackling Charlie might have been exactly what the captors needed to get away. And now he knew exactly where they were heading.

They had been walking for several hours in near silence before Charlie did trip over a tree root. The light in his hand went out, shrouding them in darkness. He pushed himself up, but his arms could barely hold his weight.

"We need to stop," said Charlie. He didn't bother getting up. He sat on the ground and rubbed his aching shoulders.

"We can't," Daniel snapped. "The longer we wait, the farther away they get. We cannot risk losing them."

"I can't. I need a break." Charlie heaved a sigh. He pushed himself to his feet and began rummaging in his saddlebags. "I just need to eat and sleep. We need to make camp or whatever you call it."

"No." Daniel grabbed Charlie's wrist and felt for Cinders' reins. "I'll lead the horses then. You rest."

"But how will you see?" Charlie didn't need to ask.

A ball of fire appeared in Daniel's hand. He used it to find a rope hidden in the saddlebags that he shoved into Charlie's chest.

"Tie yourself on. I'll wake you when we get there."

Charlie didn't move. He couldn't move. Not even Ailinn had said Daniel had magic. Charlie felt a twinge rise in his stomach thinking back to how fiercely Daniel had fought to have Ailinn marry Merrick from the very beginning. And then there was Merrick's stance on magic. He wasn't against it, not really. If Ailinn and Merrick became king and queen, would Daniel be able to use his magic openly as Piper had? Charlie swallowed and turned to mount Cinders again.

Daniel's flame was brighter than Charlie's had been, and it bounced wildly back and forth in his palm. He tied Cinders' reins to his own horse's saddle, then continued down the path.

Charlie tied himself to Cinder's saddle and leaned forward on her neck. It wasn't comfortable, but it was rest. His body ached, his head throbbed, and his mind raced. Charlie dozed for at least a half hour, listening to the sound of hooves on the path, the creak of the leather, and wondering what he would do if he woke to find Daniel was in league with Savaric all along.

One of the horses nickered, and Charlie's eyes shot open. He sat up, still transfixed between waking and sleeping and tried to move his legs. He fell forward and barely stopped himself from smacking his face into Cinder's leg before he realized he was still tied down. He had no idea how long he had been sleeping for. It was still pitch black, and both horses seemed tethered. He worked at undoing the rope tied around his middle and looked for Daniel's flame in the darkness.

He could see the faint glow of fire far off between the trees. Charlie dismounted and created his own flame. A branch snapped under his foot as he approached. Daniel's flame immediately extinguished, and Charlie could just make out that his hand was poised above the sword at his side.

"It's me," Charlie whispered. The air was still. Even the insects had long since ceased their calls in the dark. It seemed too quiet to use his normal voice. "Why have we stopped?"

Daniel, however, had no problem speaking in a normal tone. "We're very close to the Rill of Kelf. I didn't want to attempt an invasion at night. It's too dark. We can make camp until dawn. Then we strike." He picked up a small log and added it to those already tucked under his arm.

"But won't they see our fire?" Charlie asked.

"We aren't *that* close, Charlie." Daniel chuckled. He picked up another thin branch, then headed back to the horses. Charlie rolled his eyes and rubbed a spot on his back that had started aching when he fell asleep. Sure, *now* Daniel wanted to make camp and wait.

Daniel had already cleared a space across the path and collected stones to create a fire ring. The larger stones bore scorch marks, indicating they may have been used for such before. Daniel carefully arranged the logs and kindling, then used the flame in his hand to light the fire.

The two stared at the flames until one of the horses whinnied.

Daniel sighed loudly. "We'd best get the horses untacked. I hope that beck-and of yours packed you a bedroll, because I'm not sharing." He walked to his own horse and led him closer to the light. There, he unpacked the bedroll, a waterskin, and food before removing the horse's tack.

Charlie followed suit, leading Cinders beside Daniel's gelding. It was easier for him to remove the saddlebags to rummage through them. He was glad to see Phillippe had not disappointed him. The old man packed a thin, woven mat wrapped inside a wool blanket. There was cured meat, his favorite fruit tarts, and a large chunk of cheese wrapped in a waxy cloth. Charlie chuckled to himself as he unrolled the blanket beside the fire.

Daniel finished tying his horse to a nearby tree. He turned, saw Charlie's bedroll, and huffed, aggravated.

"Some beck-and, huh?" said Charlie with a grin.

Daniel stomped to his own bedroll and began laying it out. Charlie munched on a fruit tart and watched. Finally, when Daniel had settled in, Charlie held a tart out in his hand.

"Want one?" he asked.

Daniel looked from the tart to Charlie and back again. He swallowed and accepted the food.

"Thank you," he said, biting into it fiercely. "I suppose you're going to ask me about my magic then," he added through a mouthful of food.

Charlie took a drink from his waterskin. His mouth had suddenly become very dry. He wanted to. He had at least a dozen questions he'd thought of while resting.

"I figure you'll tell me when you're ready," he said. It was what his mother would have said. He hoped it was the right thing. If Daniel *was* in league with Savaric, he didn't want Daniel to know he suspected him. Charlie swallowed another mouthful of water, then folded the blanket around himself. He dared not look at Daniel's reaction, however, Charlie heard him sigh and settle into his own bedroll.

TWENTY-ONE
THE RILL OF KELF

DESPITE HAVING SLEPT ON CINDERS, Charlie fell asleep almost at once. He woke several times throughout the night, afraid he had heard footsteps or shouting. But Daniel and the horses rested peacefully.

It was the familiar birdsong high in the treetops that woke him. He turned over on his back and stared at the trees above. He could just make out a dark gray sky through a few of the branches. It was still extremely dark, but the glowing embers of the fire gave enough light that he could dress in fresh socks and look for more food.

He rummaged through his packs again and found a small sack labeled *Cinders*. It was full of grain and dried apples. Charlie took a handful and offered it to her.

He spent the next hour looking at the various treasures Phillippe had packed him, many of which he could not identify. A salve labeled *for burns* and a collection of wooden-handled metal picks wrapped in a leather case. Charlie thought it might be some kind of lock-picking kit, but he had no idea how to use it.

As the birds began singing louder, Daniel woke with a start. He sat upright and grabbed his head, his face contorted into a silent scream.

Charlie stared at him, frozen in shock before rushing to his side.

"Daniel. Daniel!" he said, shaking the young man. Daniel's pupils were dilated, and he started rocking back and forth. Seemingly out of options, Charlie smacked Daniel across the face as hard as he could. It didn't seem to faze him. Daniel rocked harder and faster.

"Daniel! Snap out of it!" Charlie cried, and he smacked Daniel across the face again. Daniel closed his mouth and shook his head. He blinked, and his pupils returned to normal. He grabbed his cheek where Charlie had hit him, slowly turning to the boy that leaned away in fear.

"Cold water usually works much better," he snapped. Charlie looked at the waterskin lying next to Daniel.

"Oops?" said Charlie. He shrugged and forced a smile.

Daniel shook his head. He threw his blanket off his legs and stood, nonchalant.

"What was that?" Charlie asked, hurrying to reassemble his bedroll.

"What?" Daniel whipped around, looking in every direction and listening.

"What happened to you? What was that?" Charlie had managed to get the bedroll tied, but it wasn't as compact as Phillippe had tied it.

Daniel rolled his eyes and continued towards a tall tree in front of him to relieve himself.

"It was a nightmare," he replied. "That's all."

"I've never seen a nightmare do that to someone," said Charlie.

Daniel returned to the fire ring rubbing his forehead and proceeded to pour the remainder of his waterskin on the fire.

"Most people don't make a habit of watching others sleep," he snapped. "And you can't imagine the things that happen in my dreams."

Lord Kharas had shown Charlie how to tack Cinders once. But for ease of speed, he'd had the stable hands and beck-ands do it. With a bit of help from Daniel, the mare was ready as soon as Daniel had finished with his own horse.

"Do you have a plan when we get to the... ralph, or whatever it is?" Charlie asked, swinging himself into the saddle stiffly.

"My vision did not provide anything," said Daniel. He tossed the stones he had used for the fire ring haphazardly and scattered the remainder of the dead fire with his boots.

"So you don't have a plan?" Charlie asked, turning Cinders back toward the path.

"There's no way to know how many people will be guarding Ailinn. We don't know if they have magic or not. There are too many variables to try to coordinate a plan."

"So what *did* this vision show you?" Charlie asked, growing more annoyed by the minute.

"I do believe we both survive," said Daniel, and he nudged his horse into a trot.

"Well, that's comforting." Charlie scoffed before following Daniel into what he was sure was certain death.

The Rill of Kelf was a small stream that Charlie could have jumped over with a running start, though there wouldn't have been a need. Several large stepping stones were placed across it, so a traveler could easily walk from one side to the other.

Charlie and Daniel dismounted and left their horses tied and ready to depart quickly if necessary. Quietly, they approached the rill, swords drawn and ready. The trees opened just before the bank dropped down. The two walked out and saw nothing.

Charlie blinked in the bright light. Morning had fully come, and it was the first time in several days that he had been in full sunlight.

"I don't understand," Daniel whispered. He looked up and down the little stream as Charlie lifted his face to bask in the sun. "They should have been here. My dream... I saw it!" He shoved his sword back into its sheath and grabbed his head.

"You okay?" Charlie asked. He set a hand on Daniel's shoulder, but it was just as quickly shrugged off.

"I'm fine!" Daniel snapped. "Come. Perhaps they're closer to the tributary."

They set out again, ducking back under the cover of the trees. Daniel had shown Charlie how to step quietly, leading with his toes and distributing the weight across his entire foot before lifting the next. Daniel was much faster at this technique, which left Charlie to make more noise than he would have liked.

They reached the Lesser Tributary within a half hour. By then, Charlie's legs were screaming in pain. Two smaller rivers and the Rill of Kelf converged before falling over a ten-foot waterfall.

Daniel emerged once again from the tree line, but there was no sign of a camp, current or bygone. He carefully picked his way down a set of makeshift steps along the bank made to walk beside the waterfall.

"Ailinn!" he called desperately. There was no answer. He waded into the river, searching the other side of the bank in the foam of the waterfall.

"They're not here," Charlie called to him.

"Perhaps we need to wait. They may not have passed this way yet," said Daniel, shouting above the noise of the waterfall. He began wading back to the bank when he stopped.

Charlie had seen it too. A shadow beneath the water crept out from behind the waterfall and was making its way toward Daniel.

"Run, Charlie," said Daniel calmly, but Charlie did not move. Daniel looked at him, his eyes sharp with fear. He drew his sword and shouted, "Run!"

Water sprayed over Daniel as a gray and green serpent rose from the depths. It continued to push itself out of the water, slowly rising into the sky until it towered over Daniel. Its eyes were solid black, dilated to see in the murk of the water. Gills flared behind its ears and neck. It rattled its gills, making a hissing sound. Its forked tongue flicked in the air before it opened its mouth, and Charlie watched its fangs drop from its pale gums.

The snake lunged at Daniel. He dodged it, but he was slower in the water than the snake. He hurried toward the bank of the river, never taking his eyes from the serpent that twisted back around to lunge again.

"Get out of here!" Daniel screamed when he noticed Charlie was still frozen in place.

Once again, fear had overtaken him. Charlie couldn't move. His feet were glued to the ground. He couldn't even reach for his blade. His heart pounded in his chest. Every fiber of his being wanted him to run. His mind screamed louder than Daniel for him to run, but he couldn't.

Daniel tripped on something in the water, and the serpent hissed louder. His sword plunged into the rushing waters and was lost beneath the foam.

Charlie thought he heard the serpent laugh as it rattled its gills again. Slowly, it twisted its body around Daniel beneath the water. With a final jerk, the creature pulled itself taut around Daniel and lifted him from the water. Charlie saw Daniel straining against the serpent's grip.

Its tongue tasted the air around Daniel. It seemed to be studying him. It squeezed even tighter, then threw Daniel toward the bank. Daniel slammed against a tree, his head snapping back before he fell several feet to the ground, unconscious.

"No!" Charlie screamed.

The creature whipped its head around and rattled its gills again. Somewhere, a fire burned inside Charlie, starting in his chest and spreading outward. He ripped his sword from its sheath and charged down the steps to the bank.

Before he had made it halfway, he was sent flying. The serpent had smacked him with his tail, sending Charlie tumbling head over heels down the rest of the steps. He landed hard on his wrist but ignored the pain.

The serpent's tongue was searching out scents again. It seemed to have found something familiar. It hissed even more fiercely, and Charlie saw its left fang drop a little lower.

He hurried to his feet and picked up his sword. "Where's Ailinn? Where is Savaric?" he yelled.

He had no idea if the creature understood him, but at the mention of Savaric's name, it hissed and lunged. Charlie was ready. He stepped to the side, bringing his blade down with all his strength on the serpent's face. This time, he heard it growl. It pulled back, ready to strike again.

An image flashed in Charlie's mind. He stumbled back and almost dropped his sword.

What he saw was not the serpent before him. The scene was blurry and seemed to be in a different spectrum of light or heat.

A figure carrying a large, black stone entered the cave behind the waterfall. Charlie could hear the hiss of the serpent, but it felt like the sound had come from him. Suddenly, his body was wracked with pain like he'd never experienced before. He cried out, but not in his own voice.

For days the stranger returned, forcing its will upon him—upon the serpent. Each time he was somehow subdued, unable to defend himself and then tortured repeatedly.

When Charlie finally broke free of the thought, he opened his eyes and saw the creature towering above him. It had covered its eyes with a protective, red membrane, giving it the look of having cried blood. It looked down at Charlie, and he noticed it had coiled its body close to him to keep his head from going under the water.

Against every instinct in his body, Charlie threw his sword as far from him as he could. The serpent hissed and tasted the air. Charlie held his hands out, palms up, and tried to make his energies calm and compassionate.

"It wasn't me," he whispered.

The serpent's blood-red membranes flicked back and forth, and its tongue moved more vivaciously.

"How can I help you?" Charlie asked, pushing himself to stand again.

The creature dove back into the water and swam behind the waterfall. Any normal person would have taken the opportunity to run. Charlie thought about doing so. He needed to see if Daniel was still alive. But an instinct within him told him to follow the serpent.

Behind the falling water was an alcove just large enough for the serpent to curl up in. It hissed a warning with its gills as Charlie approached. He stopped and held out his hands again. The serpent quieted, and Charlie watched as it wrapped itself around a large rock.

Another image flashed into his mind. A figure ripping a scale from the serpent. The creature was aware of everything—the person, the pain, but it could not move. The stranger placed the serpent's scale on the rock and struck it with a large, black stone.

The image faded from Charlie's mind as quickly as it had come. He looked at the creature in front of him and how it wrapped itself around the rock. At first, he had no idea what he had seen, or what he was supposed to do. Then a feeling rose in his chest. It was sadness, grief, and longing. It was the feelings Charlie had almost every night when he thought of his home and his family.

"They trapped you here, didn't they?" he asked the serpent.

Its gills were flat now, and its mouth was closed. It looked so different from the menace that had almost killed him minutes before.

"I don't know what to do," Charlie whispered. Someone must have used a type of magic he was not familiar with.

The serpent uncoiled itself from the rock and moved closer to Charlie. He remained still. The serpent's head was as big as his entire body. It swam before him, its eyes level with his own. As it moved its body closer, Charlie saw a red patch along the creature's side where the scale had been ripped away.

The serpent flicked its tongue again, then turned and headed back to the boulder.

This time, Charlie followed and set a hand on the rock. Despite the damp cold of the little cave, the stone was warm. He reached another hand out for the snake. It gave a soft warning hiss but allowed Charlie to touch it.

Charlie closed his eyes and reached out with his magic. He could feel the scale imbedded in the rock, and the sharp sting of another kind of magic. He ignored the pain and forced himself to concentrate harder. Carefully, he felt for the components that made up the scale, identifying new materials he had never worked with before. When he thought he had found every piece of the scale, he moved it back onto the serpent's body.

The creature hissed, and Charlie nearly pulled his hand away. He had never worked with something that was alive before. He hoped he wasn't hurting it too much. The sharp stabs of the unfamiliar magic made his arm that touched the rock go numb. When the last remnants of the scale had been pulled from the rock, Charlie opened his eyes and collapsed across the stone.

The serpent twisted and writhed, submerging itself in the cool water. It turned back to Charlie, coming eye level with him again. It flicked its red membrane across its eyes again, then plunged itself into the water and disappeared.

TWENTY-TWO
THE GLASS LANTERN

CHARLIE WADED ACROSS THE TRIBUTARY and collapsed on the bank. He looked up and saw Daniel still lying at the base of a tree, unmoving. Charlie pushed himself to his feet and ran to him.

"Daniel!" he cried breathless, falling to his knees and shaking him.

Daniel stirred, and Charlie saw blood clotted in his hair with more seeping through the back of his tunic at his shoulder.

"Cannon—" Daniel began, but his eyes closed, and his head dropped to his chest.

"No, Daniel," said Charlie, pulling him upright. "You have to stay with me. I need you to wake up."

Daniel stirred again, groaning and reaching for his head. "Follow the main road," he whispered, his eyes fluttering for a moment. They rolled back, and Daniel was unconscious again.

Charlie looked around, hoping for some sign of what to do next. He held Daniel in his arms, his eyes searching from one tree to the next. For the first time since coming to Chartile, he was completely on his own. He laid Daniel gently on the ground and searched for his sword.

Using small sticks and branches, Charlie marked his path back to the waterfall. He didn't want to risk Ailinn's captors stumbling across the trail by being too obvious and carving Xs into trees or something. He found the horses with little effort and rode back along the path he had created.

At the edge of the bank, Charlie halted the horses and swung his legs over to dismount. A sharp jolt of pain shot up Charlie's wrist. He hissed through his teeth, pressing his wrist against his chest. He had forgotten he had hurt it during his fight with... whatever that thing was. It was beginning to swell. Cinders nudged his shoulder as though she sensed something was wrong. He patted her neck and reached for the grain bag Phillippe had packed. He grabbed a handful and fed it to the horse.

"I'm sorry, girl," he whispered, and he reached out with his mind until he could sense Cinders' thoughts. The horse whipped her head back and tried to pull away. Charlie wrapped his thoughts around her own, trying to calm her. Cinders' eyes rolled, and she stamped the ground.

Charlie wasn't sure how long it took. Probably too long. Eventually, Cinders calmed and gave in to Charlie's will, lowering herself to the ground. He offered her another handful of grain, but the mare refused it.

Charlie pulled Daniel toward Cinders and heaved him onto the saddle, strapping him on with the same rope he'd used last night. He clicked his tongue, and Cinders got to her feet, clearly unhappy with her unconscious rider. But Charlie didn't want to risk using his magic on Daniel's horse. He had a relationship with Cinders, even if it mostly involved him bouncing on her back and ending up spread-eagle on the ground. She trusted him, and he hoped she still would after all this.

Charlie pulled himself into the saddle of Daniel's gelding and made for the main road. The trees passed by in a blur, and Charlie's wrist throbbed harder. He needed to get Daniel help and fast. But Ailinn was still out there. If Daniel was working for Savaric, this may have been the plan all along. A ploy to keep Charlie from getting too close. A trap to... to kill him. Charlie shuddered at the thought of the serpent's fangs sinking into his flesh, and his wrist throbbed again. Charlie turned up the main road and headed back in the direction he hoped was toward the palace.

They could travel faster by daylight and on the wider main road. He had been stupid, utterly and completely stupid to believe he could chase down Ailinn's captors in the pitch blackness of the Belirian forest, and with the one person who seemed to hate him more than Savaric. He only hoped it wasn't too late to save her.

They rounded a corner, and Charlie saw the river turn away from the road. There was a break in the trees, and he found himself heading into the heart of a bustling town. People stared as he rode past. Charlie ignored them. There had to be some sign for a hospital or doctor or someone who could help. When his eyes landed on the sign for The Glass Lantern, his heart skipped a beat.

His father had told him about this place. Dimitri had come here looking for a way to sneak into the Lord of Cannondole's manor. If this was Cannondole, then this was where Ailinn's grandfather, Valar, lived.

Charlie pulled the horses to a stop beside the inn. He untied Daniel and watched his unconscious body slide precariously toward the ground. He tried to hook his good arm under Daniel's shoulder and felt someone else grab Daniel's other side. Charlie looked up into the gray-blue eyes of Merrick. He looked sternly at Charlie, then led the way into The Glass Lantern.

The main room was dim, lit only by two chandeliers filled with small candles. The few patrons sitting at the scrubbed wooden tables stared as Merrick and Charlie carried Daniel through the door.

"This is Prince Daniel. He is injured and needs help," Charlie breathed.

The room fell even more silent.

"That may not have been wise—" Merrick began, but his words were cut short in the clatter of plates and mugs that were knocked to the floor. A stretch of table was laid bare, and several burly men stepped forward to relieve Charlie and Merrick, placing Daniel on the table.

A curvy woman bustled out from behind the counter carrying a bowl and towels.

"Oi, now!" She scolded the men who had knocked the dishes to the floor. "What'd you mean by making a mess of my tavern room? You could have put the plates on the other table."

"I'm sorry, Addie," said one of the men, and he leaned down to pick up a now empty tankard of ale.

The woman slapped his backside with one of her towels. "Leave it. All of you. Ronan, be a love and go fetch my husband. Now, all of you, get out! The prince don't need you fussing over him when you don't even know what to do." She swatted a few more men with her towel as they made their way for the door.

"What about my soup?" one of them asked.

The woman glared at him, and the man's shoulders drooped as he turned to leave with the rest of the patrons. She pulled a large bolt shut across the door, then bustled through a door behind the counter before hurry back to Daniel. With quick, experienced fingers, she placed a towel under his head and removed his tunic. Merrick and Charlie stood by, watching in silence.

"One of you pass me that bowl," she demanded, ripping a stack of fabric into strips. Merrick handed her the bowl she had brought with her from the back. It was filled with a kind of green goo that smelled faintly of Charlie's great-grandmother's perfume. The woman heaved Daniel into a sitting position and wiped the blood from his shoulder. She scooped a glob of the green goo onto her fingers and smeared it on Daniel's back before wrapping him with the strips of fabric.

"He hurt his head too," said Charlie, pointing with his throbbing hand.

The woman's eyes lingered for a moment on his swollen wrist. She gently laid Daniel back, then reached for Charlie's arm. She grabbed him firmly by the elbow and lifted his arm so she could inspect his wrist.

"I don't think it's broken," she said. She took off behind the counter again and began filling another bowl with plants and water. When she brought it back, she set the bowl by Daniel's feet and pulled up a chair.

"Sit," she ordered, pointing at the chair. "Soak it in the water. It'll help with the pain."

Without missing a beat, she turned back to Daniel and began cleaning the wound on his head.

Charlie collapsed into the chair and placed his hand and wrist in the cool water.

"Anything more I should know about?" she asked as she cleaned up the bloody towels and leftover green goo.

Charlie felt Merrick's eyes turn to him but kept his own fixated on the plants floating in the water around his wrist.

"With the war, my lady, I do not think it wise to turn good help into an enemy," Merrick finally said. "But there are no more injuries that we are aware of."

The woman huffed and took off through a door behind the bar.

Merrick pulled up another chair beside Charlie.

"Care to tell me what happened?" he asked.

"Care to tell me how you just happened to end up here at the same time as us?" Charlie snapped. He removed his wrist from the water and wrapped it in one of the clean towels the woman had left. It wasn't as swollen, but it was beginning to throb again.

Merrick sighed. "I've been following you."

"Why didn't you say anything?" Charlie asked, still seething with anger. He could have used back up against that serpent. Had Merrick just stood on the banks and watched?

"Several hours after Ailinn was kidnapped, my father demanded he be released. He had proven all his guards were accounted for, and that it could not have been him. He wanted to leave and stay with one of his friends in Sparrowmoore. King Valin had no reason to continue to hold Savaric, and he needed as many guards as possible to search for Ailinn. When my father left, I told him I would stay and send word if there were any new developments."

"You left him by himself?" It was the loudest Charlie had been since arriving. "After everything we've tried to do to figure out what he's up to, you decide to leave him on his own to follow us?"

"My father and I have been growing more distant the last several years. It would have been suspicious for me to go with him," said Merrick, countering Charlie's anger with hushed tones. "Lord Kharas did not advise leaving my father alone, either, but I see why Valin did so. At any rate, when I saw my father leaving, I also saw Kashna flying in the same direction. Daniel never mentioned anything, and I found it very odd. I approached Lord Kharas, as I knew he was one of your friends. He told me you and Daniel had left to track Ailinn's captors. I left immediately and followed the fresh tracks. Shortly after the lanterns ended, I found two sets of tracks converge, but the tracks I suspected to be you and Daniel did not follow. I found your camp farther up the road. I heard horses on the road ahead of me and followed. I saw it was you but kept my distance. When I noticed Daniel was unconscious, I knew something must have gone wrong."

Charlie set the towel he had been using to dry his hand on the table before him. He rubbed his eyes and felt the ache of exhaustion set in to every muscle in his body.

"Something *did* go wrong. Everything's gone wrong! And now Kashna's working with Savaric?"

Merrick nodded. "It would appear so."

"I know Kashna can manipulate people's minds," said Charlie. "I've seen him do it. He... he even taught me how to do it." Charlie swallowed and rubbed his wrist. "If Kashna has been working with Savaric, that explains how Savaric knew everything. It explains Daniel's vision too."

"Vision?" Merrick asked.

Charlie nodded. "Yeah, Daniel said he had a vision. He said he knew exactly where to find Ailinn and the people who kidnapped her. He said he saw us fighting. But we went to the Rill of... of whatever, and no one was there. No one but a giant snake that tried to kill us."

Merrick scratched at the stubble on his chin. "If Kashna can manipulate our minds, he very well may have planted this vision for Daniel and intended to lead you to your death."

"Maybe that's why he gets headaches. Ailinn told me Daniel used to get headaches. He told her they got better after Savaric came, but I don't know if I believe it." Charlie sighed. All he wanted to do was sleep. His body ached, his own head hurt, and he had failed at the one mission he had been sent to Chartile for.

"If you picked up the tracks that belonged to Ailinn's kidnappers, then I bet the palace guards have found them by now."

"I don't think so," said Merrick. He rose from his chair and began pacing, his hands clasped behind his back. "The reason I continued to follow your trail instead of Ailinn's is that it stopped. I believe someone used magic to hide it. If we abandon our quest now, Ailinn may be lost forever, and my father will learn that we suspect the link between Daniel's health issues and Kashna. We risk putting both of their lives in danger."

"So you're saying we need to find a way to pick up a magically hidden trail, and find a guy who's probably half-insane, has other magic users working for him, and has a telepathic flying panther. Yeah, that's sounds like a genius idea." Charlie leaned back in his chair and let his head fall back. He sighed again and stared at the flickering candles in the chandelier above him.

"Do you have any other recommendations?" Merrick asked.

"We could help you," said a man's voice.

Merrick and Charlie looked up. The curvy woman stood in the doorway she had left by, a gruff-looking man at her side.

The woman stepped toward them, stopping beside Daniel. She placed a hand over the wound on his head. Her palm glowed faintly for a moment before she removed it. She unwound the bandage around Daniel's head, and Charlie saw the wound had completely healed.

"Brock, I think our guests could use some time to think about this. Would you mind taking the lad upstairs and helping them unpack their horses?" the woman said. She did not look at Charlie or Merrick.

"'Course, dear," said the man. He lifted Daniel from the table with ease, and Merrick followed close behind as he headed for a staircase they had not noticed before.

"May I see your wrist again?" the woman asked, stopping Charlie before he rose from his chair to follow. She smiled warmly at him and held out her calloused hand. "My name is Atana Garrison. You can call me Addie. And that's my husband, Brodrick. He's the seneschal here in Cannondole, appointed by the king himself. 'Afore he was king, mind you."

Charlie held out his hand to Addie. He fought the urge to pull away when he felt the woman's magic reach into his flesh and bone.

"It's not broken," she said. "But you have strained it. I can reduce the swelling, but it would take too long to repair the damage inside the muscle. I will do my best, but you need to rest it."

Charlie felt his wrist turn cold, as he watched Addie. Her face was gentle, and the lines around her mouth and eyes seemed to disappear while she worked her magic. When she had finished, she smiled and helped Charlie to his feet.

Brock and Merrick were coming back down the stairs as Addie guided Charlie toward it.

"If you two can handle the horses, this boy needs a hot meal and a long rest," she said, then she followed Charlie up the stairs. She led him down a narrow hall with several doors Charlie assumed were bedrooms for the guests. She opened the door to one of the rooms. There were two small beds with Daniel lying unconscious in one.

"Is he going to be okay?" Charlie asked.

"I believe so," said Addie. She turned down the sheets and blanket on the bed across from Daniel. "His wound was not severe, but if what you say is true, he's fighting more demons in that mind than we can scarcely imagine."

"He told me he has nightmares. He wakes up screaming. I think it has to do with Kashna and Savaric. Do you know how to put a block on his mind or something?" Charlie asked.

Addie shook her head. "I know some magic as I taught myself. I learned about herbs and healing the body from Mathilda, the healing woman and my sister, Almara. Ally took over after Mathilda died a few years back. But I don't know about putting up blocks or anything of the like."

Charlie nodded. He tried to pull his boots off but cried out when he twisted his wrist. Addie knelt on the floor, pulling each boot off and setting them neatly beside the bed.

"Why do you want to help us?" Charlie asked.

"Because that bastard Savaric has my son." Addie's gentle face turned hard, and her light brown eyes became cold. She looked at Charlie for a moment, and he thought he saw tears begin to shine against her eyes. She turned away and closed the door behind her.

TWENTY-THREE
MOTHERS AND MERSPEECH

ADDIE AND BROCK INSISTED THAT Charlie, Daniel, and Merrick remain out of sight. They even took their meals in their room, which was now extremely cramped.

Word of the incident had spread. Even the Sisters of the Chantry came seeking an audience with Daniel hoping to hear news of what the crown was doing to sate the situation regarding the rebels. Brock and Atana insisted the whole incident had been a false alarm. Weary and injured travelers who hoped to get help sooner by posing as royalty. It had worked, and they were now paying a rather large sum for the inconvenience. Everyone who had been in the tavern that night was offered a free ale and soup. Addie said it was paid for by the three travelers, but truly she would not accept any coin from them.

Daniel woke the next morning, the light shining through the shutters nearly blinding him as he had grown accustom to the darkness of the palace deep in the Belirian Forest. Charlie was pulling on his boots when he saw Daniel sit up, and he accidentally kicked Merrick's sleeping pallet in the process. Merrick's eyes shot open. He sat up as well, his eyes flitting back and forth between Charlie and Daniel.

Daniel stiffened and finally seemed to take in his surroundings.

"I believe I've missed something," he said.

Charlie tried to stifle a laugh but couldn't. He guffawed so loud, he worried the patrons in the tavern below would hear him. He clasped his hands to his mouth, but the laughter wouldn't stop. It was the first time he had laughed in a long time.

Red faced and out of breath, he answered, "You could say that."

"I don't see what's so amusing about this," said Merrick and he frowned at Charlie, who was still chuckling.

"It's *not* amusing. None of it is. I think that's why it's so funny," said Charlie.

Merrick and Daniel looked at each other, neither seeming to understand Charlie's amusement.

"What are you doing here?" Daniel asked, turning to Merrick and leaving Charlie to figure out his hiccups.

"I was attempting to pick up the trail to Ailinn's captors when I saw Charlie headed for town and I followed," said Merrick.

"I killed the serpent," Charlie lied. "You were hurt pretty bad. I thought I was heading back to the palace, but I ended up here instead."

"Here?" Daniel asked.

"Cannondole," Merrick answered.

"Cannondole?" Daniel asked. "Is this my grandfather's house?"

Merrick shook his head. "No. It was important to keep our identities a secret in case my father had spies set here. We're in The Glass Lantern."

"A lot of good that does us now," Charlie mumbled.

"I must see my grandfather at once," said Daniel. He tried to stand but immediately sat again, holding his head.

"It's too dangerous," said Merrick, rising from his pallet and resting a hand on Daniel's shoulder. "Brock can arrange sending him a letter, but we need to leave tonight and continue after my father."

Daniel shook his head, his hand still over his forehead. "I hate when I can't remember things," he said. "Do we know yet where they've taken Ailinn?"

"We have a pretty good idea," Charlie lied again. Merrick shot him a confused look, but Charlie ignored him. He stood and pulled on a thin cord that ran through a tiny hole in the floor.

"Rest for now," said Merrick. "There is little we can do until nightfall."

"But we need to leave immediately!" said Daniel. "Ailinn—"

"He won't kill her. I'm sure of it," Merrick said, holding up a hand to silence him. "How else would I become king? He is using her for something else. What, I do not know, but she will be alive when we find her. Rest easy."

There was a knock on the door. Charlie carefully stepped over Merrick's pallet and opened it.

Addie stood in the hall holding a tray of food. She squeezed her way in as the door would only open halfway due to the sleeping pallet.

"You're awake," she said to Daniel. "Good. Let me have a look at you."

Addie shuffled her way toward Daniel. She sat on the edge of the bed and reached for the bandage over his shoulder wound. Daniel pulled back.

"I beg your—who are—?" he stammered.

"My name is Atana, but you can call me Addie. You'll remember my husband, Brodrick. He's seneschal here, appointed by your father."

"They're all right, Daniel," said Merrick gently. "They're with us."

Daniel allowed Addie to check his wound, though his body never relaxed. He watched her carefully, his dark eyes as harsh as Charlie remembered them when they'd first met.

"Oh, that looks much better," she said, pulling the strips of cloth back. Charlie saw a lighter brown, almost pink marking across Daniel's shoulder blade. If anyone had seen it, they would have guessed it had been healing for weeks. In truth, Addie had called on her sister, who'd used her own magic on Daniel after the boys had settled into their rooms.

Daniel shrugged his shirt back over his shoulder and pulled away. "Thank you, madam," he said stiffly.

Addie sighed loudly. "Well, I brought you some soup and bread. Eat up and rest. I've told the workers my father-in-law has fallen ill, and I need to visit him. Brock is finishing the preparations for our departure tonight."

"Thank you, Atana," said Merrick, inclining his head to her.

"Could you have a message sent to Lord Valar?" Charlie asked quickly.

Addie furrowed her brow. "Of course. I could send Brock to deliver it today."

"Wait," said Daniel, "*our* departure?"

Silence fell in the room. The only sound was the creaking of the bed as Daniel turned to stare at Charlie and Merrick.

"We hadn't decided yet," said Charlie, casting a sheepish look at the woman poised beside the door.

"Decided what?" Daniel demanded.

"If Brodrick and Atana are joining us," said Merrick.

"Joining—how many more people have you told of our plan? Should we alert the town crier and announce our intentions to the whole of Chartile?"

"Daniel, we can't do everything by ourselves," said Charlie, sitting on his bed in a huff.

"We need allies if we are to bring this war to an end," said Merrick gently.

Daniel reached for his forehead again and winced.

"I promise you, we have no ill intentions toward you," Addie reassured. "I just want my son back, and if that means saving the princess, then we'll save her as well."

"What... What happened to your son?" Charlie asked.

Addie removed her hand from the doorknob. She straightened her shoulders and turned to face the room again.

"I suppose it's only fair you know," she said. She cracked her knuckles and took a deep breath. "Three years ago, Bastian, my son, and I were collecting herbs for me sister. She'd just taken over as our healer, and half the town had fallen ill with blood lung. We'd heard about several children being kidnapped from some of the neighboring towns. So when I heard someone coming, I used my magic to hide us."

She swallowed but did not break her stare. "But Bastian, the little bur. I suppose I only have myself to blame, what with teaching him to look after others. A little girl from town must have wandered off. He saw her and darted out of the protective circle I had made. He had only just grabbed her and set her in my arms when the men came. Those bastards tore out of the trees so fast, they had him before I could do anything."

This time, she did look away. She wiped the tears in her eyes and blew her nose on a handkerchief she'd produced from the pocket of her skirts.

"I ran to him. I watched as they used magic to put him to sleep. I tried to scream, but I couldn't. I tried to get to him, but I couldn't move. My legs were like stone, and the more I tried, the more my body stopped moving. They looked right at me, *right at me*. They knew Bastian was mine. They tossed him over their shoulders and walked off with my boy. When their magic wore off, I ran back to town. I told everyone who would listen that Bastian had been taken. We looked—every person in Cannondole. Even Lord Valar took his horse into the forest. No one could find a trail anywhere.

"So I asked Ally for our mother's scrying mirror. When I used it, I saw my boy in the back of a wagon, still sleeping. The two men who had taken him were talking to another man. And when that man turned, I saw him. It was Savaric as the stars in the sky shine. But I couldn't tell anyone what I saw. Magic is outlawed, including my mother's mirror.

"I told Brock, of course, and he rode to Harpy's Pointe. Lord Savaric wasn't in residence and they turned him away. Brock sat outside that door for days, pounding and screaming. When he came back, his hands were bloodied and bruised, and his left one was broken. We tried to confide in the few people we knew who had magic, but no one would believe us. Savaric had begun helping the cause to have magic made legal again. He wouldn't have a reason to kidnap a young boy."

"Surely, there were others who suspected my fa—Lord Savaric. Why not come to the king?" Merrick asked.

Addie smiled gently. "People like us don't get an audience with the king, my lord." She blew her nose again and cleared her throat. "Bastian has the gift of magic. That's why they took him. I don't know how they knew it, but I know that's why. If we find the children, I would bet my last pint every one of them has the gift. Savaric might be punished, but so would my Bastian and all the other children."

Charlie didn't speak for several long moments. He clenched his teeth together so tight his jaw hurt. "How do you know he's still alive?" he finally dared to ask.

Addie turned to him. The tears were gone now, replaced with the kind gaze they had become familiar with. "A mother knows these things. No matter how long he's been gone, or how far away, I know."

Daniel leaned forward and grabbed his head.

"I'll bring you some tea for that headache, your Highness," she said, her tone also returning to its gentle insistence.

"There's no need. It won't help," said Daniel.

Addie looked over her shoulder, her eyebrows raised.

"Is that so? You've never had one of Addie's Adler Mind Mender teas then. I'll be back in just a moment. When would you like me to send your letter?"

"We'll let you know when it's ready," said Charlie, his voice quieter than he expected.

"I'll leave you in peace, then," she said as she closed the door quietly behind her.

They waited until her footfalls had faded down the hall.

"We have to help them get their son back," said Charlie.

Daniel tried to stand again, but his headache seemed to keep him down. "We can't save everyone, Charlie!" he spat. "Right now, Ailinn is our priority. We can't afford two tagalong peasants who only care about themselves. It's too risky."

There was a knock on the door again and Addie entered with a cup of tea.

"Here you are, Highness," she said, handing him the tea. "Now, I won't lie, it tastes terrible, but it helps."

"Thank you," said Daniel. He took the tea and set it on the table between the two beds.

Addie smiled at him, her hands clasped before her. "You know, Brock helped your father once. Your real father, that is."

The pain on Daniel's face was instantly replaced with shock. Addie immediately held up her hands. "Oh, it's all right, your Highness. Everyone knows. We don't think no less of you. But I just wanted to say it, if it means anything to you. We may be peasants, as you say, but we're good folk here. I do want my son home, but I have a care for the princess as well. I wouldn't want to see anyone harmed by that gorkin bastard of a man. You think on it and drink your tea now."

Addie quietly left the room, leaving Daniel with a look of shock still plastered across his face.

"Well, there ya go," said Charlie with a devilish smirk.

"There is one thing I want to discuss in private," said Merrick, cutting across whatever retort Daniel was about to make. He reached for his bag and produced a large tome from its depths.

"Is that what I think it is?" Charlie asked, knocking into Daniel's knees in his haste to get a closer look. Merrick tentatively handed Charlie the book. It was lighter than he'd expected. It was bound in a smooth, silver metal and engraved with strange symbols that looked haphazardly placed.

Merrick nodded. "It is. I haven't had much time yet to read it, but I think it may produce some answers."

Charlie opened the book, and the same haphazard lettering was scrawled across the pages alongside drawings of plants, animals, even machines that would have rivaled Leonardo da Vinci.

"You're wasting your time," Daniel quipped, bringing Charlie back to the conversation at hand. "As soon as we find Ailinn, I know Savaric's plans will be made clear."

"There may be clues in this thing that could help us rescue her," Charlie protested.

Daniel shook his head and turned away from the pair. "Suit yourself," he muttered. He lifted the cup of tea to his lips and slurped a taste.

"Urgh! This *is* awful!" he cried.

Both Merrick and Charlie stifled laughs, though Daniel didn't notice.

Charlie cleared his throat. "I'm going to spend some time with Cinders. Give her a good brushing out," he said. "Addie said there's usually no one downstairs during the day." He nodded at Merrick and hoped he understood the intention he tried to send. He gathered his cloak and closed the door behind him.

Charlie crept down the wooden stair. He peeked through the railings and saw the room was indeed empty. He could hear Addie humming to herself in the kitchen below and smelled something cooking on the stove. He headed for the door hidden under the stair and through to the stables.

The stable was larger than Charlie had expected. There were at least ten large stalls, enough for two horses each if necessary. Cinders was nose-deep in a trough of hay when Charlie approached.

"Hey, girl," he said.

The horse lifted her head at his voice and hurried to the stall door.

"Do you forgive me then?" he asked and stroked her velvet nose. "I'm sorry about yesterday. I didn't know what else to do."

Cinders dropped a mouthful of hay on Charlie's head as she nipped at his hair. Charlie laughed and grabbed a brush from a little bucket of tools in the aisle. Cinders returned to her hay as Charlie began a thorough brushing. It wasn't long before he heard the stable door open and close.

Merrick grabbed a brush from the bucket as well and joined Charlie in Cinders' stall. The horse nickered at the attention when Merrick took up brushing out her other side.

"I can't believe you stole that book!" Charlie whispered.

"It wasn't by choice," Merrick whispered back. "I had broken into my father's room while he was entertaining one of the Conclave nobles in the common room. I heard one of the guards come to the door and tell my father someone had kidnapped the princess. I knew he'd come into his room immediately. There wasn't time for me to arrange the book back at the bottom of the trunk. I took it with me and hurried back to my room before he knew I had been in there."

"Do you think he knows it's missing?"

"I'm sure of it," said Merrick matter-of-factly. "He reads it every day."

"Well, we have it now, I guess. What are we going to do with it?"

Merrick knelt and began picking stones out of Cinders' hooves. "It will take me some time to sift through everything. I haven't read Merspeech or Draconian in a long time. But I found several pages on joining minds that looked well read."

Charlie stopped brushing. He bent to look at Merrick beneath Cinders' belly and the horse immediately smacked Charlie in the back of the head with her jaw.

"What did they say?" Charlie asked, pushing Cinders' head away and massaging the lump rising on the back of his head.

"It was… disturbing to say the least. There were many species of old that could join minds. Willingly, of course. It's said the dragons did not even communicate through a spoken language but projected their thoughts through your mind."

Merrick stood and glanced into the aisle beyond. The stables were still and silent save for the stamping and munching of the horses.

"When you start to join more than one being together, it can cause problems. Especially with whoever is the… *anchor*, is the best translation. The Merfolk were seafarers. We took over most of their towns along the river when they disappeared. Their speech is full of water and nautical references, with many different meanings depending on the context. Draconian is even more complicated."

"But this anchor-thing. What kind of problems did it refer to?"

Merrick closed his eyes. "It's complicated. It spoke of the unraveling of the minds. It said the farthest links were the first to go. I don't know what that means."

"Did it say anything about symptoms?"

Merrick shook his head. "It doesn't appear to be a medical book, unfortunately."

The two brushed Cinders in silence, both of their minds racing. Charlie thought of Daniel and Kashna's connection, and he wondered which of them could be the anchor. He thought about how he had joined minds with the snake. Had it been the snake forcing its visions onto Charlie? No, the thing had definitely wanted to kill him. But then it would mean Charlie had forced the snake to connect with him. Forced or asked, Charlie wasn't sure, but he felt his stomach sink like a stone at the thought.

"Did it mention anything about water snakes?" Charlie asked.

Merrick furrowed his brow. "I can't say I've seen anything yet. Why?"

"Daniel's vision. He said he knew where they had taken Ailinn. I'm pretty sure Kashna sent him that vision. I think he was trying to kill us, or me at least."

Merrick leaned across Cinders' back. "What happened?"

This time, Charlie checked for any listeners in the stable. "There was this huge snake. Like a water serpent. It was as big as a tree, I swear!"

Merrick's eyes widened. "A Lyndormn?" he asked with an excited whisper.

Charlie shrugged. "I don't know. What's that?"

"An ancient creature. One of the Lost Legends. It's said one of the foals of the Silver Unicorn refused to leave the sea foam after it had grown. So the creator punished it, taking it's legs so it could never walk on land again and banished it to the depths of the Deep of Tomorrow."

"Maybe," said Charlie. "I don't know anything about that. We have lost legends on Earth too. Well, kind of. Some people don't believe they really exist or ever did at all. But, anyway, I connected with it, like Kashna taught me. Someone had done something to it, something really bad. They used magic to sort of bind the snake to that place, to keep it from leaving."

"How do you know this?" Merrick asked, his eyes widening the more Charlie spoke.

"I saw it. I *felt* it. When I was joined with the snake, I guess, but not permanently or anything. I don't think so, anyway. Someone came into that cave and tortured the thing for days. Then they ripped off one of its scales and… it's complicated. The point is, I freed the thing. It's not under Savaric or whoever's control anymore."

Merrick rubbed his chin and leaned into Cinders more. The horse stamped her foot, nearly smashing the young man's toe. He stood straight and tossed his brush into the bucket in the aisle.

"I can look, but I think you're right that someone was trying to kill you. I only hope it wasn't my father."

The door to the stables opened and slammed closed. Charlie tossed his brush into the bucket as well, and Merrick quickly exited the stall.

"I'll be back later," Charlie whispered to Cinders, and he snuck her a piece of sugar he had nicked from the tea tray that morning. He closed the stall door behind him and found Merrick locked in conversation with Brock. The man was tall and broad, and he had the look of someone who had worked hard labor most of his life. His brown hair was thinning at the temples, but his beard was full and streaked with gray.

"I'm afraid Lord Valar is not here," said Brock as Charlie approached.

"Where is he?" Charlie asked.

Brock smiled beneath his bushy beard. "It's nothing like that. He's off visiting the baron of Red Grove a few towns over. Doing what he can to reassure the nobles that Chartile ain't falling apart at the seams. Ruddy lie, but eh. Helps keep the peace, I suppose."

"Daniel won't be happy," said Charlie.

"Is he ever?" Merrick asked with a grin.

TWENTY-FOUR
REFLECTIONS

IT WAS RATHER BORING WAITING in the cramped room all day for nightfall. Charlie unpacked his saddlebags and repacked them at least four times. Merrick occupied himself by throwing a small dagger at the wall until Addie scolded him for ruining the wood when she brought them lunch. He then turned his attention to his father's book, occasionally pronouncing a word out loud or scribbling a note on a piece of paper.

Daniel was quiet. He tossed and turned in his bed, alternating between staring at the ceiling and out the little window. He seemed more than just uncomfortable to Charlie and Merrick, though neither dared mention it. He seemed lost, and Charlie wondered how long he had ever been away from Kashna. They dared not tell him that his best friend had sided with the enemy.

Night fell more slowly in the town of Cannondole. Like many of the Elven towns, the trees had been cleared away, leaving the sky above open. Charlie, Daniel, and Merrick seemed to count the minutes to when the moon had fully risen and the last of the tavern patrons stumbled home. Addie knocked on the door, and they jumped to gather their things. They crept quietly through the inn, bags slung over their shoulders, heading for the stables.

Brock was already there and had finished tacking three of the horses.

"You'll have to saddle your gelding yourself, Lord Daniel," he said. "He won't let me near him."

Daniel nodded and headed for the saddle draped over the horse's stall door.

Charlie approached Cinders, a handful of grain and dried apples in his hand. Her nostrils flared as he approached, ears flicking back and forth. He offered out his hand, and Cinders lipped his fingers before taking the entire palmful into her mouth at once.

Brock and Daniel finished tacking the last of the horses as Addie locked the door to the inn behind her.

"Did you leave any food for our guests, woman?" Brock asked. He playfully swatted her backside as she walked by with a large sack full of food. Addie returned the gesture before loading her saddlebag onto a white and gray mare.

"I'm traveling with three growing young men and an old man who still thinks he's growing," she said. Despite her size, she pulled herself onto the mare with ease. Brock grunted as he mounted far less gracefully than his wife.

"Those old bones getting the better of you already?" She continued to tease.

"These old bones are telling me I should be in bed right now. Not gallivanting across the Elven territories like I was twenty years younger," Brock scoffed and continued squirming uncomfortably in his saddle.

"I still think you look like him, you know. That young lad who used to clean my pa's stable every morning." She leaned in and kissed Brock before nudging her horse into the darkness of the street.

Charlie felt a sort of numbness as he watched a smile spread across Brock's face as he followed his wife out of the stable. His parents had been outwardly affectionate. They even had an inside joke about grapes that would immediately send each of them into a fit of laughter. But it all changed after they admitted his father to the hospital. A sort of sadness settled over the house. It had been slow, but his mother laughed less often now. Chelsea was the only one who managed to stay positive. He gulped and followed Merrick out of the stable.

They rode out of Cannondole and did not stop until they reached the inner part of the forest where the trees made it too dark to see. Charlie and Addie produced flames in their hands to light the way. Immediately, Charlie noticed how hers was calm at the base, but the tip flicked back and forth like an agitated cat's tail. The group dismounted, and Addie dug a shiny, black disk from the depths of her saddlebag.

"What's that?" Daniel asked. The group had decided to tell him as little as possible for fear of tipping off Kashna or Savaric.

"This was my mother's scrying mirror," she whispered, wiping the mirror on her skirt.

"Your mother's?" Daniel's tone turned more accusatory.

"Yes," she replied gently. "Our people have had the gift of magic since before we can remember. You may have tried to stamp it out, but a gift from the gods is not so easily eradicated."

"You're playing with things you don't understand," said Daniel.

Addie chuckled. "Worried about evil spirits coming back and stealing you from your crib, Highness? My mother used this to find my sisters and I when we would run off and play," she explained. "I've been known to use it to track down a thief for Brock now and then as well." Brock grunted and scratched his beard uncomfortably. "There's no evil here, I assure you."

She extinguished the flame in her hand and wiped her palm on her skirt. The group had discussed in private while Daniel slept that they would use Addie's scrying mirror to try to locate Ailinn as she had done for Bastian.

"Can't you use it now?" Merrick had asked when she'd first showed it to them back at the inn.

"Addie!" someone had called from the tavern below.

Addie had sighed. "Not with this lot needing me to hold their hands every five minutes. What!"

"I can't find the parsley for the soup!"

"It's safer to do it outside town anyway," Brock had said. "Savaric's men found Bastian because he has magic. The last thing we need is another ruckus, especially about magic."

Charlie's insides itched at the prospect of using the mirror. He just wanted to know that Ailinn was safe, and patience wasn't a word anyone would use to describe him.

Now, under the cover of darkness in the middle of the forest, they stepped back and watched Addie work. By the dim light of Charlie's flame, they saw the surface of the mirror ripple and shimmer. Slowly, an image came into focus.

"It's her!" Charlie cried, stepping closer to Addie.

There was little doubt in Charlie's mind the girl in the mirror was Ailinn, but she was almost unrecognizable. She had been bound and gagged, but this was the least of her worries. Ailinn's clothes had been torn in several places, and small patches of blood were scattered across her body. Some of which did not appear to be her own. Her face was red and swollen, and a large, purple bruise across her jaw stood out against her pale skin.

"I can't believe they would do this to her," Merrick whispered in shock.

"If I know Ailinn, it's because she put up a fight," said Daniel.

"Why didn't they just use magic to keep her calm?" asked Charlie.

"Look," said Daniel, pointing at the mirror. "She's not wearing her orenite cuffs. They must have removed them to bind her hands. Judging by the marks around her ankles, they probably weren't able to get as tight of a grip on her wrists with the cuffs on. If they used magic on her, she could use it on them. Unless she was too weak to do so. Bastards. They beat her so she couldn't use magic!"

The wagon she rode in stopped rocking, and Ailinn opened a single eye, her other too swollen to see through. Someone approached her, and the light around her grew brighter. She nodded after a moment, and the stranger began untying the ropes on her ankles. As soon as she was free, Ailinn kicked the stranger and rolled out of the wagon. She was barefoot but ran across the rocky terrain as quickly as she could. She didn't get far before something knocked her down. With her hands bound, she twisted and slammed hard into the ground, but she didn't stop moving. She tried to stand to run again, but the stranger who had untied her feet caught her by her messy hair and lifted her from the ground.

Though they could not hear, the group watched her cry out in pain. Tears rolled down her cheeks as she continued to pull, kick, and twist away from her captor. The stranger brought his face close to her and she spit at him before twisting to bite at his arm. The stranger smacked her across her already swollen cheek and tossed her over his shoulder. He walked past the wagon and joined a small group. Together, they began to climb a narrow walk up a steep incline.

Ailinn no longer struggled. She lay limp and unmoving across the stranger's shoulder. The group spread out and walked single-file as the path narrowed even more.

"Wait," said Merrick, and he leaned close to the mirror. "I know where they've taken her."

"Where? Is it Sparrowmoore? That's where your dad was heading, right?" Charlie asked.

Merrick shook his head. "They're taking her to Harpy's Pointe."

"Your father's castle?" Daniel asked. "Why would he deny he had any involvement in her kidnapping and then have her taken back to Harpy's Pointe?"

"I don't know," said Merrick, continuing to shake his head. "My father has been growing more unstable the longer this war goes on. I fear he is involved in something far greater than he realizes. But what it has to do with Ailinn, I cannot say."

"How did he get to his castle so fast?" Charlie asked.

"Probably magic," Brock muttered under his breath. He pulled at his beard and scowled at the mirror.

"It doesn't matter," said Addie as the mirror faded to black again. "We're going to get her back, and I'm going to find my son."

Addie carefully repacked her mirror and pulled out a short torch instead. She lit it with the flame in her hand, then held it aloft so Brock could retrieve and light two more torches they had packed.

"Won't we stand out a bit?" Charlie asked as Merrick helped him into the saddle again.

"Would you rather the horses be running into the trees?" Addie turned and asked. "If you're lucky to get them to move at all."

Charlie shrugged in agreement. They had five horses to manage now, and the light he and Addie created would only spread so far without draining their energy.

They rode through the night, stopping only for a short meal break. Before they reached the Great River, the path forked, running opposite the river.

"This way," said Merrick, leading them down the narrower road that followed close to the river.

"What's Harpy's Pointe like?" Charlie asked, following close behind.

Merrick smiled, his mind recalling a happier time. "The castle is perched atop a high cliff above the Harpy's Bracken," he said.

"A bracken?" asked Charlie. "Like, salt water."

Merrick nodded. "It's an estuary between the Great River and the Neverending Sea. It's almost always dark and gray with a single footpath leading up to the castle. This is the only way in or out."

"Well, that's stupid," said Charlie, and Cinders snorted beneath him. "See, even Cinders agrees. Doesn't sound very welcoming."

Merrick chuckled. "It wasn't meant to be. It was built centuries ago during the time of the Great War as a fortress against invaders from both land and sea. It's nearly impossible to penetrate."

"Nearly, but not completely," said Brock from behind Charlie.

"No, not completely," said Merrick, and he shot a look at Daniel, who rode behind Brock.

They rode quietly again until the sky above turned to gray, and they were able to put their torches away.

They didn't bother to light a fire, but instead ate from the bread and cured meats Addie packed.

Charlie sat at the base of a tree, his legs stretched out before him, and massaged his sore thighs.

"May I?" Merrick asked, indicating the space beside Charlie.

Charlie nodded, and Merrick joined him with a groan.

"I haven't ridden this much in a long time," said Merrick.

Charlie grumbled. "I haven't ridden this much, like, ever."

"You're doing well, then." Merrick clapped Charlie on the back. "There is something I wanted to discuss away from Daniel. No, don't look at him."

Charlie quickly rubbed his nose to hide the glance he had been about to aim at Daniel. He rummaged in his pack and pulled out a salve Addie made for his still injured wrist. "What's up?"

Merrick paused, briefly glancing at the boughs above, and continued, "I know how Ailinn got to Harpy's Pointe so quickly."

"Something in the book?"

Merrick accepted the salve from Charlie and rubbed it into his neck and shoulders. "It's called a temporal bend," he said. "I still don't understand how it works, but I believe I experienced it."

"You what?" Charlie had to fake a sneeze as Daniel looked in their direction.

"When Queen Piper died, we left the castle as soon as we received the missive. I woke one night and saw some of my father's personal beck-ands standing around the fire ring. There was wind all around the camp, but none of the leaves around us moved. When I woke, we had traveled at least a week's distance. Something similar happened on our way to the palace a few weeks ago."

Charlie's mouth fell open. "And you think it was the temporal bend thing?"

"It's the only thing that could explain it. And there's more. We have always had more beck-ands than was necessary for a castle our size. Especially because my mother insisted we pull some of our own weight with duties. But certain beck-ands seemed to disappear for a time and would reemerge. It is the custom of beck-ands not to speak, but these seemed to be caught in some kind of trance. It was so normal for me growing up, I thought nothing of it. Until I found this."

Merrick pulled his father's book from his bag and opened it to a page close to the back. This was not written in Merspeech or Draconian. It was a spikey scrawl in a thick, black ink.

"This is by my father's own hand."

Charlie saw what looked like a complicated diagram. Phrases like *Rising Nettle* and *Energy Extraction* were scrawled randomly across the page, connected by intersecting lines with the occasional rune.

"What's it mean?" Charlie asked. He had nearly fallen off Cinders from pure exhaustion before they'd stopped, and his brain was not making sense of what he was seeing.

"I believe my father has bound himself to more people than Kashna. If I'm reading this correctly, he uses the Rising Nettle to subdue the beck-ands, which allows him to control their thoughts and thus, their magic."

"That's gotta be how he kept popping up all over the palace. He was using his beck-ands to do the temporal bend thing."

"Ailinn has some of the strongest magic Chartile has seen since Queen Piper. If my father can use this technique on Ailinn, then he can control the kingdom through her. Even if I were to oppose the return of magic, Ailinn is the direct heir to the Elves. He could easily stop his support of the rebels and still get what he wants."

"What's this?" Daniel asked, making both Merrick and Charlie jump.

"Charlie was interested in learning Draconian," said Merrick, quickly turning the page.

"Well, I wish you luck. Unless you like to speak in growls and coughs, I see little point."

"Come on, boys!" Brock called. "We're making camp here for the night."

Charlie gave a sigh of relief. "I'm finally starting to feel my butt again."

Daniel chuckled and helped Charlie to his feet.

"We've made up some time. We can afford a rest," Brock said as the three approached, stiff-legged and staggering. He pulled a bedroll from the back of his saddle and spread it on the ground. "Will you two find some wood for the fire, eh? And Daniel, be a gent and help Addie with the food."

Addie made short work of preparing a small meal for them. They sat in silence, staring at the crackling fire and filling their bellies. Suddenly, Addie jumped. She looked at her hair and picked out a mushroom.

"Who?" she asked.

Brock pointed a finger at Charlie beside him.

"I did not!" Charlie cried, utterly bewildered. He glared at Brock and saw the man wink and smirk beneath his scruffy beard.

"It's all in the wrist," he whispered and sent another mushroom flying at Addie.

"No, no, you have to get one with good weight to it," said Merrick, and he flicked a mushroom at Daniel, who hadn't yet acknowledged the food fight.

"Oy!" Daniel cried when it smacked him square in the face.

"It was Addie!" Merrick cried, and they all doubled over in a fit of laughter, leaving Daniel quite confused.

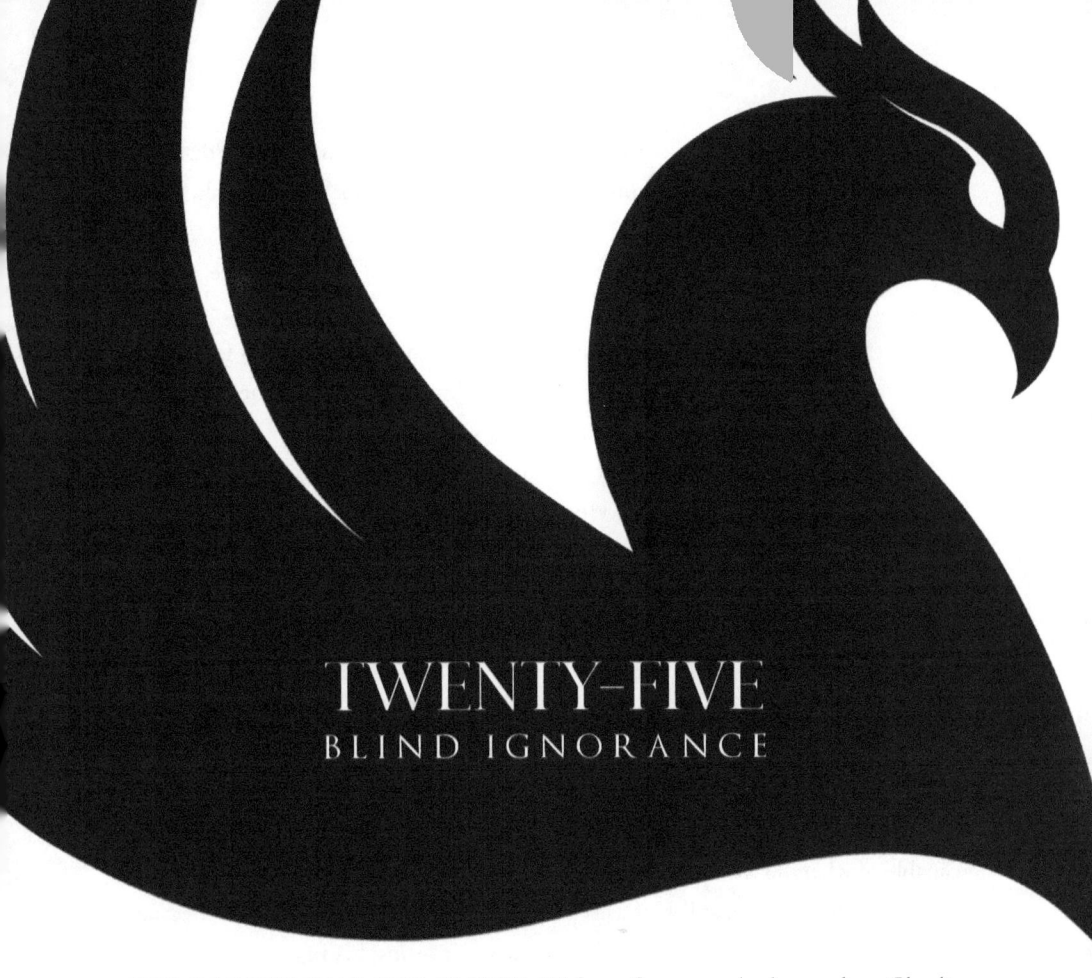

TWENTY-FIVE
BLIND IGNORANCE

THE FOREST WAS SHROUDED IN late afternoon shadows when Charlie finally opened his eyes. He reached under his bedroll and felt around for what he was sure was a giant rock. It took him a moment, but he did find a stick that was imbedded in the ground beneath him. He shrugged and tossed it into the fire.

Their camp was still rather quiet. Addie lay sleeping in Brock's bedroll, while the man sat skinning a rabbit. Merrick sat on his bedroll reading a small book. Charlie sat up and stretched.

"Why haven't we left yet?" Charlie asked.

"Addie said Daniel woke up twice from his nightmares," said Merrick, and he tucked his book back into the saddlebag that sat at his feet. "She said he looked pale and was running a fever. She insisted we stay a little longer so he could rest."

"He woke up shortly after I did," said Brock. "Addie went to sleep, and he offered to go hunting with me. He disappeared for a bit, but—"

"Why isn't anyone looking for him then?" Charlie cried. He pulled the wool blanket off his legs and quickly redressed in his socks and boots.

"He fell asleep against a tree over there," said Merrick, pointing in the distance. "We didn't want to disturb him to make him come back. Brock took him a blanket. He's all right."

Charlie could see a figure hunched on the ground against a large tree. Daniel stirred slightly, then settled. Charlie rummaged in his own saddlebag for some of the fruit tarts Phillippe had packed and a jar of horrid-smelling cream for muscle aches. As Brock arranged the freshly skinned rabbit on a stick over the fire, Addie sat up and rubbed her eyes.

"Oh, dear," she whispered. "Have I slept too long?"

"You're fine, dear," said Brock. He poured some water from his waterskin over his hands and wiped them clean. "The boy's finally resting. We decided to let him be for a bit."

Addie turned in the direction Brock had pointed and shook her head. "The poor lad," she said, more to herself than those around her. "I can't imagine what he's been through to be haunted so." She ran her fingers through her tangled mess of hair and turned to her husband. "Someone should wake him."

"I'll go," said Charlie. He rose stiffly and headed for the slouched figure. He approached cautiously, not wanting to startle Daniel. Charlie knew what he was capable of when he was in his right mind. He didn't want to find out what Daniel could do when he was still half-asleep and feeling suddenly threatened. Because Addie was right, Charlie didn't know what was causing his nightmares and his strange shifts in personality. And he didn't want to find out the hard way.

"Make it end. Make them end. All of it. Them. All of it."

Charlie heard the faintest whisper as he approached Daniel. He stopped and watched Daniel's hands shake and trembled.

"Never know. Never see," Daniel muttered. Charlie dared a step closer.

"Daniel?" Charlie whispered. He looked back at the camp. Everyone was on their feet watching him. Brock had picked up Charlie's sword, heading toward him.

"Daniel," said Charlie more loudly. Daniel's entire body jerked, and his eyes snapped open. But they were not Daniel's eyes. They were bright and golden. Daniel's lip curled, and he lunged for Charlie. Charlie ducked, and Brock slammed his fist into Daniel's teeth.

Daniel stumbled back and fell to the ground with a loud *thud*. Brock pushed himself between Charlie and Daniel, holding the sword in front of him. Daniel did not stir. Gently, Brock nudged Daniel with the blade, but he appeared unconscious.

"What happened?" Addie rushed to Daniel's side. She rolled him over and saw a small cut against his bottom lip.

"Blindfold him," said Charlie quite suddenly.

"What?" asked Addie, her brow furrowed.

"Blindfold him," Charlie repeated. "Those weren't Daniel's eyes."

Brock hurried back to camp and grabbed a strip of fabric from Addie's injury kit. The woman tenderly wrapped the cloth around Daniel's eyes, his head cradled in her lap.

Merrick grabbed Charlie's shoulder, leading him away from Daniel. "What did you see?" he asked, his face more stern than Charlie had ever seen it.

Charlie dared a glance at Daniel. He was definitely unconscious. "It was Kashna."

"What?" Merrick asked.

"I know it sounds crazy, but trust me, I'll never forget those eyes as long as I live. Those were Kashna's eyes looking at me, not Daniel's."

"How is that possible?" Addie asked, rising from the ground.

"If Kashna is working for Savaric, he could be using some sort of psychic connection to manipulate Daniel." Realization washed over Charlie, and he smashed his face into his palm. "That's why he kept threatening me and trying to beat me to a pulp. It wasn't Daniel. He was being controlled."

"My father's known everything all along," Merrick said softly. "Before we even came to the palace. He was using Kashna as a connection to get to Daniel."

"I didn't know what it was at first, but I think I know now," said Charlie. He looked up, daring a glance at Daniel. "When Kashna and I... mind melded or whatever, I saw through Kashna's eyes when he was a baby. Merrick, did your father, like, nurse and care for Kashna when he first found him?"

Merrick nodded. "Of course. He was far too young to survive on his own."

Charlie nodded. "I think Savaric used magic to connect himself to Kashna all that time ago. He's been planning to spy on the royal family for years. And now, everything we say and do, Kashna can tell Savaric."

"How are we to formulate any plans, then?" asked Merrick.

"He's a danger to all of us, and even the princess," said Brock. "We need to get rid of him."

"We can't just leave him here!" Charlie cried.

"What else can we do?" said Brock.

"Can someone escort him back to the palace?" Merrick suggested.

"He'll never give up on Ailinn," said Charlie. "She's the only person who really cares about him anymore. Valin only put up with him because of Piper. Now that she's gone, Ailinn's all he's got."

Daniel stirred beside them. Addie quickly knelt again, resting a gentle hand on his shoulder. He reached for the blindfold, but she grabbed his hands in hers.

"Leave that now, dear," she said softly.

"What's going on? Where am I?" Daniel asked, his voice high in panic.

"What's the last thing you remember?" Charlie asked, kneeling beside him as well.

Daniel turned his head towards Charlie. "I—I was hunting. With Brock in the forest," he said. "There were two different tracks and we decided to split up. I— it's a little—I'm not sure. Why can't I remember?"

"You came back to camp and tripped over Merrick into the fire," Charlie lied. "You hurt your head pretty bad. Addie did some healing on your eye, but you need to leave the bandage on." After years of trying to avoid confrontations with Malcolm Darcy and even his father, Charlie had perfected the art of lying. It still left an uncomfortable feeling in the pit of his stomach.

"We need to get you back to the palace—"

"No! Just tie me to my horse. I can't leave Ailinn!" Daniel interrupted Merrick.

"Shh," Addie whispered. She squeezed his hand and stroked his hair. A single tear fell down her cheek. "You may have made your concussion from earlier worse. You need to rest. I'm going to put you to sleep now, all right, dear? We'll take care of you."

"Please don't send me back," Daniel pleaded. They watched tears begin to seep through the bandage around his eyes.

"I promise we won't," said Merrick.

Addie laid her hand over Daniel's forehead. His body went limp, and she leaned down to kiss his forehead.

"We have to make his injuries believable," said Charlie. "Can… can you give him a black eye?"

Addie lifted her head, the fear in her eyes speaking before Brock did.

"We don't use magic to hurt people," he said.

Charlie nodded. "I know. I get it. But this is different. It's for the greater good, or whatever. We have to convince Daniel to keep that blindfold on so Kashna and Savaric don't know where we are. He'll only do that if he feels the pain."

"Won't Savaric suspect if Kashna can no longer see through Daniel's eyes?" Merrick asked.

"Not if we feed him wrong information," said Charlie. "If he won't go back to the castle, then we can't tell him what's really going on."

"This is all too risky," said Brock, shaking his head and pulling at his beard. "We should all go back. Report what we know to the king and let him handle it."

"Treacherous though my words may be, our king is useless," said Merrick. "If he wanted to hold his position, he wouldn't be trying to arrange a marriage with someone like my father. King Valin cannot help us."

Charlie had fallen silent at Brock's words. His mind was racing. He took off toward the camp area, the rest of the party yelling after him. He fell to his knees on his bedroll, sure he had found that dratted stone again, and began tossing things out of his saddlebags. He pulled out a few leaves of paper and ran back to the group.

"Does anyone have a pen or pencil?" he asked before remembering such things did not exist in Chartile.

"What are you thinking, Charlie?" Merrick asked.

"I'm going to send a message to my friends. If the king doesn't know what to do with the information we send him, Jock and Drustad will think of a plan, and they'll tell Valin. It's a long shot in case something goes really bad, maybe they can send reinforcements or something."

"And how do you know Savaric won't intercept this message?" asked Brock.

"Because I'm going to use magic," said Charlie.

Brock showed Charlie how to burn the end of a small stick to create a char that would write. As he wrote, Addie worked her magic, giving Daniel a swollen black eye. He could hear her sobbing through it all. He felt awful, but it was the only thing he could think to do. When he finished, he reached out with his magic.

One of the birds that flitted in the treetops above landed on a low-hanging branch. Charlie remembered his father had used a similar trick and hoped it would work for him too. The bird tilted its head and turned a beady black eye on him. Charlie tied the note to the bird's leg and received a light peck on the hand before it took flight. By the time he returned to camp, half the horses were already tacked, though Daniel still lay sleeping.

"How long will your sleep thing last?" Charlie asked as he bridled Cinders.

"I don't know," said Addie. "I've only done it for those who are ill. They usually sleep through the night at least."

"Let's hope he's better when he wakes up," Merrick muttered.

Charlie watched as he and Brock tied Daniel to his horse. When Brock and

Addie learned who Charlie was—or rather who his father had been—they had been even more eager to help. They were all older than him, even Daniel. He wished that one of them would step forward instead to finish fulfilling the prophecy. Merrick seemed more destined to do so than Charlie.

He mounted Cinders, and the mare nickered beneath him. He patted her neck and sighed. Whoever was going to fulfill the prophecy didn't matter. They were going to rescue Ailinn. He'd work on figuring out the rest later.

THE GROUP RODE AS QUICKLY as they dared. Though they stopped and retied him several times, Daniel's unconscious body bounced more than any of them felt comfortable with. He woke with a start several hours in but insisted they keep going.

"You have to eat, and you *will* eat if I have anything to say about it," Addie said sternly, shoving a piece of bread and an apple into his hand.

"We rested too long. Ailinn—"

"You aren't any good to Ailinn if you don't take care of yourself," said Merrick.

Daniel huffed. "I'm no good to her at all," he said, indicating the bandage around his eyes. "Savaric is at least three days ahead of us. Who knows what he could be doing to her?"

"We should make camp," said Brock, cutting the tension. "The horses need a rest."

"And we cannot hope to confront Savaric or whatever persons he has working for him if we are not rested," Merrick reiterated as he and Charlie exchanged an uncomfortable glance.

"You mean those with magic," Charlie said flatly.

"There is a difference between someone who possesses magic and someone who uses magic," said Merrick. "I know there are some who possess magical abilities that would wish for it to remain outlawed."

"Those who do not wish to use their magic should not be forcing the rest of us to endure a lifetime of holding back what we were born with," snapped Addie. Her eyes widened, and she covered her hand with her mouth. Even in the dim light from the flame dancing in her hand, they could see her blushing.

"Would you wish the humans' rights restored the same as elves and dwarves, then?" asked Merrick.

No!" cried Addie and her flame flickered even faster. "No, that is a different matter entirely. Humans can't control the effects magic has on the mind. The power and manipulation it can cause. They don't have the ability to keep it in check as elves do."

"How do you know?" Charlie asked abruptly. Addie, Brock, and Merrick furrowed their brows at him, and Daniel cocked an ear to listen. He fed Cinders the apple core Daniel had tossed to the ground before turning back to them. "I mean, how long have they been forced to wear those cuff things? How do you know they haven't learned to control it? Have you given them a chance?"

"There are plenty of reports that come from the Chamberlain in Duneland about rogue humans," said Daniel. "They pick the locks on their cuffs and attempt to escape. They use their magic to take down anyone in their path, including innocent bystanders."

"If you had been chained your whole life, wouldn't you do whatever it took to be free?" said Charlie. He removed his boots and pulled a piece of cured meat from his bag.

"Being powerless can make one as mad as someone with power," said Merrick quietly.

There was no more discussion. One by one, they settled into their bedrolls, with Merrick taking the first watch, and drifted into uncomfortable sleep.

Charlie lay awake, staring into the fire. His father had spoken very little of the palace beck-ands when Charlie was a child. And when he had, it had made everyone uncomfortable. Yet Charlie had fallen into the status quo of Chartile. He did not demand Phillippe or Saajee'a's orenite cuffs be removed. He had allowed himself to be caught up in the acceptance of the enslavement of an entire race. He tossed and turned until he heard Merrick change watch with Addie.

Merrick's words echoed in Charlie's mind. *Being powerless can make one as mad as someone with power.*

TWENTY-SIX
CHOOSING

THE GENERAL MOOD AMONG THE travelers slowly improved as they rode toward Harpy's Pointe over the next two days. Brock and Merrick established an ongoing arm-wrestling battle that occurred at the beginning of each rest point they took, and Addie started training Charlie to use her scrying mirror. It took several attempts before he made anything appear. The mirror seemed to have its own sort of magic, and Charlie could not force his will upon an inanimate object.

Daniel had grown quiet, at least towards his friends. They often heard him muttering to himself and whispering in his sleep. Their fear increased with each mumbled word. They may be walking into a trap—or worse.

They halted to make camp at sunset of the third day. Merrick and Addie estimated they were close to half a day's ride from Harpy's Pointe.

"You can't face Savaric with saddle sore," he said, dismounting more gracefully than he had their first day.

"Why are we stopping so often?" Daniel asked, his voice cold and sharp. He swung his leg over to dismount and nearly fell. Brock reached for his arm to steady him. "Get off me!" he cried, pushing Brock away.

Daniel ripped the blindfold from his eyes. The black eye Addie had made was still prominent, but he could open both eyes now.

"Daniel," said Addie, her voice worried. "Dear, you need to put that back on. Your eye—"

"My eye is fine," said Daniel. "What's going on? Are you all in league with Savaric?"

"What are you going on about?" Brock asked, his hands on his hips.

"That's it, isn't it? You're keeping me from Ailinn. All of you, you're working for him." Daniel reached for his sword tied to the back of his saddle.

"Daniel, that's not true," said Charlie. He placed a hand on Merrick's elbow, and Merrick's grip on the hilt of his own sword lessened.

"We could have been to Harpy's Pointe before now. Why are you delaying us?" Daniel demanded, dropping his sword sheath to the ground and holding the blade before him at arm's length.

"Daniel, we need to be rested," said Merrick, his voice calmer than the grip on his hilt had indicated. "We cannot know what we will be up against to get Ailinn back."

"Dear, please listen," said Addie gently. She stepped forward and stood between her husband and the end of Daniel's blade. She reached out a hand, inching closer to Daniel, who seemed frozen with confusion. "I know you want to get your sister back. I want to find my son. Believe me, a mother's love is greater than you could ever know."

"Lies!" said Daniel, and he turned his blade toward Addie. "My mother didn't care about me. She let the king strip me of my rights as the heir to the throne and told me to hide my magic! She said my real father was half-human. She said they'd kill me if they ever found out—or worse! She doted on Ailinn, taught her how to use her magic."

"Your mother was protecting you in the best way she could," said Addie, her voice smooth and clear. Merrick's hand trembled as she inched closer. "If your lineage is not pure Elven, she did what she had to to keep you alive. And she did the same for Ailinn. Do you think Ailinn would have the spirit to survive through all this if your mother hadn't taught her how to use her magic? There's more to magic than working with fire and making people do what you want them to. You have to know who *you* are to reach your greatest potential."

Daniel's eyes rolled back in his head, and his sword fell to the ground. Addie's movements had been so slow, no one noticed when she placed a hand on Daniel's arm. He crumpled into her arms, unconscious once more. Merrick and Brock hurried forward to relieve her and placed Daniel gently on the ground.

Addie fell to her knees. She buried her face in her hands, and Charlie could hear her crying.

"Addie?" Charlie asked. "Are you okay?"

Addie took a deep breath. She lifted her head from her hands, and Brock kissed the top of her head before retrieving Daniel's bedroll.

"My mother warned me when I was little. She said magic could be used for good or ill, and sometimes that line was a hard one to see." She rose and wiped the dirt and leaves from her knees. "Keeping that boy asleep is the best thing for all of us, but I question if it's what's best for him." She walked to her horse and began untacking her.

Charlie sat wide awake that night. He was on last watch, though he had hardly slept. The closer they were to Savaric and Harpy's Pointe, the more his stomach churned. Several scenarios played through his mind as he stared into the flames before him. He wondered how they would get into Harpy's Pointe. He wondered if Daniel would turn on them once they did. He wondered if his magic was strong enough to beat Savaric. Mostly, he thought of his father's war stories. He thought about the times Jayson told him of the dying enemy soldiers that had pleaded for their lives. They believed they were doing the right thing. They believed it was right. Some of them had had no choice. They'd joined the army to save their families.

Jayson had killed people when he'd been in Chartile. Two people, in fact. He seemed to become his fourteen-year-old self again when he told Charlie the tale—just once, though.

Charlie never wanted to be like his father before he'd come to Chartile. *He* would never abandon his family. *He* would never selfishly do or say things that he knew could hurt the people he loved. But now, in some ways, he wanted to be exactly like his father. He wanted to be a hero. He wanted to be the one to save Ailinn and prove he could take care of her. He wanted to be somebody worthwhile, but not if it meant killing someone.

Daniel sat up in his bedroll. He did not have the silent scream plastered on his face this time. Instead, he grabbed his sword and headed into the trees. Charlie reached over to Brock sleeping beside him. He shook the man's shoulder but did not take his eyes off Daniel.

"Already?" Brock grumbled.

"Shh," said Charlie.

Brock was still for a moment, then followed Charlie's gaze. He grabbed the sword beside him, quietly rising from his bedroll, and ran after Daniel.

Charlie stayed back as Brock approached Daniel. He didn't want him to feel ganged up on. He watched as Daniel drew his sword, but Brock was faster. He blocked Daniel's attack, dodging aside with surprising speed. Daniel relentlessly attacked over and over, ignoring Brock's words to him.

"Guys!" Charlie shouted. He reached for his own blade as Merrick and Addie were jarred awake. He was halfway to Brock and Daniel when he caught movement beside him. He froze and saw three cloaked figures converged on Brock and Daniel.

One sent a blue ball of light toward Daniel, and he immediately fell limp. His assailant moved in a blur and caught him before he hit the ground. The stranger lifted Daniel with ease and took off into the darkness. The two remaining figures united against Brock. He swung his blade at them, shouting, "You bloody bastards! Come on!"

One of the figures lifted a hand, and Brock's sword leapt from his grasp. It hung in the air between them, slowly spinning. It was like watching a scene in slow-motion, and Charlie was powerless to stop it. His legs had become like jelly again. He couldn't move. He couldn't think.

Brock's sword stopped spinning, the tip level with his face. Charlie could hear his heart pounding in his ears. He saw Merrick and Addie out of the corner of his eye. They all stopped, not daring to breathe. The sword moved faster than if someone had been holding it. It sliced through the air before landing tip down into the ground. Brock's body crumpled beside it, his head completely severed at the neck.

"NO!" Charlie wasn't sure if it was his own scream or Addie's. She sent several balls of fire blazing toward her husband's killers. As swiftly as they had come, the cloaked figures disappeared into the night.

Addie ran after them, screaming insults and continuing to throw fireballs. She stopped when she reached Brock's body and fell into a heap on the ground. Merrick rushed to her. He dropped to his knees and pulled her head to him, covering her eyes from the scene before them.

"Charlie!" Merrick called.

Charlie tried putting one foot in front of the other. He managed a few steps before leaning against a tree and bringing up his dinner. He felt hot tears running down his cheeks. His head was spinning and his whole body shook. He screamed and closed his eyes against the lightheaded feeling that was starting to overpower him.

He wasn't sure how long he stayed that way, screaming into the bark of a Belirian tree. When he lifted his head, the sky was turning pink and orange.

Merrick had wrapped Brock's body in several blankets. He knelt beside Charlie, holding out a waterskin. Charlie accepted it and sat up. He realized he was back in his bedroll.

"What happened?" Charlie asked.

"You collapsed," said Merrick, but his voice was not angry. "Are you all right?"

Charlie nodded. He looked across the fire and saw Addie curled beneath her blanket, staring into the flames.

"How's—?" Charlie began, but Merrick shook his head. He motioned for Charlie to follow him and walked deeper into the forest.

"Addie's not coming with us," Merrick whispered when Charlie had caught up to him. Charlie swallowed and nodded. "She needs to return Brock's body to the priestesses in thirteen days to avoid the wrath of the gods." Charlie nodded again. "That means it's just us now. I understand if this is too much for you. You aren't part of our world, and you didn't ask for this."

"I didn't ask to come to Chartile at all," Charlie snapped, "but I did come on this trip on my own." His eyes met Merrick's, but he saw only kindness returned.

"I know," said Merrick, resting his hands on Charlie's shoulders, "and I can't imagine this is what you anticipated. Charlie, if you're coming with me, then I need to know I can count on you. If you want to go with Addie, I will understand."

Charlie chewed at his nails. He looked at Addie, still staring into the fire, and the bundle of blankets that contained Brock's body.

"What about Ailinn?" Charlie asked. "You can't save her by yourself. How will you even get in?"

"There is one other way into Harpy's Pointe, but I didn't know how to tell everyone with Daniel's condition," Merrick said, his voice hushing even more. "I assumed I would find a way when we came closer. We can get in and at least send messages back to the palace if we can't get back out."

Behind them, Addie suddenly rose from her bedroll. Merrick and Charlie watched as she led Brock's horse toward her husband's body. She knelt beside him, her head bowed as if in prayer. Then, with careful determination, she tried to lift his body.

Merrick and Charlie hurried to her.

"No, I can do it." Addie's voice trembled.

"I know you can," said Merrick gently. "But let us help."

Addie's eyes filled with tears. She stepped aside and allowed Merrick and Charlie to place Brock's body on the horse.

"There's a small town only three or four hours from here," said Merrick after he tied the last knot. "You can ride there and barter for a wagon to get Brock home." He slipped a small coin purse into Addie's hand.

"I don't need your money, young man," said Addie with a gentle smile. "I have friends in Portswitch. I will manage." She kissed him on the cheek, then led the horse back to her own.

Charlie watched as she began packing, every moment trembling and shaking. He walked toward Cinders, unsure what to do or say. He patted the horse's jaw and buried his face in her neck. He had never envied the sights his father had seen as a medic during the war. Chartile had been his family's personal fairy tale, a place of escape and wonder. But this series of events had become much darker than its fantastical retelling.

"He said he didn't believe Bastian was still alive, but I always knew better," said Addie as she tightened the girth on her saddle. "He wanted to protect me, to keep me from trying to go after Bastian. He didn't want to lose me too."

Charlie looked up and watched as she pulled the scrying mirror from her saddlebag. She stroked it with her thumb before turning to place the mirror in Charlie's hands.

"Addie, I don't think I'm the one who's supposed to fulfill this prophecy," he whispered. He saw Merrick over her shoulder gathering the remainder of Daniel's things from the campsite.

Addie chuckled and brushed Charlie's hair from his eyes. "We never are, dear," she said. She kissed Charlie's forehead and mounted her horse.

"Young man," she called to Merrick, who had moved on to saddling his own horse. "If you find my son, bring him home to me."

Merrick nodded, and Addie turned her horses back toward the main path. Charlie watched her leave, and for a moment, he wondered why he wasn't following her. He felt his legs begin to move as he ran after her. His mouth opened, ready to call out her name, and Ailinn's smiling face flashed into his mind. He stopped, watching Addie turn the horses down the path and urge them into a trot. He could almost hear Ailinn's laugh.

Merrick placed a hand on his shoulder, and Charlie turned to see him smiling. A pang of guilt tightened his stomach, and he looked away.

"Let's keep moving," said Merrick. "I have a plan."

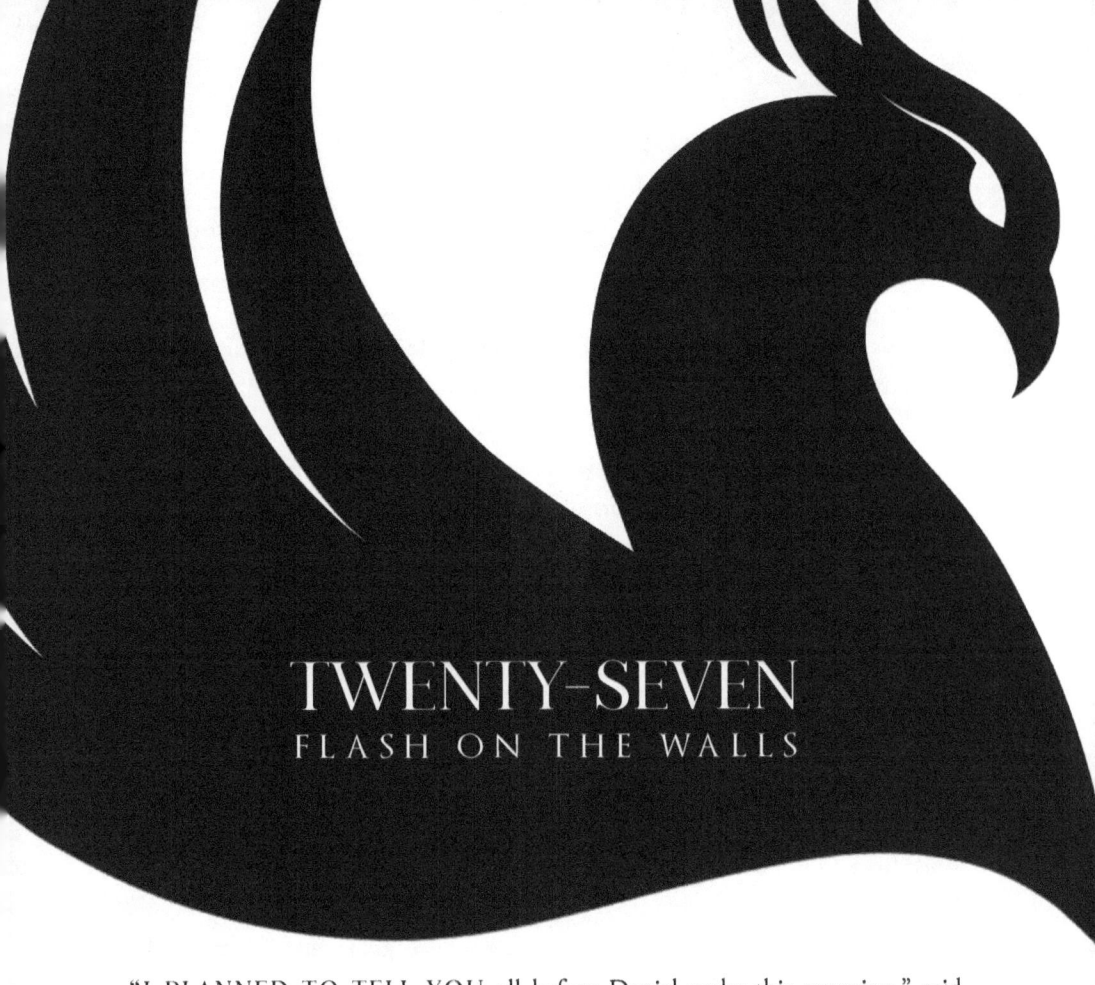

TWENTY-SEVEN
FLASH ON THE WALLS

"I PLANNED TO TELL YOU all before Daniel woke this morning," said Merrick as they finished packing the horses. "I wanted to wait as long as possible. If anyone tried to discuss the plan, there would have been too many opportunities for Daniel to overhear and report to my father."

Charlie only nodded. They were a few short hours from Harpy's Pointe and whatever confrontation lay ahead. Seeing Brock die right in front of him had somehow made the situation more real to Charlie. He could die. Ailinn could die. Someone else could die because of him. The thought made his stomach churn. It was safer not to speak. When the embers from the fire had been smothered and the last signs of any camp dispersed, they mounted their horses and headed back toward the main road with Daniel's horse in tow.

"There is one more way into the castle," Merrick continued. "There is a small tunnel that leads to the base of the cliff and the shoreline. It allowed the nobility to escape unnoticed if Harpy's Pointe was ever attacked. We were not permitted to speak of it to anyone except our family. As children, we were told tales that the passage was cursed, and whoever you told would die a horrible death."

Charlie's eyes widened, and he forced his mouth closed.

"They were only tales, Charlie." Merrick chuckled. "Don't worry yourself."

Charlie turned away, but his hands shook more.

"There are cliffs that overhang the shore close to the castle. We will need to leave the horses behind, but the cliffs should provide enough cover for sneaking in, as they do for the nobility sneaking out. There is one thing I will need your help with, though."

"Mm-hmm," said Charlie. He was only half-listening to Merrick now. His mind had wandered to the horrors of a cursed passage and what sort of magic Savaric may have invented to guard it.

"What's wrong?" Merrick asked, halting his horse, and Cinders stopped before Charlie even pulled on her reins.

"I don't think I can do this," Charlie blurted out before he could stop himself. He finally met Merrick's eyes for the first time since Brock's death.

Merrick watched Charlie's face blanch even whiter, but he did not look away. Charlie sighed and fidgeted with the reins in his hand. "I'm scared, okay! I just stood there and watched Brock die. Every time some fight or something happens, I just freeze! I'm not the chosen one or whatever, Merrick. I can't do this. I—I just can't."

Merrick nodded and pulled a flask from his saddlebag. He offered it to Charlie as he spoke. "I'm scared too, Charlie. Very scared."

A sharp taste burned Charlie's tongue and throat as he drank. He coughed, recognizing the smell as some kind of alcohol. He took another drink before handing it back to Merrick.

"You are?" he asked.

"Of course I am." Merrick returned the flask to his saddlebag and nudged his horse forward again. "I only discovered days ago that the rumors about my father are likely true. He kidnapped my friend and possibly future wife, and I suspect the reason that scrying mirror can no longer see Ailinn is because he has put magical barriers in place to keep others from spying on his activities. I'm afraid my fears have been confirmed. My father is not the same man he was before my mother died. He has fallen down a very dark path, and I don't know if I can bring him back through it. And if I am successful, he has committed more acts of treason than I can count. They will try him for his crimes, and I will be powerless to do anything. I'm afraid we will find Ailinn dead or worse, and I'm afraid my own father may turn against me. I am very afraid, Charlie. But my fear is not keeping me from doing what I believe is right. If I am to be the future king of the elves, I cannot turn aside and let such atrocities continue."

"But I'm not like you," said Charlie meekly.

"Of course you aren't. If you were to turn back now, I would hold no ill will against you. I said as much back at camp before Addie left. Yet here you are. It is the beliefs in my heart that keep me moving forward. There must be something for you as well."

"It's Ailinn," Charlie said. He blushed, but Merrick took no notice. "Every time I get scared, I think about her. I can't leave her to die without trying to do something. But…"

"But…?" Merrick urged.

"But Ailinn's going to be Queen someday."

Charlie heard Merrick inhale and nod. "Ah. I understand," he said. "That is a decision only you and Ailinn can make."

It was not the response that Charlie had expected, though he wasn't exactly sure *what* he had expected. Merrick had not participated in the same crimes as his father. He could still be king one day, and he knew it. He had every right and advantage to sweep Ailinn out from under him. Charlie's chances of building a relationship with Ailinn were worse than his chances at making it on his school's football team, and yet Merrick never discouraged him.

"Why are you so nice?" Charlie asked.

"I'm sorry?" Merrick turned in his saddle and looked at Charlie with a furrowed brow.

"I mean, your dad. How come you didn't turn out like him?"

"We are not defined by our families, Charlie," said Merrick calmly. "I think you of all people would understand that. And love can do strange things to someone. I believe you can understand that too."

The road they traveled climbed higher and higher above the river that ran beside them. Soon the gradual decline toward the rocky shoreline below was gone, and only a straight drop-off to the bottom remained. The wind had picked up, and the air grew chill.

"We'll stop here," said Merrick. "We can climb down the cliff and follow this to the castle. From there, we'll need your magic to get in."

"My magic?" Charlie called above the wind as he dismounted.

"The door cannot be opened from the outside," said Merrick. "That is why I need your help to get in." He pulled a thick traveling cloak from his saddlebag and began loading a shoulder bag with his waterskin, flask, and various other tools. Charlie did the same.

"What about the horses?" Charlie asked. "I mean, if they're tied up, they'll die if we never come back."

Merrick nodded. "Can you use your magic to make them stay in the area?"

The hair on Charlie's neck stood up, and it had nothing to do with the icy ocean wind. He looked at Cinders, his mind racing with thoughts of how she had fought against him when he had forced her to kneel so he could save Daniel.

"I can try," he said, pulling the last apple out of the bag. He offered it to Cinders, who ate it greedily. As she ate, Charlie reached out with his mind once more, connecting to hers. Cinders tossed her head but did not try to bolt. Charlie could feel her unease.

She wouldn't understand him if he tried to use words with her, and who knew how long it would be before his magic wore off if he forced her to stay? Instead, Charlie formed an image in his mind. Cinders stomped hard on the ground and tossed her head more violently. Charlie stroked her velvet nose and continued to concentrate. Instead of forcing her to stay, he asked her to, using images. He showed her Merrick and Charlie walking along the beach below them. He created an image of Cinders and the other horses eating the grass and mushrooms that grew along the path. He showed several day and night cycles before showing Cinders that he and Merrick would return.

Charlie released his mind from hers and took several deep breaths. Cinders relaxed as well and butted Charlie in the chest with her nose. She blew hot air in his face and nipped at the strap on his shoulder. He patted her neck and moved on to Merrick's and Daniel's horses.

Several minutes later, Charlie joined Merrick at the edge of the cliff.

"I think they'll stay," he told Merrick.

Merrick smiled and clapped Charlie on the back. "You did your best. That's all we can ask." He carefully lowered himself over the edge of the precipice, feeling for footholds among the dirt and rocks. When he reached the bottom, he waved up at Charlie to join him.

Charlie was sure Merrick had spent many days climbing the small cliffs along the river as a child. Charlie wasn't afraid of heights, but Merrick made it look easy. He swung over the edge as gracefully as walking. For Charlie, it was anything but graceful. He was sure he would have fallen to his death—four times—if he hadn't clung to a root that grew vertically beside him.

"You're doing great, Charlie!" Merrick called to him.

"Yeah, great. Amazing. I'm fantastic," Charlie mumbled to himself.

When he finally made it to the ground, sweat and dirt clung to every inch of his bare skin, and he sported a scratch across his cheek.

"Well done," said Merrick, clapping his shoulder again.

"Yeah, sure." Charlie scoffed and adjusted Phillippe's pack on his back. "We could have used a rope or something."

Merrick smiled. "Someone might have noticed if they are patrolling the shoreline. Besides, you're still alive." Merrick winked and headed up the rocky shoreline.

They walked in silence for nearly a half hour under the cover of the overhanging cliffs. The icy waters of the river lapped against the rock-strewn shore. Between the trees and a few breaks in the cliffs, Charlie could just make out Harpy's Pointe castle.

It was a towering black spire and sat precariously on the edge of the cliffs overlooking where the river widened into the estuary. It appeared to have been built from the same rocks and cliffs it sat upon.

The sky was a gloomy gray when they reached the cliffs at the base of the castle.

"Now we climb," Merrick whispered as he began scaling the cliffs once more.

Charlie nodded and shivered against the cold. As they climbed higher, he could see a circle of worn stone on a jut of land he thought may have been a lighthouse at one time. The wind whipped against his traveling cloak and sent him clutching for the rock face again. He gasped and steadied himself before continuing on.

When they neared the top of the precipice, Charlie watched Merrick squeeze himself through a small opening. He reached a hand out for Charlie and pulled him onto sturdier ground. The silence was almost deafening now that they were out of the wind and cold.

"Come," whispered Merrick, leading the way along a narrow tunnel. After only a few steps, it was completely black, but the strain in Charlie's legs told him the path was inclining. He created a small flame in his hand and followed close behind Merrick.

They walked farther than Charlie had expected. The flame in his hand pulsed in time with his heart. Without warning, the passage before them stopped, and Charlie nearly caught Merrick's cloak on fire. Merrick reached his hands out, feeling along the solid stone wall and looking more puzzled by the minute.

"Did we take a wrong turn?" asked Charlie.

"No," said Merrick. "No, this isn't supposed to be here. The tunnel goes much farther in. I used to climb this way as a child. It was a favorite hiding spot of mine. I—I don't understand."

"Maybe your dad blocked it up. Maybe he knew someone would try to come this way." Charlie replied with a shrug before realizing Merrick wasn't looking at him.

"Wait. There's something." Merrick ran his fingers along the stone again. Charlie held his flame higher and saw the faint outline of a door. Merrick turned to Charlie, a slight smirk pulling at the corner of his mouth.

"Are you ready, Charlie?"

Charlie swallowed and nodded. He extinguished the flame in his hand and took a deep breath. Carefully, he felt around the edges of the door with his magic until he found the latch. The tumblers were very large but were made of the same metal as his chalice had been. He took another breath and moved them as he would have moved the candles through the air when he'd practiced with Ailinn. The lock clicked loudly, and the door swung toward them.

Light flooded the tunnel, blinding both Charlie and Merrick. A man standing beside the door stepped back. His hand flew to his hip, and he grabbed a small hatchet.

"Charlie! Now!" Merrick shouted beside him.

Charlie reached out his hand, and the hatchet jumped to his palm. The man seemed unsurprised. He raised his hands, and Charlie felt as though the wind had been knocked out of him. He fell back, landing hard in the darkness of the tunnel.

Merrick leapt forward. He raised his sword and knocked the man on the head with his hilt. Once again, the man was not fazed. Merrick stood dumbfounded as the man turned to him, blood trickling down his temple and a blank stare in his eyes.

Another guard ran down the corridor toward them, a similar blank stare on his face. Charlie struggled to his feet, his chest and lungs still sore from whatever the guard had done to him. He reached out his hand again and lifted both guards into the air. They stopped struggling and stared emotionless at Merrick and Charlie below them.

Charlie closed his eyes, and the two men dipped slightly in the air. Within moments, the guards' eyes drooped, and they drifted into sleep. Charlie lowered them to the ground and dropped to his knees.

Merrick placed a hand on his shoulder. "That was incredible, Charlie."

"I—" Charlie panted. "I didn't want to hurt them."

Merrick stepped toward the guards and rolled one onto his back. "Such an act is more noble than you can know." He worked at the clasp of the cape at the guard's throat. "When your life is threatened, it is an instinct to defend yourself and meet violence with violence. It takes great courage to do what you did."

Merrick tossed the cloak at Charlie and began untying the guard's belt to remove his tabard next.

"What are you doing?" Charlie asked, finally getting to his feet. He felt lightheaded, and his hands trembled.

"We need to blend in," said Merrick, and he pulled the tabard over the guard's head before tossing it to Charlie.

Charlie grimaced. The tabard was slightly damp under the arms. "But you live here."

"*Lived*," Merrick corrected him, moving on to the second guard's cloak clasp. "My father and I—well, we did not agree on how to handle the rebellion. I left a few years ago, remember?"

"Don't you think they'll still recognize you?"

Merrick stood, the second guard's tabard pulled over his head. He secured his belt, readjusting the sword and scabbard back into place. He looked at Charlie and smiled, scratching at the short beard on his chin. "Not since the man in me came out." He winked at Charlie and carefully pulled one of the guards through the door to the dark tunnel outside. Charlie followed with the second guard, and they shut the door.

An unease settled in Charlie's stomach, and he grabbed at his own smooth chin as he followed behind Merrick.

The tunnels were roughly carved, very unlike the smooth, perfect structures of the Dwarvik mountain Charlie's father had described. They were lit by strange glowing orbs that hung against the stone wall. On either side ran long, thin rails of some sort of brassy metal. Charlie thought they looked like a form of electrical conduits, but his father never mentioned anything like them before.

"What are those?" he asked Merrick.

Merrick glanced where Charlie pointed. "Likely some of my father's inventions," he said.

"Inventions?" Charlie's voice was barely a whisper as they continued down the long corridor.

"Discoveries, creations. My father has always been a tinkerer. They look like some of the drawings I came across in his book."

Charlie looked at the metal rails again, and his stomach churned once more. They rounded a corner and immediately stopped.

This hall was more illuminated than the last. Charlie and Merrick stared in wonder at the line of superbly furnished alcoves on either side of the corridor. Brightly colored pillows and rugs, raised cots, and shelves of books adorned each small room. There were no doors or curtains, but the residents seemed content to remain within. A few glanced their way as Merrick and Charlie finally sauntered forward and attempted not to look too stunned.

In one alcove, a young woman sat on a small stool, her eyes blank, staring through Merrick and Charlie as they passed.

"Hello?" Charlie whispered to her. He waved a hand in front of her, but the woman did not respond. Charlie glanced back at Merrick. His once-confident air was slowly diminishing as he shifted uncomfortably.

"What's happening here?" Merrick whispered.

"Oy! When are you lot bringing the shoddy excuse you call food 'round here, eh? I can't replenish me magic without food, you dragon dingleberries."

A boy dressed in a simple tunic and trousers leaned against the edge of one alcove. He glared at Merrick and Charlie with a devilish grin, and his blue eyes sparkled with mischief.

"Charlie, we need to keep moving. We cannot know if my father has these prisoners linked to Kashna as Daniel is. If he learns we're here now, we may never get Ailinn back."

Charlie stood defiantly, looking from Merrick to the boy now picking at his nails against the alcove wall. The Harpy's Pointe guards had already injured Ailinn. They had seen that in Addie's scrying mirror. Charlie pulled his arm free from Merrick's grip and stood straighter.

"Ailinn's taken care of herself so far. If we have the chance to find out where she is, we need to take it. Besides," Charlie looked back down the hall from where they had come, "that fight with the guards couldn't have been quiet. They might already know we're here, anyway."

"Eh, no worries, mate," the boy said, his sly grin deepening. "They won't hear you down here."

"What is this place?" Merrick asked. "The escape passage. What happened?"

"Nice, 'innit?" the boy said as he looked down the hall. Every ten feet, another opening revealed an alcove like the one the boy stood in. "Better than those dungeons we were in a year ago. Almost makes the experiments worth it."

He stood straight again and casually walked farther into the tiny room. A small mattress lay on the floor by the back wall surrounded by colorful pillows, blankets, and rugs. He fluffed one of the pillows and leaned back against it.

"Have you seen a girl come in here? It would have been a few days ago?" Charlie asked.

The boy grabbed his chin and thought a moment. The black orenite cuffs on his wrists shifted, revealing worn and pale skin beneath. He had likely worn them for years.

"I ain't seen no one, but I heard a guard talking. Said something about 'her' this morning."

"What else did they say? Where is she? Please tell me, and I promise I'll get you out of here." Charlie took a step forward and immediately fell back. Merrick caught him as sparks flashed at the entrance to the alcove. Shouts of concern farther down the tunnel echoed off the stone as Merrick pulled Charlie to his feet again.

"Flash on the walls, and the fresh meat's still raw!" the boy shouted. They heard several laughs from the other alcoves, and Charlie felt his cheeks flush red.

"Fresh meat got the fixins, Bastian?" A girl in the alcove next to the boy giggled.

He laughed and replied, "Raw from the sea. Don't know the flavor yet. Got a spyglass for a doe. You smelled any such nonsense?"

Nonsense was right. Charlie had no idea what the boy was going on about. He looked at Merrick, but the young man's eyes had grown wide.

"Bastian?" Merrick asked.

The boy whipped around.

"Bastian Garrison?" Charlie now recognized him. Brock's eyes. Addie's nose. "You're coming with us. We're getting you out of here." Charlie took a step forward again, then stopped. He looked at the entrance to the alcove. Strange runes carved into the rock face glowed dimly, and Charlie watched as they faded into innocent scratches on the stone.

"Now you're understanding," said Bastian. He leaned against the back wall, his arms folded and smirking. "Those runes are what keep us in here. One wrong step and you get more than a light show."

"Seems to keep people out nicely as well," said Merrick. He ran a hand along the outer edge of the stone, careful not to cross the threshold that would activate the runes.

"Aye," said Bastian, "if you ain't one of Lord Sparky's chosen guards, you can't get through."

"But obviously, they take you in and out of here," said Charlie. "I promised your mom and dad I'd save you if I could. How do they get you out?"

Bastian shrugged. "Different runes, I think. They counter the ones carved here or something of the sort."

"And they just keep you locked up in here?" Despite the luxurious pillows and books, Charlie felt a sense of barbarity that was quietly being brushed under the lavish rugs.

The girl in the neighboring alcove spoke again. "We've all been here since we was little. Most of us anyways." She nodded toward Bastian, who had suddenly fallen silent. "This is our life now. Some of us is meant for great things and some of us is needed to help with the greater good."

"The greater good?" asked Merrick. His voice trembled, and his hands shook. "That sounds an awful lot like something my father would say." He stepped away from the alcove, pacing back and forth, fists clenched. "I have no words for the horror of what my father has done—what he *is* doing." He turned to Charlie, his eyes as fierce as Savaric's when Charlie had first met him. "Charlie, you go on ahead. Find Ailinn. I'll find a way to rescue these people."

"What!" Charlie cried. "You want me to go up there by myself? Are you crazy?"

"And what if I don't want to be rescued?" a boy in the alcove across from Bastian chided. He'd moved to the front of his room, his arms crossed and eyebrow raised.

Merrick turned to him, stunned. "You would rather stay here? To never see the sun again or feel the wind on your skin?" He turned to Bastian again. "Brock and Addie have never given up on getting you back. They love you, Bastian, and we promised we would do everything we could to return you to them."

A smile spread across Bastian's face. "We might be magic fodder, but we ain't savages. You get us out of here, and we'll help you take down Master Magic Balls."

TWENTY-EIGHT
THE FALL OF THE BRAVE

THE HALLWAYS OF HARPY'S POINTE were made from the same large, gray stones that littered the coastline. Charlie had expected it to be dark and ominous, but the strange glowing orbs and metal rails were found in every passage he turned down. The familiar Belirian wood columns like those at the Elven palace lined every corridor, but the ceiling was not made from tree boughs here. Instead, the tree trunks held up a low ceiling, and its top boughs had been plastered to the stone above. It blended with the gray rock and looked as though the trees were turning to stone.

Every guard that Charlie passed wore the same gambeson emblazoned with the Harpy's Pointe crest. He saw a handful of beck-ands dressed in the familiar dirty white tunics and dresses. No one gave a second glance at him, and for this, Charlie was grateful.

He relaxed as he wound his way farther up to the higher stories of the castle. He kept one hand on his sword hilt, and the other stiff at his side as he had seen the other guards do. Blending in wasn't as difficult as he had thought but finding

Ailinn was proving almost impossible.

Most of the doors he passed were magically locked. Guards and beck-ands passed in and out with ease, but Charlie could not get the doors to budge. At one door, Charlie tried to use his magic to move the locking mechanism. A tiny rune carved into the metal of the door handle glowed and sent tiny sparks flying. He leapt back, batting out the ember that had landed on his gambeson.

A door farther up the hall creaked open, and Charlie glanced over his shoulder. A disheveled-looking Savaric exited the room, followed closely by two guards. It took every ounce of Charlie's willpower not to run. He turned from the door as casually as possible and headed down a hall in the opposite direction.

The door Savaric had exited from was closing gently on its squeaky hinge. Charlie knew he could not magically manipulate the locking mechanism. But the hinge...

He closed his eyes and searched for the energy of the metal at the inner edge of the door. He tightened the bolt, and the door creaked more fiercely as it inched closer and closer to shutting completely. The squeaking stopped, and Charlie peered around the corner. The door had halted inches from latching.

He breathed an audible sigh of relief and hurried back into the wide hallway, stopping beside one of the tree pillars to listen. There was pacing from within the room. His heart leapt as he thought of Ailinn and trudged on.

Charlie stopped outside the wooden door. He peered in, waiting to see Ailinn. Instead, he jumped back. It was Kashna. Deep lashes openly bled across his body. His tattered wings drooped with exhaustion, and Charlie watched his muscles tremor beneath the missing fur and feathers. He laid before the blazing hearth, breathing deep and ragged breaths.

Kashna lifted his head, as though sensing Charlie's presence. His nostrils flared, and Charlie froze. Kashna rested his head on his paws and closed his eyes.

"Come no closer, whoever you are," he said. His voice had lost its confident air, and for the first time he sounded defeated. "If I do not know who you are, then Savaric cannot know. If you wish to remain unknown, you would be wise to leave."

Charlie stared at Kashna, his heart breaking. Kashna had been his greatest mentor. He had taught Charlie more about magic in two days than Ailinn had taught him in a week. Charlie watched as Kashna lifted a paw to rub at a gash across his muzzle and found he could not pull himself away.

Kashna lifted his head again and turned an ear toward the door.

"Still here, I see. Come to watch the once-great Kashna reduced to nothing more than a broken lap cat? You couldn't possibly understand what I have been through. I was used, and I did not realize it. How could I? Savaric was all I had ever known. But he wanted Queen Piper, and when that plan failed, he set his sights on the princess. He needed her. He still needs her. And just as her mother was too stubborn to cooperate, so too is Princess Ailinn. But what would you know? Are you a beck-and? Service is what you were bred for. A curious guard perhaps. More service. But service through manipulation? Manipulation I was an accessory to. Daniel was my friend. I love him. What Savaric made me do…"

Charlie swallowed, and he felt his hands shake. He turned from the door as Kashna stood and began pacing once more.

"He knew. Savaric knew I loved him. But he also knew Daniel loved his sister. When the son of our returned kings came to Chartile, Savaric knew he had to have them both."

Charlie did not believe it was possible, but Kashna's wings dipped more. He circled before the fire and repositioned on the stone before the flames again. "I deserve this. I deserve every slash and drop of my blood that was spilled. But not for denying Savaric. For turning my back on my friends." Kashna laid his head upon his paws again. Charlie thought he saw a silvery tear run down the creature's snout. "Whoever you are and whatever you want, run as far from here as you can. Savaric has more magic at his disposal than even he understands. Learning how to link the Draconian runes was only the first step. Discard any runes he has given you and run."

The door slammed in Charlie's face, and he was left stunned and rubbing the end of his nose. He stared at the back of the door for several minutes, then took off through the hallways and back to the prisoner area.

He tore down the hallway of alcoves. Nearly all the prisoners were at the front of their rooms, whispering to each other. They watched intently as Merrick paced back and forth with his father's book in hand, discussing something with Bastian. Charlie stopped and bent double, clutching at a stitch in his side.

"What's happened?" Merrick rushed to Charlie's side.

"Nothing, I mean—I saw Kashna—"

"What!" Merrick cried.

"No! He didn't see me," Charlie reassured the panicked Merrick.

"Did you find Ailinn?" Merrick asked more calmly.

"No," said Charlie, and Merrick hung his head. "But I have an idea how to get everyone out of here."

"Then some good has come from your exploits. We haven't been able to think of anything."

Merrick and Charlie returned to Bastian's alcove. Bastian leaned against the wall again, though his mischievous smirk was gone.

"Cat's been talking," he said, "and little lord here says you're the son of Jayson Hill."

Charlie swallowed. "Yeah. So?" He cleared his throat. "I'm not my dad, okay? I can't bring in twenty bad guys by myself or shoot a bow from a hundred yards away. But I've got an idea to get you out of here. You still wanna help or are you just gonna stay in your little cage and call people names for the rest of your life?"

Now it was Merrick's turn to smirk. Bastian stared at Charlie a moment, his eyes narrowing. Charlie refused to break his gaze.

"Anything the toothy-bird told you can't be trusted," said Bastian. "He's with Savaric—"

"And Savaric has manipulated him just as much as anyone else. He's lying in a room right now, cut to pieces and bleeding. I don't know what he did, but he stood up to Savaric somehow."

The other prisoners had gone quiet, and Bastian shifted uncomfortably.

"Kashna is my friend. He taught me the magic I'm gonna use to get you out of here."

"You can't, mate," Bastian said with a shrug. "I told you, those runes are activated by magic."

"Kashna said Savaric linked the Draconian runes. He said to discard any runes I was given and to run."

"Best bit of dung he's every given," the girl beside them muttered.

"No, it wasn't, but if I'm right..." He stepped back and closed his eyes. The runes carved into the rock face around Bastian's alcove gave off a sharp energy.

Charlie turned to Merrick, the book still open in his hand. "Have you been able to decipher what the runes are?"

Merrick looked back at the book, turning a few pages in. "You are correct that they are Draconian. They were often used against trespassers who tried to enter the dragon's caves without permission. If you were a friend of a dragon, they would gift you with..." Merrick looked at the book again, pointing at a handful of runes on the page. "Usually it was jewelry. Gold seems to be their preferred metal. It must compliment the runes."

Charlie glanced up at the runes scratched on the surface of the stone again.

They had glowed a golden color when they'd been activated, but the stone itself was completely ordinary.

"Okay," said Charlie, taking a deep breath and rubbing his hands together. "I think I got this." He closed his eyes and reached out with his mind.

Merrick and Bastian watched as the Draconian runes began to glow at the top of the arch. The air around the stone pulsed and warped, and the runes glowed brighter.

"Flash on the walls!" Bastian shouted. He ran farther into the room and lifted his bed mat, shielding himself between it and the back wall.

"Charlie," Merrick said warningly. Charlie ignored him. The stone was beginning to bend to his will, despite the fighting forces of the runes. Merrick watched as the stone around the runes appeared to melt. A crack formed beneath them with a great clap that echoed loudly. One by one, small cracks formed between each of the runes, cutting them off from each other. The runes sparked one last time, and Charlie fell to his knees.

Murmurs from the other prisoners started. Charlie could see them coming to the front of their alcoves again. Bastian peeked from behind his mattress as Charlie stumbled to his feet.

"Come on," Charlie said, breathless. "You should be able to pass through now."

Bastian tossed the mattress aside and walked tentatively toward the entrance.

"You sure?" he asked.

Charlie wiped sweat from his brow. "Not like a hundred percent or anything, but I think so."

Bastian reached a hand toward the arch. The runes did not glow. He passed a single toe over the threshold and pulled it back. Nothing happened. He took a deep breath and walked back to the far side of the little room. He ran full-out, gritting his teeth. He passed beneath the arch unharmed and nearly slammed into the far wall on the opposite side of the hallway.

A collective gasp could be heard from the onlookers within the other alcoves. Bastian looked at the orenite cuffs on his wrists and then at Charlie.

"How did you...?" he asked.

Charlie smiled. "Kashna."

A door opened in the hallway around the corner, and Bastian ran back to his room. Charlie and Merrick took refuge around the corner of another hallway. They peered around the corner and watched two guards drag an unconscious Daniel down the corridor. One of the guards reached out a hand toward the runes of an empty alcove. The runes glowed but did not spark. The second guard tossed Daniel inside, and the two men left without a word.

As soon as the sound of a door closing filled the hall, Charlie rushed to Daniel's alcove.

"Oy! You nutters?" Bastian shouted after him before remembering he could leave his room and followed close behind.

Charlie skidded to a stop, and Bastian immediately pulled him back.

"He's one of Lord Sparky's mates," Bastian whispered.

"He's right, Charlie," Merrick whispered. "If Daniel sees us, Savaric will know we are here."

"And how do we know *they* aren't linked to Lord Sparky?" Charlie snapped, pointing at the line of prisoners that continued to watch from their cells.

"Because this place would have been swarming with guards to toss you in one of your own," said one of the prisoners. Charlie nodded in agreement.

"At some point, we gotta start taking some risks," Charlie said, though he couldn't believe it. Risk was not a word he would have associated with himself. But this wasn't about him anymore. He pulled his arm from Bastian's grasp and walked back to Daniel's alcove.

Daniel lay on the floor, his face, arms and hands covered in blood. Charlie closed his eyes and removed the link between the Draconian runes. He ran to Daniel and hauled him to the mattress at the other end of the room.

"Merrick!" Charlie called. The young man barreled down the line of alcoves, Bastian close on his heel. Merrick gasped when he saw Daniel. He slid his bag from beneath his cloak, rummaging for bandages and ointment.

"We need water!" Charlie shouted. Bastian ran into the hall and returned moments later with a pitcher of water and a clean tunic. Merrick cocked his head in surprise.

"I told you we ain't savages, little lord."

Merrick took the pitcher and tunic, his eyes lingering on Bastian with skepticism. He poured water on the tunic and wiped the blood from Daniel's face and neck.

"What happened to him?" Charlie asked.

"Looks like Savaric put him on his machine. Probably tried to torture information out of him. He's bloody strong as a dragon if he's still alive."

"What machine?" Merrick asked, wiping ointment onto Daniel's cuts and bruises.

Bastian sighed and rolled his eyes. "Lord Sparky built a machine that takes our magic and transfers it to him."

Charlie and Merrick exchanged worried glances.

"Our scouts at the palace couldn't find any traces of magic on Savaric," said Charlie.

"It doesn't last," said Bastian, handing Merrick another wet tunic. "And it depends on the person, how long they've had to rest and so on. Some of us are better with some kinds of magic than others. Davish's got the touch for moving stuff. And Gallia has the gift of sight. If Savior Sav wants to try raising his wife again, he won't get as much power if he uses Gallia's power verses mine or Davish."

Merrick had stopped in the middle of capping the ointment container. He turned back to Bastian, and Charlie could feel the tension in the air.

"Raising his wife?" Merrick's voice was low and cut through the silence with a cold grind.

Bastian recoiled. "He ain't been successful yet, mate. Mostly he just likes to experiment with magic, see what it can do and can't do."

Merrick stood, pacing the small space beside Daniel. He grabbed his thick, blond hair in his fists and what sounded like a growl escaped his throat.

"He's mad," he whispered. "I thought this was a simple matter of viewpoint, of how to approach the rise of magic in our world again. But raising the dead..."

Charlie stood touched Merrick's shoulder. He snapped around, and for a moment, Charlie saw the same wild look in his eyes that Savaric often had. Merrick's face softened, and Charlie squeezed his shoulder.

"I don't know if magic is the answer to this whole thing, the rebellion and all, but it's our best chance against Savaric. Merrick, I know he's your dad—"

Merrick raised his hand to silence him. "No. We must end this, Charlie. This prison, this machine." Merrick pulled his father's book from his bag once more. He flipped through until he found the pages with the strange machines Charlie had seen back at the Glass Lantern.

"That's the one!" Bastian said, pointing to one particular picture. "Well, sort of. I think he's made some modifications."

"You're okay with this, Merrick?" Charlie asked.

Merrick bit his lip and replied, "My father had his chance. Several, in fact. Now, can you teach Bastian and the others your magic techniques? We need all the help we can get."

TWENTY-NINE
FAULT AND FEALTY

CHARLIE FOUND A NEW RESPECT for Kashna. It took him two hours to sever the ties of the Draconian runes in all the prisoners' alcoves. There was a small interruption during which a guard passed through the hall, seemingly on some sort of security round. It took several minutes to refocus the prisoners, who became enthralled with Charlie's ability to make the guard believe he had not seen a group of fifteen prisoners loose in the hall, and instead that he urgently needed a ham sandwich.

Despite having their magic taken from them for years, none of the prisoners knew anything about using it. The orenite cuffs prevented them from performing any magic and were only removed when the person was connected to Savaric's magic machine.

Merrick used the lock pick set Phillippe had packed to remove the prisoners' orenite cuffs. Charlie stood behind him and grounded the surge of energy that occurred when the locks were disturbed.

Charlie spent the remainder of the day teaching the prisoners how to use their magic. They started with moving objects, which most learned quickly. They heard the bell for the evening meal toll in the far distance, and Charlie instructed them to return to their rooms to practice while he rested. He collapsed on the rug beside Daniel's mattress, tuning out the excited chatter that echoed off the stone walls. Merrick entered moments later and offered him a large chunk of bread and the last of Phillippe's tarts.

"Thanks," Charlie muttered as he sat up.

"You're doing wonderful, Charlie," Merrick replied quietly. He grabbed a pink satin pillow and sat beside him on the floor.

Charlie shrugged. "It's no big deal. I'm just showing them what Kashna and Ailinn taught me."

Merrick exhaled, chuckling, and shook his head. "You don't understand how incredible you are, do you?"

Charlie stopped chewing and raised a skeptical eyebrow.

"To learn magic as quickly as you have—"

"They've learned it just as fast as me. If not faster!" Charlie cried. "I couldn't have learned magic without Ailinn and Kashna. I would never have gotten here if it weren't for you and Addie and Brock. And I definitely don't stand a chance against Savaric without all those people out there. All this hero stuff, and me finishing the prophecy my dad started, that's not me."

Merrick smiled again. "It's more of who you are than you know, Charlie. What would have happened to these people had you not come to Chartile? They may have eventually found a means of escape, but at what cost? How many would have died in the process without your help? Ailinn's spirit was slowly fading before you arrived. And I... I would have gone with my father's plan to do whatever it took to bring peace to the kingdom again. Heroes are not made by their great deeds of individual triumph. They are defined by their small acts and influence upon the world."

Charlie grunted and swallowed his last bit of tart. "Then I guess everybody's a hero in some way by your logic."

Merrick nodded. "That is true. Even my father."

A strained silence fell between them as the excited whispers of the prisoners continued to fill the stone hall outside. Daniel slept unmoving beside them, and Merrick took a swig from his flask.

"So what happened between you and your dad, anyway?" Charlie finally broke the tension.

Merrick turned his gaze to the hall. Two young women moved a pillow back and forth between them with their magic. "We did not agree on how to handle the rebellion. So I left."

Charlie rolled his eyes. "No, like, what *really* happened?"

Merrick turned back to Charlie and shifted uncomfortably. "It's not something I am proud of, Charlie. You must know, I have learned from my actions, and I hope to be a better person for it."

Charlie waved off his comments. "Whatever. Nobody's perfect."

"The trouble is I was supposed to be." Merrick took another drink from his flask, and his cheeks flushed. Charlie wondered if the alcohol had more to do with calming Merrick's nerves than it did with helping him stay warm.

"I found my father in his study one day reading from an ancient scroll. He always had an affinity for antiques, and I thought little of it until I looked more closely. It showed a crudely drawn image of someone strapped to a wheel screaming in pain."

Charlie gasped. "The machine?"

"I believe so." Merrick looked at the book still in his lap and ran his fingers over the picture. "I had a terrible feeling then about that scroll. I wanted to throw it in the fire. But I didn't. It would seem he made some modifications. He must have added to this book on his own."

"You didn't know what would happen," said Charlie, setting a hand on Merrick's arm. "It's not your fault."

"Sometimes I think it is," Merrick whispered. He sighed, shutting the book and putting it back in his bag. "We argued. Quite severely. Father said learning more could help bring about a new era of magic, where everyone could exist together in peace. He wanted to prevent what happened to my mother from happening to anyone else."

"But your mom was sick. Magic wouldn't have helped with that, would it?" asked Charlie.

"We don't know. We'll never know. There are theories about how to use magic in ways we cannot yet comprehend. Without research, without experimenting, how can we know?" There was silence again as Charlie mulled over Merrick's words. "But I knew this wasn't the way. The image I saw on that scroll was pure torture. Finally, we came to blows, and I left."

"Left? What, like, you just ran away? Where'd you go?"

Merrick smiled. "I tried to take some inspiration from our dear Queen Piper. She had lived for three years at the base of Mount Kelsii on the outskirts of

Outland Post. After four days, I was too hungry to try to make it on my own. I walked into the local tavern in Harpy's Pointe and found a job working as a porter at the docks. I changed my name, but they knew who I was."

"Why did you go back?" Charlie reached out a hand and took the flask Merrick offered him. The liquid burned his mouth and throat like fire but seemed to warm him as soon as it hit his stomach. He handed the flask back with a twisted face and a cough.

"Peace. It's all any of us really want. We simply have different ideas of how it should be done. Ailinn and I were arranged to be married long before I had run away. When that treaty was rekindled, I knew I would have the opportunity to stop the fighting. Or at least try."

"Oy, you two palace pickles finished your cavorting? We think we might have a plan," said Bastian.

Merrick and Charlie rose. They had only walked a few paces when they heard a pained groan behind them.

Charlie whipped around and ran to Daniel's side.

"No, Charlie!" Merrick cried.

"Charlie?" Daniel whispered weakly.

"Hey," Charlie whispered back. "Yeah. Are you okay?"

"What happened?" Daniel tried to sit up and immediately stiffened, his face contorted in agonizing pain.

"I don't know exactly. The others, they said something about Savaric's machine."

"Charlie, his connection to my father," Merrick urged him.

"It's gone," Daniel said, his breath coming faster now. "He severed the connection. He says I'm no longer a use to him. He is keeping me alive only as leverage against Ailinn."

"Have you seen her? Ailinn? Is she all right?" asked Charlie.

Daniel shook his head. Charlie barely noticed. "I have not, but she must be alive at the very least." Daniel closed his eyes and released a deep, audible breath. "What are you going to do?"

Charlie glanced up at Merrick. His jaw was set, and his eyes searched Charlie's face.

"I'm going to end this, Daniel. I'm going to finish what my dad started."

Daniel coughed and groaned again. A small dot of fresh blood appeared in the corner of his nose. "If anyone can do it, you can. I am sorry, Charlie. For all of it.

I don't know everything I did or said to you. It's coming back to me in flashes—nightmares. But whatever I may have said or done, I believe in you."

His face relaxed, and Daniel fell into unconsciousness again.

THIRTY
THE FALL OF NEW MAGIC

THE HALLS OF HARPY'S POINTE were dark and silent once more. The orbs along the walls had dimmed, and Charlie could see the sun setting through the narrow windows at the end of the hallways. Merrick walked close to his side, and Charlie could feel the tension within him. The plan seemed simple enough, but Merrick had been struggling with what he would say to his father from the moment they discussed it.

Somewhere up ahead, a door closed, and Merrick and Charlie darted behind the tree pillars.

"You'll never break me, Savaric! By my mother's blood, I will die before I let you take my magic!"

Charlie's eyes widened at the sound of the voice. Merrick grabbed the back of his tunic before he darted from behind the pillar. A door creaked open, and Charlie stopped struggling against Merrick's grip.

"It is by your blood that you are here, your Highness. In time, you will understand. Your magical contribution is far greater than any political decisions

247

you could have ever made. I am sorry it had to come to this. I will send someone to tend to your wounds soon."

The door closed more gently this time, and Savaric's footfalls faded down a set of stairs at the other end of the hall.

Charlie bolted for the door before Merrick could reach for him again. He did not have to worry about finding a way through the doors this time. They had nicked the gold cuffs from the guards who remained unconscious in the passage beyond the alcoves. The door opened easily with the runes inscribed on the guard's cuffs.

He stood transfixed, his legs unable to move. Part of him expected to see Savaric standing in the middle of the room with his smug smirk and gray eyes. It would not have surprised him if this were a trap, and all his hopes of ever seeing Ailinn again would disappear as his life flashed before his eyes.

But there she was. Her royal gown had been replaced with a simple beck-and dress. Her face was gaunt, and her once-wild hair hung limp down her back. Her wrists and forearms were red and raw, and in the dim light from the setting sun, Charlie could make out long gashes on her back that had bled through her dress. She turned, and the fire that burned in her eyes softened. The two stood in silence, eyes locked and unbelieving. Charlie stepped cautiously toward her, then stopped when he saw her recoil.

"Ailinn, it's me," he said.

Ailinn's eyes looked over his shoulder. Charlie heard footsteps in the doorway, and he turned to see Merrick enter the room. Ailinn turned her gaze back to Charlie, searching his face for any sign that what she was seeing was a lie. Carefully, she lifted her hand and touched his face with trembling fingers. Charlie took her hand in his, careful to avoid the burned looking flesh.

"Let's get you out of—" Charlie's words were cut short as Ailinn threw herself into his arms. She buried her face in his stolen gambeson and squeezed him tighter than she ever had. He hugged her back, unsure of what to say.

Merrick shut the door behind him and began a security sweep of the space. It was a single room, like the one Charlie found Kashna in, with a hearth, a small bed, and dressing table. The crank to open the window had been covered in orenite and carved with more Draconian runes.

Ailinn loosened her grip and looked at Merrick as he laid a comforting hand on her back. She smiled weakly and leaned in to hug her childhood friend.

"I promised I would always be here for you," Merrick said into her hair, kissing the top of her head.

"How are we going to escape?" she asked. Her voice was dry and had lost the strength she had used when speaking to Savaric only moments before. "I cannot imagine getting out will be as simple as getting in."

Charlie laughed. "Getting in was definitely not simple."

Every muscle in Charlie's body suddenly tightened. He watched as Merrick's and Ailinn's bodies stiffened in the positions they had been standing in. Very slowly, Charlie felt his arms move straight to his sides, though he was not the one controlling them. In front of him, Ailinn's arms were forced down to her sides and her back straightened from where she had been leaning into Merrick. Her lower lip trembled, and Charlie could see tears glazing over her frightened eyes.

"Oh, but getting out was never part of the plan," said a smooth voice from the door.

Charlie's body moved upward until his feet dangled inches above the floor. All three of them turned to face the open door. There stood Savaric, his smug smile more menacing than mischievous. Behind him stood the girl who had been Bastian's neighbor.

"Why?" Merrick whispered, and the girl disappeared up the hall.

"Never underestimate the power of luxury and convenience, my son. For a little pain every few days, these people are afforded every indulgence I can bring to them. They never want for food, and they are not ravaged by illness. Had they continued to live their lives in the villages and towns, they would have died from injuries, disease, childbirth. Here they are safe. And it is here they wish to stay."

"Not all of them," Charlie choked out.

Savaric chuckled, but the grip of his stolen magic did not lessen upon Charlie.

"No, not all of them, little king. But those who would defy me are dealt with accordingly."

"Like those people you brought to the palace?" Charlie snapped. He felt the muscles in his throat tighten as if Savaric were trying to squeeze the life from him.

"Your magic is as wild as your tongue, little king," Savaric snapped. "And now that I have both the princess and the son of Jayson Hill, I can complete my work."

Charlie's body jerked. He felt himself rise higher into the air, Merrick and Ailinn beside him. Savaric lifted his hand, and they floated through the air toward him.

The glowing orbs along the halls brightened and dimmed again as Savaric passed with his new prisoners in tow. They passed through the deserted halls and down winding stone steps. The corridors were quiet—too quiet, and Charlie realized this must have been in part what tipped Savaric off. Bastian and the prisoners had done their job well. They had quietly infiltrated the castle and put every guard and beck-and they encountered to sleep, allowing Charlie and Merrick to pass without confrontation. He wondered how many more of the prisoners had sided with Savaric.

The last hall was lined with several windows that faced the small port town of Harpy's Pointe. The waves crashed against the docks, and Charlie saw dark clouds forming in the distance.

Savaric lifted his other hand, and the heavy door before him opened. He passed through, his three captives still floating through the air behind him. Ailinn's fingers twitched, and her eyes widened as she fought against Savaric's magical grasp.

The orbs around the room brightened, and Charlie gasped. It was something out of a science-fiction laboratory. Wires, wheels, and metal contraptions littered the large room. Towering bookshelves lined the far walls, and a wooden desk piled high with scrolls, books, and parchment sat in the corner. Perched on top was the book Merrick had stolen and had left hidden in Daniel's alcove.

"No," Merrick breathed.

Charlie couldn't move his head, but his eyes shifted, and he knew exactly what Merrick had referred to. Beneath the only window in the room was a glass case on a small platform. Beneath the glass was the perfectly preserved body of a blonde-haired woman, Merrick's mother.

The magical tension within Charlie's muscles lessened. He assumed the same was true for Ailinn as she struggled more fiercely beside him. The three suddenly dropped to the floor, and a heavy cage collapsed over top of them.

"Father, this is wrong! All of this!" Merrick cried. He pulled at the bars of the cage, but it didn't move.

"And who decides what is right and wrong?" Savaric shouted back. "Our kings? The chosen ones?"

Savaric headed toward the giant wheel beside his desk and pulled a lever on a large box. The hairs on Charlie's body stood on end, though there was no sound. He could feel an electricity in the air, and his heart pounded faster.

"For too long we have lived in fear of something that could save lives, and all because we do not understand it." Savaric peered inside the glass casket at his wife and ran his fingers gently across the top.

"She's gone, Father. Let her be at peace. I promised I would work to lift the legalities against magic, but not like this. *You* need peace."

"I will have my peace when I can hold my wife in my arms once more."

Savaric turned back to the wheel. He pulled more levers and Charlie saw several smaller cogs at the base of the machine begin to move and spark. At the top of the wheel frame was a circle of gold inset with the largest orenite stones he had yet seen.

Ailinn must have followed his gaze. Through her tears, she whispered, "It's the royal circlet. The one the four kings used to remove magic from the elves."

Charlie backed away from the bars of the cage. His father had never found the circlet. They had defeated Taraniz and Noraedin in other ways.

"He's modified it to remove magic instead of hold it within." Ailinn fell to her knees and held her injured arms close to her. Merrick knelt beside her and wrapped his arms around her.

"We're going to figure a way out of here, Ailinn. He won't hurt you again."

"Maybe if all of us try to lift this thing," Charlie said, staring at the metal cage around them.

"It's no use," Ailinn said weakly, burying her face in her knees.

"We have to think of something," Merrick said to Charlie.

Savaric turned from the book on his desk and approached a long table filled with glass vials and tubes. They couldn't see what he had done, but one of the vials began to smoke. They watched a blue liquid run through the tubes and disappear behind the great wheel. Moments later, the blue liquid appeared in a glass tube around the perimeter of the wheel and the circlet. They watched with bated breath as the liquid slowly completed its circuit of the wheel and touched the orenite cuffs. The liquid turned a bright red, and the orenite changed to a strange green tinge.

Savaric breathed heavily, turning back to the cage behind him. His eyes narrowed, and his face turned red as he strained to lift the cage again. His stolen magic was draining.

Charlie and Merrick tried to run. Charlie made it halfway to the door when he felt Savaric's magical grip tighten on his body again, and he heard Merrick and Ailinn cry out behind him. He fought the man's weakening magic enough to turn and see them lying flat on the stone floor and the cage swaying above them.

"Let them go!" Charlie cried, pushing the energy of Savaric's magic from his body. He ran back to the cage, reaching for the sword that still hung at his side. Just as he wrapped his fingers around the hilt, the cage slammed to the ground, and

Ailinn screamed. Merrick scrambled and held her tightly against him once more.

"Not yet, little king."

Charlie felt his throat tighten. The sword he held clattered to the ground, and he reached for his neck, unable to breathe. He looked at Savaric, and the man's red face had turned nearly purple with the effort of using the fading magic. Charlie felt his feet rise off the floor again and inch toward the giant wheel.

"No!" Ailinn screamed. She beat feverishly against the metal bars before Merrick pulled her into his arms again. "I'll do what you ask! Let him go!" she pleaded, her face half buried against Merrick.

"You think this is love, princess?" Savaric sneered at her, though his voice was strained with pain. "The panic in your heart? The fear in your mind? You know nothing of love, child. This! All of this! I did for my Merra, and until you understand that, you do not understand love."

Savaric swung his arm toward the wheel, and Charlie slammed into the hard wood. Ailinn continued to shout, and Merrick attempted to calm her to no avail. Her pretty face was blotched with tears, and her wrists had started bleeding again. The orenite cuffs snapped shut around Charlie's ankles and wrists, and Savaric collapsed, breathless, on the stone floor.

"You don't have to do this, Savaric. There's gotta be another way. Something you haven't found yet," said Charlie. He pushed against the cuffs, hoping his voice sounded calmer than he felt.

"Unlike you, little king, I am not content to sit idly by and allow others to choose my fate." Savaric pushed himself to his knees, his breathing labored. "Perhaps there is another way, but if I discover it too late..." He staggered to his feet and stared at Merra's glass casket once more. He turned another lever, and Charlie heard the creak of gears and the grind of metal on metal from somewhere behind him.

The hair on Charlie's body stood on end more. Even his thick, red hair began to rise. His entire body tingled with a static that came from all around him. Savaric lifted a pair of green-tinged orenite cuffs from his desk, snapping them around his own wrists.

"Please. *Please*, Savaric," Ailinn begged. "I'll do it. Take me instead. I was the one you wanted all along."

"No!" Charlie cried. He locked his eyes to hers and shook his head. The fire in her was gone. She closed her eyes and leaned into Merrick's shoulder, sobbing once more.

Savaric laughed a cold, merciless laugh. "I wanted you both, princess," he said sweetly. "The only way to have you both was to bring you here myself. I knew the silly boy would follow you, and like his father, he would come alone."

"He's not alone. He's never been alone. And neither have you, Father." Merrick's voice had changed, but Charlie barely noticed. The orenite cuffs were turning hot against his skin.

"Merrick, I commend your ability to ride the line with this war on magic. I can only credit your mother for it. But it has blinded you to the true benefits of understanding what magic could bring to this world. Even those fighting against the crown do not understand as deeply as I do. My son, I have been alone since your mother died. But no longer."

Savaric pulled another lever, and Charlie felt a sharp pain run down his spine. It did not lessen but continued to build. His scream intermingled with Savaric's and Ailinn's. His vision blurred, the edges black and yellow, and the weight on his chest was growing worse. In a few short moments, he knew he wouldn't be able to breathe anymore.

The blackness across his sight was almost complete, and the pounding in his ears drowned out all else. Charlie felt himself take a deep breath and realized he had passed out. He heard Ailinn crying from what seemed like miles away and Merrick calling his name.

Charlie tried to lift his head, but his muscles screamed with agony.

"He's alive," he heard Merrick say, and Ailinn let out a single sobbing gasp.

"Father!" Merrick called to Savaric now. Charlie could only guess he had fallen unconscious as well. He heard movement from somewhere below him. His eyes flicked open, and he saw Savaric stagger to his feet.

Savaric stared at his hands and flexed his fingers. He removed the orenite cuffs from his wrists, and they clattered to the floor with a flash of sparks. Carefully, he lifted his hand, and the cage that still trapped Merrick and Ailinn rose on its chain into the air. Both remained still and staring.

Savaric flicked his wrist, and Merrick's body was thrown flat on the stone floor again. He slowly turned his wrist, and Ailinn rose into the air, floating toward him with such speed, she cried out. Savaric wrapped his hand around her throat and eased her to the floor.

"I may not even need you anymore, little princess," he said. The corners of his lips curled into a satisfied smile, then his eyes rolled back. He released his grip on Ailinn and she crumpled to the floor. Savaric screamed and held the back of his now-bleeding head.

Daniel stood towering over him, a sword held tightly in one hand.

"Go, Ailinn!" he shouted.

Ailinn scrambled to her feet and ran to Charlie.

"No! What are you doing?" said Charlie, frantic. "Get out of here! The horses are wait—"

"You are more than naïve if you think I'm going to leave you," she seethed as she pulled at the orenite cuffs.

"Ailinn! Behind you!" Merrick cried. A blur of black fur and feathers leapt over Ailinn, pushing her to the ground. Kashna landed hard on top of Charlie, the mechanical wheel swaying under his weight. Kashna slashed again and again at the cuffs until deep gouges ran the length of the metal.

Charlie struggled to remain awake. He heard rather than saw Daniel and Savaric exchanging both physical and magical blows. A loud crash made his eyes shoot open. Savaric lay in a pile of glass from Merra's casket.

Daniel used his magic to lift the cage that still enclosed Merrick. The young man darted beneath the bars before Savaric hit Daniel with a blast of magical energy, causing the cage to fall again.

Merrick rushed to Ailinn and pulled her to her feet. "Please, get out of here, Ailinn. I promise I won't leave Charlie behind," said Merrick.

"Run, young princess," Kashna said, leaping to the floor beside Ailinn. "Your people must know what has happened here." Kashna roared and took off to join the fight against Savaric.

Charlie felt the giant wheel lurch as Merrick climbed toward him. He pulled hard against the slashed cuffs, his teeth clenching with the effort. Finally, the metal gave way. Charlie squeezed his wrist through the opening and pulled at the metal of the other wrist cuff. Ailinn ignored both Merrick and Kashna and was working at the orenite cuffs that bound Charlie's ankles.

Kashna's deafening roar made them all turn as he was hurled through the air. He slammed into the stone floor just feet from them. Charlie looked into the creature's bright golden eyes. There was a carnal wildness he had never seen before. The qarveena turned from Charlie and ran for Savaric again.

The last of the cuffs gave way around Charlie's right ankle and he felt himself falling face-first toward the floor. Merrick and Ailinn caught him and pushed themselves beneath his arms to support him. Charlie's body felt weaker without the cuffs to hold his weight, but at least his mind was growing sharper.

He watched as Savaric used his stolen magic to raise Daniel toward the ceiling.

Daniel writhed in pain, his hands clasped over his throat, and his face turning red. Kashna pounced on Savaric, pushing him to the ground. Charlie was sure he heard bones crack as Savaric's mouth collided with the floor. Kashna bounded off the man's back and into the air to catch Daniel.

Ailinn pushed Charlie into Merrick. They watched as she rushed toward Savaric, picking up the large tome from his desk as she went. She raised the book over the man's head and came down hard on the base of his skull. Savaric fell, sprawling on the floor as Kashna landed with Daniel safely in tow.

Ailinn threw the book to the ground, the sound echoing off the stone walls. Merrick and Charlie watched the fire return to her bright green eyes. She turned to the giant wheel, her arms still bleeding, and climbed precariously to the top. The wood creaked beneath her, and Merrick saw the base begin to splinter.

"Ailinn, get off there!" Daniel cried, climbing from Kashna's back.

Ailinn snatched the orenite circlet from between the glass tubing and leapt to the floor.

Savaric grunted and groaned as he pushed himself to his knees. Ailinn hurried back to him, the circlet held over his head. Without warning, Savaric sat up. He reached for Ailinn's wrist and pulled her down with him, twisting her arms behind her back.

"Anyone moves and she dies," he said, the circlet now poised above Ailinn's head. He spit a mouthful of blood on the floor, his breath coming in heaving ragged gasps.

Daniel, Merrick, and Charlie did not move. Kashna growled beside them and flexed his claws against the stone floor.

"You will return to the holding cell. Now," he said, and he gestured toward the cage behind them. "I will not give a second war—Ah!" Savaric yelped and Ailinn leapt to her feet as the man batted at the fire quickly spreading across his tunic. Charlie couldn't help but smile at her quick thinking.

As Savaric patted out the fire, Ailinn snatched the circlet away from him again, slamming it onto his head. Savaric froze, and the fire continued to spread. With a strained effort, she eased Savaric through the air with what little magic she had left and into the orenite cuffs of the strange wheel contraption. The cuffs closed around his wrists and ankles, and Ailinn released her magic from him.

Daniel, no longer paralyzed with shock, hurried to his sister. "Come on, Ailinn," he whispered.

Ailinn pushed him away. "I am in no need of saving, Daniel."

She pulled every lever she could find on the wooden boxes beside Savaric's desk.

The scream that reverberated throughout the room was almost deafening. The second pair of orenite cuffs sparked and hummed on the floor. The air around Savaric rippled, slowly spreading throughout the room.

A window close to Savaric exploded, showering them all with glass. Ailinn fell back, and Daniel caught her just before she hit the ground.

"He'll bring down the entire castle if this continues!" Merrick shouted over Savaric's scream.

Daniel turned to Kashna. "Get them out," he said, and he tossed his sister haphazardly toward the creature.

Kashna grabbed the back of Ailinn's dress in his teeth and dragged her toward the door.

"No! Daniel!" she screamed, fighting to free herself from Kashna's grasp.

"Daniel, what are you doing?" Merrick called. He took a step toward him. Another window shattered, and he stopped short of the magical aura that continued to grow around his father.

"It's what my father did to save my mother and the kings. The magic needs to be grounded. Tell Ailinn I'm sorry. Tell her—tell her I love her, and I'm sorry for leaving her. Like Mother." He picked up the orenite cuffs, his screams joining Savaric's.

Charlie pulled himself from beneath Merrick's arm and stumbled toward Daniel. Blood was forming around his eyes, nose and mouth.

"Daniel, no!" Charlie cried. "I'm supposed to be the chosen one!"

Merrick grabbed Charlie's bleeding wrist.

"We have to get out of here!" he yelled over the sound of more shattering glass.

"I can't let him die!" Charlie shouted.

"We can't let her die, either," said Merrick, nodding toward Ailinn. He glanced painfully toward his mother's casket. Her once perfectly preserved body seemed to deteriorate before their eyes.

Charlie tore his eyes from the scene and followed Kashna out of the room.

THIRTY-ONE
HEROES AND HESITATION

MERRICK LED THE WAY THROUGH the darkened hallways and stairwells. Charlie sat upon the great qarveena's back, gripping the fur and feathers at the nape of Kashna's neck. Ailinn struggled against Kashna, who still held her tunic between his teeth. The screams from Savaric and Daniel had faded, but the hum of magical energy still reverberated in the air.

The whole castle shook violently, throwing everyone to the ground. Ailinn was the first to her feet and began running back up the corridor.

"Ailinn!" Kashna growled after her. She stopped, turning slowly back to him. Her eyes were bloodshot, and her face red from tears.

"Please, Kashna," she whispered to him. The two stared at each other for several long moments. Ailinn fell to her knees. "Let me go to him. You have to let me save him."

Kashna turned to look at Charlie out of the corner of his eye. Without a word, Charlie climbed from Kashna's back, and the creature leapt past Ailinn back up the corridor.

"Come on," Merrick urged as she stared after Kashna. "He'll save him."

"We have to keep moving," said Charlie.

They each grabbed one of Ailinn's hands and led her down a winding stair. Merrick resumed the lead and led them to the main hall of the castle. A scared group of beck-ands and prisoners congregated before the main doors.

"Master Merrick," said one of the older beck-ands, and the group turned as one to see the three running toward them.

"Thank the gods!" said Bastian, pushing his way through the crowd.

"Is there anyone left in the castle?" Merrick called to the group. Several shook their heads in reply. Others continued to cower in terror.

"This is the last of them," said Bastian. "Bloody guards took off as soon as they realized they had a magical mutiny on their hands."

"What about—?" Charlie began when his eyes fell on the girl who had betrayed them to Savaric. "You..." He took a step toward her, but Bastian held up his hands.

"Easy there, you little love-struck lordy," said Bastian. "She'll be dealt with," Charlie saw a pair of orenite cuffs and a piece of rope around her wrists.

The assembly shrieked as the castle shook again, and dust and tiny pebbles fell from the ceiling above them.

"Everyone out!" Merrick called.

The double entry doors were swung wide, and the throng of people dashed one by one down the small trail that led from the castle to the forest's edge. The sound of breaking glass and crumbling stone followed them as they ran. Lord, beck-and, and prisoner had no meaning as they gathered in the small clearing at the base of the path. They turned to each other, tending to wounds and emotions alike.

Merrick took charge, leaving Charlie sitting on the ground against a small Belirian tree. Ailinn sat beside him, curled in his arms and staring at the castle above them. There was no sign of Daniel or Kashna.

Merrick touched Charlie's shoulder, and the boy started.

"I'm moving everyone to the main docks in town. King Valin would have mounted his own search for us not long after we departed. I cannot imagine they are too far behind, especially after your correspondence with Jock and Drustad."

Charlie nodded. A loud crack broke the quiet tension of the crowd, and they turned to watch as the castle began to crumble into the sea.

Ailinn stood and stared, unmoving. The plume of dust that rose into the air could have easily hidden Kashna if he had found Daniel and escaped. She stood frozen with the rest of the beck-ands and prisoners, watching and waiting.

"Oy! Rickon!" a gruff voice called from between the trees.

Merrick whipped around, and relief spread across his face.

"Seamus!" said Merrick as several men on horseback emerged from the forest. Four of them dismounted, and three turned their attention to the beck-ands and prisoners with medical supplies and food. The last man embraced Merrick heartily.

"I knew you and your father did not see eye to eye, but—" started Seamus.

Merrick held up a hand to silence him, and the teasing grin quickly disappeared from Seamus's face.

"There was always a part of me that believed I could save him," Merrick whispered.

"You're too soft, Rickon," said Seamus, and he patted Merrick on the back.

"I want to move these people away from here," said Merrick, his voice stronger. "Can you help?"

Seamus nodded and turned his attention back to the prisoners and beck-ands. Merrick exhaled, then squared his shoulders before joining Charlie and Ailinn once more.

"Who's that?" Charlie asked.

"Seamus. He works at the docks. He gave me a job when I left my father. He knew who I was, but he never said anything."

"Rickon?" Charlie raised an eyebrow at Merrick.

"The name I chose when I left. I didn't want anyone to know who I was. I wanted to be normal." Merrick glanced over his shoulder at the people gathered at the forest's edge. Several beck-and women crowded around a heavily pregnant girl. "I realize now that is not who I am. It never was."

The two turned to Ailinn, who had not stopped staring at the crumbling castle in the distance.

"Ailinn," said Merrick gently. "We need to go. These people need food and shelter."

Ailinn's eyes darted between Merrick and Charlie. "Daniel," she croaked and swallowed hard.

"Ailinn, I don't know if..." Charlie trailed off as Ailinn's gaze fell.

Merrick stepped toward her, his hand outstretched. She pulled away, her brows knitted in anger.

"Rickon!" Seamus called to Merrick. Most of the men had remounted their horses, and the prisoners and beck-ands were congregating around them.

Merrick nodded and raised his hand to Seamus. He turned back to Charlie, but the boy interrupted him before he could speak.

"You go do your thing," said Charlie. "You're the leader here, not me. I'll take care of her."

Merrick smiled weakly, his eyes closing in relief. He squared his shoulders and held out his hand to Charlie.

"You're not the only one capable of learning about other worlds." Merrick's smile turned wry as he gripped and shook Charlie's hand. He squeezed Ailinn's shoulder in comfort. She had resumed staring into the cloud of dust that had once been Harpy's Pointe castle. She did not move. Merrick nodded to Charlie and joined Seamus.

Charlie sat again at the base of the Belirian tree. Ailinn eventually joined him, and the two watched as the dust slowly settled against the backdrop of the setting sun.

When the sun turned a bright orange and hung low in the sky, Charlie spoke. "Do you think maybe they ran away or something?" There was a moment's pause, and he wondered if Ailinn had heard him at all, or if her mind had finally drifted far enough away.

"I never said goodbye," she said several minutes later. "He wouldn't have left me without..." She looked at her hands, which had remained clenched in her lap for hours.

Charlie was sure he knew what she was thinking. Daniel had many reasons to leave—if he were even still alive. And Kashna was now free to return to his family and the other lost legends of Chartile. It was like some sort of secret, happily ever after to a fairy tale. All Charlie could do was hold on to the hope that he was right. If he thought too long about the alternative, he knew he wouldn't be strong enough for Ailinn.

Charlie stood, fighting the pain and tingling in his feet from sitting in one place for hours. He reached a hand out to her. Hesitantly, Ailinn took it, and Charlie pulled her to her feet. Hand in hand, the two walked away from the sight of the crumbling castle and toward Harpy's Pointe.

It was near dark when they reached the town's edge where tents that were normally used for war battles and tournaments had been erected. The town was busy despite the growing darkness. Campfires had been dug and lit with pots of steaming stew bubbling over them. From every home and shop, the citizens of Harpy's Pointe hurried back and forth, carrying everything from clothes and blankets to food and even chamber pots.

As Charlie and Ailinn rounded the corner of one tent, they saw Merrick and

Bastian standing at the inland edge of the largest dock. People hurried to them, exchanged information, then bustled off again.

Charlie pushed his way through the crowds, Ailinn's hand still tightly in his own.

"Oy! You finally made it, I see. All the hard work's been done. Mostly anyway. You wouldn't know anything about making cots with your magic, would you?" Bastian asked them before the two had even reached the dock. Merrick turned away from his conversation with Seamus as they approached. He sighed with relief when he set eyes on them.

"Did he—?" Merrick began. Charlie shook his head. Merrick was politely silent for a moment, then continued. "We need help. The town has done all they can, but there are just not enough beds, and the ground is too wet from the storm that passed through."

"What can we do?" Ailinn asked, her voice cracking.

"I can't allow the prison—the magically gifted—to use their magic. It's still outlawed, and I will not take my father's place in this war, even if I believe we should lift the ban," said Merrick quietly. "Charlie, you are the one destined to finish this prophecy. If anyone has a right to magic, it would be you."

"Do you forget my mother was the reincarnated soul of one of the ancient kings?" Ailinn snapped. "I am just as destined as Charlie to help in this."

Merrick squeezed Ailinn's shoulder. "The last thing we need is for you to become a martyr like Queen Piper. She died because some people felt she shouldn't be allowed to use her magic if others couldn't. If we allowed everyone here to use their magic, it would open the floodgates against none other than your own father and the Conclave."

Ailinn shrugged Merrick's hand away, her eyes turning cold again. She opened her mouth to speak, and Merrick placed a finger to her lips.

"Please, Ailinn. I know you want to help, and I wish you to do so. But not with this task. You are our princess, and I believe your role in this to be much greater than magic alone. My father was wrong about you. Very, very wrong."

Ailinn softened, and Merrick removed his finger from her lips. Charlie shifted uncomfortably as he watched them. He never thought it was possible to temper Ailinn's fire. She squared her shoulders and pushed her chin in the air.

"Very well. What did you have in mind? This is your town, Merrick. I am but a guest here."

Merrick smiled and kissed her forehead. "We may not be defined by our family, but we cannot deny what is in our blood. I see the same fire in you that your mother had. As well as the kindness I have heard of Runa. Go to your people. Be among them. Care for them."

Ailinn paused and stared into Merrick's gray-blue eyes. Charlie sensed a confidence and reassurance from him. Ailinn must have sensed it too. She hugged him warmly, a smile she had not held since before Savaric arrived spreading across her face.

She broke from Merrick and hugged Charlie as well. But there was something different about her touch this time. With her dress still seeped in blood, and her wrists and ankles raw and red, she disappeared into the darkness toward the large tents.

Charlie watched until she disappeared among the crowds. He felt a hand touch his shoulder. He turned, expecting to see Merrick, but it was Bastian who smiled at him.

"Trouble with the ladies, mate?" he asked.

Charlie didn't answer. He looked at Merrick, who had returned to his conversation with Seamus.

"I guess we have our orders then," said Bastian. His hand pressed against Charlie's shoulder as he led him away from Merrick and Seamus.

"*Our* orders?" Charlie asked him.

Bastian smirked. "Eh, what the boss man don't know won't hurt him."

They walked through the crowd of townsfolk unnoticed. Charlie felt numb. His hands shook, and fear and confusion suddenly overwhelmed him. When they reached the edge of the forest, all Charlie could do was stare at the mud pit before them.

"So, how we doing this?" Bastian pushed up the sleeves of his plain tunic and shook out his arms. When Charlie didn't answer, he looked at him. "Oy. Mate. Are you with me?"

In the deepening darkness, Charlie saw how young Bastian truly was. Perhaps only twelve years old. But his eyes carried a wisdom as deep as Brock's, and his smile was as gentle as Addie's.

"I guess I can't believe everything that happened. Like, all the stuff I did," Charlie whispered. Bastian remained silent, his eyes coaxing Charlie's emotions to the surface. "But the thing is, I didn't really do anything. Daniel, he—and now Merrick. Did I fulfill the prophecy? Was I the one all along?"

Bastian shifted and scratched at the side of his nose. Charlie remembered Brock doing the same thing, and he wondered how many of Jayson's traits he himself carried without realizing it.

"Well, that's about as deep as a wargler's pit, mate, and I ain't no wargler to be investigating such things. But I'll tell you this, it doesn't matter what happened before. It's just the here and the after. I haven't felt the wind on my face in years but thinking about that now's no help to me or anyone else. So, Daniel was the one who killed Lord Sparky. Maybe he had his own prophecy or destiny or something of the sort. And Lord Merrick's been running things since before he got the first tingle in his belly for a girl. It's what them fancy folk do. Don't make it right or wrong. It's just the way of things."

Charlie sighed. Somehow, the wisdom of a twelve-year-old seemed to leave him even more confused. A light appeared to Charlie's left, and he turned to see Bastian standing beside him with a fistful of fire. He grinned eagerly.

"The night is getting on, Charlie. I, for one, would quite enjoy a place to rest."

"Bastian, wait," said Charlie.

The young boy's face fell, and he extinguished his light.

"Something the matter?" he asked.

Charlie opened and closed his mouth several times, shifting his weight back and forth at the edge of the mud pit. Bastian deserved to know. He'd find out sooner than later, anyway.

"You should know that it was your parents who helped us," Charlie began. Bastian squinted, his eyes surveying Charlie just as Brock had done. Charlie's stomach flopped. He swallowed and continued. "Without them, we never would have made it to Harpy's Pointe. Your mom, she's an amazing healer. You can learn a lot from her. And, your da—"

Charlie's voice trembled. The memory of Brock's final stand flashed through his mind. He felt his knees buckle under him. He sat on the wet earth, his arms wrapped around himself.

Bastian knelt beside him, his light reappearing in the palm of his hand, but softer this time. "My dad's gone, isn't he?"

The wetness from the ground was seeping through Charlie's pants, but he didn't care. He looked at Bastian and saw Addie's strong kindness staring back at him.

"He's one of the bravest people I've ever known, Bastian."

The boy smiled. "Well, 'in't that saying something, then? And you know Jayson of the Hill."

"They would have gone with us to the very end, Bastian. They never gave up on you."

Bastian nodded. "In truth, I never gave up on them either. But here's the thing, they also wouldn't have us blubbering over them. Tis nothing to be done except move on and help the people who are here right now."

"So, you're not mad at me?" Charlie asked, wiping a tear from his eye.

Bastian stood and held out his free hand to Charlie. "Ain't nothing to be mad about. My dad's a hero, like yours now. You and me? We're brothers like that now. So, help a brother out? Help me dry this marsh of a mud pit. A good night sleep will get me on the road home sooner."

Bastian held his light aloft as he and Charlie surveyed the ground. They took turns providing light for each other, which was a much easier task than forcing the small molecules of water through the ground to dry the area. Bastian learned quickly, and Charlie was pleasantly surprised how easy teaching seemed to come to him. After only an hour, the area was dry, and Bastian and Charlie headed back toward the town.

It was quieter, and most of the homes that lined the main street were dark. As they rounded the corner, a scream broke through the night. Charlie didn't stop to think. The fire he had created in his hand immediately disappeared, and he ran full-out toward the scream.

A crowd was gathered outside the main tent, chattering excitedly. Charlie saw Merrick heading toward the crowd as well.

"Where's Ailinn?" he shouted to Merrick. No one answered. Charlie pushed his way through the crowd, barreling toward the tent flap.

"Charlie, no!" Merrick called after him as he tore through the opening.

Charlie stopped dead in his tracks. The pregnant beck-and stood over a large bucket. A woman knelt on the ground at her feet, while two more held her up, one under each arm. One of them was Ailinn.

The crowd of women looked up as Charlie entered, and the pregnant girl screamed again.

"Charlie!" Ailinn shouted, but Charlie barely registered.

"Young man, bring me those towels!" said the woman kneeling on the ground. Charlie felt his stomach begin to turn. "Now!" the woman cried again.

Charlie ran to the corner of the tent, his legs threatening to give way under him. He could barely grasp the towels and resorted to carrying them against his wrists to keep from dropping them.

"You're doing wonderful, U'maaya. Just hold on," he heard Ailinn say to the beck-and.

Charlie handed the kneeling woman the stack of cloth and dared a glance at Ailinn. She smiled at him and dabbed a wet cloth across the woman's forehead.

As quickly as he had darted in, Charlie ran from the tent, stopping only when he felt himself collide into someone. He looked up and saw Merrick staring down at him. He still felt numb and had no idea why Merrick suddenly burst into laughter.

"A drink for our hero!" Merrick called, and he guided Charlie through the crowd toward the town tavern.

THIRTY-TWO
CHOICES

AILINN EMERGED FROM THE TENT four hours later. She beamed and escorted the beck-and and her baby toward one of the still-lit homes. Charlie was amazed she could even walk, let alone that she was smiling. He shuddered.

He watched as Merrick caught Ailinn before she entered the little house. They talked for several minutes. About what, Charlie did not know. Before they departed, Ailinn kissed Merrick's cheek. Charlie's stomach churned, and he hurried off before Ailinn saw him.

Charlie barely slept that night. The local tavern's mead and stew seemed to give him a renewed vigor. Or it could have been every time he closed his eyes, all he could think about was that scene from the old *Alien* movie and the pregnant beck-and.

By morning, he found himself sitting at the end of one of the docks. He stared into the haze above the water's surface. Several birds called back and forth to each other, diving into the water and flying back to the trees with their catches.

He heard footsteps approaching from the end of the dock. They were slow and soft, unlike the boots of the guards or other men. Ailinn pulled her skirts in front of her and sat beside him. She had been given a simple dress from one of the townswomen, and her wrists had finally been wrapped and bandaged. She shifted uncomfortably, sitting straighter than normal and moving her shoulders back and forth. Charlie saw the outline of bandaging beneath her dress where the wounds on her back had been dressed.

She settled after a moment, folding her hands in her lap, staring at the fog and diving birds as well. "My father's here," she said quietly.

Charlie turned to look at her for the first time. Her hair was pulled back and piled on top of her head, though several strands had broken free. Her bright green eyes were soft and gentle. She no longer looked wild or royal. She wasn't the Ailinn whom Charlie knew.

"Your father?" he asked.

Ailinn nodded. "When they learned I had been taken, they came after me."

Charlie huffed. "Took 'em long enough."

Ailinn rolled her eyes. "Have you ever been part of a royal caravan—never mind."

They sat in silence again, her words hanging in the air between them. Yet another reminder of just how different they were.

"He wants to speak with you," she finally said. "And Jock and Drustad as well."

"Jock and Drustad are here?"

Ailinn nodded.

Charlie rose to his feet, his legs stiff from sitting so long. He rubbed his eyes and squared his shoulders, then started up the dock toward the shore. Ailinn followed a few paces behind until they reached the town's center.

Horses were tied along either side of the main road, and they had erected a round pavilion with a small flag emblazoned with the Elven crest where the main road dipped down toward the water. Ailinn took the lead this time, heading straight for the round tent. They had barely made it ten feet when two palace guards intercepted them.

"Master Charlie!"

A weight lifted from Charlie when he saw Jock and Drustad, the reins of a familiar graying mare held in one's hand. He smiled as both guards embraced him at once. When they pulled away, even their beards could not hide their smiles.

"We knew you would do it," said Drustad. He tousled Charlie's hair as the boy wrapped his arms around his horse's neck. She nickered softly to him and lipped at his hair.

Charlie pulled away, his face falling. "I don't know what everyone's been saying, but I didn't really do much of anything," he said quietly.

"Didn't do anything?" Jock asked.

"That's not true, Charlie," said Ailinn, placing a hand on Charlie's shoulder. Charlie shrugged her off and turned back to Cinders, stroking the velvet hair of her nose.

"Phil did more than me. I mean, he prepared for it anyway. Man, I miss those fruit tarts. How is Phil?" Charlie hoped the change of subject would help them avoid any uncomfortable discussions, but Jock and Drustad exchanged uneasy looks. Charlie's heart skipped a beat.

"Your beck-and, he..." Drustad looked at Jock.

"When you left, Lord Savaric was still at the palace. He immediately accused you, of course. Your room was searched, and Phillippe was questioned." Jock swallowed hard.

"Your beck-and was faithful to the end," Drustad finished.

"To the end?" Ailinn asked.

Jock nodded. "It was needless cruelty, even for a beck-and. Even if they aren't as intelligent as the rest of us, it was unnecessarily forceful."

"What happened to him?" Charlie asked. His hands shook so violently, Cinders stamped her feet in annoyance.

"He did not survive the interrogation," said Drustad. "But he never gave you up, Master Charlie. Never once did he break."

The world around Charlie spun. Jock and Ailinn caught him and lowered him to the ground. He felt suddenly ill.

It wasn't enough that Brock had died to save them. Daniel and Kashna had likely died because Charlie was useless in the fight against Savaric. And now Phillippe was dead because Charlie had run off on a wild adventure, leaving the man who had been his constant companion alone and unarmed. He had not been the one who'd made the final blow to end someone's life, but the weight on his heart seemed just as heavy. His father's face flashed before him, Jayson's sad eyes boring into him from somewhere he had no idea how to return to. A pang of guilt and understanding tugged behind his stomach.

"Charlie," said a gentle voice in his ear. He looked up into Ailinn's bright green eyes. He stood, and Ailinn reached toward him to embrace him, but he pushed her away. He swung himself into the saddle still on Cinder's back and took off toward the Belirian Forest.

"Charlie!" Ailinn, Jock, and Drustad called after him. He ignored them. His vision was beginning to blur as the tears welled in his eyes. He tore through the town, urging Cinders to run faster and faster. He followed the road out of Harpy's Pointe, until the sounds of the town had completely died away behind him. He pulled Cinders to a halt and dismounted before she had stopped. He ripped through the tree line and pushed his way past the bushes and tall grasses until he could go no farther. He collapsed in a cluster of weeds and cried.

After several minutes, he had no more tears left in him. He gasped and spluttered and coughed. The crying had done nothing to relieve his pain. It only brought his emotions closer to the surface, leaving him raw and vulnerable. He heard the gentle hoofbeats of Cinders approach, and she stopped before him, pushing her nose against his face.

A shadow passed overhead, and something landed in the clearing beside him. Charlie looked up, squinting through his tears. A pair of golden eyes loomed out of the morning fog as Kashna walked toward him. His deep black fur was nearly gray from the dust and dirt that covered his body. He limped on his back paw, and several of his wounds still bled.

The two stared at each other, motionless, not speaking. An image of Daniel, severely injured and unmoving, flashed across Charlie's mind. Charlie hung his head. He knew what Kashna was trying to tell him.

"I tried to save him," Kashna whispered so quietly Charlie wasn't sure if he was speaking aloud or within his mind. "I wanted to find my family. I wished to take Daniel with me. I... I attempted to heal his injuries. I worked all night. In the end, he wanted to go, but he wished his body returned to his sister."

Charlie was silent for several long moments. He watched as Kashna lowered himself to the ground and lay on his side, exhausted. A cool breeze wove its way through the trees, leaving goosebumps along his skin. But Charlie shivered from more than just the cold.

"Do not blame yourself, Charlie," said Kashna.

Charlie looked again into the qarveena's golden eyes. "How?" he asked. "I have done nothing but cause trouble. Ailinn would have never been kidnapped if Savaric hadn't felt threatened by me. Phillippe wouldn't have died trying to keep secret where I was. Even Daniel died because I was stuck on that stupid wheel. Merrick and Ailinn pretty much had to carry me out of the castle. What have I done that's good, Kashna? I'm no better than my dad now and all the turmoil he brought here."

Kashna heaved himself upright, his breathing labored. "No one can know what good or ill their actions and inactions have upon the world at large. All we can ever hope to do is the best we can in the moment."

Charlie didn't answer. He felt a single tear run down his cheek.

"A commander may not be the one to land the final blow, but without their strength and spirit, the army can never hope to win," said Kashna. "We do not praise the wind that carries the seeds, making it possible for the flowers to grow. But without it, the insects that feast upon their nectar would surely perish."

Perhaps it was his moments of telepathic connection with Kashna, or spending so much time trying to decipher what he meant, but Charlie seemed to understand.

"What are you going to do now?" Charlie asked. "Savaric's gone. The link between you and him, and even Daniel, is gone. I'm sure Ailinn would—"

Kashna shook his head. "I know little of who I am, and what I am. I have lived most of my life under the influence of another. It is time for me to reunite with others like me. I wish to learn what they know, and perhaps I can teach them of the goodness of the elves."

"What about the bad stuff?"

Kashna grinned. "Good, bad. Light, dark. It all depends on how you see it, Charlie. Is it a bowl, or is it a disfigured chalice?"

Charlie felt himself smile as he wiped away his tears.

Kashna rose unsteadily to his feet, and Charlie watched a single feather fall from his wing. Kashna followed his gaze, then picked up the feather with surprising gentleness in his teeth before laying it at the boy's feet.

"I know your kind is sentimental," he said. He turned and walked back through the grass to where Charlie supposed Daniel's body lay. A moment later, there was a rush of wind and a flap of wings. Charlie watched Kashna rise into the air and through the boughs of the Belirian trees.

FROM THAT MOMENT ON, EVERYTHING was a blur to Charlie. Daniel's body was more than severely injured. It was mangled in ways Charlie wished to have removed from his mind. Ailinn was stronger than he expected when she saw her brother's body. Charlie wondered if it was Merrick who gave her the strength as he stood beside her.

King Valin seemed to struggle with how to react to Daniel's death. He left Ailinn in charge of the preparations and quickly turned his attention to Charlie.

Inside the king's pavilion, the air was humid and stuffy. It was also very dark, as Valin kept all the tent flaps closed. Only two lanterns illuminated the entire space. It was surprisingly well-furnished. A full bed, chairs, table, and even a small desk were scattered around the perimeter. This must have been what Ailinn meant. No wonder it had taken them so long to organize. Charlie stood just inside the main entrance as King Valin paced back and forth.

"I find myself in quite the predicament, Charlie," he said. "I'm not sure if our goal was ever to kill Savaric. Then again, I cannot say what our end goal truly was. I don't think I had ever gotten that far. I needed to know what he was up to first."

Charlie listened as Valin seemed to ramble. His pacing came faster and slower as his stream of consciousness came and went.

"What I need to know is whether to continue with the agreement to marry Ailinn to Merrick." Valin stopped pacing, but he still swayed as he looked at Charlie.

Charlie shrugged. "I dunno. Why don't you ask them?"

Valin waved his hand in the air. "It does not work this way, Charlie. Then again, she wished to marry you at one time. Yes, we could spin things this way. The princess and the one destined to fulfill the prophec—Charlie?"

Charlie turned abruptly, stopping only when he reached the tent flap.

"Since the moment I came here, everyone has been telling me what I should and should not be doing, who I should and should not be. My dad got one thing right. He didn't let anyone boss him around." The tent flap closed behind him, and Charlie was relieved King Valin did not follow.

He headed toward the tent that had been erected close to the edge of the forest. He had refused the lodgings at the local inn alongside Ailinn and Merrick and instead decided to sleep with the prisoners and beck-ands. He was tired of being treated like someone special. He rounded the corner of the main road out of Harpy's Pointe and nearly ran into a palace soldier.

"Apologies, Master Charlie," said the guard, and he bowed low. Charlie held up a hand, trying to signal for the man to stop.

"No, it's all right. I wasn't watching where I was going." He glanced over the man's shoulder and locked eyes with Ailinn's. His stomach churned, and he swallowed hard as he watched her push her way past her guards.

"May I speak with you?" she asked, her voice gentle.

Charlie nodded. Ailinn mumbled something to her guards, then walked several paces away beneath the boughs of the outlying trees.

He crossed his arms and shifted back and forth. Ailinn's hands were folded elegantly before her, though she wouldn't meet his eye. Charlie had a feeling he knew what was coming.

"I—I have been talking to my father," she began.

"Yeah." Charlie shrugged.

"And Merrick." This time, she did catch his eye. Charlie tried hard not to glare. "There are many strategic reasons for continuing with my marriage to him. He's open to finding a solution for those with magic, and I was betrothed to him many years ago. The arrangement is almost expected."

"And you love him," Charlie added more curtly than he had intended.

Ailinn licked her lips and rubbed her hands together. "It's different than that. It's complicated. It's nothing like how I felt with you."

"Fine, then you're comfortable with him. I get it." Charlie shifted his weight. He plucked a leaf from the tree beside him and tore it into little pieces.

"Charlie, please. There is the risk you could leave at any moment. If the stories I heard from my mother are true, you have only to yearn enough for your own world, and you could be gone in an instant. I cannot marry someone who would leave me and leave our kingdom."

The last bits of the leaf fell to the ground. Charlie brushed his hands on the tight trousers he had been given and sighed.

"Just tell me one thing," he said. Ailinn pressed her lips together. Her eyes searched his face, and her brows raised. "If you weren't a princess, if you didn't *have* to marry someone because a kingdom depended on it, would you... would you consider...?"

"I cannot say, Charlie. I have never been anything other than a princess. I suppose it's something I would be willing to—"

Charlie reached for Ailinn's shoulders and pulled her close to him. He pressed his lips to hers and kissed her fiercely. He felt the tension leave her body, and she wrapped her arms around his neck.

They stayed this way for several long minutes, not caring who saw them as they passed by on the road. Charlie finally pulled away, taking one last look into her eyes.

"I know how sentimental your kind is," he said, "But the wind cannot control the seeds it spreads, or the direction it will take." He turned and headed back toward the town's tavern for a very large pint of mead.

THIRTY-THREE
BETWEEN TIME

WHEN CHARLIE STUMBLED INTO THE communal tent that night, he wasn't sure whether it had been the mead or something else that had lifted a weight from his shoulders. A pang of guilt for those who had died still pulled behind his navel, but that too could have been the mead.

He flopped onto his makeshift cot and stared at the canvas above him. The summer air was much more tolerable this close to the water, especially compared to the stuffiness of the Elven palace. He watched the shadow of a leaf fall on the roof of the tent. It reminded him of the leaves that had gathered on the fabric above his four-poster in the palace. As his eyes closed, he almost thought he could hear the creak of Phillippe's little door in the distance.

A hand on his shoulder shook him violently. "Charlie! Charlie!" A male voice yelled his name.

Charlie opened his eyes and immediately shut them again. A familiar face slowly came into focus above his own.

"Charlie!" It was Malcolm Darcy's father.

273

Charlie jumped, and his hands slipped on the plastic arm of the Swansdale High School office chair.

"We only have four minutes," said the man, pulling at Charlie's arm.

Charlie stood. Mr. Darcy walked right through the office door, pulling Charlie along behind him. Charlie yanked his arm free, and the two skidded to a stop in the school hallway. Charlie blinked in the white, artificial light. The school was exactly as he remembered, though it was eerily quiet. He glanced down and was thankful he was not naked this time. He still wore his clothes from Chartile, and his sword hung at his side. He glanced back at the door he had just walked through, then back at the man who stood impatiently before him.

"Come on," the man urged, then hurried through the front doors of the school. Charlie followed, hesitant at first and afraid he was about to run headlong into a thick metal door. He passed through them all with ease and followed Mr. Darcy to the antique white Cadillac he now rummaged in.

Mr. Darcy pulled a bag from the back of his car and handed it to Charlie.

"Three minutes. Hurry up and change."

Charlie hastily removed his leather belt and tunic, pulling a T-shirt over his head.

"How—?"

"We're in between time right now. The last thing those school cameras saw was a boy in Earth clothes, not Chartilian tunics and hose."

Charlie's head snapped up. He stopped mid-button as he pulled a pair of loose jeans on over his trousers.

"Two minutes. Hurry!" said the man. Charlie finished dressing, and Mr. Darcy threw Charlie's Chartilian clothes in the back of his car. He grabbed Charlie's arm again. This time, he did not bother with the doors. He pulled the boy through the mulberry bush at the base of the office window and through the side of the brick building.

"On my mark, sit down," the man said, looking at a very large watch on his wrist. "Three, two, one. Okay, sit."

Charlie sat and was relieved when he did not fall through and land on the floor. Mr. Darcy had walked back into the principal's office just as Charlie sat.

A moment later, Deb walked into the office, a stack of books and papers in her hand. Charlie watched as she placed the pile into his backpack and laid it on the counter in front of her.

"Here you are, dear," she said. Charlie rose and stared at the door to the principal's office through which Mr. Darcy had just disappeared. More shouting had started again. The door flew open, and Principal Umpree ran out in a huff.

"Did Malcolm come this way?" he shouted. Deb pushed her chair back and blinked.

"I thought he was with you," she said.

Mr. Darcy stepped out of the room and gave Charlie a stern look. Charlie returned the look and remained silent.

"Mr. Darrow," said Deb. "I didn't see you come in."

"Darrow?" Charlie blurted out.

"I'm Malcolm's mentor for his parole program," the man Charlie thought was Malcolm's father replied sternly.

"He's gone!" Principal Umpree shouted. "I don't understand. Boy!" he rounded on Charlie. "Did you see him leave? Did you see anything?"

Charlie looked at Mr. Darrow, and, so as not to give anything away, glanced at Deb before meeting Principal Umpree's eye. "No, sir. But I was starting to fall asleep, so maybe he ran off."

Principal Umpree threw his arms in the air and sighed loudly before heading back into his office. Mr. Darrow smirked and winked at Charlie and followed behind Principal Umpree.

Charlie watched the door close, more confused than ever. More headlights flashed into the small office, and Charlie turned to see his mother's van pulling up.

"Charlie, where are your glasses?" Deb asked.

Charlie lifted a hand to his face. He hadn't worn them in so long, he had forgotten.

"They were covered in milk, so I just took them off," he lied. Deb nodded.

Moments later, Mrs. Hill opened the office door. Before he could stop himself, Charlie ran full-on into her arms, nearly knocking the woman off her feet.

"Baby!" she said, hugging him back. Principal Umpree's door opened again, and Mr. Darrow stepped out.

"Mrs. Hill," he said, nodding. The woman's eyes narrowed suspiciously.

"I'm sorry, do I—?"

"I'm Mr. Darrow. I'm an old friend of your husband's. Please tell him I said hello when you see him next." The man nodded again and left the office. This time, he pulled on the door handles and did not walk through.

Charlie watched him through the office window as Deb and his mother spoke feverishly behind him. Mr. Darrow gave Charlie a kind of salute before climbing into his car and driving away. He looked down at the chair he had sat in and saw Kashna's black feather perched perfectly in the center of the seat. He snatched it up and tucked it inside his shirt.

"Mom," said Charlie, "I want to go visit dad."

EPILOGUE

THE BURLY MALE NURSE TAPPED a series of numbers on the panel outside the visiting room. Charlie stepped through the heavy metal door, waiting for it to close completely.

Jayson Hill sat at the same table, working on the same puzzle. He did not look up when Charlie joined him. He held a single, tiny puzzle piece in his hand. Charlie took the piece from his father's fingers and placed it perfectly along the left side of the puzzle.

Finally, Jayson looked at his son. The two stared on in silence, blue eyes meeting blue. Jayson looked away and picked up another puzzle piece.

"I suppose your mother made you come to apologize," he said. "You don't have to, Charlie—"

"I need to tell you something, Dad," Charlie said, interrupting. He placed Kashna's black feather on the half-finished puzzle. Jayson dropped the puzzle piece in his hand and gently picked up the feather.

"It's about Chartile," Charlie continued. Jayson dropped the feather, his eyes wide and his hands trembling. "It was amazing."

MORE FROM CASSANDRA MORGAN

The Witch of Eisenwald Forest
Dreams of Darkness Anthology by Dragon Storm Press
Available on Amazon

COMING SOON

Gathering Storms
Book Three of the Kingdoms of Chartile
2023

CASSANDRA MORGAN WRITES AS C.P. MORGAN

A new Paranormal Cozy Mystery Novella
"…like *Warehouse 13* and *Sherlock Holmes*, with cats!"

Spring 2018

EXCERPT FROM GATHERING STORMS
BOOK THREE OF THE KINGDOMS OF CHARTILE

THE SOUND OF FALLING RUBBLE was deafening. Jack reached for Gemari's hand. He pulled her to him, lifting her easily into his arms and running as far as he could from the cascade of rocks and boulders that blocked the tunnel entrance she had been standing in moments before. Slowly, the crashing and shifting of rocks subsided, and Jack found himself curled around Gemari, the princess trembling in his arms.

"Princess!" one of Gemari's guards called, but she could not answer them.

"Over here!" Jack called back as loud as his strained voice would allow.

Gemari's guards ran to them, their burly Dwarvik frames quickly blocking the view of the pile of boulders behind them.

"Well done, my lord," one of the guards whispered to Jack as the others pulled Gemari to her feet.

Jack turned to smile at him but noticed they only numbered five.

"Where's Halil?" Jack's eyes widened. He looked past the man before him and saw a single, dark skinned hand sticking out from the pile of rocks. The scene swam before him. He thought he heard the distant rumble of another cave in, but it was the sound of his own screaming. He fell to his knees, the sound of the guards' voices indiscernible with his own cries of anguish and terror.

Jack rolled over and fell off the couch onto the carpeted floor. His phone alarm blared in his ear, and he found the television remote underneath his left thigh, the volume turned to max. He scrambled for the remote, pushing buttons blindly through his still-blurry vision until the television powered off.

He breathed an exasperated sigh, turning off the alarm on his phone and glanced at the time. 10:02 AM. Jack freed himself from the mess of blankets, throwing on a bathrobe that was draped over the living room chair, and tore off down the hall.

DOROTHY CLAES

AND THE

PRISON OF THENEMI

"MS. CLAES, I AM AFRAID THERE ARE MANY THINGS ABOUT RICHARD Van Damme that you do not know. But they are all things he wished to pass on to you. Now, it is very cold out here, madam. I would love nothing more than to discuss this further with you over a cup of tea."

"Who are you?" Dorothy asked in an awed whisper.

"My name is Destin. Destin Hollanday. I work as a consultant, mostly to the Worchester Museum of Art. You are more than welcome to look up my credentials, but I would beg you to do so after you have let me in out of the cold."

Dorothy slammed the phone down and bolted up the winding stairs. She was thankful she had maintained a very active lifestyle, even into her elder years. Her knees creaked at the effort, but she was barely out of breath when she reached the top of the stairs. Solomon bounded through the bookcase and Dorothy pushed it shut. She ran back to her father's desk and pulled a tiny Smith and Wesson she carried with her from her purse. She locked Solomon in the bathroom to keep him out of the way before heading down the apartment stairs.

A gentleman in his late fifties stood outside the front door of the little shop. He wore a woolen trench coat and a black homburg. He smiled and waved when he saw her. Dorothy clutched the pistol even tighter in her pocket. She unlocked the door and Destin Hollanday pushed it open.

"Thank you, dear lady," he said.

The tea kettle began to whistle upstairs, and Destin smiled. "What wonderful timing," he said, and headed for the avocado-green door. His hand had barely rested on the knob when he stopped abruptly. Dorothy held her gun between his shoulder blades.

"I don't know what's going on here, but you're going to tell me everything right now," she seethed.

Destin sighed. His hands slowly moved above his head in surrender. Without warning, he spun around faster than Dorothy would have expected of a man his age. He twisted the gun from her grasp and immediately emptied the chamber into his palm before tossing the gun back to her.

"My dear woman, I promise you have no idea what you are dealing with."

ABOUT THE AUTHOR

When she's not rescuing orphan kittens or doing voice acting for villainous purple mermaids, CASSANDRA MORGAN can be found creating worlds of magic, suspense and friendship. A lover of doughnuts and a self-proclaimed Coffee Connoisseur, Cassandra Morgan hails from a family of writers, authors and journalists.

The idea for Chartile (pronounced KAR-tyl) came to Cassie when she was thirteen years old. It is loosely based on some of the games she and her friends would play. She lives in NW Ohio with her hubby, five fabulous felines, and any number of foster kittens.

Connect with Cassandra!

WWW.AUTHORCASSANDRAMORGAN.COM

WWW.AUTHORCPMORGAN.COM

CONTACT@AUTHORCASSANDRAMORGAN.COM

WWW.FACEBOOK.COM/AUTHOR.CASSANDRA.MORGAN

TWITTER: @AUTHORCASMORGAN

INSTAGRAM: @MORGAN_CASSANDRA